DRACULA LIVES

Robert Ryan

Edited By: Brian Moreland
http://brianmoreland.com/

Book Design: Polgarus Studio
http://www.polgarusstudio.com/

Cover Design: Natasha Snow
http://natashasnowdesigns.com/

Contact the author:
www.robertryanwriter.com

Facebook:
http://bit.ly/1TUbaEt

This novel is dedicated to all those who love the classic monsters from Universal Studios.

Where is the line between movies and real life?
Perhaps there isn't one.

CHAPTER 1

The severed hand hitched its way up the stairs in its relentless drive to kill the person it was directed to kill.

The hand was not human. It was a webbed humanoid thing. Long, scaly fingers with inch-long, needle-sharp claws deftly hooked into the carpet covering the stairs, again and again, until the hand flopped onto the landing. It scuttled across the Persian rug to the closed wooden door of the bedchamber. Catlike, the hand used its claws to dig into the wood and skitter up the door. The instant it reached the top, it released its grip and began falling. With a precision that spoke of long practice, it broke its fall by grabbing the handle. The maneuver turned the handle and jostled the door open a crack.

The hand dropped noiselessly onto the rug. Righting itself, it squeezed through the crack and scrabbled across the floor as though possessed. Clamping onto the wooden bedpost of the canopied four-poster, it wriggled up and flopped onto the bed.

The sleeper lay face up, under a satin sheet pulled up to just below the neck.

A few feet away, a tall man dressed in black stood beside

the bed, watching the scene unfold through a pair of oversized goggles. A large glove on his right hand mimicked the movements of the beast with five fingers.

The hand clawed its way across the sheet with deadly purpose. Seconds later, it reached the exposed neck and clamped down.

The sleeper's eyes shot open.

The tall man dropped his gloved hand to his side. "Cut!" he said.

The hand from some alien world squeezed harder.

The sleeper's eyes widened in alarm.

"*Cut, I said!*" The tall man yanked off the glove.

The sleeper struggled to pull the hand off, moaning in pain as the tugging only made the maniacal thing tighten its grip.

After an intense battle the tall man managed to pry the hand loose and toss it to the floor. Its fingers twitched erratically for a few seconds, then made a wobbly effort to crawl back to the bedpost. As the man bent to grab it, the hand fell over on its back and lay still.

Looking back at the sleeper, the man saw spots of red where some of the claws had pierced the flesh.

Annoyed, the tall man stared at his glove. "We shall have to test it again. All must be in readiness for our guest. There will be no time for retakes."

CHAPTER 2

It was a scene straight out of a horror movie.

Somehow, in the wilds of New England, a man claiming to have worked on the 1931 version of *Dracula* had re-created the setting from the film's famous opening sequence. An exhilarating mix of curiosity and trepidation scurried through the veins of the lone passenger in the horse-drawn carriage. He was living out one of his all-time favorite movie fantasies: to be Renfield taking that maniacal ride through the Borgo Pass into the heart of vampire country.

Transylvania.

Castle Dracula.

Adam Quinn stuck his head out the window, wanting to fully savor the moment.

Seemingly in a race against the setting sun, the four-horse team sped along the top of a narrow, craggy ridge that ran down the middle of a deep gorge. Steep drop-offs on both sides meant almost certain death if they went over.

Quinn drew his head back inside the coach, amazed that his lifelong love of old Universal horror classics and obsessive research into their history—*Dracula* in particular—had led him to this.

The original production notes for *Dracula* listed a man named George Tilton as "production assistant." Quinn's exhaustive search for anyone associated with the horror classic had uncovered no mention of Tilton after the movie was released in 1931.

Until now.

George Tilton was still alive. He'd changed names, but Quinn's work as a consultant to law enforcement had gained him access to their databases. Tilton's paper trail was sparse, almost as though he'd tried to erase any record of his existence. No birth certificate, no marriage or driver's licenses, no credit cards, no bank accounts. What little there was ended with two legal documents filed in Boston in 1954.

On Halloween of that year, George had posted bail for Max Tilton. His fourteen-year-old son had been arrested for attempted murder. A search for the outcome of the case had led nowhere, and Quinn had wondered if some law favoring juveniles might have been used to get the records expunged.

The second document, dated in November, was the official record of George Tilton's name change to Frederick Schreck. Quinn had recognized the significance of the alias at once.

The first screen version of Dracula had been the silent classic *Nosferatu*, in which Max Schreck had played the vampire. But Schreck's first name wasn't Max. It was Friedrich. Tilton had simply Americanized it to Frederick. First he'd named his son after the mysterious German actor, then he'd later done the same for himself.

Schreck was also the German word for *fear*.

It smacked of obsession.

Quinn took a slip of paper from the pocket of his fleece jacket. Unable to read the message in the feeble twilight, from another pocket he pulled out his keychain, which had a small flashlight attached. The incessant bumping of the coach forced him to steady his hand to keep the light focused. He re-read the printout of the e-mail he'd already read at least a dozen times since receiving it a few days ago.

Dear Mr. Quinn:

I have found your knowledge of Dracula and film background to be most interesting. As it happens, I am deep into the final edit of a horror film I have been working on for quite some time. The editing will keep me occupied until Sunday evening. Then on Monday I must shoot the final sequence of what I like to think of as the greatest horror film ever made. This would not give us as much time as one might like for a leisurely visit, but if you would like to come Sunday evening and stay through Monday, aside from lively discussions about the glory days of Universal horror—which of course would include telling you the story of my connection to Dracula, and the powerful impact it has had on my life—your film background could be useful during the shoot.

If this is acceptable, you must agree to certain conditions.

My driver will pick you up at a time and place I will specify in a future e-mail. Your vehicle will be left at the meeting place and you will be brought to my home. You must agree to be blindfolded for the first leg of the journey. My driver will tell you when it is permissible to remove the blindfold. To borrow a phrase from Morbius in Forbidden Planet, please forgive the ill manners of an old recluse, but as far as is humanly possible, I like to keep the location of my sanctuary a secret.

Come at your own risk.

He had signed with the cryptic name *Markov*.

Quinn's initial reaction had been annoyance at being ordered what to do, but the apology by way of *Forbidden Planet* had won him over, and on further reflection he had understood. Beyond the fact that decades of seclusion had obviously dulled the man's social skills, his desire to protect his privacy was understandable. For all Quinn knew, he might be the first person allowed to visit in years. Maybe ever.

It was that final line that had bothered him the most:

Come at your own risk.

What risk could there be in going to visit a man who had to be somewhere around a hundred years old?

A mile or so back, the driver had pulled over to remove Quinn's blindfold. Now, glancing uneasily at the precipice a few feet away, Quinn decided his host must have been referring to this dangerous ride.

He looked out at the ominous clouds beginning to roil in the darkening sky. Night was fast approaching, but at least the storm was holding off. This late in October the temperature hovered around freezing, which meant ice storms: mixtures of rain, sleet, and snow that made for the worst possible travel conditions.

A particularly severe bump launched him straight up from his seat. He landed with a thud and stuck his head out the window. He almost expected to see a bat at the reins, but the mysterious driver still clutched them in one hand, while the other hand whipped the horses as though getting to their destination was a matter of life or death. Unlike Bela Lugosi, whose face was visible in the carriage ride to the castle, this driver's face was concealed by a cap and scarf. Only the eyes were visible.

Just as written in the original script.

The first fat drops of rain splatted against Quinn's face, but he kept his head outside the window, wanting to take it all in: the strained clanking of the harness, the puffs of smoke coming from the nostrils of the hell-bent horses, the clatter of the wheels as they bumped and rattled over the dangerous terrain.

The carriage slid around a turn in the snaking path and gained speed. Massive black thunderclouds seethed and spread across the sky to smother the last gasp of the dying sun. Quinn's eyes strained to follow the path ahead.

Perhaps a mile away stood the castle.

It appeared to be an exact replica of the one in the movie Quinn had watched dozens of times. Silhouetted against the encroaching darkness, it stood on a finger of rock that dropped precipitously away on all sides. Looming like a sinister shadow, the sprawling, jagged outline of turrets and battlements was not the product of any castle architect. Tilton/Schreck/Markov had faithfully reproduced the art design of *Dracula*. A red-tinged moon hovering over the gloom-shrouded pile perfectly complemented the sense of brooding menace.

A sudden spider web of lightning erupted around the moon and shot its filaments toward the roof, making the scene appear more out of *Frankenstein* than *Dracula*. In Quinn's horror-steeped imagination, either the castle was a ground drawing electricity into itself, or the moon was the eye of God, hurling down His wrath against the evil within.

A single light shining in one of the rectangular upper windows sent a thrill of anticipation through Quinn. This wildly improbable journey into the world of movie horror he'd loved since childhood was exactly the escape he needed from the real horror of his everyday life.

The coachman eased to a stop in the porte-cochère at the entrance to the castle.

Gaslight from wall lanterns affixed to the four corners of the overhanging shelter made it a glowing oasis in the storm-wracked night. Quinn glanced at the huge wooden door with its large round iron knocker and smiled. He'd seen versions of that door in countless haunted castle movies.

He had barely clambered out of the coach with his two bags before the driver cracked the whip and the carriage disappeared into the night.

Quinn lingered at the bottom of the stone steps that led up to the door. He took one last look around before his surroundings surrendered to the embracing cloak of darkness. A light fog was creeping in. From somewhere close an animal howled, its shriek either a protest or warning against this intrusion into its domain. Quinn cocked his ears.

Coyote?

Wolf?

A flash of lightning cast a shadow on the wall. Canine. Large. Not quite right for a coyote or wolf.

Quinn jerked his head around, peering into the fog to find the source.

Nothing there. The lightning and boom of thunder might have scared whatever it was away. The rumbling across the sky died out and silence returned.

Thinking of Tilton's movie background, and the obvious pains he'd taken to replicate the *Dracula* setting, Quinn wondered if machines were providing the special effects. Whatever the case, the creepy atmosphere heightened the feeling that he'd actually stepped into the classic horror movie.

A creaking noise made him look up. The huge door was opening, slowly. Cobwebs hung in the nooks and crannies around the entranceway. *Set decoration?* Spiders were rare this far north, even more so as winter approached. Tod Browning, director of *Dracula*, had used spider webs often in his movies as an atmospheric touch.

Quinn grabbed his bags and hurried up the front steps, curious to see if, in keeping with the theme, the door had opened itself.

He reached the doorway. No one was there.

"Enter freely and go safely."

The strong resonant voice came from a considerable distance beyond the threshold.

The speaker was paraphrasing Dracula's greeting from the novel. Quinn looked past the open door before entering, almost expecting to step onto a movie set.

He crossed the threshold.

The groan of the door closing sounded like a moan of despair. It sent a chill fluttering across Quinn's back. Scanning the cavernous space before him, he took a moment to drink it all in.

The huge great hall was straight out of *Dracula*. A row of tall columns to the left supported arches that led to unseen rooms. High above and to the right, moonlight shone through large mullioned windows that conveyed the feeling of a cathedral. Cobwebs were everywhere.

As Quinn began walking in the direction the voice had come from, the feeling grew that he had indeed entered a movie set.

Dead ahead was a faithful reproduction of the huge winding staircase on which Dracula had made his immortal entrance. At the bottom of the staircase, a large movie camera dating from the early days of cinema stood atop a wooden tripod. A boom mike hovered in its stand. Jarringly, empty Coors beer cans were scattered about.

A tall, slender man dressed in black stood on the bottom landing of the staircase, holding an ornate candle holder. The half-melted candle burned with a steady flame. Above and behind the commanding figure, the iconic giant spider web from *Dracula* stretched across the next landing up the stairs.

Quinn stopped at the bottom of the staircase and looked up at his host. Even if Tilton/Schreck/Markov had been only a teenager in 1931, he had to be at least a hundred now. But he looked decades younger. Not much older than Quinn, who was almost fifty-five.

Tilton was not the repulsive Nosferatu of Max Schreck. He was well-groomed and dressed in an elegant loungewear ensemble of smoking jacket, slacks, socks, and slippers. All black, except for the white ruffled shirt and the gold edging along the pockets and lapels of the jacket. The material was velvet, judging from the way it reflected the candlelight. Aside from the gold trim and white shirt, a blood-red ascot was the only splash of color. Staring down with an unnaturally intense gaze, he clearly fancied himself a reincarnation of Lugosi. Although his black hair was not slicked back, there was even a slight resemblance.

"*I* ... am Markov. I bid you welcome."

Was calling himself Markov an in-joke to himself? J. Carrol Naish had played the mad Doctor Markoff in a poverty row production called *The Monster Maker*. Quinn's confusion over the alias was superseded by Markov's perfect imitation of Lugosi's sepulchral voice.

"You do a great Bela Lugosi," Quinn said.

This time Markov spoke in what was presumably his own voice, standard American with no discernible accent.

"I am not an impressionist. I am a re-creationist." Markov let his Lugosi gaze bore into Quinn before going on. "Do you believe in monsters, Mr. Quinn?"

CHAPTER 3

It took a moment to process the unexpected question.

"Human monsters, yes," Quinn said. "I hunt them for a living."

"Interesting. Perhaps we are kindred spirits, although I take it you do not believe in actual monsters."

"Like vampires and werewolves? No."

"Then we shall have much to discuss. Come. Let us get to know one another in my den."

He turned and walked with a deliberate tread back up the stairs. Quinn followed, half-expecting the famous wolf howl from the movie, but none came. Remembering the howl he'd heard on the way in, he said, "Do you have wolves up here?"

Markov glanced over his shoulder while continuing up the stairs. "One. He is very troublesome."

The cryptic statement registered for only a second as Quinn's attention stayed on Markov. He'd reached the gigantic spider web that blocked his path. Would he walk through it? He stopped as if deliberating, then stepped through a gap between the edge of the web and the column to which some of its silky threads clung for support. With a hint of an enigmatic smile, he beckoned Quinn through the same opening.

They reached the top of the stairs. Markov's black velvet slippers moved noiselessly across an expansive landing inlaid with large rectangular stones. Quinn followed to an intricately carved wooden door. Markov turned the handle and gave the door a gentle push, inviting his guest in with a theatrical sweep of his arm, made more dramatic by the groaning accompaniment of the hinges.

Because Markov had referred to this space as his den, Quinn had expected something small, but at roughly thirty yards square, the chamber was bordering on vast. His library took up the entire right wall. Rich mahogany shelves were filled with books, many appearing to be quite old. Ahead, a fire blazed invitingly from a large fireplace embellished with elaborately carved scrollwork. High-backed chairs on either side of a black granite table formed a seating area on the hearth. Dozens of candles burned in wall sconces and candelabra around the room.

Much of the wall space was taken up by framed movie posters and stills from the glory days of Universal horror. Quinn quickly became absorbed by several that were from silent films on which Lon Chaney and Tod Browning had worked together.

Markov came up beside him, and for the first time it fully registered how tall he was. Quinn stood six one, and Markov was a few inches taller.

"I hope you were comfortable enough in the horse-drawn carriage," his mysterious host said. "I could have sent our horseless carriage, but I thought you would appreciate being transported to the castle in *Dracula* fashion."

"It was perfect. As was your re-creation of Borgo Pass. I felt like Renfield."

"It is nice to meet someone who can fully appreciate the pains I have taken to re-create the *Dracula* experience. In that spirit, this would be the moment when Dracula asks Renfield if he is hungry."

"No, I'm fine."

"Drinks, then. Contrary to what Bela Lugosi might have led you to expect, I do drink … wine."

Quinn smiled an acknowledgement of the famous *Dracula* line. "This room reminds me so much of those Vincent Price-Poe movies, it seems like a snifter of brandy is the way to go."

"Make yourself comfortable while I take care of it."

A tasseled velvet bell rope hung beside the door. He gave it a gentle tug and less than a minute later there was a knock. Markov opened the door a crack, muttered to some unseen person beyond, then rejoined Quinn, who had again turned his attention to the posters and stills.

"Johnny will take care of us," Markov said. "My right arm. The one who tends to the considerable details of maintaining this estate with impeccable discretion."

Quinn nodded distractedly, continuing to stare at the posters. "All the ones in this section are from Tod Browning movies," he said. "*Dracula*, of course. *Freaks*." He pointed to one of the stills. "I love this picture of Lon Chaney flashing that famous sawtooth grin from *London After Midnight*. It's a shame that movie is lost. It's probably the most sought-after lost film."

"I worked on all those pictures."

London After Midnight had been released in 1927. How old *was* this man?

"How was working with Tod Browning?"

"We were very close. I became like the son he never had.

14

And he was like a father to me."

A flicker of emotion gave Quinn his first peek at the human being behind the Markov persona. George Tilton had loved Browning deeply. In an instant the mask was back.

"Once he left the picture business and moved to Malibu, he never wanted to leave his home. So as often as I could, I flew out to see him."

There was a knock at the door.

"Come in," Markov said.

Johnny was thick through the chest and walked with a pronounced limp. The sole of one slipper was a few inches thick, apparently compensating for one leg being shorter than the other. The shorter leg seemed to bend at an unnatural angle, but it was difficult to tell through the baggy legs of pantaloons that gathered at the ankles. A loose-fitting blouse with decorative stitching combined with the pantaloons to form a kind of uniform.

Despite the attendant's hitching gait, the silver tray with two snifters of brandy and a carafe of water remained rock steady on an upturned palm, while a garment draped over the other forearm never fluttered. As Johnny deftly placed the brandies in front of the two men, Quinn noticed a cauliflower ear and wondered if the servant had been a boxer in a previous life.

With a flourish Johnny set the tray aside and held out the garment for Quinn to slip into. The burgundy smoking jacket had black silk lapels and pocket flaps, trimmed in gold. Quinn ran his hands over the impeccably tailored velvet, admiring the styling and craftsmanship. It fit him perfectly.

"Excellent," he said. "Thank you."

Johnny made a slight nod and withdrew.

Quinn and Markov swirled the amber liquid, clinked

snifters, and drank. Markov cut an elegant figure as he relaxed into his chair, crossing his legs at the knee and cradling his brandy. "How did you come to believe in human monsters, Mr. Quinn?"

"My answer to that would be a long and rather dark tale."

"We have brandy, a warm fire, and nowhere else to be. This is our time to get to know one another, and I'm sure your tale can hardly be darker than mine. My home was built for dark tales."

"A House of Dark Shadows?"

"Indeed. I could have been the script consultant for that show."

"As someone who worked in Castle Dracula, with the greatest of all vampires, I'm sure you could have." Quinn held up his snifter. "To you and your house of dark shadows."

Markov held up his glass in acknowledgement.

After they had taken a moment to savor their brandy, Quinn began. "The answer to your question begins with my love of horror movies. Since I was born on Halloween to a father who loved them, it seems I was destined to become a horror fan."

"Did you inherit your love of the old classics from him?"

"Absolutely. He was an English professor, with a very keen critical mind. Among other things he taught classes on horror literature, which always included showing the movie version, if there was one. I was six when he started my horror film education. This was in the early '60s, before home video, so my introduction to the old classics was through Shock Theater on television. Dad and I watched them so many times over the years that I just about knew every line by heart. When I was little, he got a kick out of having me get up and act out famous lines when we had company over."

"Did that embarrass you?"

"No. I loved it. I'm kind of a ham. For a while I had thought of pursuing acting."

Quinn watched Markov centering his face in the square he'd formed with his thumbs and forefingers, a director framing his shot. "Yes," he said, peering through the frame. "I think the camera would like you."

Quinn gave a wistful smile. "One of the roads not taken."

"We all have those. I've chosen to believe that something keeps us on the one we are meant to be on."

Quinn didn't agree. He'd known plenty of people who'd gone down all sorts of wrong roads. He'd been on a few himself. He said nothing, not wanting to waste time on pointless philosophical digressions.

Markov cradled his glass. "Is your father a fan of *Dracula* like yourself?"

"It was his favorite."

"'Was'? Is he no longer with us?"

"Sadly, no. He ... passed away several years ago."

Passed away. Quinn had chosen the euphemism because he wasn't ready to stir up the ashes of a burning regret that were just now starting to cool. The truth would cast its own dark shadow over a weekend he had been looking forward to, a chance to hear the experiences of a man who had worked on *Dracula.* Knowing that their time would be limited, and wanting to maximize his once-in-a-lifetime opportunity, Quinn had even made sure to get plenty of sleep in anticipation of lively all-night discussion. Just picking Markov's brain about working with the legendary

Lon Chaney, going back to the silent era, could take hours. Quinn didn't want to seem impatient by looking at his watch, but it had to be somewhere around seven. They only had one more day, and Markov had said he would be using it to shoot the climax of his film.

Talking about personal tragedies could wait.

Markov held out his snifter. "Here's to the spirit of your father that lives on in you." After they drank to the somber toast, Markov said, "So. Your Dracula roots run deep."

"Not as deep as yours, obviously, but yes. Very."

"Do go on."

"I idolized my father and had always wanted to do something with that love of the genre that he had instilled in me, something that would make him proud. I majored in film in college, thinking I might become the next great horror director. I made a few short student films, won a couple local awards, but never pursued it. Watching movies and critiquing them appealed more to the analytical nature I had also gotten from him. So I concentrated on the film study courses, with some vague idea that I might become a critic or cinema scholar.

"But—there's always a 'but' in life, isn't there?—as I got deeper into the study of horror movies, I became fascinated by the legends the monsters were based on, to the point where I ended up pursuing a second major in folklore.

"I was having a good career as a college professor, teaching courses on the horror film, writing for various film magazines, spending most of my summers tracking down one legend or another. My father was still teaching at Maryland when I became a part of the faculty. Our minds thought so much alike that we always had to get together before planning our courses for the next semester, to make sure we didn't both end up teaching the same thing. With my background in folklore, I always taught the Ray Harryhausen course, since he used those stories from Greek Mythology."

"I knew Ray Harryhausen's mentor. Willis O'Brien. Tod got me in to see him when O'Brien was working on *King Kong*. He showed me how he did his stop-motion technique."

Quinn was much more interested in hearing those kinds of behind-the-scenes stories—from what had to be the only person still alive to tell them—than in talking about himself, but he understood the desire of a recluse to get to know the stranger he had risked inviting into his home. As much as he wanted to take Markov's fascinating tidbit about Willis O'Brien and run with it, he needed to finish his story.

As though reading his mind, Markov said, "Please— continue."

"You asked if I believed in monsters. No, I don't, but I've become fascinated by humanity's obsession with them, going back to Beowulf and Grendel and beyond, to the oral traditions when the tales first got told around the campfire. Why did we invent monsters for all the ills that plague us? Why have we been drawn to scary stories from the very beginning, like Poe's Imp of the Perverse? Why do we like to be scared? There have been a lot of attempts to explain it, but no one really knows.

"I put together a graduate course that was my attempt to shed some light on the subject: *Monsters and Why We Need Them*. My research led me to write a book with the same title. The book did well and the course was extremely popular. They both traced the evolution of monsters from their origins in folklore to the present day. In the graduate course,

I had the added advantage of being able to have lively discussions of books that had played a part, and screenings of horror movies that had done the same. I had an entire two-week unit devoted to the mythology of vampires—which means, by the way, that I've watched and discussed *Dracula* many, many times."

"It sounds as though your Dracula—would *obsession* be too strong a word?—might be second only to mine."

"No, it wouldn't be, and yes, you're probably right."

"Are you still teaching?"

"No. My studies had led me down an unexpected path: investigating the belief among a growing segment of the population that these creatures are *real*. That unnameable monsters lurk in all the hidden realms on earth. What I have dubbed the Shadowland. The belief has become so widespread that it has spawned countless TV shows documenting the search for these creatures. A field of pseudoscience has developed to explore it."

"Cryptozoology," Markov said.

"Yes. Every place on earth has legends about creatures living in its uncharted regions. Mothman, Bigfoot, Wolf Men, vampires, creatures from the deep. But the line between legend and reality has always been blurred. Has it all been superstition? Were these all the fanciful tales of writers, the wild imaginings of unenlightened explorers, or … *were* there dragons? Was there a Grendel? A Cyclops? Were there night prowlers and shadow creatures from another dimension? Finding those answers has become my life's work."

"It is a subject in which I, too, have a great interest," Markov said.

"In any case, over the years I've watched creatures of

superstition and legend and fiction evolve into becoming accepted as real beings. In some cases more than accepted. Admired. Worshipped. Facebook pages devoted to vampires, werewolves, demons. In the worst cases, it has led to bondage, torture, killing. An unmistakable trend has developed in our society. More and more, people have been acting out the horror they see in books and movies. Particularly movies, where seeing and hearing the horror can affect us far more profoundly than printed words on a page."

"Movie horror bleeding into real life," Markov observed.

"Aptly put." Quinn inwardly winced at the memory of how his father had died.

"Another concept with which I am very familiar," Markov said.

What did that mean? Again Quinn stifled the urge to respond, not wanting to derail the conversation. "In my case," he continued, "the unanticipated outcome of all that research was my realization that I had opened a Pandora's Box. In this day of social media, out there in the vast unpoliced regions of cyberspace, virtual cults have been developing. A parallel universe, where a love of horror stories has mutated into monster worship. Admiring conversations in chat rooms about the darkest aspects of humanity. The deeper you dig, the darker it gets. It goes from talking to doing. Groups believing they *are* these creatures, emulating them, engaging in their practices."

Markov's gaze narrowed. "Such as?"

"You find grave robbers. Ghouls. Zombies. Flesh eaters. Blood drinkers. Sex with corpses. Then, in the comments, people saying how funny they find it all."

Markov's gaze became more penetrating. "We shall

indeed have much to discuss. As one who has spent his life creating movie monsters, and collecting them in my Chamber of Horrors, I am all too familiar with the influence of movies on human behavior."

Creating movie monsters? Chamber of Horrors? Markov's comments screamed for responses, and Quinn had come to the point in his story where he'd be happy to change the subject. "I'm eager to have those discussions," he said, "but if you'd like me to go on, this is the point in my rather long-winded tale where, as you so aptly put it, movie horror bleeds into real life."

"I do not find your tale long-winded at all. I am finding it most interesting, especially since your life seems to have many parallels to mine. And—you may already know this—but it has taken me a very long life to accept an inescapable truth: one can never be truly happy until one makes peace with whatever is hidden away in the secret chambers of the heart."

"There is wisdom in that, certainly."

"I must hear how your story ends. Then I will tell you mine."

"Very well. Five years ago, two things happened that made me take stock of my life. I turned fifty, and my father …" He started to say "passed away" again, but what Markov had just said made him reconsider. After keeping what had happened that night inside all these years, this might be the right time and place to unlock that secret chamber in his heart. Maybe finally talking about his father's death would start to pull him out of the downward spiral his life had become since that night. "… my father was murdered."

Hearing himself use the correct word roused him into plunging ahead with ruthless honesty. "We had gone to a horror movie on Halloween for our annual father/son birthday ritual. We'd gotten too old for costumes, but most of the audience was wearing one. The movie wasn't very good, but we were old-school moviegoers. We never left our seats until the last credit disappeared from the screen.

"This particular night, one other person was still in the theater when we got up. Several rows back. A man wearing the same mask Michael Myers wore in *Halloween*. Just before we got to his row, he stepped into the aisle and blocked our path." Despite his steely effort to maintain composure, a hollow sigh escaped. He gathered himself to say something he'd only said once before: on the witness stand. "He stabbed my father in the heart."

Markov made a small groan. Quinn went on.

"At the trial, the killer said the rubber mask had actually been used in one of the *Halloween* movies. He had gotten it at an auction, and whenever he put it on, he claimed the spirit of Michael Myers got into him. A medical expert for the defense presented a very artfully constructed argument for his 'personality disorder,' but to me it was all just courtroom bullshit. There is only one explanation for something like that: pure wanton evil."

Markov made a small shake of his head and closed his eyes. When he opened them, his eyes were filled with genuine sadness. "You have my condolences, Mr. Quinn. Something similar happened to me years ago. It ripped my family apart."

"What happened?"

"That would be one dark tale too many for our first night together. I will let you finish yours, then we can move on to lighter matters. There will be time later to go digging into the secret chambers of my heart."

Quinn nodded. "That night affected me profoundly. It was ironic, because even though my father loved horror, a generally amoral genre, he was a very moral man. He abhorred movies with no conscience, where evil went unpunished. He hated what he called the slice 'n' dice movies that became fashionable in the '70s, when filmmakers started trying to outdo each other with gratuitous buckets of gore and thinking up new ways to show the human body being mutilated."

"Slasher films," Markov said. "They started to show the things Tod had cut away from. Even in the pre-code days, you could only go so far."

"Would he have shown it if he could?"

Markov considered the idea. "An interesting question. Knowing the sadistic paths his muse took him down, yes, I think he would."

"I think you're probably right. In any case, what happened that night made me think long and hard about my father's keen sense of right and wrong—another of his traits he'd passed on to me. I decided that, if his death was going to have any meaning, I could no longer simply sit in the safe halls of academia, intellectualizing about fictional horrors, while watching those horrors becoming real enough to kill. It was time to see if there was a way to combat the evil he and I had spent so many hours lamenting.

"So, I quit teaching to become a consultant for law enforcement. Because of my background in folklore, my area of expertise became murder cases that had a ritual or occult aspect. Of which, sadly, not only has there been an endless supply, but the cases keep getting sicker and sicker. It's a shocking eye-opener. I came to realize that evil is not just an abstract notion for academics to ponder. Evil *exists*.

The impulse to commit the most appalling atrocities is *real*. No one knows where this impulse comes from, whether from within or without. All we know is that, every day, it overtakes countless human beings around the world to leave behind a trail of blood and death. I was hoping that a better understanding of what made people do these horrific things might be able to prevent some of them from happening. Might help to put the lid back on Pandora's Box."

"And has it?"

"Not to any noticeable degree. My last case was particularly appalling. A satanic cult making child-porn snuff films, where after the child was violated, the boy or girl was killed and offered up as a sacrifice." Another despairing sigh escaped. "Just when you think it's gotten as bad as it can get, it seems there's always a deeper level of Hell."

"Yet another thing we have in common."

"What's that?"

"Our journey into the deepest levels of Hell."

Quinn couldn't imagine a deeper level than satanic child porn. He started to say something about his Hell being real and Markov's only being in the movies, but he wanted to steer the conversation away from the depressing turn it had taken. He had come here to pick the brain of a man who had to be a treasure trove of stories from Universal's golden age of horror, not discuss the real-life horrors his work as a consultant made him desperately want to forget.

"Movies influencing behavior is far from new," Markov said. "*London After Midnight* came out in 1927. The makeup Lon came up with for that part—especially that hideous rictus—scared people out of their wits. To the point where a man in London killed a woman, claiming he had a vision of Lon Chaney goading him into it."

"I read about that case. He slashed her throat with a razor. But until recently, such cases were relatively rare. Now they're all too common."

"Life imitating art," Markov said.

"Something like that. Be that as it may, my last case was so horrific I'm taking a hiatus. Trying to decide what I want to do with the rest of my life."

The sound of a log rustling in the fireplace got their attention, and they turned to watch it slide off the grate amid a shower of sparks.

"It warms the body but not the soul," Markov said.

Quinn glanced at his empty snifter. "Depends on the soul, I suppose. Some are harder to warm than others. In some of the killers I've seen, their soul had become a permanently frozen wasteland. If they ever had one."

Markov swirled his brandy with an air of melancholy, then took a deliberate sip to savor its passage into his system. "So. You have given up on the horror film?"

"No, I still watch them, but not as much. Most of the newer ones are terrible, and I won't watch the slice 'n' dice ones. I don't want to be repulsed. I want to be *scared*. When I get in the mood for a horror movie now, I usually just watch one of the old ones for the umpteenth time."

"And yet you are bothered by their consequences for society. How do you reconcile those conflicting viewpoints?"

"They're not reconcilable. I live with it by knowing I've at least tried to do something to stop human monsters."

"Yours is an interesting story, Mr. Quinn. One, it seems, that ultimately comes down to what is at the core of every story: good versus evil."

"Ultimately, yes."

Markov stood, and Quinn was again impressed by his erect posture and general sturdiness for his age. "Let's pause for refreshment." He tugged on the rope bell and gave instructions at the door. Moments later Johnny returned with a platter of cheese, crackers, fruit, and ice water. The caretaker refilled snifters, poured water, rekindled the fire, and left.

The two men picked at the snacks in silence, sipping their drinks and gazing at the fire. Quinn stole a sidelong glance at Markov and noticed that his vague resemblance to Lugosi had disappeared, at least from this angle. Seeing him in profile, Quinn did a furtive double take.

Now, with his face partially in shadow, he seemed to resemble another Universal horror legend: Lon Chaney Jr., who portrayed the Wolf Man in the black and white classic. Markov's large face seemed fuller, rounder, his prominent nose a bit wider.

Quinn turned his gaze back to the fire, silently chiding himself. After watching those movies so many times, he had to be engaging in a self-fulfilling prophecy. Almost willing the monsters to show up.

He stole another glance. The resemblance was still there. Another possibility struck him. Markov had been with Tod Browning on his collaborations with Lon Chaney's father. Maybe he'd picked up a quick magician's move for changing identities from "the Man of a Thousand Faces."

As if on cue, a flash of lightning came through the window. These atmospheric touches pulled Quinn deeper into the *mise-en-scène* of this real-life movie world. Caressed by the warm embrace of the fire, soothed and warmed from within by the brandy, he savored the pleasure he'd experienced vicariously so many times while watching movie scenes played out by the hearth. Now, instead of *watching* the scene, he was *in* it.

In one deft movement Markov pushed his plate aside, nestled his snifter in one hand, and melded himself into his chair. Swirling and sniffing the amber liquid, he lifted his glass in salute and took a deliberate sip. "You appear to be in very good shape, Mr. Quinn."

"I decided years ago I wasn't going to be the nerdy, rumpled stereotype of the college professor. I run and I work out. In what some of my colleagues used to tell me was an overcompensating move, I played rugby for several years. I'd rather wear out than rust out."

"A good philosophy," Markov said. After they each sipped their brandies, he said, "Now I shall tell you about my *Dracula* experience—in its own way a tale of good versus evil."

CHAPTER 4

Hypnotic reflections from the fire animated Markov's chameleonic expression as he began to weave his tale.

"I believe in destiny, Mr. Quinn. And just as destiny has led you to me, destiny led me to *Dracula*. As a boy, I'd had a love of movies since the first moment I went to one. This was during the silent era.

"My childhood was not a happy one. Cruel father, weak mother. As destiny would have it, not only did we live in Los Angeles, we lived only a few blocks from Broadway. One movie palace after another got built on that street. The public couldn't get enough. My father was happy to have me out of the house, and my mother let me do anything, so from the time I was six they would give me the money and let me go by myself.

"I would sit in the magnificent *Orpheum*—a gold-lined movie kingdom, I its little king—watching whatever was showing over and over. Wishing I could trade places with the people up on the screen. I wanted to stay there and never leave. To be *in* the movies up on the screen, literally. Of course, even then I knew that wasn't possible. Some part of my young brain knew that the people up there weren't real, that they somehow materialized on the screen. I became obsessed with knowing how movie magic was done.

"I began pestering the projectionist. He took me under his wing, showed me how film worked, how movies were really a series of still photos creating the illusion of movement. I would become mesmerized looking at those small individual frames of my movie idols, bits of their lives frozen forever.

"I hung around the theater every spare moment, eventually working there during summer vacations from school. I saw every movie over and over, studying them, watching how the camera was set up, how it moved, where the cuts were. That was the beginning of my film education. I devoured every word I could find on filmmaking. There wasn't much in those days, but there was enough to give me the basic idea.

"In 1918, I sneaked into the premiere at the first *Grauman's*. I remember it vividly. So many stars and famous directors, I thought I had died and gone to heaven. Charlie Chaplin. D. W. Griffith. Cecil B. DeMille. Tod later told me he was there, although I didn't know him then.

"I got a job there that summer. It was thrilling to be working in what was then the state-of-the-art in motion picture exhibition. My film education was developing right along with the development of cinema.

"The next summer I graduated from high school with one burning goal: to work at a Hollywood studio. Security seemed more lax at Universal, and from reading the trades I knew Tod Browning was filming his latest picture there. I'd been following his work since *The Eyes of Mystery*. It was the type of film I loved: a spooky gothic chiller, full of hidden sliding doors, secret passages, all of that. From reading all the movie gossip, I'd also learned that Tod was a huge baseball fan, and that since he was from Louisville, he rooted for the Cincinnati Reds. Armed with that bit of information, I hatched a plan that might get me in to see him. I knew very little about baseball, but I made it my business to learn everything I could, especially about the Cincinnati team.

"Again, as fate would have it, they were running away with the National League that year. 1919. Tod was thirty-nine, which meant he had probably been rooting for them for thirty years or so, and they had always been mediocre. Now that they would almost certainly be going to the World Series for the first time, I knew the fan part of him had to be very excited. Since timing is everything, I gambled on waiting to see if the Reds would win the pennant, which I knew would put him in a great mood and help my plan. They were so much better than the other teams that year that they clinched the pennant by mid-September.

"First thing the next morning, I put my plan in motion. I played hooky and went to the nearest Western Union office to send a telegram to Tod. But instead of having them deliver it to the studio, I gave them the address of a ne'er-do-well school chum. Jed Prater. His parents never seemed to be around, and he was always ready to skip school for any shady scheme.

"A couple weeks earlier, I had bought a Western Union uniform from one of the ushers I worked with at *Grauman's*. He worked for Western Union part-time and was happy to sell me one of his old uniforms for the then-astronomical sum of ten dollars. So after receiving the telegram at Jed's, I donned the uniform and marched confidently up to Universal's front gate, telling the guard I had a telegram for Mr. Browning that had to be signed for by him personally."

A hint of an appreciative smile tilted Markov's mouth.

"All those hours I had spent in front of the mirror imitating my favorite actors must have paid off, because the guard sent for a production assistant to escort me to Mr. Browning, no questions asked."

"What did the telegram say?"

"Something like, 'Dear Mr. Browning: You probably don't remember me, but we met at one of your premieres and talked about our love of the Cincinnati Reds. Looks like our boys finally made it. Just wanted to share the moment with someone who has suffered for as long as I have. Maybe you can make a movie about this year's team one of these days.'

"I had signed it George Smith, purposely choosing the commonest name I could think of to avoid being traced. I knew he must meet so many people he'd never remember this person. I had also planned the timing very carefully. From reading the trades I knew that productions took a break for lunch. I also knew that, at Universal at least, stars and directors often had their own bungalows. If I could catch Tod there, I might have him all to myself for a few minutes to make my pitch. I arrived at the gate at exactly 12:05, to allow him time to get to his bungalow and get settled in. I was indeed taken to his bungalow. Again destiny took me by the hand.

"Just as I was about to go in Tod's bungalow, Irving Thalberg was coming out. The 'Boy Wonder' himself. I recognized him instantly from having seen his picture so often in the trades. Tod waved me over, smiling from ear to ear. After he read the telegram, he looked me up and down.

'Son,' he said, 'you must be my lucky charm. Do you know who that man was who just walked out?'

'Certainly, sir. Irving Thalberg. He's in charge of production at Universal.'

'Indeed he is. And for my next picture he just assigned me to direct Universal's biggest production ever.'

"With just the right note of breathless admiration, I said, 'A Jewel DeLuxe Production?'"

'You seem to know the moving picture business very well, young man.'

"I assured him that I did, quickly rattling off my experience, telling him I wanted moviemaking to be my life, and that if he could give me a job I would do anything that needed doing to make his life easier. I remember him fiddling with his mustache for a moment, then saying the words that changed my life forever: 'Maybe I could use a good-luck charm when I'm getting ready to start the biggest picture of my career.'

"He told me to report to the gate the next morning and he would find something for me to do. From that point on he always called me Lucky."

Quinn cocked his head. "That's interesting. Tod's biography mentions that, after he retired to Malibu, he became very fond of a house painter named Lucky. They became drinking buddies, to the point where Tod told Lucky that, when he died, he wanted him to come to his funeral and spend the night toasting him with Coors. Which supposedly actually happened."

"That wasn't the house painter drinking those toasts at his funeral. That was me. The painter and I looked a little alike, and people didn't know either of us very well. Tod told me he called that man Lucky sometimes, because with me no longer around, he hoped using the name would bring him luck."

That explained all the Coors cans he'd seen earlier. They were a tribute to Browning.

"I became Tod's right arm," Markov continued. "No one could have had a better film education. For years I was at his side, learning everything conceivable about filmmaking, from the best in the business. When he was sure no producers were around, he even let me direct a few scenes. I was with him on all the Chaney-Browning films, which were largely manifestations of Tod's sadistic, twisted view of life—a vision I shared. Tod had been called the Edgar Allan Poe of the cinema. He considered that a great compliment, since he thought Poe was one of the great masters of horror. So did I. I wanted to follow in Tod's footsteps, become the ultimate horror director, make the ultimate horror picture. Thus began my—to borrow Poe's phrase—descent into the maelstrom."

He fell silent as Johnny came in without being summoned, tending to the fire and their drinks, gathering up empty plates. The caretaker stopped near Markov, gaze directed toward the floor, posture slightly tilted by the bad leg. "Will there be anything else?"

"No, thank you, Johnny. We shall take care of ourselves for the rest of the evening."

The servant nodded and cast a quick glance at Quinn. In the seconds that they held each other's gaze, Quinn sensed Johnny trying to convey something, perhaps a desire to talk privately. He watched the steward of the castle shuffle away, wanting to see if there would be a second glance to strengthen the vague hint of the first, but Johnny never turned around.

Markov made a point of waiting until the door was closed before going on. "Tod and Lon had been talking about doing *Dracula* for years. Since Bram Stoker's widow was keeping an iron grip on the movie rights, in 1927 they made their cleverly disguised version: *London After Midnight.* The first American vampire film," he added with a trace of pride. "Not only did it scare audiences to death, it was their biggest box-office smash. We all figured that sooner or later someone would get the rights to *Dracula*, so while we were shooting *London After Midnight,* Lon started to develop his Dracula makeup. Finally Universal got the rights, and Carl Laemmle gave his son the green light to make the picture— with the stipulation that Lon Chaney play Dracula. Unfortunately, Lon died before production began."

Quinn said, "Which opened the door that led to Bela Lugosi's screen immortality."

A hint of the Transylvanian actor flickered across Markov's face and quickly disappeared. "He certainly put his stamp on the role, but we'll never know what Lon might have done. Although I have a short he made that gives a good idea."

"I would love to see it."

Markov nodded. "In any case, we filmed *Dracula* with Lugosi, and by the time we were done, I felt my film education was complete. My mind was brimming with creative ways to use the camera—and now, sound—to scare people. Filmmaking is a technology-driven art and, as fate would have it, I had a genius for technology. I could instantly grasp how things worked, and I had been tutored by the best as each new innovation came in. I had learned how to record sound, for example, by sitting at the elbow of Douglas Shearer when we were at MGM."

"Douglas Shearer," Quinn said. "An absolute giant in the development of sound. His name is in the credits of virtually every MGM film for decades."

"Yes. He and many other pioneers of film were the professors who taught me every aspect of moviemaking. I learned makeup, for example, from Lon Chaney himself."

"Really? Chaney was notoriously secretive about his makeup."

"True. And he kept his secrets. I'm talking about the basics, a few tricks here and there. Sometimes I would approximate some of his grotesqueries as his stand-in while he was getting ready for the next shot."

Quinn felt as though he'd entered a time machine and been transported to one of his favorite moments in history. The fact that he was talking to the one man in the world who had been privy to even the most rudimentary of Lon Chaney's makeup secrets shook loose an avalanche of questions, but he didn't want to disrupt the flow of the evening. He forced himself to keep quiet and let his strange host tell his tale in his own way.

"I was anxious to start making my own films," Markov went on, "but Tod and I seemed to need each other, so I stayed by his side. Probably longer than I should have." A barely perceptible wistful sigh escaped before he added, "But those are stories for another time. You asked about my involvement with *Dracula*. As you can see, it was really an involvement with Tod Browning that eventually led to *Dracula*. I can regale you with anecdotes from the set later, if you wish, but it is getting late, and there are other things we need to discuss."

"However you want to tell your story is fine with me," Quinn said. "I find it all quite fascinating."

"Very well. One moment while I tend to my duties as a stoker."

He gave a wry grin, and Quinn made an appreciative nod at his pun. As Markov prodded the fire and effortlessly added two more large logs, Quinn marveled at how physically sound he was at such an advanced age. Johnny had also appeared very sturdy, and Quinn wondered how the elderly hermit and his servant kept so fit.

The fire leapt back to life. Markov's expression hardened as he resumed his story. "When we were shooting *Dracula* I'd had an unpleasant exchange with Junior."

"Carl Laemmle's son."

Markov nodded.

"In my research that led me to you," Quinn said, "I got access to all of Universal's production notes on *Dracula*. I read Carl Junior's memo to Browning, asking him to keep an eye on you, because you were—in his words—'taking liberties.'"

The first hint of color came onto Markov's pale face, but he remained otherwise inscrutable. "Indeed," he said coolly. "What else did he say?"

"He said he walked in on you in Lugosi's dressing room when Lugosi wasn't there. You were wearing his cape and standing in front of the mirror saying, 'I ... am Dracula.' Which of course Lugosi often did between takes to stay in character. Laemmle also said you were 'haunting' the Spanish production that was shooting on the same sets at night. That you sometimes spent the night sleeping in Dracula's coffin. Laemmle was concerned that you would disrupt the production, upset the artists."

Quinn didn't mention another memo he'd discovered when researching Browning's productions at MGM. During the shooting of *London After Midnight*, Irving Thalberg had cautioned Browning about Tilton, who had been seen rummaging around in "something even God cannot touch. Lon Chaney's makeup kit."

"Yes," Markov said defiantly. "I did those things. Being a part of *Dracula* was the ultimate dream come true for me. I had been obsessed by the Dracula/vampire mystique since reading Bram Stoker's novel as a boy. I'd probably read the book at least a dozen times. And, yes. While the others were laughing and joking between takes, I took it *very* seriously. It was real to me. I felt evil on that set. It emanated from Lugosi, because he took his character so seriously. For me, that opening line of his is still the most powerful in the history of cinema:

"I am … Dracula."

CHAPTER 5

Markov delivered the line perfectly. Possibly even more chillingly than Lugosi.

"I was completely in Lugosi's thrall. My God, I helped set up the lighting for those famous close-ups of his eyes. Those *eyes*."

Markov's gaze shifted from Quinn to the empty space behind Quinn's back, as though Lugosi were back there pulling him in with that mesmeric stare. A few seconds later he blinked, and whatever he'd seen or imagined lost its hold. "There were many such moments," he went on. "Another was when I helped set up the famous shot looking down on Dwight Frye in the hold, and he gives that maniacal laugh."

"An iconic shot. Arguably the creepiest laugh in cinema history. Did it seem that way at the time?"

"Of course, we didn't think of it in those terms, but yes. It was chilling. Give Dwight Frye credit. That laugh was his invention. He was a highly dedicated stage actor whose star had been rising on Broadway. One critic had compared him to Barrymore. Tod had told him that, for that shot, they needed the insane look and laugh of a person becoming a vampire, a good man who had been turned into something evil, and that's what Dwight came up with.

"And Lugosi. His very presence in that role was chilling. And not just because he had the look and the voice. None of that would have mattered if he hadn't been the dedicated actor he was, who took his role so seriously. Some of the other actors made fun of him standing in front of the mirror during breaks, practicing his entrance line: 'I am … Dracula.' But that's why it's remembered as one of the most famous moments in cinema history, while their careers are entirely forgotten. Lugosi wasn't just hitting his mark and saying his lines. He knew he was playing a role he was born to play. My experience on *Dracula* was the most powerful of my life. It haunts me to this day."

With a move obviously perfected through long practice, he swirled and drank his brandy, as though anesthetizing eighty-year-old ghosts.

"When *Dracula* turned out to be a smash, studios realized there was big money to be made in horror. I was putting together my pitch to persuade the Laemmles to let me direct, but Thalberg had gone to MGM, and when he offered Tod a deal to come over there, I reconsidered. I'd been in Tod's shadow for so long at Universal, they probably just considered me a gopher. And since Tod had gotten the okay to bring me with him to MGM, I decided one picture would get us established and I could make my pitch there. Unfortunately, that one picture was *Freaks*."

Markov shook his head, the regret still fresh after all these years. "Tod had been determined to do it for years, and on the heels of his *Dracula* success, Thalberg humored him. The movie was an utter disaster. People ran from the theater at the preview. Watching those real-life sideshow freaks was unbearable to most people. Tod's career never recovered. He and everyone associated with him fell into disfavor. I stuck around, visions of directing burning in my head, but nowhere to take them. MGM certainly didn't want to hear from Tod Browning's 'personal assistant,' and I was sure that going back to Universal would be a dead end.

"As eager as I was to start my own career, I couldn't bring myself to abandon him when he was at his lowest. I stayed with him, hoping I could help him turn it around. But the handwriting was on the wall. MGM only gave him four pictures in the next seven years. For me the best part of that whole miserable period was learning more about the camera from James Wong Howe when he shot *Mark of the Vampire*."

"One of the all-time great cinematographers."

"Without question. He told me Lon knew more about the camera than any actor he ever worked with. In the early days at Universal, Lon had done some directing. He loved to make home movies. Sometimes he'd film things between takes, some short scenario he'd concocted. When we finish here I can show you the one I mentioned earlier."

"I'm looking forward to it," Quinn said.

Markov nodded, gazing sadly at his brandy but leaving it on the table, as though some memories were beyond its capacity to heal.

"In 1941, Tod finally gave up and retired to Malibu. I stayed in Los Angeles to pitch whatever stories I came up with. I didn't need the work or the money. I'd gotten rich by using my insider knowledge to invest in sure things in the film industry—technological breakthroughs, productions I knew would make money. So I spent my time writing.

"My obsession with the Dracula legend had always made me want to make my own version. I saw what Tod did wrong—the staginess, the slow, talky pace, unimaginative camera work, and so on—and was convinced I could do much better.

"My Dracula couldn't be a remake. Aside from copyright issues, I didn't want to be bound by the story as Stoker told it in his novel, or the stage version that had been adapted for the movie. Both were severely flawed, as far as I was concerned. I wanted to make a sequel. That way I could tell whatever Dracula story *I* wanted to tell. At that point, I didn't know what that story would be. All I knew was that it would pick up where *Dracula* had left off—right after Van Helsing had driven the stake into his heart. Unfortunately, Universal was thinking the same thing. While I was still trying to come up with a good scenario, they came out with their sequel."

"*Dracula's Daughter*," Quinn said. "1936. Gloria Holden played the part."

"Yes. And she had cremated his remains. How could I bring him back to life after that? I kept groping for a plausible premise. Then, in 1938, Universal re-released their biggest box-office hits as a double bill—*Dracula* and *Frankenstein*. When I saw the blockbuster business they did all over the country, I had a eureka moment: combine the central ideas of the two most popular horror stories. I wouldn't *need* Dracula's body. I could use the dead to create the undead. An entirely *new* Dracula. Not the suave Lugosi. More like Nosferatu, only worse. A hideous vampire of pure evil. Instead of lightning, I would use the blood of the original Dracula to bring him to life as a vampire."

"But if he's been cremated, how would you come up with his blood?"

"I mean the *original* Dracula. The one that inspired Bram Stoker. The Prince of Wallachia. Vlad Dracula III. Vlad the Impaler."

"Even more of a challenge. He's been dead for five hundred years."

"A challenge, yes, but not an insurmountable one. The historical record tells us Vlad Dracula was beheaded in a battle against the Turks. The body was supposedly found, but the head never was. For the purposes of my story, the head would have been recovered and kept alive. Severed heads being kept alive for some nefarious purpose is a plot device that's been used many times."

"True. That would certainly add an interesting element. Stoker used his name, which was one of the best decisions in the history of literature, and fictionalized him into a vampire, but there is no evidence that Vlad Dracula ever engaged in vampirism."

"My research had proven otherwise," Markov said.

Quinn knew how thorough his own research had been. There were apocryphal mentions of an occasional sip of blood taken from one of his impalement victims, but nothing substantiating the idea that the Wallachian ruler had been a vampire. Nevertheless, Quinn allowed for the possibility that Markov's Dracula obsession could have uncovered something he'd missed. "How so?"

"I can show you my proof later. For now, suffice it to say that this is one of the plausibility issues I agonized over. Even when I knew I was writing nonsense, such as the ridiculous notion that a brain and heart could be kept alive indefinitely in a jar, inserted into sewn-together dead tissue taken from corpses, then bombarded with electricity to create a fully-functioning human being—never mind the question of all the other internal organs that would have been needed—the scientist in me kept trying to make everything at least remotely physically possible.

"So the writing dragged on, until I saw the monster rally pictures Universal started making in the '40s. You are familiar with them, I'm sure."

"Very. Frankenstein meets the Wolf Man meets Dracula and so on. They're riddled with inconsistencies, especially the lame explanations of how monsters who seemingly died in the previous movie not only didn't die, they somehow all ended up in the same place."

"If they bothered to explain at all. When I saw *House of Dracula*, I finally accepted the fact that you could happily throw plausibility out the window."

Quinn smiled knowingly. "You must be talking about how a perfectly healthy Dracula shows up after he had gotten caught in the sunlight and turned to a skeleton in *House of Frankenstein*."

Markov sighed and shook his head. "Just waltzes in without a word of explanation, as if it never happened. I wish John Carradine's vastly overrated performance had never happened, but that's neither here nor there. The audience didn't care. They just wanted to eat popcorn while being scared by their favorite monsters, no matter who was playing them or how illogical the story was. Their appetite for horror was insatiable."

"It always has been," Quinn said. "We see it not just in movies, but whenever there's a car accident and people slow down to gawk. Or in the media's endless highlighting of real-life horrors. 'If it bleeds it leads.'"

"Indeed," Markov said. "In my case, blood *was* the lead. The crux of the story. I had made it part of the title: *The Blood of Dracula*.

"Even so, I went through countless drafts until I had a script that satisfied me. By the time I did the final re-write, the war had just ended, and I started thinking of my Dracula as a kind of Hitler. But instead of an Aryan master race, his master race would be vampires. Thus Dracula would remain the supreme ruler for all eternity of the most powerful race on earth. A master race of vampires."

"An interesting approach," Quinn said. As he tried to guess where that angle might have taken Markov's Dracula, he felt the same excitement he'd often felt during one of the exercises he'd conducted in his screenwriting class. He and his students would invent a premise for a horror movie, then see how far they could take it in one session. Ideas for plot elements would start bouncing around the room, coming faster and faster, until the more dramatic students couldn't sit still and began acting out moments. Especially the scary ones.

"So did your movie get made?" Quinn asked.

Markov's sip of brandy was apparently to steel himself for the next part of the story.

"The furor over *Freaks* had died down, so I made the rounds of the major studios, hat in hand. Producers kept me dangling, waiting for phone calls that never came." Bitterness tightened his features. "I got disgusted. With myself for groveling, as much as with the benighted fools who had been given the keys to the kingdom. I shoved the script into a drawer and left it there. But I couldn't get it out of my mind.

"Finally I swallowed my pride and made the rounds again—this time to the poverty row studios. I reached the bottom of the barrel and persuaded Midnight Pictures to let me make it. They gave me two weeks and thirty thousand dollars. It was barely released in 1947. My *magnum opus*. And, until now, my swan song."

"I would love to see it."

Markov seemed to be deciding how much of his life to reveal. "We shall see. That film is so painful for me that I haven't watched it since the initial screening."

"I understand."

"I kept waiting to see if it would bring me any offers, but none came and I was pushing fifty. I'd had enough of Hollywood, and New York's film industry was taking off, so I moved my family there. More promises that were never kept. My monomania drove us to Boston, thinking I might be a bigger fish in a smaller pond. More lies."

Maybe you just weren't good enough, Quinn thought. Whatever the reason, Markov couldn't be telling him the whole story.

"Finally I decided to do what Carl Laemmle had done: create my own studio with its own backlot. A self-contained world for making movies. Of course, mine is much bigger. He started Universal on a 230-acre lot. My property here is almost 7,000 acres."

"But why here? It's virtually inaccessible. The long, harsh winters would make outdoor shooting difficult. There's no talent pool—"

"I had my reasons. I wanted to be left alone to do things my own way. As for talent and accessibility, I wrote treatments that wouldn't need a big cast and could be shot mostly indoors. I did my casting in Boston and brought everyone here. For them it was a chance to go on location. And the price for the property was right. The state was practically giving land away when I bought it in 1955.

"Five years and two million dollars later, I moved in with my second wife and two grown children. I had been grooming them as filmmakers and actors since they were little, even teaching them things like swordplay and horseback riding for the action scenes we might one day shoot. My hope was that they would eventually take over whatever I was able to build, but, alas, only one of the projects I planned has ever gotten off the ground. There were ... family problems. I will not burden you with those. They are my cross to bear."

He waved the topic away, but Quinn remembered the son who had been charged with attempted murder in Boston in 1954.

"I have many treasures and secrets I will reveal to you," Markov continued. "Some are quite dark."

A weariness had settled onto him that went beyond merely physical. Beneath his polished air, Quinn had gotten glimpses of something troubling him deep down in his soul. Markov closed his eyes and tried to massage it away. When he opened them again, a slight tremor rippled across his face. For one flicker of an instant, Quinn thought he glimpsed Lon Chaney Jr.

There was much more going on here than the nostalgia of an impossibly old eccentric. Quinn's curiosity about the supernatural and the occult sprang to life. He needed to know more. "I would like to learn as much as you care to tell me about your 'treasures and secrets.' Even the dark ones."

Markov leaned forward, alert. "Your visit has gotten the blood flowing in these old veins. When I read your background in your initial inquiry, I realized you could be the perfect person to assist in culminating my cinematic legacy."

"How so?"

"You and I are kindred spirits. You said you once

harbored the dream of becoming a great horror director. The same dream I have harbored all my life. It is too late for me to have a career, but I am almost finished making the ultimate horror film. A monster rally to end all monster rallies."

"With all of the classic Universal monsters?" Quinn asked.

"Yes, but with all of the hokiness removed. I have had to work like Orson Welles did on some of his ill-fated projects, shooting scenes off and on for years. All of that footage has been edited and is ready to go. All that remains is to shoot the climactic sequence. If it comes off as planned, it will secure my cinematic immortality. The moment my life's work has been aiming for. My Rosebud."

He leaned closer. "You have walked into the ultimate reality show, Mr. Quinn. Cinéma vérité. With special effects far beyond 3D. My house and grounds are the set. Before the digital revolution, shooting our scenes was slow and cumbersome, because I had to hire a crew to drag all the equipment around for each setup. But now Johnny and I can do it all ourselves. I have installed fifty high-definition digital cameras throughout the castle and grounds that we can control from my state-of-the-art studio. We can adjust the ambient lighting, get just about any angle from wherever the scene is taking place, and so forth. Which, of course, virtually eliminates the need for setups. In this way we have been able to shoot nearly the entire film—the horror story that has been our lives. Except, as I said, the final sequence. And you are now in it."

His expression turned more serious than Quinn had yet seen it. "I had not realized until now that incorporating you into that sequence could mean danger for us all. Your very emanations could upset the delicate balance of natural and unnatural forces I have combined to create this world where … the line between movies and reality sometimes seems blurred."

Emanations upsetting unnatural forces? That sounded like the wild imaginings of a mind left alone too long to create a world of movie fantasy, but Quinn couldn't dismiss it.

"What exactly is this danger my being here could cause?" he asked.

"I cannot say precisely, because I do not know. What I *do* know is that your being here will test my creations in ways they've never been tested."

"Are you saying your castle is haunted?"

His gaze narrowed. "Extremely."

"By what?"

The intense gaze shifted inward to some troubling place. "Bad deeds," he said. "Remnants of things I have done."

"We're all haunted by those."

"Not like mine. They have begun to take on a life of their own."

That sounded impossible, but for now Quinn had to take him at his word. "If you think my being here puts any of us in jeopardy, then perhaps I should leave."

"*No,*" Markov said, a little too emphatically. "I think that would be premature. If I can find a way to write you into the final sequence, it could add a great deal of excitement. And totally aside from that, I have been looking forward to lively discussions with someone so knowledgeable about the glory days of Universal."

"As have I," Quinn said, wondering how Markov thought he could do all this after having invited him for only two days—one of which was already almost gone. Maybe he was thinking of asking him to stay longer.

The vague hint of a smile came onto Markov's lips. "In those old movies we both love—*The Most Dangerous Game* comes to mind—the mad eccentric would lock his guests in the castle for his villainous purposes. I could certainly do that, but ... while I am undeniably eccentric, I am not mad, Mr. Quinn. Like everyone I have the capacity for evil within me, but ... I am *not* evil." He sounded as though he were trying to convince himself more than Quinn. "I will not force you to stay. You must do so of your own free will."

Suppressing annoyance at the notion that he could so easily be taken prisoner, Quinn stayed focused on his mysterious host's explanation of the evil that he believed dwelled—not just in the castle—but within himself.

"In *The Most Dangerous Game*," Markov continued, "Count Zaroff was the madman behind it all. Here, of course, that would be me. My castle is my laboratory."

He tried to lighten the moment by using the comical British pronunciation—luh-BORE-uh-tree—and raising an exaggeratedly sinister eyebrow, conjuring the stereotype of countless mad movie scientists and their stock line that "I must never be disturbed when the door to my luh-BORE-uh-tree is closed."

He held the pose for a long beat before turning serious again.

"But even the mad Zaroff gave Joel McCrea and Fay Wray a sporting chance. If you recall, he had them trapped in a cave with a bow and arrow but walked away, saying he would 'hunt them like a leopard.'"

"I do recall." *You and I are kindred spirits*, Markov had said. Count Zaroff said the same thing to Joel McCrea. "So is this our version of *The Most Dangerous Game*?"

"Not exactly. But your threshold for terror may be tested. For you to make a fully informed decision about whether to stay or leave, I must show you the monsters I have created in this shrine to madness. But the things I have to show you are so far outside the boundaries of reality, our minds must be fresh. I know you must be fatigued after the rather grueling trip in the carriage, so tonight I will only show you Lon's short—a behind-the-scenes look at one of the movie moments that fueled my Dracula obsession. A Preview of Coming Attractions, if you will. I will give you the full studio tour after you have had a chance to sleep."

"I'm not fatigued," Quinn said. He looked at his watch. "It's not quite eight o'clock yet. Why not give me the full tour now? Trust me: I've spent a good chunk of my life exploring the world outside the boundaries of reality, and that's not a nine-to-five world. Besides, I didn't come here to sleep. I'll get plenty of sleep when I'm dead."

"Ah. It seems everything reminds me of a moment in *Dracula*." In an instant he arranged his facial features into a passing resemblance of Lugosi and said the famous line in the actor's voice: "To die … to be *really* dead … that must be glorious."

"One my favorite lines. Dracula says it to Mina when they're in their box at the opera."

"I'm impressed. You were born too late to be in Tod's *Dracula*, but now perhaps you can be in mine. Very well. I will give you the tour now. If you decide to stay after it is complete, I would need some time to write you into the final sequence. A few hours, at most. But it would have to be with the understanding that you cannot leave until it is done."

"So I would join you in your 'cinematic immortality?'"

"A compelling offer, I would think, for a Draculaphile

like yourself. Like me, you have followed the path that leads from the original Dracula—Vlad the Impaler—to Bram Stoker to Tod Browning and Bela Lugosi. It is not a Yellow Brick Road that leads to Oz. It is a blood-stained road that leads to Castle Markov. I have also come to think of this ill-fated pile as my version of the House of Usher. The doomed House of Markov, hidden away in 'the ghoul-haunted woodland of Weir.'"

"Another one of my favorite lines," Quinn said, trying gamely to keep the conversation on more pleasant topics. "From *Ulalume*. One of Poe's best poems."

"You share my love of Poe?"

"Yes."

Markov gave him the stare. "Can you walk out on the chance to live forever in the greatest horror movie ever made?"

Quinn was beginning to see what lay beneath Markov's polished rationale for inviting him.

Ego. He wanted an audience.

"Your offer is compelling," Quinn said. "A tad Faustian, but compelling."

"Faustian. I have found exploring the work of the devil much more interesting than exploring the work of angels. And, after all, we are talking about a path forged by one whose name means son of the Devil." A lifetime spent in a world of virtual horror tainted Markov's smile. "Of course, the path of evil is the one fraught with danger. The one I have gotten the distinct impression it has become your life's mission to follow."

Despite Markov's talk of monsters and blurring the line between movies and real life, Quinn couldn't see how being in his movie could put them all in danger. Then he remembered the night his father died, almost as if the psycho from *Halloween* had stepped off the screen to stab him. That thought triggered another one.

Being in Markov's movie, after all his dire warnings, would in a sense be a way of avenging his father's death. It would be like spitting in the eye of the man who killed him and used the movies as an excuse. *"See, you sick son of a bitch? I was in the worst horror movie ever, and it didn't make me go out and kill somebody."* It would be Quinn's way of saying that, no matter how much movies influenced real life, no matter how powerful Markov's movie monsters might be, no movie had the power to control *him*.

Another thought flashed into his brain: the memory of how much his father had loved *Dracula*, and all the happy times they'd watched it together. The chance to be in the ultimate Dracula movie, directed by a man who had been a part of the original production, would be a fitting final tribute to the memory of his father. A much better eulogy than the one he'd given in a daze at the funeral.

But as tempting as Markov's offer was, Quinn couldn't put his life on hold forever. He needed to get back and figure out what he wanted to do with the rest of it.

"I have other commitments I can't put off indefinitely," he said. "Before I make my decision I'd need at least a rough idea of how long you would need me."

"I can tell you exactly. I am determined to end the greatest horror movie ever made on the night of the next full moon, because it is known as the Blood Moon. It will add the final note of perfection—because everything in the film will have *really happened*. No stock footage of the moon. No movie hokum with stunt men and actors acting."

"When is the Blood Moon?"

"Tomorrow."

Quinn couldn't keep a skeptical look off his face. "You think you can get a monster rally sequence written and shot—with me coming into it ice cold—in one day?"

Markov smiled that unwholesome smile. "When one is driven by monsters, anything is possible."

What had struck the filmmaker part of Quinn's brain as merely impossible was beginning to sound delusional. No filmmaker in his right mind would put more pressure on himself by setting a deadline based on the name of the full moon. But the chance to bring meaning to his father's death kept Quinn from dismissing the idea, no matter how implausible.

If all the time-consuming setups had been eliminated, and Markov was an extremely fast director with the genius for special effects he claimed, maybe he could just shoot the footage of Quinn he needed by midnight. That would let him tell himself he had wrapped on the night of the Blood Moon. Then, since all the previous footage had already been edited, all he'd have to do was edit in the final sequence. It still sounded ludicrous, but maybe.

"Your shooting schedule certainly doesn't leave any margin for error," Quinn said. "Minutes are going to count. Which means the sooner we get started with the tour, the sooner I can give your proposal my full consideration."

"Fair enough. We will begin by screening Lon's short. It is a vital link in the chain of events that have led to my Dracula obsession."

He started to rise but stopped, again fixing his guest with his Dracula stare. Quinn stared back, fascinated, as he watched Markov almost imperceptibly transform himself into a stand-in for Lugosi.

I am not an impressionist. I am a re-creationist.

In his uncanny imitation of the actor's distinctive voice, Markov recited another of Dracula's lines to Renfield: "I trust you have kept your comink here a secret."

Quinn played along and gave him Renfield's slightly effeminate response. "I followed your instructions implicitly."

Markov picked up his cue. "Excellent, Mr. Quinn. Excellent."

He stood and beckoned for his guest to follow. As they exited the study, Markov spoke in his own voice. "Now I will show you the Dracula that never was."

CHAPTER 6

Markov's screening room was a large modern theater that rivaled any state-of-the-art multiplex at a mall. Its sense of spaciousness was enhanced by a floor plan that was more square than the typical rectangular design.

"I don't like long narrow rooms," Markov said. "They feel claustrophobic."

Quinn caught the obvious implication—that he shared Dracula's aversion to being enclosed in coffinlike spaces—but dismissed it as another example of his movie-influenced flair for melodrama. Instead Quinn focused on the details of the nicest home theater he had ever seen.

Everything looked new. Plush carpet covered the floor and walls, no doubt to enhance the acoustics. Several speakers embedded along each side wall meant surround sound. The floor was empty, save for two leather recliners on either side of a low table, about two-thirds of the way back from the screen. "Many more seats can be added when necessary," Markov said, "but … it has seldom been necessary." He gestured toward the rear of the theater. "First we must get our refreshments. No matter how dark life becomes, it can always be brightened with popcorn."

"Amen to that," Quinn said, following him to a small, fully-stocked refreshment counter. Several kinds of movie candy were neatly arrayed in a glass case, behind which gleamed a soda dispenser. Markov started a popcorn machine. "It will only take a few minutes. Help yourself to some candy and soda while I set things up."

Markov disappeared up a carpeted stairway behind the counter.

Quinn poured himself a large Coke and got a box of Sno-Caps. Popcorn never seemed to smell as good as when it was popping at the movies, and that smell hit him full force now. It triggered a sense memory of all those Saturdays when he was a kid, happily munching popcorn and candy while watching monsters stomp through cities and eat people.

Markov reappeared and went straight to the popcorn machine, which had just finished popping. "Butter?"

"Of course."

Markov filled two large tubs, then got a soda and a box of Raisinets for himself. He led the way to the seating area and took the recliner on the right. A black console attached to the floor beside it had several buttons on top. "My control panel," he said.

"You can start the film from here?"

Markov nodded.

"Won't you still have to get up to start the projector?"

"No. I have digitally remastered my film library onto Blu-ray discs."

"You mentioned Morbius from *Forbidden Planet* in one of your e-mails. Apparently you share Morbius's genius for technology."

Markov waved away the compliment. "Mere child's play,

as Morbius said about having 'tinkered' Robby the Robot together."

When they were settled into their seats, Markov gave a brief introduction.

"Lon made this during the shooting of *London After Midnight*. He shot it on one of the sets after everyone had gone home. He and Tod had long wanted to do *Dracula*. They had been very impressed by Murnau's unauthorized version—*Nosferatu*."

So were you, Quinn thought. *You changed your name to Schreck and named your son Max. And your belief in destiny*…. Had he adopted that belief after watching *Nosferatu*? At the very beginning of the film, Harker is accosted by a man who tells him he cannot escape his destiny by running away….

"Max Schreck is unquestionably the creepiest Dracula," Quinn said.

"Unquestionably. Tod and Lon wanted to make their version of Dracula much creepier, but since they couldn't get the rights, *London After Midnight* was their rather watered-down attempt to do as much of it as they could get away with without getting sued. Lon's sawtoothed vampire had scared people to death, but he wanted to come up with something that would outdo Schreck's Nosferatu."

"A tall order."

"Indeed, but the Man of a Thousand Faces was the man for the job." His hand went to his control panel. "Judge for yourself. This short was Lon working out some of his ideas to show Tod and the Laemmles, in case they ever got those rights. Without further ado, then." He stabbed a button and the house lights went out.

As they stared at the black screen, a single shivery violin tremolo created an air of creeping menace. The opening titles slowly materialized, indistinguishable at first until they became stark white lettering on the black background:

THE UN-DEAD
A Lon Chaney Production
Written and Directed by Lon Chaney
Guest Appearance by…?
Sound by Douglas Shearer

Sound?

The first talkie, *The Jazz Singer*, had come out just before *London After Midnight*, but Browning's film had been silent. And it couldn't have been an accident that Chaney used Bram Stoker's original title for *Dracula*. Chaney was known for thorough research that always included reading the literary sources for his projects, if there was one.

The title faded in on an opening shot of Chaney sitting in a director's chair, smiling for the camera. Quinn had been prepared by the "Sound" credit, but it was still startling when Chaney opened his mouth and spoke with a mysterious-sounding, Eastern European accent that hinted at British:

"I am Lon Chaney. I bid you welcome."

A sweeping hand gesture invited the viewer in. That shot dissolved into a long shot of a man in a cape with his back to the camera. He stood in the center of the study of the haunted estate from *London After Midnight*. Beside him, a wine glass half-filled with dark liquid sat on a table.

The man slowly began turning his head at the same time that the camera crept in for a close-up. When the face reached profile, the camera was still too far away to pick up any detail, but it was close enough to see that the face was deathly pale.

A sound like a groan of evil erupted from the speakers—the single sustained note of a cello. In the same instant, the man's head whipped full front and the camera shot forward until his face filled the screen.

Quinn flinched and felt his heart pounding. After the initial jolt, the full horror of the face burrowed into him.

Chaney's Dracula was more hideous than Max Schreck's Nosferatu. Chaney had concocted a makeup that showed the putrid decay of death that lay just beneath a ghastly veneer of life. His vampire brilliantly captured the idea of a demonic creature from the netherworld between the living and the dead.

Bits of bone were visible under skin that looked thin and taut, as if unable to regenerate itself enough to completely cover the skull. Swollen veins zigzagged along each temple and both sides of the neck. He had taken the goggle-eyed effect from *London After Midnight* much further.

Rather than applying the dark circles around the eyes that had become the stereotype for movie monstrosities, he had encircled them with orbits of bone, creating an effect of eyes staring from the empty sockets of a decomposed corpse. Beyond the mesmeric pull of the stare was a bloodless face, whose furrows and wrinkles had been darkened into an expression of jaded contempt. The thin black lips formed into a sardonic smile. They parted to reveal a set of teeth that, in such a hideous decaying face, were jarring in their perfection. He held this grin while the camera pulled back to reveal his hands, folded across his chest in the manner of a corpse.

Like Nosferatu, he had made the fingers long. But unlike Nosferatu's rotting clawlike fingernails, Chaney's were polished black and perfectly manicured into long points. Still grinning, he drummed his fingertips playfully against his chest to showcase the fingers, then lifted a hand and pointed toward his mouth.

Two fangs suddenly popped down—curved white needles like the fangs of a snake. He moved his finger to point directly at the camera.

"You, who try to steal what is left of my soul with your magic box. Come here."

He beckoned with the finger.

The camera began shakily advancing. It stopped and steadied several feet short of Chaney and waited. "Leave your magic box behind," he said. "I have an earth box that will give you a much more satisfying immortality than your little picture show. Come." He beckoned again.

The camera jiggled slightly but kept running from the same spot. Seconds later the cameraman came into the shot, facing Chaney, back to the camera.

"Ah," Chaney said to the figure, who was dressed in a cape. "I see you are already one of us. Good. A cameraman who can help me steal the souls of the living. Show the audience the eyes through which they will watch our race take over."

The cameraman moved to stand beside Chaney, then spun around.

He was the sawtoothed vampire from *London After Midnight*.

Chaney put an arm around the man's shoulders, then beckoned for the camera to come closer. It moved in until the two hideous faces filled the screen like masks from the Grand Guignol. The camera held on that disturbing image for several seconds, then inched ever closer until only their hypnotic eyes filled the screen. An iris fade-out began, stopping to hold on the demonic stares. In a blink the iris closed, the screen went black, and the evil cello note burst from the speakers. An instant later the final title came on:

The Beginning

Markov brought up the house lights and waited.

"Brilliant," Quinn said. "Much creepier than Nosferatu. I think it's the best makeup Chaney ever did. Scarier than his Phantom of the Opera, and that's saying something. The scene where the Phantom was unveiled is one of the scariest moments in film history."

"I know. I was at the premiere. You could hear thumping throughout the theater as kids flung themselves to the floor. Some people even fled the theater."

A thrill coursed through Quinn. Markov's statement reminded him that he was talking to the only living eyewitness to many of the pivotal moments in the history of horror cinema.

"Chaney's Dracula would have been groundbreaking," Quinn said. "The camera work was very sophisticated. Especially that lightning fast camera movement into a close-up of Chaney's face."

Pride brightened Markov's somber visage. "I was the cameraman. Until the last moment when Tod took over so I could get into the shot."

"That was you?"

"Yes. As I said, I was often Lon's stand-in."

"Very effective. In fact, the whole film was doing things that would have been groundbreaking. Sound, of course. Using those sudden musical notes to heighten the shocks. The dialogue was impressive as well. Very sophisticated. Chaney was a good writer. Those had to be the first words he ever spoke on-screen."

"They were."

"How did he make those fangs pop down?"

"He had them fitted onto a spring mechanism that retracted up close to the roof of his mouth. When the time came he would slip his tongue over the mechanism and press until the spring kicked in, and the teeth would pop down."

"Way ahead of its time in depicting vampire fangs."

"Chaney was way ahead of his time in many ways," Markov said. "The way he immersed himself in his characters, he was essentially a method actor long before anyone had heard of such a thing. I worked with some greats."

"You did indeed."

"I can regale you with some of those stories later," he said. "Now we must move to my studio. In the old days studios were called 'dream factories.' Mine is a nightmare factory. The place where I make my monsters."

"Your luh-BORE-uh-tree?"

Markov didn't smile. "Indeed."

CHAPTER 7

The flickering gaslights created a jittery shadow dance as the two men headed down the long corridor. Holding a candle lantern in front of them for added illumination in the gloomy passage, Markov led the way.

They hadn't gone far when they came to an elaborately carved wooden door on the left. "The entrance to your bedchamber," Markov said without slowing. A short distance beyond the door, they reached a corner where the corridor they were on intersected with another that ran to the right. Quinn stopped when he saw what was standing on a pedestal in the corner.

Shrouded in a black cowl, a grinning skeleton holding a scythe in one hand and brandishing a crucifix in the other stared from eyeless sockets.

Markov held the light closer to the figure. "One of my most prized pieces from my collection of movie memorabilia." The strobe effect of the candlelight animated the lifeless skull.

Quinn searched the film archives in his brain for which movie this would have come from. "Is this from the opening cemetery sequence in *Frankenstein?*"

"The very same."

"But Browning didn't direct that. James Whale did. I would think each set would have been closely guarded."

"They were. I didn't take it from the set. I got it years later at an auction. I paid a king's ransom for it, but I had to have it."

Still holding the light in front of the skull, he said, "All of my set decorations are placed with a particular thought in mind. I added the scythe, meaning to suggest the Grim Reaper. The idea behind placing him at this intersection is that he is poised at the threshold between the living and the dead, waiting for new souls to harvest."

"Not a comforting thought for your guests, to have him right outside their door."

"True. Consider that a small test of your love of horror."

They rounded the corner and headed down another long, windowless corridor. Quinn began counting his paces, wanting to create a mental map of the layout. He had counted thirty when they came to another finely crafted wooden door on the right.

"Johnny's quarters," Markov said without slowing.

Thirty-one paces later they came to a similar door and stopped.

Markov pulled out a skeleton key. "Not exactly the most sophisticated locking system, but I didn't want to keep track of countless keys. This way I need only one. There was also the matter of not violating the set design. The movie of my life is a period piece."

"I thought I saw a modern lock on the door to Johnny's quarters."

"Everyone needs their privacy. The need is especially acute for two people in such an … unusual relationship, so cut off from the world. Johnny's apartment is the only exception to my one-lock rule."

"A good policy," Quinn said. "By the way, I must compliment you on your Art Direction and Set Decoration. Cedric Gibbons would approve."

"Oh, come now. I have a high opinion of my talents, but Gibbons is the god of art directors. He won eleven Oscars. You flatter me."

"No, I don't. You've done an excellent job of designing a home that blurs the line between movies and real life."

Markov gave him the now-familiar stare. "In my case there isn't one. My horror film is the record of the horror of my life. They are one and the same."

CHAPTER 8

Johnny sat at the control panel in the steward's quarters, watching them on one of two dozen large monitors that gave views of every part of the castle and grounds. Markov and Quinn had stopped by the Grim Reaper to discuss something. Alongside the bank of monitors was an array of controls for everything from panning or tilting a particular camera to starting the coffee in the kitchen. Johnny pushed a button.

A tiny camera embedded in one of the eye sockets of the Grim Reaper took a picture that would enable it to instantly recognize the new soul that had come into their realm.

Markov led them into his laboratory. After he closed the door, Johnny pushed another button.

The scythe made a vicious *whoosh* as it rent the air.

Practice.

CHAPTER 9

Markov unlocked the door and pressed a button on the inside wall. Fluorescent light bathed a vast studio. The windowless square, filled with modern audiovisual equipment, was a jarring contrast to the gloomy Gothic design of the rest of the castle. Walls and floor were carpeted, no doubt to improve the acoustics. The wall to the left was mostly shelving. Quinn glimpsed cans of film and blank recording media.

Markov led him past a huge instrument panel on the wall to the right, filled with monitors, gauges, and dials.

He gestured at the panel without stopping. "Master control for all the various systems of the estate."

A plush leather swivel chair on casters for tending to the impressive array made Quinn think of Captain Kirk in *Star Trek*.

Labels under each monitor told which part of the castle or grounds it showed. Two in all capital letters under much larger monitors caught Quinn's eye: LAGOON and GARDEN. Unlike the other monitors, these were turned off, their screens black.

After the instrument panel came a door. On the way here

they'd passed Johnny's quarters. The two spaces must be adjoining. Markov seemed to like keeping his steward nearby.

A few steps past the door, they stopped at a bank of half a dozen computers, their widescreen monitors resting on a shelf built into the wall. To the left of the computers, a 35-millimeter projector faced a five-foot screen. Everything was immaculate and precisely arranged. This was the workspace of a perfectionist.

"My remastering/editing console," Markov said.

Quinn made a polite nod. His attention kept being drawn to the lurid horror movie posters arrayed on the carpeted wall behind the console: *Horror of Dracula, The Mummy's Ghost, House of Horrors, Creature from the Black Lagoon, Man-Made Monster, The Monster Maker.*

"My wall of inspiration," Markov said. "Come. Let me show you how the 21st-century version of the mad movie scientist creates his monsters."

He led them to an area that looked like the place where a kid who loved monster movies kept his toys. There were reproduced miniatures of King Kong, Dracula, the Wolf Man, the Creature from the Black Lagoon, Robby the Robot, and several others.

"For whatever reason," Markov began, "people are given certain abilities. I have already mentioned my genius for technology. From my first day at Universal, I understood the importance of technology to filmmaking, so I made it my business to learn each new innovation. In particular I wanted to learn how to make the most realistic movie monsters the world had ever seen. In the '60s, I taught myself robotic animation and started with Robby. I was able to move my creations around, and they were very good, but never quite realistic enough to suit me. Then the digital revolution begat computer animation, and …" he gestured at the array of miniatures "… these creatures became extinct."

"Are they still functional?"

"Oh yes. As are some other robotic things I keep around for my amusement. I was in my seventies when home computers came in, but I didn't run from them like most people my age. I couldn't wait to get one. In 1975, I ordered the Altair 8800 from *Popular Electronics*. The model generally considered to have launched the home computer revolution. You 'tinkered it together' from a kit."

"Quoting Morbius again," Quinn said.

"I still think *Forbidden Planet* is one of the best sci-fi films. Way ahead of its time."

"Maybe the inventor of the Altair 8800 loved it, too, since Morbius lived on the planet Altair 4."

"The thought crossed my mind," Markov said. "I also found it an interesting coincidence that your name is Quinn. There's a character named Quinn in *Forbidden Planet*."

"Yes. The engineer. When I first saw *Forbidden Planet* as a kid, I thought it was cool to have the same name as one of the guys on the spaceship. Until he gets killed by the Monster from Morbius's Id."

"One of the great movie monsters," Markov said.

"Absolutely."

"When I first started to teach myself computer technology, I did indeed fancy myself as a kind of Morbius. I learned everything there was to learn, down to the last bit and pixel. When the first DVDs hit the market, I knew a revolution had begun. I immersed myself in learning all the digital possibilities for filmmakers. Come. Let me show you the *pièces de résistance*."

They went back to the editing console and sat side by side in two rolling office chairs. Markov put his hand on an unusually large mouse with several buttons. Clearly relishing the chance to tell someone of his accomplishments, he became more animated than Quinn had yet seen him.

"The process I am about to show you has taken countless thousands of hours, spread out over decades, to develop. Along the way I created this mouse, which can give the computer commands unique to my operation. Here's the map of the castle I use to place my creations wherever I need them."

A click of the mouse brought up a stunning, high-definition image of the exterior of castle.

"The master shot, so to speak. I have a separate page for each area of the castle. Each page has a grid dividing it into squares. Standard letter and number coordinates along the sides allow me to pinpoint any square."

A series of clicks brought up images of the entrance, the stairs, the study, the screening room. He stopped at the one showing the inside of Quinn's apartment. "You get the idea."

"Yes."

"Once a film is digitally remastered, I can pause it at any point. I then very precisely highlight the part of the image I need, pixel by pixel, and extract it from the picture. I can then paste that into my digital editing program and make it larger, make it appear more vicious—the possibilities are endless. Once the enhancement is finished, I can then place the enhanced version wherever I want it in the castle by entering the coordinates of that particular square in the grid. Animating them requires another step, which I will show you in a moment. Before we get to that, you commented upon the excellence of my Bela Lugosi voice. Let me show you how that is achieved."

A few mouse clicks brought up a freeze-frame of Lugosi standing on the stairs in *Dracula*. Beneath the image was the track of the editing software that would graphically display the peaks and valleys of the sound. "Watch what happens when he speaks." He clicked the mouse and the movie came to life. Lugosi spoke his famous opening line:

"I am ... Dracula."

The line on the sound track zigzagged as it registered the highs and lows of the soundwave created by Lugosi's voice.

"I put on earphones and record my version on a new track directly beneath his, watching both of the graphic displays, doing it over and over, continually modulating my voice until the graph of my voice matches the graph of his as closely as possible."

"Ingenious."

Markov quoted Morbius again. "Mere child's play. I can do it with any of the actors if I take the time."

"You could sell your secrets to Hollywood and be a very rich man."

"I am already a very rich man. I am only interested in culminating my life's work. Besides, there are aspects to what I do that are very dangerous."

"Dangerous? How so?"

"You shall see. Come. Let me show you the rest of the process."

They went to the far end of the room. An oversized recliner faced a full-sized movie screen. On a small table next to the recliner was an unusual pair of large gloves and large tinted goggles. The goggles were clearly designed for some kind of specialized viewing. The temples that secured them over the ears were much larger than regular temples, to accommodate a series of small lights that continually pulsated along one, and a series of buttons that ran along the other. Beside them was an oversized mouse similar to the one at the remastering console.

"First I bring up the location where I want to insert my digital creature." He clicked the mouse and the exterior of the castle again came onto the screen. "The master shot." Another few clicks brought up the grounds that ran along the right wall of the castle. A short distance beyond the access road, the clearing was bordered by thick woods.

"Now I insert whatever digitally-enhanced creature I have extracted from a movie."

A couple slight finger movements on the mouse made a huge black dog appear at the edge of the woods. "From the 1939 version of *The Hound of the Baskervilles*. I have greatly enhanced him for my purposes. Made him much larger and more fearsome."

"He's definitely fearsome," Quinn said. "Almost as big as a bear."

"Now we come to the most formidable obstacle: animation. Not animation as we know it, where the character's movements are done once and remain the same forever. I wanted my creations to be independent entities. Things I could move about at will, while giving them whatever life was needed to suit the situation."

He donned the gloves and goggles.

"These are essentially integrated computers of my own design, able to process nearly a trillion bits of data per second. Twenty-five years ago you would have needed a central processing unit the size of this room to even approach that capacity. I can use one or both of the gloves, depending on the needs of the scene. The gloves have sensors that can transmit any of my body movements to the creatures. Instead of cells, their millions of digital bits are the receptors. Watch."

He pressed the fingertips and thumb of one hand against the fingertips and thumb of the other. Markov and the hound slowly swiveled their heads in unison. "Repetitive movements like walking are easy. I simply program them into the creature, then I activate the program here." He held a finger poised over a button on the goggles. "Each push makes it go faster, from walking to an all-out run."

He pushed the button and the hound began walking. He pushed another button and the hound stopped. Markov sat. The hound sat. Markov looked around, sniffing. The hound did the exact same.

"You get the idea," Markov said. He removed the gloves and goggles with the theatrical flair of a lead actor holding for applause at the curtain call. Quinn almost expected him to bow.

"You make a very convincing hound," Quinn said.

"In acting out the parts for my movie, I have had to learn to move—even think—like a dog, or whatever the part calls for. Which, of course, is something it seems I was born to do. I've been mimicking actors my whole life."

"Impressive," Quinn said. "Your technology goes far beyond computer animation. Even George Lucas and his team at Skywalker haven't been able to do this."

"It took me years to perfect. I spent enough hours studying the neurosciences to have earned a Ph.D., learning everything there is to know about how the brain functions and how it controls what we do.

"In the simplest layman's terms, all activity in the brain

translates into electrical, chemical, and magnetic impulses that course through our nervous system and control all of our bodily functions. In essence, I was the transmitter and my digital creation was the receiver. The missing link was how to connect the two so that I could use the energy from my brain to animate the digital creation. My theory was, that if I could somehow harness those brain waves and conduct them into my digital creations, I could bring them to a close approximation of life."

"So what did you do?" Quinn asked.

"The theory was sound, but I reached an impasse. No computer was powerful enough—fast enough—to process the billions of bits of data required for such complex operations. Nanotechnology changed everything. Silicon Valley was getting more and more data onto smaller and smaller chips, increasing their processing speed exponentially. It was clear that this was the quantum leap that would propel the computer revolution into unimaginable realms of possibility. One of the reasons I'm so rich is the investments I made in computers and computer technology from the very beginning. Intel and Microsoft paid for this estate many times over."

Markov handed him the gloves and goggles for closer inspection.

"They're like a more advanced virtual reality setup," Quinn said.

"My goal is to take the 'virtual' out of that phrase. I am very close. Too close, perhaps."

Quinn's impatience at one cryptic remark too many slammed head-on into his need to remain diplomatic so that he could get the full story. "Meaning what, exactly?"

"I sense your frustration with all my veiled references to

danger, but it had to be so. Before I could reveal the dark secrets of a very unorthodox life, I needed to assure myself that you were not merely some awestruck fan. I have had to deal with a number of those over the years. Despite the enormous pains I have taken not to be hounded because of my *Dracula* connection, it seems that in this age of the Internet no secret is safe. Whatever the case, somehow overzealous fans find out, and I am forced to get rid of them. This is why I have been purposely keeping my cards close to the vest.

"Now that I see the seriousness of your interest, and that your knowledge of horror and filmmaking fits in very well with my situation, I shall start putting those cards on the table. Come. I will turn over the next one in answer to your question, about my perhaps coming too close to creating cinema reality."

CHAPTER 10

When they were seated back at the editing/remastering console, Markov saw Quinn staring at the framed quotation centered beneath the movie posters:

"My terror is not of Germany. It is of the soul."
—Poe—

Quinn gestured at the quotation. "A line well-known to Poe aficionados. It's from an essay in which Poe defended himself against charges of 'Germanism' in his horror tales."

"What I am about to show you gives Poe's statement a whole new level of meaning," Markov said. "As a folklorist, you may be familiar with a superstition that developed in the early days of photography: the notion that a photograph permanently captured some of a person's soul."

Quinn nodded. "I researched it extensively when I was studying the influence of movies on real life. The illusion of reality was so shocking in the earliest days of moving pictures that some actors refused to do them, for fear that their soul might forever be trapped in the film."

What passed for lightheartedness in Markov's solemn

nature had evaporated. "Quite by accident during the remastering process, I discovered that their fears were not groundless."

"You discovered that an actor's soul *is* retained in the film?"

"At least to some degree, yes. The first film I remastered was, of course, *Dracula*. One night after I turned off the computer, I noticed ghostly images of the actors continuing to move around the screen. I began to explore how this could be. I was very aware of 'burn-in'—the potential for a digital image left frozen on the screen too long to leave an afterimage of itself. But these were *moving* images, and they were moving around exactly as the actors had during the scene. No other part of the scene had remained; only the actors. Why? Screen immortality had always fascinated me, the fact that we can watch people long dead still living their lives, laughing, loving, having adventures. Was there more to it than simply images captured on film? Had I discovered a new form of animation? More than that: a way to bring actors back from the dead?

"So I tried an experiment. I froze a particular scene with Lugosi and Dwight Frye and highlighted them pixel by pixel. I then extracted them from the picture, leaving a blank space where they had been. There was no movement, no afterimage. I pasted the actors onto a blank page in another computer, and turned the computer off.

"The ghostly images of the actors played out the scene exactly as they had before."

The faint hum of the computers in the otherwise silent room conveyed an eerie feeling of soulless life. The drone was so hypnotic that Quinn was mildly startled when Markov went on.

"I tried to find a way to determine whether this same phenomenon existed in the original film, or if it was some kind of anomaly that only manifested itself in the digitized version. I tried running the film, then stopping it and examining the frames for any sign of continued movement. I did this in light and darkness, through all kinds of filters—infrared, ultraviolet, polarizing. I examined the frames with a microscope, searching for signs of anything unusual within the actors—a glow, a spark, something not visible to the naked eye.

"There was nothing. Yet somehow, the digitizing process had brought something dormant in the celluloid to life. What? How did the digital recording process differ from film?

"The answer immediately became clear: magnetism. Digital recording is done on magnetic media—hard drives, thumb drives, disks. And science has long proven that electromagnetism is one of the primal forces that give us life, going back at least to Mesmer's early 19th-century attempts to manipulate our magnetic aura. Animal magnetism, he called it. His experiments, and the intense scientific study of the phenomenon at the time, were a major source of inspiration for Mary Shelley in creating Frankenstein's Monster."

Markov's steady gaze wandered to some troubling inner place before returning with a heightened intensity. Quinn had gotten used to his pauses for effect, but this was not the melodramatic Lugosi stare. For the first time Quinn saw uncertainty. It was only there for an instant before Markov gathered himself and went on.

"My theory was that the human soul, like all other things, has a molecular structure. Because motion pictures are actually 24 still frames per second creating the illusion of motion, the silver nitrate that captured the original images on film trapped those molecules into permanent stasis within each individual still frame. But digitization eliminated the split-second between each frame to give the lives of the characters a continuous flow. It created *reality* instead of the 24-frames-per-second *illusion* of reality. At the same time, the magnetism inherent in that process excited the static molecules of each frame back into life."

Whatever was troubling Markov flickered across his expression again. Before, Quinn had read it as uncertainty. Now he thought he saw something else: remorse.

"I have reached the line you spoke of, Mr. Quinn. The line between movies and real life. The line I have spent my life trying to make disappear."

He paused, choosing his words carefully. The glow of the monitors combined with the fluorescent lighting to lend an air of surrealism to the scene.

"This is where we enter the realm of true horror," Markov continued. "Magnetism had caused an unforeseen side effect. During my countless hours of remastering, the magnetism of my body had acted as a kind of hard drive, drawing some of those digitized bits into me. I began to notice changes in the mirror. Fleeting resemblances to Lugosi, Karloff, Lon Chaney, Lon Chaney Jr., many others. I was becoming them. I began to *feel* what they were feeling. Not the actors. Their *characters*. I would catch glimpses of the Frankenstein Monster, the Wolf Man. Even though I couldn't see him in the mirror, I could *feel* Dracula's growing need for blood."

Markov cast a glance at his large remastering monitor. In the few seconds that he stared at the black screen, Quinn wondered if he was looking for his reflection. Or signs of movement. Markov got up and took a few steps until he was directly between Quinn and the Poe quote—an actor taking stage.

"Rather than being appalled, as any sane person would be, I was thrilled. If I could harness that magnetism, I might somehow become a conduit for the most realistic special effects the world had ever seen.

"Over a period of weeks I took readings of my personal magnetic field with a magnetometer. It was getting stronger. Even so, the manifestations were still weak and fleeting. Two factors came into play that boosted them to full strength.

"The first was not intentional. Too many trespassers had forced me to take a drastic step to protect my privacy—and to protect the trespassers from my wrath. I installed several extremely powerful electromagnetic transmitters around my property, creating a kind of force field. Compasses couldn't find north, and the wave transmission necessary for modern devices would be disrupted—GPS, cell phones, and the like. Johnny or I turn the system off when we need to communicate with the outside world. Since we rarely need to do that, the system is on most of the time. Again I theorize, but I believe that years of those magnetic waves seeping into my body strengthened the magnetism within me, causing the digital bits I have absorbed to stay integrated as a unified entity. In other words, it gave the creatures life."

Henry Frankenstein's mad shout when his creation first shows movement after the bombardment of lightning came into Quinn's head: *"It's alive!"*

"What was the other factor?" he said.

"My invention of those gloves and goggles. When I put

them on I can become the creatures on the screen."

"You mean a digital version of them. Like the Hound of the Baserkvilles."

"Yes and no," Markov said.

Quinn forced himself to wait for the explanation.

Markov gestured toward the gloves and goggles. "At first, yes. As soon as I took them off, the image disintegrated into its digital bits. But over time—years—a transformation began to take place. The digital image would disintegrate, but its spirit had clung to me. I was becoming evil incarnate. I *was* each monster that overtook me. At first the manifestations would last only a few seconds, and only affect part of my body. The face, a hand, a foot. But the more I continued the process, the stronger the mutations became. Not just physically, but psychically. I began to *feel* what the monsters felt: a thirst for blood, a hunger for vengeance."

Again a hint of remorse flickered across his features, but in the space of a breath the stoic mask was back.

"The scientist in me groped for an explanation. My hypothesis was that, powered by the electrical and magnetic and chemical impulses that continually course through us all, the bits of the characters' souls that had seeped into me were combining with the molecular structure of *my* soul. In effect becoming digital recombinant DNA to create a new life form within me. An unthinkable computer virus, if you will, using me as a host to replicate itself.

"Of course, I could not prove this. No one can. To this day, science does not fully understand the workings of the human psyche. Of these animating forces that give us life. It was moot in any case. I knew I had left the realm of science and entered the realm of nightmare. I also knew that I should stop, that it could lead to no good end."

"But you haven't," Quinn said.

"My superego—my conscience—was no match for my id. The 'mindless primitive,' as Morbius called it. Home to my uncontrollable urge to prove that I was not just Lucky— the gopher, the mascot. I was George Tilton, *genius*. Remastered into the greatest horror director the world had never seen. Markov.

"And so I changed my name and built this house of horrors. Oh yes, there is horror here. Because I still cannot make myself stop, even though the horror continues to get progressively worse."

Worse? Quinn's mind had already been racing to imagine the dangers of a psychotic mimicking the behaviors of movie monsters. What could be worse? "How so?" he asked.

"I am no longer in complete control of the monsters inside me. Most of the time this virus within me lays dormant. But like any virus, there are triggers."

"Such as?" Quinn said.

"Anger. Stress. The moon."

The full moon was tomorrow night. The night Markov was determined to end his movie with a monster rally to end all monster rallies.

With me in the middle of it, if I decide to stay.

"Sometimes the mindless primitive takes over completely," Markov went on, "and I cannot be stayed from committing its atrocities."

"Atrocities?"

"Yes." A flare of anger burned away the Markov persona long enough to reveal the tortured soul that had been George Tilton, struggling to come to grips with the havoc wreaked not only by monsters he had created, but apparently by monsters that were sometimes *him*.

He closed his eyes and took a moment to collect himself. The moment lasted so long Quinn began to think he had fallen asleep or gone into some kind of trance. "Markov?"

He opened his eyes and spoke with great effort. "There is more to the story. My transformation into something not completely human had begun long before." He seemed to be pulling the words from some long-unopened vault in his soul. "It is time to reveal my darkest secrets. The ones I keep hidden away in my version of Pandora's box. Only then can you fully understand how George Tilton became Markov, Maker of Monsters."

Something not completely human. Whatever forces had come together to make him describe himself that way, Quinn knew from Markov's offer to let him leave, and other hints and glimpses he'd gotten, that there might still be enough of George Tilton left to save him. Watching his struggle against whatever abyss his demons were pulling him into, Quinn threw him a lifeline.

"In the Pandora myth," he said, "when she reaches the bottom of her box, she finds Hope."

"Ah. I never knew that. Then perhaps there will be a happy ending to my horror story?"

"As the writer you can make the ending whatever you want it to be. Whatever makes *you* happy."

"That is very much the ending I have planned. I just need to work out the final sequence that will make it a reality."

Having seen how intensely Markov believed in the "nightmare factory" he had created, Quinn expected that whatever dark secrets he was about to see would be disturbing. But the compulsion to explore dark secrets was the story of Quinn's life. In his work searching for the origins of monsters, he'd come to many moments of decision like this, when it was time either to do the sensible thing and turn back, or plunge ahead into almost certain danger. When he'd realized a fundamental truth about himself—that some irresistible urge in his nature made him invariably plunge ahead—he'd developed a mental ritual to lighten the moment, and he engaged in it now:

Poe's *Imp of the Perverse* popped into his head like a demonic jack-in-the-box, goading him into it.

"Open the lid," Quinn said. "Let's get to the bottom of your box and see if we find Hope."

Markov moved to stand but stopped when another thought struck him. "Earlier you asked if my castle is a house of dark shadows."

"I was being tongue-in-cheek."

"Yes, but your observation was dead-on. My house—my *life*—is a creation of the movies. And movies are, as you well know, light and shadow. The light is those 24 still frames per second that create the *illusion* of life. The shadow is the spaces between those frames, where there is no life. I have lived my life in those shadows, yearning to be among the living in those 24 frames. For you to fully understand the bizarre path of that life, I must show you the film I have never shown anyone since its ill-fated release. The one that has cast the darkest shadow, from which I have spent my life trying to escape."

"*The Blood of Dracula*," Quinn said. "I've been looking forward to it."

Markov pulled up the time on his computer. "It is almost eleven," he said. "That screening and the rest of the tour will have to wait until morning. We must at least try to get a few hours sleep for what will be a long and grueling day. The most important one of my life. As you said, minutes count. Can you be ready by four?"

"Absolutely," Quinn said.

"Good. Meet me in the den. After the tour I can give you some time to make your decision—but not much."

"Understood," Quinn said.

"Very well. Then let me show you to your bedchamber."

Despite Markov's dire warnings, Quinn found himself perversely excited to see what monsters his eccentric host had unleashed in his "extremely" haunted castle. Haunted castle movies had always been his favorites. Now, according to Markov, he was *in* one.

He'd had many philosophical discussions with his father about what it would be like to actually confront movie monsters in real life, as opposed to watching them in the safety of a theater while happily munching popcorn. Now, according to Markov, if he decided to stay, he was going to find out.

CHAPTER 11

Markov led Quinn into the spacious bedchamber. He lit a taper and went around the room lighting candles in copper wall sconces, fashioned into sinister gargoyle faces. As each candle winked to life, it animated its gargoyle into an eerie semblance of life. On the wall beneath the gargoyles were slanted, disorienting shadows—odd geometrical shapes that hinted at some approaching alien menace, made more sinister because they remained perfectly still. The candlelight should be making them flutter.

Quinn looked for the source of the shadows but could find none. Finally he realized they had been painted on for effect. Markov had clearly been influenced by German expressionism. And Jack Otterson's unsettling set design for *Son of Frankenstein*.

Markov finished lighting the candles and showed his guest the accommodations.

The four-poster bed was a perfect reproduction of those found in medieval bedchambers. A sheer linen curtain hung from a gold-fringed canopy, and the bed had been turned down to show a crisp white sheet under a black coverlet so luxurious it almost glowed. At the foot of the bed, Quinn's bags rested on the velvet-upholstered bench where Johnny had neatly placed them.

Markov led the way into an inviting open room off the main chamber. "The oriel," he explained. "One of my favorite parts of the castle. A good place for study, for writing, or simply to sit and reflect."

Its main feature was a huge bay window consisting of three panes at least twenty feet tall and ten wide. Near the center pane, a gold-plated telescope rested on a tripod. The entire roof of the oriel was a skylight. A fireplace of ornamental brick had been built into the wall beside the bay window.

Quinn admired the skylight. "I would imagine that on a clear night the stargazing is excellent."

"On a clear night it is superb."

A comfortable retreat had been set up in the alcove surrounded by the window. A Persian rug covered most of the wooden floor. To the left, a loveseat and two high-backed chairs were arranged around a wooden table. To the right was a wooden desk and beautifully upholstered armchair. Atop the desk, a thick half-melted candle rested in a brass chamberstick holder—19th-century, Quinn guessed. Near the candle, a large quill pen stuck up from its inkwell, along with several sheets of vellum writing paper. Gas lamps at the seating area and desk gave a soft pleasing glow. A few steps beyond the seating area, a bookshelf was filled with books.

Quinn went to take in the view through the bay window. The brunt of the storm had passed, but in its wake the wind bent the thinnest trunks of a few leafless trees and whistled against the windows. About fifty yards from the base of the castle, sporadic glimmers of light looked like reflections of the Blood Moon off a body of water. "Is that a pond?"

"In 'House of Usher' Roderick had his tarn. At the House of Markov, I have my lagoon." He moved quickly to the right edge of the fireplace. "The last thing I need to show you."

Quinn stood beside him and waited.

"The third brick down." Markov pressed it. To the right of the fireplace, an undetectable wall panel slid open to reveal a small bathroom. He explained that he couldn't have anything modern appearing in any of his scenes.

Back in the main chamber, Quinn noticed a suit of armor with its halberd held high standing in the corner to the right of the door. "Another piece from your collection?"

Markov nodded as they continued toward the door. "From *London After Midnight*. We can continue our discussion after we rest. I will meet you in the study at four. If you get there before me, simply ring the bell and Johnny can fix you breakfast or take care of whatever you need."

He paused in the doorway. "I know you must be wondering about the age of someone who worked on *Dracula* in 1931." He leaned forward, clear shining eyes boring into Quinn. "I passed the century mark a while ago."

Quinn had done the math when Markov mentioned graduating from high school in 1919, but it was still shocking to hear him say that he was over a hundred years old. What made it even more so was that he looked barely sixty.

Markov spoke as if reading his mind. "I know I look much younger. My lifestyle helps retard the aging process."

Without any apparent awareness or effort by him, his features again took on an aspect of Lugosi. Quinn wasn't ready to accept the notion that parts of movie characters had seeped into him, but whatever was going on, he would have been the envy of any impressionist. His eyes again widened in the famous stare, and as Lugosi he said the well-known line perfectly: "The blood is the life, Mr. Quinn."

"A great line, but how do you mean it?"

He reverted to his own voice. "Tomorrow. As part of the tour." Markov gave a curt bow. "I will meet you in the den at four. Till then, I bid you goodnight."

As Quinn watched him disappear around the corner guarded by the Grim Reaper, he thought about how excited he'd been to meet this man. But the person he'd been expecting to meet, George Tilton/Frederick Schreck, was buried somewhere deep inside a man who had spent his entire life under the dominion of a fictional creation called Dracula. With a heavy dose of Poe and Morbius thrown in.

It struck Quinn that it went much deeper than that. *I am not an impressionist*, Markov had said. *I am a re-creationist.*

The fact that he'd gone to such enormous pains and expense to create his own Borgo Pass, and a castle that was a virtual duplicate of the one in the movie, meant he'd spent over eighty years—his entire adult life—consumed by his *Dracula* experience.

Quinn turned back into the bedchamber, wondering what dark secrets an old filmmaker obsessed with monsters might reveal. He wondered if he had left behind the deepest level of his own private Hell, only to have entered a deeper one here.

CHAPTER 12

Still standing inside his chamber door, Quinn decided he needed to know his exact location before making up his mind whether to stay or leave. If he stayed, and his situation became truly dangerous, knowing how far he was from his vehicle, and having a map that showed him how to get there, could be vital information.

He went to his duffel bag at the foot of the bed and pulled out an object about the size of an e-book reader. His most valuable tool in tracking down legends, it was a powerful state-of-the-art GPS unit that had kept him on track in the deepest wilderness. He turned it on and waited for the default map that would show him exactly where he was.

Searching for satellites….

It was a message he was used to getting in heavily wooded areas. A few minutes later he got a message he'd never gotten, even in the remotest locations:

Cannot find satellites….

It didn't make sense. He'd been in woods as dense as these and never had a problem. Maybe the thunderstorm was interfering with the signal. All that lightning, especially around the castle.… Then he remembered:

Markov's electromagnetic barrier.

That had to be it. He'd talk to Markov about it later. For now all he could do was extrapolate from what he knew to make a rough guess at where he was.

Markov's driver had picked him up in the woods a few miles from the small Vermont village of Riverdale, fifteen miles south of the Canadian border. The trip from there to the castle had taken a little over two hours. In a horse-drawn carriage, maneuvering through dense woods, five miles an hour was probably the best they could have done. That would put them about five miles from the Canadian border, more or less. He'd not felt any severe deviations from straight ahead, but they could easily have angled west and gone deeper into Vermont, or east into New Hampshire. Either way, this was all sparsely populated wilderness. Factoring in Markov's extreme desire for privacy, Quinn leaned toward Vermont. There were fewer villages there than in New Hampshire, and those small outposts were scattered around the edges of fifty square miles of dense, virtually uninhabited forest in the remotest part of the state. His best guess was that he was somewhere in the least populous, northeastern corner of Vermont. It was never good not know where you were, but for now that was the best he could do.

Wanting to clear his head before attempting sleep, he went into the oriel and gravitated to the bay window. As he scanned the night-shrouded landscape, his gaze was drawn to the faint glimmers of moonlight that winked like fireflies on the lagoon. He half-expected a creature to rise up, but nothing stirred, and he began a closer inspection of his apartment.

He went to the suit of armor and smiled at the memory of all the scenes in haunted castle movies, where the halberd would take a swipe at an unwary passerby and just miss. Invariably there would be eyes watching through the visor. He lifted it and peered inside.

The suit of armor was empty.

Above the large fireplace hung a portrait of a man disintegrating into madness. It reminded him of the one from Roger Corman's *House of Usher*, which in turn had always made him think of the one from *The Picture of Dorian Gray* that showed Dorian's serene expression becoming hideous as the evil within overtook him.

Dorian Gray. A man who had sold his soul to the devil for eternal youth.

Quinn's gaze automatically went to the eyes, looking for peepholes through which real eyes would follow him around the room. He walked a few steps, then abruptly turned back to stare at the painting.

The eyes hadn't moved.

He inspected the gargoyle wall sconces, counting as he made his circuit of the room. Thirteen. Each sconce had been meticulously crafted into a different monstrous visage. Almond-shaped holes had been cut out to indicate eyes. Thirteen potential sets of peepholes. Scanning the disturbing collection of leers, hatred, and evil intent, Quinn felt as though he were being scrutinized by a demonic conclave, trying to decide whether they should allow him into their netherworld.

He went to the bookshelves recessed into a wall of the oriel and flicked a switch, cleverly concealed to blend in with the shelving. Lights recessed into the ceiling bathed the shelves in a soft, bright glow.

Quinn immediately became absorbed in a connoisseur's collection of horror literature, fiction on the upper shelves, non-fiction on the lower. Most of the non-fiction was either biographies of the best-known writers in the genre or scholarly works on its history and significance. Many of the titles were intriguing, but Quinn's first love was fiction, and his attention quickly focused on the upper shelves.

The first two books on the top shelf were first editions of *Dracula* and *Frankenstein*. From there the books seemed loosely grouped in chronological order, going through the 19th century and into the 20th. The essential authors were all there—Poe, Wilkie Collins, H.P. Lovecraft, Robert Bloch—along with many other important but lesser-known names. Books by Dean Koontz and Stephen King took up an entire shelf. Anne Rice and several other contemporary authors took up three more. A first edition of *The Exorcist* had been autographed by William Peter Blatty. Books upon which Tod Browning's movies had been based were grouped together, including another copy of *Dracula*.

The next section was dedicated to short stories. A scan of their contents showed a definitive collection of titles and authors. It took considerable willpower to resist the urge to start a fire, take several volumes to the inviting love seat, and become lost in pleasurable hours of reading.

Quinn looked at his watch. A few minutes past eleven. There wasn't time. He needed to get some sleep before his meeting with Markov.

He started to leave but stopped when a whimsical thought came into his head.

Markov seemed to be incorporating all the stock elements from every haunted castle movie into his set design. Which meant there had to be a secret passage. And the entrance to the secret passage always seemed to be hidden among the bookshelves.

Quinn looked for anything in the woodwork that might be a knob or switch in disguise. Finding none, he went to the unlit torches in brackets on either side of the entrance to the recess. In the movies, a torch often turned out to be the lever that opened the hidden panel.

He tugged the one on the left.

Nothing.

Pulled the one on the right.

Nothing.

He considered other possibilities.

Sometimes things were hidden in hollowed-out books. Acting on his first impulse, he opened the first edition of *Dracula*. It was a real book, nothing hidden inside or on the shelf behind it. He put it back and opened the other copy on a lower shelf. Again, nothing.

He thought for a moment. The books relating to Tod Browning and his movies.

A thorough search of them revealed no hidden mechanism.

Markov had mentioned that he and Browning shared a reverence for Poe. Quinn removed a beautifully bound copy of *The Complete Works of Edgar Allan Poe*, burgundy with gold edging. A quick inspection revealed nothing odd about the book. When he went to put it back, however, he noticed something hidden behind it. A shadowy cylindrical shape, about the size of a forefinger, jutted up from the shelf.

He removed a few more books to make the space wide enough for his hand. Wondering if it could actually be a finger, he gently poked and squeezed. A wooden peg. He gave it a gentle tug.

There was the slight hum of machinery as the entire bookcase slid into the wall.

Quinn couldn't repress a smile as he stared into the opening to a secret passageway.

CHAPTER 13

Markov stood in his bedchamber, staring at himself in the full-length mirror.

"Have you truly created monsters? Or are you yourself the monster?"

Shortly after moving here, he'd installed the mirror as a lark, thinking he would channel Lugosi by mimicking his practice of standing in front of his dressing-room mirror saying, "I am … Dracula."

But when Markov had started remastering the old films, hints of other monsters began to appear, gradually becoming more than hints, as though they were somehow seeping in to him. Except for Dracula. Since a vampire casts no reflection in a mirror, as the spirit of Lugosi's performance had gotten stronger within him, the Dracula reflection had gotten weaker.

As he continued to stare at the mirror, he watched a series of dissolves in which, for one fleeting moment, his reflection became one movie horror after another.

First a faint image of Lon Chaney's Dracula from *The Un-Dead*.

Then an even fainter image of Lugosi's Dracula.

Karloff's Frankenstein Monster.

Lon Chaney Jr.'s Wolf Man.

As Markov watched the werewolf revert to its human self, he saw hints of his own face mixed in with Lon Chaney Jr.'s. But it was conscience-tormented Lawrence Talbot's voice pleading inside his head: *Save me. Please! The full moon is coming. The worst one of all. The Blood Moon.*

Markov struggled for dominance until the tortured Lawrence Talbot persona dissolved, and he was himself again.

Himself.

Who was he?

He probed his eyes in the mirror, searching for the lost soul of George Tilton, seeing instead only fading split-second flashes of the monsters that triggered a surge of self-loathing.

Unlike Lawrence Talbot, the hapless victim of a werewolf, Markov had knowingly sold his soul to chase the dream of screen immortality. But like Lawrence Talbot, he despised the beasts within that would devour human life to perpetuate their unnatural existence.

The faint image of another face slowly became visible in the mirror until Bram Stoker's original inspiration for Dracula was staring back at him. Vlad the Impaler, eyes red with bloodlust. Against his will, Markov followed the eyes as they shifted their focus from him to the ten-foot-long wooden stake propped upright in the corner—as though willing him to use it.

No. That was only a prop for set decoration.

Markov tore his gaze away from the stake and looked back at the mirror.

Now the eyes were those of George Tilton. There was pleading in them.

Could a soul be reclaimed from the Devil?

CHAPTER 14

Quinn walked into the small antechamber that had been hollowed out of the solid rock upon which the castle had been built. At the far edge of the cavity, a large opening loomed. The light from the bookshelves barely reached it, but there was enough to see the top of a staircase leading down into a black void. Unlit torches stood in brackets on either side of the entrance.

He took a tentative step onto one of the large stone tiles covering the floor, then another, half-expecting a trapdoor or some other movie trickery. A few steps later, a spiral staircase cut into the stone disappeared around a bend. He went down far enough to look at the section beyond the curve. Slanting, uneven stairs continued through a crudely hand-hewn tunnel. A craggy, unfinished ceiling hung down into the opening, and chiseled ridges on the stone walls created sharp, sinister shadows.

Markov had called his movie set/castle a shrine to madness. If what waited below was the inner sanctum of that shrine, the disorienting staircase perfectly conveyed the feeling of entering an underworld where sanity no longer prevailed. Like the bizarre shadows painted on the wall beneath the gargoyle sconces, the staircase clearly had been influenced by the expressionistic design of *Son of Frankenstein*. That thought made Quinn wonder if another of *Son of Frankenstein*'s design elements might await in the forbidden chamber below: the sulfuric lava pit.

Only a few steps were visible before the light from the library died, and jagged, lurking shadows merged into one and swallowed the staircase. Quinn stared into the black void below. Concern over what might hide in that darkness wrestled with his lifelong impulse to explore the hidden realms where monsters supposedly lurked. He remained frozen on the top step, debating whether he should head down the stairs.

Markov kept warning me about monsters. I need to know just how vulnerable I am from this direction.

But he's beginning to trust me, and I don't want to violate that trust.

But he made a point of quoting Dracula's line about "enter freely and go safely."

That's not the same as saying "Go freely." I can probably find out whatever I need to know when we talk later....

But he keeps warning about serious danger. If serious danger lurks in the castle, surely it will lurk in a hidden subterranean chamber.

That thought ended his mental tug-of-war.

I've got to know what I'm getting involved in.

He retrieved his small powerful flashlight from the nightstand. Following its bright beam, treading carefully on the uneven stairs, he began his descent into the black maw that led to whatever waited below.

After the curve, the disorienting staircase went straight down. Other than unlit gas torches in wall brackets at regular intervals, nothing adorned the bare stone. Quinn constantly scanned the space ahead, uncertain of what might lay beyond the ten-foot range of his light. His descent took him deep into the bowels of the castle.

Finally he reached bottom. He took a few tentative steps into the chamber beyond, then stood still while his senses adjusted to the oppressive underground environment. Casting his light about, he saw nothing but hard-packed barren earth. A heavy musty smell hung in the damp stale air. He detected some other pungent odor he couldn't identify mixed in with the smell of mold. Decaying plant matter, perhaps.

A faint sound disturbed the tomblike silence. He cocked his head.

A distant, barely audible moaning. The low keening had a sad, human quality, but it could be the wind. It had been blowing hard upstairs, and a chamber like this, with all its unsealed nooks and crannies, might make the ideal amplifier.

After decades of methodically seeking the reality behind superstitions and myths, and debunking most of them, Quinn had learned to consider only concrete, provable facts. Which, so far, amounted to nothing. If the noise came from something other than the wind, the only way to find out was to follow it to its source.

Advancing warily, he followed his shaft of light deeper into the Stygian gloom. He counted his paces, wanting to establish the dimensions of a space whose boundaries were invisible in the darkness. The moaning got slightly louder, but still seemed to be coming from a considerable distance ahead. Judging from the brown barren earth, strewn here and there with bits of rubble, nothing had been done to make this part of the castle liveable.

Forty-one steps later, his light fell on a large wrought iron gate. A heavy padlock held it closed.

He shone his light through the gate's bars. At the far edge of a shallow antechamber where his light barely reached, the shadowy outline of a gaping entrance to yet another chamber loomed. Faint light glowed from somewhere beyond.

Quinn shifted his attention back to the gate and noticed lettering affixed to the top:

Les Fleurs du Mal

The Flowers of Evil. Why had Markov chosen the title of Baudelaire's infamous book of poetry for the entrance to this particular chamber? The book George Sanders was reading in the very first shot of *The Picture of Dorian Gray*. The question was quickly swept aside by a wave of sensory impressions. The moaning had gotten louder and the smell stronger. The earthy smell was almost certainly some kind of weed or plant matter.

He pricked his ears to concentrate on the sound.

Definitely not the wind. It sounded like the sibilant babble of many voices whispering, as of a crowd reacting to the approach of a stranger.

A figure emerged from the darkness.

"You should not have come down here."

CHAPTER 15

Johnny had a flashlight in one hand and a gun in the other. Both were aimed at Quinn. The voices had abruptly stopped, as though the whisperers from beyond the gloom were listening.

Markov's vigilant steward shambled toward him until they were staring at each other from a few feet apart.

"You weren't planning on shooting me, were you?" Quinn said.

Johnny lowered the flashlight and gun. "Merely a precaution."

"Against what?"

"Creatures of the night."

Quinn noticed the pectoral cross around the steward's neck. It instantly made him think of the pectoral star Bela Lugosi wore on his very first appearance in the movie. Quinn pointed to it, then gestured at the inscription above the gate. "Is that for protection against the Flowers of Evil?"

"Not exactly."

"Johnny, I need some straight answers. Markov has been talking in riddles all night. He says I'm in a horror movie that's been his lifelong dream, at the same time telling me the castle is haunted and warning me about how dangerous it might be. I need to know what I'm getting into."

"The secrets of the castle can only come from the lord of the manor."

"Not good enough."

Johnny paused as though searching for the right thing to say. The neutral mask quickly returned. "I am sure your questions will be answered when you meet with Markov."

"How did you know I was down here?" Quinn pressed, hoping to pry something from the servant.

"Among my many duties, I am head of security. We have cameras throughout the castle."

Quinn pointed to a device clipped to the steward's waist, about the size of a paperback book but very thin. "What's that?"

"My portable master control. It allows me to check all the monitors and other systems of the castle, and to communicate with Markov. I keep it on me at all times."

"Is home invasion a problem in such a remote place?"

"Trespassers of one sort or another. Hikers, skiers who get lost. Curiosity seekers who have somehow found out about Markov's *Dracula* connection. I have intercepted many over the years when I am patrolling the woods. Sometimes I have actually come upon them wandering around inside, claiming they thought the castle was abandoned."

"Do you have them arrested?"

"We tend to them." Johnny's evasive gaze suddenly focused on him with uncharacteristic intensity. "If Markov wasn't watching you, and doesn't already know, I shall let your trespass go this time. There must be no others."

Annoyed at being ordered what to do, Quinn bit back a snappy retort. It wouldn't be right to kill the messenger. "I'll take it up with Markov."

"Good. Come. I will escort you back to your room."

When they reached the top of the stairs and stepped back into the bedchamber, Johnny pressed a button disguised as a knot in the wood paneling. The bookcase slid back into place.

Quinn followed Johnny to the door. "Lock this," the head of security said, then quickly rounded the corner where the Grim Reaper maintained its eternal eyeless vigil.

Eager for sleep, Quinn locked the door and returned to bed. He was halfway under the sheets when he stopped with a groan. The candles in the wall sconces still needed to be extinguished.

He grabbed his flashlight and pulled the snuffer from the receptacle that held the fireplace implements. As each candle winked out, there was an eerie moment when its gargoyle holder was swallowed by the darkness.

Quinn was glad to see them go. He went back to bed, slipped under the covers, and clicked off his flashlight.

From behind the wall, eyes stared at him through the eye slits of one of the gargoyles.

Eyes accustomed to the darkness.

Johnny's eyes.

CHAPTER 16

Quinn barely managed to get a couple hours of fitful sleep. Now he lay on his back, eyes open as they adjusted to the darkness. They probed for a glimmer of light. Moonglow coming through the large bay window dimly lit the oriel, but his bedchamber remained in total darkness. The unrelieved gloom seemed to muffle sound, for the silence was absolute. In what almost amounted to a sensory deprivation chamber, he closed his eyes.

The utter stillness gradually seeped into him until it blotted out the disturbing moments that kept echoing in his brain:

"You have walked into the ultimate reality show, Mr. Quinn…."

"I have many secrets … some are quite dark…."

"… descent into the maelstrom…."

Finally the echoes died out. Somewhere in the uncharted region between wakefulness and sleep, Quinn saw himself fleeing for his life.

Something was chasing him through deep woods. Hopelessly lost, he kept changing direction but could find no way out. No footpath, no light hinting at a clearing or civilization in the vast impenetrable forest.

Where was he?

Behind him heavy footsteps crashed through the thick underbrush. Faster. Closer.

His eyes sprang open wide.

Quinn stared into the darkness for a long time, seeing nothing. Then a flash of light appeared beyond the foot of the bed, in the direction of the fireplace. The burst came and went so quickly he thought he'd imagined it. His eyes stayed fixed on the spot to see if there would be another.

Yes. Bright white. This time it didn't go away. The light hung suspended in the middle of the fireplace. Not quite round. More elliptical. Indistinct shadows inside it.

Again the light vanished, plunging the room into darkness.

It flashed again. Bigger. Closer.

Again.

Closer.

Now the shape stayed visible. Hovering in midair, flickering like the hand-cranked image from a silent film, a head floated slowly toward the bed. No body, just a disembodied head.

It was the hideous vampire from the short they had just watched. Lon Chaney's *Un-Dead*. The perfect teeth were bared in a malevolent grin. Suddenly, as they had done in the film, fangs popped down. The head floated toward him until it got almost close enough to touch.

Quinn leapt from the bed, shooting both palms at the face like a pile driver. His hands went through it and the face blinked out. Unexpectedly meeting no resistance, Quinn stumbled forward. When he turned around, the face was back again, only a few steps away, eyes boring into him, lustful predatory grin sending icy splinters up his neck and across his scalp.

The lips began to move. The mouth opened. It spoke a single word.

"Beware."

The eyes stayed locked onto his for a long, unsettling moment before the face began disintegrating into tiny squares like tiles from a mosaic, as a satellite television image does during a thunderstorm. The face expanded and distorted as the space between the bits increased. Eyes that had been as big as quarters stretched into insanely misshapen saucers. The hellish grin broadened from a few inches to a foot wide. As the disintegration continued, the fangs elongated and the mouth opened into a gaping maw. The head kept swelling like something out of a funhouse nightmare until it silently exploded and thousands of bits were flung into the darkness.

Quinn kept turning in circles, expecting some new horror to come from any direction. None came, and the heavy mantle of dark silence settled back over him. He groped blindly through the room until he reached the bed. From there he used the glow from his digital traveling clock to find the nightstand where he'd left his flashlight. He grabbed it and noted the time before clicking it on.

Almost one-thirty. Time was running out for him to get some sleep before meeting Markov.

Simmering anger at apparently being used for Markov's amusement smothered a spark of reluctant admiration for his special effects wizardry. The anger drained away as Quinn remembered that Markov had warned him about potential danger in the castle.

He began walking around the chamber, probing the darkness with his flashlight, trying to convince himself that the leers of the gargoyles hadn't become more sinister, that the disembodied vampire head had been part of his dream. Wanting to clear his head for whatever chance he had at sleep, he went to the window in the oriel.

The light of the waxing Blood Moon was strong. The way it fell on the gnarled leafless branches of the trees created an eerie tapestry of shadows on the ground below. Occasional flickers of moonlight reflected on the surface of the otherwise black lagoon. Shadowy movement at its far end caught his eye.

For one fleeting moment, a single wave rose above the surface like a mound. Quinn thought it might be the tide, pulling the water across a large rock or boulder, but that theory quickly faded as the swell rose higher and assumed a more definite shape. It was too far and too dark to make out clearly, but for an instant the watery silhouette vaguely resembled the head and shoulders of something almost human but not quite.

Humanoid.

He rubbed his eyes. When he looked again the shape was gone.

Is Markov playing tricks again? How could he know that I'd be standing here looking at the lagoon?

Quinn glanced around, looking for a camera but finding none. That didn't mean one couldn't be hidden somewhere.

He remembered coming home from horror movies when he was little and seeing monsters in the wallpaper when he went to bed. Here he was, fifty years later, a grown man, professional folklorist, debunker of legends, still turning shadows into monsters.

Unless there actually was a Creature in Markov's Black Lagoon.

Quinn focused on the spot where he'd seen the shape.

The water's surface was smooth.

Move along, Adam. Would you even be thinking this if Markov called his body of water a tarn instead of a lagoon? Go to bed.

He set his alarm for 3:35 and lay in darkness for what seemed like a long time before finally sinking into sleep. In his dream world, another scene unfolded in the projection booth inside his head:

A handheld shot from Quinn's point of view edged up to the yawning mouth of the secret passage, stopping to peer into darkness that would be the perfect shroud for the creeping undead.

A slow iris fade-out began. Before closing all the way it froze, taking one long last look to be sure nothing lurked in the ominous gloom.

Two disembodied eyes began to glow in the blackness below. Dimly at first, but getting brighter and larger as they came steadily closer, their sinister gaze exerting a magnetic pull.

Quinn's closed eyelids clenched tighter, and the fade-out went to black.

CHAPTER 17

Quinn's attempt at sleep didn't last long.

With his eyes still closed, he sensed movement in the darkness. His eyes popped open and probed for the source.

To his left, on the far side of the chamber, an indistinct shadow shifted on the oriel wall.

He shot a glance at the clock.

3:12.

Could the shadow be from one of the tree branches blowing in the wind?

The shadow moved a little farther along the wall and became utterly still.

It can't be from a tree. A tree blowing in the wind would flutter, not stay perfectly still like that.

He went to the oriel.

Nothing was amiss. All was still, including the shadow.

Quinn had almost convinced himself the movement must have been a trick of the moonlight as it filtered through the fluttering branches—until it began moving again. He snapped his head around to find the source.

Outside the right edge of the bay window, along the ledge that jutted out from the castle wall, a hulking figure emerged from the darkness. Moving slowly toward him. Its shadow preceded it, creeping across the floor with jerky, ungainly movements. Quinn strained to make out what was coming toward him, but in the murky light could see only the silhouette of something very large.

Something not human.

When it got within a few feet of the window, he stumbled back. Heart pounding, he stared in awe.

A large, black, unblinking, predatory eye stared back at him. The eye was imbedded in the face of a creature that didn't exist. Clinging to crevices in the stonework, the nightmare held perfectly still, its evil eye riveted on him.

The beast was huge—at least ten feet from top to bottom. Its pointed beak was several feet long, and a swordlike crest of equal length protruded from the back of its head. The beak was open enough to reveal rows of savage teeth like conical needles. Its wings were bent in half and held tight against the sides. At the midpoint where each wing folded, talons atop the wing opened and closed, as if questing for prey.

The thing began to move.

It shifted itself around so the talons on top of the wings could find purchase on the stonework. Clinging to the castle wall, the huge creature contorted its body until the lower talons came to within a foot of Quinn on the other side of the window, snapping open and closed, as if eager to snatch him up.

Suddenly the nightmare beast released its hold on the wall and spread its enormous wings. Quinn watched in disbelief as it glided across the face of the Blood Moon, a creature of the night returning to its lair.

Even as the chills ran down his neck and spread across

his back, he knew the vision couldn't have been real. It had to be one of Markov's special effects.

Because this creature existed only in dinosaur movies.

The pterodactyl was extinct.

CHAPTER 18

Johnny responded promptly to Quinn's pull on the rope bell. Judging from the puffy eyes, he had awakened the steward from a deep sleep. He briefly described the Chaney and pterodactyl visions. "Markov said I'd be dealing with monsters, but I thought he'd wait until I agreed to be in his film. Is he toying with me for his amusement?"

Johnny gave another pat response. "He told me he is meeting you at four, to show you what you are getting involved in, should you agree to be in his movie. He will tell you whatever he thinks you need to know."

"You're right, Johnny. I shouldn't have called you. Go to back to bed."

"If you decide to stay, he will need some time to write you into whatever climactic sequence he comes up with. He is very fast, but that would still take at least a couple hours." The caretaker made pointed eye contact. "I'm sure he has told you that you are free to enter any unlocked doors."

"Yes, he has."

"After your meeting, if you decide to stay, that would be a good time to take him up on his offer. Familiarity with your acting space can only help. If there is time, you should explore the grounds as well. The sun starts coming up around seven."

"I'll do that."

When Johnny made no move to leave, Quinn thought the caretaker might be waiting to be formally dismissed. "Get some sleep, Johnny."

"Very well. I shall leave you to your own devices. Take care that you do not become lost in your wanderings. Particularly outside, if you are here when night approaches. Especially this night. The nocturnal creatures that haunt our woods seem to be more active when the moon is full."

Knowing how steeped Johnny must be in the Universal classics, Quinn tried to lighten the moment by reciting the famous rhyme from *The Wolf Man*: "Even a man who is pure in heart, and says his prayers by night, can become a wolf, when the wolfbane blooms, and the autumn moon is bright."

Quinn waited for a reaction. Other than a slight narrowing of the eyes, Johnny gave none, so he went on. "The autumn moon will be at its brightest tonight. Is Markov … pure in heart?"

Johnny hesitated. "Is anyone?"

"Touché," Quinn said.

"If there is nothing else," Johnny said.

"No, thank you. I need to get ready for that meeting."

Johnny went to the door. "Keep this locked." The steward took a step to leave but stopped again, apparently wanting to say something else, but searching for the right words. "I wish I could help you more." Johnny quickly turned and left.

In that brief hesitation, Quinn had seen something churning beneath the neutral mask, something hinting at troubling secrets too long held inside. He sensed a rift between the Lord of the Manor and his loyal servant—a growing fissure that ran deep, perhaps deep enough to threaten the foundation of the cloistered fantasy world they'd lived in for half a century—the strange edifice Markov had referred to as his version of the House of Usher, calling it his doomed House of Markov.

Did Markov actually believe he was headed for an ill-fated destiny, or was his characterization simply his tendency toward melodrama, derived from a lifetime of movies and Poe?

Whatever the case, somewhere in Johnny's furtive glances and veiled statements, Quinn thought he saw a cry for help.

CHAPTER 19

Johnny had just gotten back into bed when the buzzer on the nightstand made its irritating short burst: Markov summoning his "right arm" to the laboratory. Slipping back into clothes just taken off, Johnny entered through the door connecting the two adjoining spaces and a moment later was at Markov's side, dreading his instructions if he had seen his guest's trespass.

Markov stood in front of his control panel. An array of monitors and gauges and buttons took up a third of the long wall adjoining Johnny's apartment. On the shelf that extended out beneath the monitors were the gloves and goggles he used to manipulate his special effects. He pointed to the monitor showing Quinn's bedchamber. "I have been watching our guest's reaction to my creations. He handled them reasonably well, but then he went into the oriel and seemed to become fixated on the lagoon."

Johnny showed no reaction but was inwardly relieved. Markov must not have been watching when Quinn entered the forbidden chamber. If he had been, he'd be in a rage now and demanding punishment.

Markov nodded toward one of the monitors that was larger than the others. The label underneath it said

LAGOON. "I pulled it up on the infrared camera and noticed a shape that seemed to be moving under the water. Have you been doing your inspections to make sure all is well down there?"

"Yes. Weekly." Of all the tasks necessary for maintaining the security of their hellhole, Johnny hated the underwater inspection of the lagoon the most. Even more so at night. "All is ... I wouldn't say 'well,' but all is as it should be."

"I'm in no mood to argue semantics, Johnny. Please go check to make sure nothing has gotten loose from its moorings. Woe betide anything—or anyone—that interrupts us now that we are so close to the end."

The end. The two words Johnny most longed to see in the horror movie that had been their life. It was impossible to know what the ending would be, because real life wasn't a movie. It couldn't be storyboarded, no matter how much Markov tried. Still, he hated improvisation. He would certainly have a plan—a plan that no doubt would include putting their guest in peril.

On the long walk to the outbuilding they used for storage, Johnny tried to work out the details of a real-life ending that would undoubtedly be far different from whatever twisted Tod Browning-influenced movie version Markov had in mind. But it was hard to concentrate while having to listen for any unusual sounds in the surrounding woods. Still, one image remained unwavering in Johnny's brain: those two words, emblazoned over a beautiful natural landscape, while a lush string orchestra played a sound track of soaring happy-ending music.

The End

For Johnny, those two words couldn't come soon enough.

CHAPTER 20

Quinn took a quick shower, got dressed, and headed for his four o'clock meeting with Markov in the den. It was only 3:40, but he wanted to have time to mull over his decision about whether to stay or leave. Ten minutes later, he had finished his pastry and was sitting at the hearth by the fire, sipping coffee as he contemplated the irony of his situation.

He'd come here to get away from the ever-darker evil he'd been seeing in his work with law enforcement, excited about a chance to escape into the world of someone who had not only worked on one of his all-time favorite movies, but had to be a treasure trove of behind-the-scenes stories going back to the dawn of motion pictures.

Instead he had walked into a world so warped by the movies that it rivaled Norma Desmond's in *Sunset Boulevard*. But where she had preserved her dead pet monkey, Markov seemed to be preserving his dead pet monsters. He had said his castle was "extremely haunted" by his "bad deeds." Was there any genuine danger here, or was Markov merely preparing Quinn for his role in the movie?

The floating Chaney head and the pterodactyl had been special effects. Surely all the monsters in and around this castle were nothing more than digital smoke and mirrors.

But that moaning sound coming from the forbidden chamber below.... Another special effect?

In his years of studying the horror genre, Quinn had given a lot of thought to the nature of evil, especially as it manifested itself in movies and books. That line of reasoning had invariably led his philosophical nature to contemplate the much larger picture: why does evil exist, and where does it come from? Even staring into its darkest face as a consultant on the sickest murder cases, he'd never come up with any satisfactory answers to those questions, finally deciding they were probably unanswerable.

But working on those cases had opened his eyes to an obvious, inescapable truth—a truth he'd known all along, but never seen so clearly. More than opened his eyes. Had driven the truth home like a stake through the heart.

Evil thrived in the hidden places where no one ever went, when no one was looking. Or—much worse—when people saw it and looked the other way. Whenever any of us comes face to face with evil, there are only two choices: face it head-on, or look away. Confront it or turn and run. Fight or flight. It was that simple.

If, after Markov gave him the full tour, it became clear that this was truly a house where evil dwelled, Quinn would become the only witness. The only one who could stop it. Leaving would not be an option.

And if he decided to stay, Johnny was right. It would be time to find out all he could about his "acting space"—a lost world where pterodactyls still existed, and something moaned in a forbidden chamber.

CHAPTER 21

Feeling ridiculous dressed in a diving outfit and carrying a spear gun, Johnny came to the end of the underground passage that connected the outbuilding to the lagoon. Markov's tortured rationale for having the tunnel dug was as a security measure for keeping their clandestine activities out of sight. As though anyone would ever see or care.

When the tunnel had been completed, Markov had indulged his *auteur* fantasy and had a second one dug. Connecting the lagoon to the castle's subterranean chamber, he'd envisioned it as a setting for spooky, atmospheric scenes—especially ones showing creatures from the lagoon creeping along it to infiltrate the castle and threaten its inhabitants.

Like so many of his harebrained ideas, those scenarios had never materialized.

Johnny hesitated a few feet from the water's edge. It wasn't the plunge into the cold water that was causing the hesitation, although even with the insulation provided by the full-body dry suit, a water temperature around forty degrees would not be pleasant.

The hesitation was dread over what might be waiting at

the bottom. In Markov's insane desire to create the most realistic movie monsters ever—unstoppable killing machines he tried to bring to some semblance of actual life—Johnny could never be sure that the corpses of the failed experiments down there hadn't come back from the dead.

When Markov had first bought this property with the intention of creating a self-contained world for making movies, he'd hired an excavator to create the lagoon. Aside from lending atmosphere to the Universal-inspired horror movies he planned on making, it could also be used for any water scenes.

But the road to Hell is paved with good intentions, and as Markov began to see himself as "the Orson Welles of horror," those movies never got made. Instead he had spent—*wasted*—their lives, trying to create a single horror masterpiece that would give him the screen immortality he so dearly coveted.

The problem, Johnny had wanted to scream at him, was that—aside from the fact that Markov was no Orson Welles—he could never figure out the story he wanted to tell. All he knew was that he wanted to make the ultimate monster rally picture with the most realistic monsters the world had ever seen. That, too, was the problem. The monsters would be the stars. Humans, for him, were only fodder for the monsters.

Several times Markov had started production only to shut it down because he wasn't happy with the robotic monsters he'd created. By the time he finished tinkering with them and was ready to resume shooting, his contract with the actors would have expired and he'd have to recast. The result was a bunch of interesting but disjointed scenes that no amount of clever editing or scriptwriting could pull into a coherent narrative.

He had finally put the picture on hold while he spent decades in his laboratory, trying to develop more realistic monsters he could insert anywhere in the film and make them do anything. But the more real they became, the deeper Markov slipped into madness.

Not long after they'd moved here, he'd summoned Johnny to his laboratory in a panic, pointing to two of his earliest creations that lay dormant on the floor: The Watcher in the Crypt, and his much more terrifying version of the Gill Man. Full-scale models of robotic monsters he'd built, for scenes that would feature the lagoon.

"I no longer have complete control," Markov had said. "They must be destroyed while they are sleeping. Nothing can live if it cannot breathe. Drown them. And weigh them down somehow, so that if whatever infernal spark of life is in them flares up, they will not be able to come up for air."

With the usual feelings of self-loathing at continuing to be a party to such madness, Johnny had done his bidding, tying the monstrosities to cinder blocks to keep them from floating to the top. When Markov heard how flimsily they'd been weighted down, he'd immediately hired a heavy equipment operator to deposit a block of granite in the lagoon and instructed Johnny to chain them to that.

Now, awkwardly high-stepping because of the flippers, Johnny took the last few steps, hesitating briefly to quiet the whisper that always came at the water's edge:

It's only the current that makes them twitch and float upward, like they're straining to break free.

Johnny clicked on the diver's light secured to the forehead like a miner's and jumped in feet first, quickly sinking to the bottom ten feet away. After taking a moment to stabilize, the usual inspection began, which consisted of floating around the aborted monsters as they gently swayed in the current, making sure they were still chained to the block while looking for anything unusual. When the circuit around the granite slab was complete, Johnny resisted the powerful urge to be gone and took a moment to study the things for any sign of life.

Disturbing as it was, their ghostly swaying was only the normal ebb and flow to be expected underwater. There was no twitching or otherwise unnatural movement. Finally came the most hated part of this task: looking into the eyes to make sure they were still closed.

They were.

Johnny's feeling of relief was abruptly cut short by an odd movement. The Creature from the Black Lagoon's arms started drifting upward, as though reaching for the surface. Then the Creature itself starting floating toward the top. Johnny hadn't noticed if the monster's slow ascent had been aided by a kick of the scaly webbed foot.

The Gill Man's head was nearing the surface when the chain became taut. From several feet below in the murky water, it was impossible to tell, but the head might be poking through. Alarmed, Johnny swam up fast to check.

The head was below the surface. Its eyes were still closed.

Johnny looked down.

Visibility was too poor to tell if the thing was straining against the chain. The arms slowly floated back down to the sides, and the Creature just hung there, a few feet below the surface—not alive, but seeming as though any moment it might be.

Markov had said nothing can live without air, but the

Creature was amphibious.

Johnny finned to the bottom and used the chain to pull it back down, then coiled the chain to make it shorter and wedged it under the block of granite, knowing it would eventually come loose again and making a mental note to get a shorter chain. Far from convinced that the thing was dead, the head of security swam not to the surface, but to the ten-foot wide opening into the underground tunnels. Eager to be away from robotic corpses that may have been prematurely buried, Johnny plunged into the hole and swam into the tunnel on the left that led to the castle.

A short distance in, the upward-sloping tunnel became free of water except for a trickle glimmering along the bottom. Pieces of slimy marine vegetation were scattered here and there, but there were no signs of life. Johnny replaced the flippers with sturdy slip-ons and moved up the passage.

Moments later, it opened into the Garden. Hastening through the nightmare chamber, Johnny went up a stone staircase that led to the only safe haven in the castle—the private apartment Markov had so generously included for his steward.

Steward. Caretaker. Head of Security. Groundskeeper.

Servant? Slave? Prisoner?

What am I? Johnny thought. A human being. Trapped in a world of the inhuman.

CHAPTER 22

Markov joined Quinn in the den promptly at four. He fixed himself a coffee and pulled the other chair around, until they sat facing one another from a few feet apart. "How did you sleep?"

"Not well."

"Oh? Were the accommodations not to your liking?"

"The accommodations were fine. But there were some disturbances."

"Disturbances?"

"Lon Chaney and a pterodactyl made appearances." Uncertainty about the shape he thought he'd seen in the lagoon kept him from mentioning it.

Markov showed the vaguest hint of a smile. "I told you there would be previews of coming attractions."

"So they were your handiwork." Again Quinn's flare of annoyance at being manipulated was quickly extinguished by the truth of the matter: he'd been warned. "Impressive," he said. "Revolutionary. The ability to project a special effect like a hologram anywhere you want and control its movement. But why a pterodactyl? Are you making a dinosaur movie?"

"No. That was just me showing off, I'm afraid. One's ego can become quite large, living alone for so many years."

Quinn resisted saying something about becoming a legend in one's own mind. "Mr. Markov—should I call you Mister? There was a *Doctor* Markoff in *The Monster Maker*."

"I am no doctor, and Count or Baron would be such a cliché. I thought of Morbius, living on his own Forbidden Planet, but that seemed too … on the nose. Markov will suffice."

"I know that is not your original name. Did you take it from that movie?"

"You are most well-informed. Yes. Given the movie reality I have created, it seemed appropriate. And it has that eastern European ring to it."

"You keep hinting at all sorts of dangers—monsters, ghosts, some alternate reality. I had been looking forward to a companionable weekend, discussing your experience on *Dracula* and whatever else you wanted to share. But our visit seems to be turning into something else. If this is your version of *The Most Dangerous Game*, then I need to know exactly what the rules are."

"And so you shall. You have studied the power of movies to influence real life. The story of my life is that power taken to the nth degree—with, as Poe said in *The Conqueror Worm*, 'much of Madness, and more of Sin, and Horror the soul of the plot.'

"I have my flaws, Mr. Quinn. Some quite grievous. But make no mistake: I am not the mad castle recluse one might assume. Nor am I the eccentric reincarnation of Bela Lugosi I sometimes present myself to be.

"It is impossible to know all the countless factors that combine to make us who we are. I believe the overriding force behind it all is Destiny. Some call it God. But if there is a God, then perhaps the evil part of my nature was created by the Powers of Darkness. Whatever the case, I am certain of the *primary* factors that have combined in my warped psyche to turn me into Markov—Maker of Monsters."

"Someone had scrawled those words on Henry Frankenstein's tomb in *Son of Frankenstein*," Quinn said.

"Another of my cinematic ancestors. I am the offspring of those movies. *Frankenstein, Dracula, The Wolf Man.* They created me. And now I am creating them. A maker of monsters for the digital age."

"What are these 'factors' that compel you to create monsters?"

"There at least three of which I am certain. The two most dominant are unquestionably my obsession with Dracula, and my genius in applying technology to filmmaking. I say this latter not as braggadocio, but simply to help you fully understand the things that have shaped my life."

"What is the third factor?" Quinn was doggedly trying to forge a path of reason into the dark forests of Markov's mental wilderness.

"We shall come to that at our final stop in the tour. My Chamber of Horrors. Forgive my reticence, but I'm sure you can appreciate my filmmaker's love of the dramatic reveal."

"You're the tour guide. I'm eager to see what comes next."

"Very well. It is time to dig deeper into *my* Pandora's box. The lid is the door to my screening room. The story of my life starts and ends with the movies."

CHAPTER 23

Inside the screening room, they once again got candy, buckets of popcorn, and drinks. When they were comfortably settled into their seats, Markov began his introduction.

"We saw Lon's short last night. Now it is time for the feature. The one film I was able to make. The poverty row picture we talked about earlier."

"*The Blood of Dracula*," Quinn said.

"Yes. This is the version that was never shown in theaters. Some of the footage was too grim and taken out before release. My goal was to make the most frightening, disturbing film I could. To out-Tod Tod. Even allowing for what had always been considered unacceptable, I'd always thought horror films shied away from showing the genuine horror. They were too timid. Too formulaic. Too unimaginative in their presentation. I had decided long ago, that if I only had one chance to make my mark, I was going to hold nothing back. You will be the first person outside of the people who worked on the film to see the uncut version. I myself have not watched it since. The memories it conjures are too painful."

Markov's dire introduction only made Quinn more curious to see what he had done with the Dracula story.

"I'm sure you are familiar with a program on Turner Classic Movies called *The Essentials*," Markov said.

"Very."

"Then I give you a never-before-seen look at an absolute essential if you are to truly understand the depth of my Dracula obsession: *The Blood of Dracula*. Shot for thirty thousand dollars in 1947." His hand hovered over the button that would start the movie. "We talked of the power of movies to influence real life. This is the film that changed mine forever."

From the opening credits it was clear that Markov had not exaggerated his skill as a writer/director. Instead of the standard fade-in, the title burst onto the screen accompanied by the jarring screech of a violin that reminded Quinn of *Psycho*—he quickly did the math—thirteen years before *Psycho* came out.

The lettering of the title and credits dripped blood. In brief intervals between each section of the credits, body parts and monstrous faces whirled in and out of disturbing juxtapositions. It was a kaleidoscopic preview of the horror about to unfold.

After the final credit there was a dedication:

This motion picture is dedicated to the memory of Lon Chaney, the Man of a Thousand Faces, whose genius was the inspiration for this Dracula.

The dedication faded, leaving only a blank white screen that stayed on for what seemed like too long, until Quinn began to wonder if there was a technical problem.

Suddenly a huge knife slashed through the screen and jolted him back in his seat. The torn remnants of the screen fell away to reveal the opening of the movie. A dizzying montage quickly established the plot:

A prisoner strapped into an electric chair.

CUT TO

A switch being thrown.

CUT TO

The prisoner's shadow on the wall twitching violently while the current buzzes loudly.

CUT TO

The prison doctor confirming death.

CUT TO

Prison attendants hauling the carcass away as a newspaper headline swirls into view:

"DUTCH" BURKHARDT FRIES IN CHAIR!
MONSTER MOLESTED, KILLED CHILDREN

CUT TO

Shovels of dirt being thrown on the coffin in the graveyard.

DISSOLVE TO

The body being snatched that night by a couple of goons and taken to the lair of a mad doctor.

The camera dollied into a fixed position in the operating room of the cadaverous Doctor Montescu, whose sharp Germanic features reminded Quinn of Otto Kruger. The corpse was strapped to the operating table, and one of the goons left while the other, Klaus, hovered nearby to assist. At Montescu's nod he plucked a chainsaw from a table full of gruesome-looking instruments, got it started, and reverently handed it to his master. Montescu displayed no emotion as he sawed off the arms, the legs, and finally the head. Each time the saw was just about to touch flesh, a cutaway to the doctor's face avoided showing the incision.

Despite Markov's criticism of horror movies for not showing the genuine horror, in 1947 spurting blood would never have gotten past the Breen Office. Quinn was glad. Buckets of blood weren't necessary for the audience to get the full effect.

Intercut with the severing of the body parts were shots of them being stitched onto a new muscular torso. When the recycled body was completely assembled, small sheets concealed the face, chest, and genital area.

From a large bell jar of some clear liquid, Montescu lovingly removed a beating heart. He nodded at Klaus, and the oafish assistant pulled the small sheet from the chest to reveal a gaping incision. Montescu inserted the heart into the hole. Quickly sewing it closed, he went to a glass case a few steps away.

Inside was a severed head wearing a crown. The head was still alive and watching his every move. Montescu opened the case and inserted a needle into the neck, explaining to the uncomprehending but worshipful Klaus as the glass cylinder filled with blood.

"This is the head of the original Vlad Dracula, Klaus. For five hundred years it has been kept alive and passed down by his loyal descendants." When the needle was full, Montescu pulled it out and held it poised over the arm of the reconstructed corpse. "The blood of Dracula," he proclaimed. "It will transform this imperfect creature into the *new* Dracula—patriarch and supreme ruler of a new race. A race that shall live forever. *A race of vampires!*"

He jammed the needle into the vein.

A series of dissolves showed the moment of truth: the arm ... the needle emptying ... the clock on the wall ... the empty needle.

The camera moved farther back to see if the creature would come to life. After a suitably long wait to drag out the tension, the reassembled cadaver began to twitch and stir. Finally, remaining ramrod straight the entire time, it rose into a standing position, exactly as Nosferatu had done in the iconic shot of him rising in his coffin. The cloths over the face and genitals had remained in place. The vampire reached up and yanked the one from his face, staring directly into the camera—in effect directly into the eyes of the viewer.

"Dracula lives!" Montescu shouted. "Forever shall his bloodline rule the earth!"

The reveal had jolted Quinn back in his seat. Not just because of the sudden direct confrontation by the vampire. The countenance Markov had chosen for his Dracula was shocking.

It was the hideous vampire from Lon Chaney's short. *The Un-Dead.* The scariest vampire Quinn had ever seen. Worse than Max Schreck's Nosferatu.

The thin black lips parted to reveal the same set of jarringly perfect teeth. As they had in *The Un-Dead,* two snake-like fangs popped into place. The vampire's smile was that of a demon.

Montescu's moment of triumph was cut short by a knock at the operating room door. He stepped in front of his monster to shield him from view. "Send them away!" he ordered Klaus.

Klaus opened the door a crack and peeked through. The voice of a young child came from behind the door. "It's me, Daddy."

Still facing the monster with his back to the door, Montescu told the child he'd be out in a moment.

"Can't I come in?"

From the unmuffled sound of the voice, the youngster had apparently managed to poke through the crack in the door. Silently cursing Klaus for letting it happen, Montescu pulled himself up to his fullest possible height to block the hideous face from view. Dracula moved his head to peer over Montescu's shoulder at the child. An unsavory spark came into the vampire's eyes.

A quick cut showed a close-up of the adorable child's beautiful face. "Who's your friend, Daddy?"

"No one you know, sweetheart. We have a private matter to discuss. *Klaus!* Take Donnie to the study!"

Quinn set the last of his popcorn aside, anxious to see if Donnie would come bursting in. Instead there was the sound of Klaus muttering as Donnie withdrew and the door closed.

Montescu and Dracula stood a few feet apart, creator and his creation, eyeing each other with an unwavering stare.

"You shall be Dracula, master of all vampires," Montescu said. "But always remember: without me, you would still be lying in the grave. I am *your* master. I created you to do *my* bidding. Do you understand?"

Dracula held the stare for a very long, defiant moment before making a reluctant, barely perceptible nod.

A long dissolve gave way to a night scene at the edge of deep woods. Montescu commanded his Dracula:

"Go. Feed. Feed on them all."

Dracula spoke his first words—*"Yes, Master"*—and dropped to all fours.

A quick cutaway to Montescu's reaction avoided the expensive and time-consuming transformation scene of Dracula turning into a wolf. In the next shot the wolf was simply there, artfully underlit to conceal the fact that it was probably a large dog. Its long, rumbling growl, a mixture of deep menace and predatory lust, sent a chill scurrying through Quinn. The growl died out and the wolf bolted into the woods.

Dracula returned to human form as he approached a village. A tension-filled sequence followed, showing him skulking through the shadows to feed on one hapless soul after another. Each feeding made him stronger and more confident, and a disturbing pattern began to emerge.

Apparently the child molester influence of Dutch Burkhardt's body parts made the vampire feed only on children.

Montescu found this out when he ventured into the village to see if his experiment had been a success. Sitting alone at a table in the pub, he overheard snippets of conversation from the terrified villagers, uttered with a vague Eastern European accent:

"Calls himself Dracula!"

"Says he has risen to become our supreme ruler!"

"Ya!" a beefy villager chimed in. "Yosef escaped his clutches," he said, crossing himself. "But before he did, dis Dracula boasted to him dat he vus going to be da Prince of Darkness, as soon as he could destroy da vun who stood between him and da throne."

Montescu's eyes widened when he heard this.

Dracula's lust for power meant he would be coming to destroy his creator.

"He sucks da blood of children!" someone shouted.

Fear contorted Montescu's face. He bolted from the pub and hastened back to the castle. "The devil cannot take my angel!" he said, running to Donnie's bedroom with a desperate urgency.

After placing garlic and wolfbane and crucifixes all around the room, Montescu pulled up a chair and kept watch by the sleeping child's bedside.

Suddenly the wolf burst through the window in a shower of glass. After a quick cutaway for a reaction shot, Dracula was standing there, drawn up to his full height, leaving no doubt that he was now the master of all.

"I am Dracula. Son of the Devil. Your banes cannot stop me. You have made me too strong." He pointed at the crucifix on the wall above Donnie's head. "Stronger even than Him!" He looked at Montescu and made a sweeping movement with his arm. "Step aside, mortal. Your child shall carry on *my* bloodline, not yours."

Montescu plucked a sword from the wall. "Never! No creature can live without its head!"

Dracula ducked and the vicious swipe just missed. In one fluid motion the vampire snatched Donnie while leaping across the bed. Landing on his feet, he struggled to maneuver the screaming and wriggling child into position as a human shield. Montescu saw that he must act fast, while the vampire's neck was still exposed.

He rounded the bed and drew back the sword. But just as he began the killing stroke, Dracula stumbled backward over a toy left on the floor. Instead of landing on the vampire's neck, the sword sliced deeply into the thigh of the child, who let out an agonized scream as blood spurted everywhere.

In the screening room, Quinn's arm shot up to shield him from the splatter but he quickly caught himself and pulled it back down. *Jesus Christ, that looks real. No child actor could be that convincing.* He cast a furtive glance at Markov, whose attention was riveted on the screen, a pained look on his face.

136

Troubling thoughts nagged Quinn as he watched Donnie's all-too-realistic agony.

Is this a snuff film? How sick is Markov? How did he get that blood past the Breen office?

Unable to tear his eyes away, he watched as an enraged Montescu drew back for a second stroke at the neck of the vampire. Just as the downstroke began the screen went black. In the blackout Quinn heard the *whoosh*, followed by Dracula's agonized death groans.

The blackout faded in to a denouement that lasted barely a minute, obviously meant to reassure the audience that the child would be alright. Compared to the seamlessness of the rest of the film, the series of clumsily edited shots had the air of having been hastily tacked on.

A medium shot showed Donnie lying in a hospital bed, Montescu sitting close and holding his child's hand. A close-up of Montescu looking down at Donnie with a relieved smile was followed by an extreme close-up of the child's smiling face, incongruously showing no reaction to having almost lost a leg.

The angelic face dissolved into Dracula's severed head. The final shot held on the hideous dead face of the vampire for a disturbingly long time, tension mounting every second as Quinn wondered: *will those eyes pop open?*

Instead, the screen suddenly went black. The blackout lasted just long enough to lull the audience into thinking the film was over, then—

The same knife from the opening slashed through the screen, accompanied by the same screeching violin. The torn halves of the blackout fell away to reveal the blank white screen that had begun the movie. A splash of color in the completely black-and-white film burst onto the stark whiteness—two red words dripping blood:

THE END

After a long beat, two of the blood trails beneath the letters began to move. They slithered up alongside the *D*, then wriggled into the shape of a question mark.

THE END?

An iris fade-out held on the blood-red words before a quick blackout.

The theater was plunged into complete darkness except for the dim lighting in Markov's control panel. In its faint glow he appeared as a shadow. Whether he was in a daze or engaging in his flair for melodrama, he sat utterly still for a long moment.

Finally he activated the house lights and turned to face Quinn, clearly waiting for his reaction.

Quinn sorted through the jumble of impressions swirling in his head, thinking of how best to begin. "It is indeed the *Citizen Kane* of poverty row pictures."

A glow of pride chased the shadow from Markov's face. "Do go on."

"Truly shocking. Decades ahead of its time. There are elements of *Psycho*—thirteen years before *Psycho* came out. That screeching violin and the final dissolve, from the beautiful Donnie to the hideous Dracula."

"My Dracula, of course, is an homage to Lon Chaney's Dracula. A way of bringing to the screen what he didn't live long enough to bring himself."

For the next fifteen minutes they discussed the film, Markov reveling in the praise of his filmmaking skills. The acting was adequate at best, but all the other elements— inventive camerawork, intelligent dialogue, creative editing, nerve-jangling music—combined to create a minor masterpiece, far beyond what should have been possible on a minuscule poverty row budget.

"The severing of the body parts," Quinn said. "You artfully cut around it, but even showing that much was unheard-of in those days. And that blood spurting at the end was completely taboo. I kept wondering how you could have gotten that past the Breen office."

"That shot was removed from the print we sent to the Breen office. And from the release print."

"Saved for the director's cut," Quinn said.

Markov winced as if the casual remark inflicted pain. He offered no explanation, so Quinn went on. "That business with the sword slicing Donnie's leg looked incredibly real."

The furrows of pain on Markov's face deepened. "That's because it was. Dracula was not supposed to trip. We had rehearsed it many times. I was going to stop the sword just before it landed, and use editing to show the head flying through the air. But when he stumbled, the child's leg got in the way before I could stop my swing...."

"We couldn't end the movie like that. Audiences would have hated us. So we had to add the last scene of the child recovering in the hospital. The close-up of Donnie's face was an insert from a scene we had shot earlier. The child was still in far too much pain for a happily-ever-after smile. I've come not to believe in happily-ever-afters."

This was obviously a very painful memory. Any further discussion of Markov's *magnum opus* could wait. But there was one more comment Quinn felt compelled to make.

"The child reminded me of a young Johnny."

Markov's hollow intonation sounded as though it came from a sepulcher deep within himself.

"That's because it is. Johnny is my daughter."

CHAPTER 24

Johnny sat on the bed in her chamber, staring at the foot-long scar on her thigh. Earlier, while her father and Quinn had been getting settled in for the screening, she had snuck into the projection booth to watch the film so often mentioned but never shown. Markov had called it "unwatchable."

Now, for the ten-thousandth time, she watched the most horrible scene in her life vividly unfold in the air above the scar, as though the puckered trail of flesh were a memory-activated 3D movie projector.

She had just opened her eyes in the recovery room. Her father sat by her bed, holding her hand. Even to a little girl recovering from shock and anesthesia, it was obvious that guilt was making him promise something that would make him feel better but do nothing for her.

"From now on I will never let you leave my side. You will be to me what I was to Tod. My permanent assistant."

Johnny watched herself make the small nod that would change her from beloved daughter into indentured servant, and the father she idolized into her Lord and Master. The moment when her leg had been saved but her life had ended.

The moment when Daddy announced that he was now Markov.

It had been Markov who had kept Daddy's promises and turned his daughter into a cringing keeper of the castle and its secrets.

Johnny. She hated her name, not only because it was no name for a girl, but because it had turned out to be so fitting. Her father, in his obsessive worship of Tod Browning, had named her after Browning's favorite freak: Johnny Eck. Half-boy. And she had turned out to be a freak. Half-girl. Living a half-life. Dead but un-dead.

In the make-believe movie life she had constructed for herself, in here she was not Johnny. In here she was Cinderella, waiting for her Prince to save her.

Tears of shame at never having the courage to save herself, to become whatever she had been put on this earth to become, filled her eyes. Her anger wouldn't let them fall. Since Quinn's arrival, her prematurely buried soul had been clamoring for release from its gilded coffin.

This travesty of life must end. It had been artificially prolonged—for what? To make any of her dreams come true? No. To help a madman's nightmare come true. Allowing it to go on would only perpetuate the evil.

All these years on this earth, yet I have never truly lived. For fifty years I have been trapped in this world of Gothic movie horror. A crypt for the un-dead. The half-dead.

She traced her finger back and forth along the scar, as though erasing it. It was too late for tears. It was time for action.

CHAPTER 25

"Daughter?"

The word set off two explosions in Quinn's mind.

The first was the revelation that Johnny was female. His mental scramble to see how he could have mistaken a woman for a man all this time was quickly shattered by the second, larger explosion.

Markov's cringing attendant wasn't just a loyal employee. In his warped version of fatherhood, he had somehow converted his daughter into a loyal subject. A servant.

But she didn't serve happily. It was clear now that her furtive overtures to Quinn—a visitor she barely knew—had been cries for help to free her from her twisted bondage.

"Yes," Markov said. "Nothing makes audiences squirm more than seeing a child put in harm's way. I'd seen it from the silent days, but most especially when the Monster drowns the little girl in *Frankenstein*. So I convinced myself that a child had to be put in extreme danger in my film. I had made little home movies with Johnny, silly things where some toy monster would be coming after her. I was always telling her she was going to be a big star, bigger than Mae Clarke or Fay Wray. By the time she was in first grade she knew who they were, because I'd taken her to see *Frankenstein* and *King Kong* and all the rest when they were re-released. She worshipped me and loved being in front of the camera. Since she had experience and we had to save every dollar we could, I decided to cast her in the part." He stared at the floor as though it were a bottomless well of regret. "I had to keep her in my care after the accident."

"Because of guilt over what you had done."

"Initially, yes. But over time our relationship evolved into what it has become. The accident has bound us together forever. I look after her and she looks after me."

"I must tell you: it's not the healthiest father/daughter relationship I've ever seen."

"We have our moments when we are alone, but this family has never been healthy. That stems from me. Rot in the trunk of the tree extends to its branches. Our family tree is like one of those twisted grotesques you see in the fog-shrouded moors of the old horror movies."

As Quinn pictured the gnarled dead branches jutting through the fog, it struck him: the make-believe world of movies had become George Tilton's reality. They had entirely consumed his life. They'd given him delusions of becoming a great director that had driven him to create his own elaborate studio and set—in a location utterly impractical for filmmaking—to record the life of a very sick character he had created, for a film that almost certainly would never be finished and never be seen.

Even adding the shocking revelation about Johnny to all the other disturbing things he'd seen and heard since coming here, Quinn felt sure he hadn't gotten close to the deepest level of Markov's Hell. With his hopes for a Universal horror lover's dream weekend escape dashed, Quinn felt far less inclined to mince words. "What happened to Johnny's ear?"

Markov closed his eyes for a few seconds. "Kong bit it."

"Kong? One of your creations?"

A single nod. "My virtual miniature. It happened a few years ago. I had extracted and enlarged a digital version of the original King Kong to include in my film. It was about two feet tall. I needed to shoot some test footage, to see if I could find a setup that would let me have Kong and Johnny in the same shot while disguising their difference in size.

"The thing worked perfectly. Its movements were completely convincing. With my gloves and goggles I could control its every movement, including the opening and closing of the mouth. The shot I had set up called for Kong to lean in close to Johnny's face, curious to inspect this strange creature."

He took a moment to gather himself. "There was a malfunction. I have relived that scene a thousand times. I had rehearsed every move to a fare-thee-well. I made no mistakes. In effect, I was Kong. He was a digital extension of myself. The shot was going beautifully. He loved her at first sight, just as Kong did Fay Wray, just as I had when Johnny was born. Tears came to my eyes as he tenderly studied her. But while he hovered several inches from her face, something came into his eyes. They moved in their sockets, surveying her, becoming excited.

"He was alive, Mr. Quinn. I know I sound like Colin Clive in *Frankenstein*. Make of it what you will. Unlike James Whale, I have not created Gods and Monsters. Only monsters. And unfortunately I can no longer make it all stop simply by yelling 'Cut!'"

In the waves of turmoil washing over Markov with increasing frequency, Quinn glimpsed the lost soul of

George Tilton, struggling against a rising tide of inner horror. Horror caused by alter egos he'd created that had begun to feed on the evil within himself. The day he'd become Lucky, he'd entered Tod Browning's world of cinematic cruelty and freaks and never escaped. Lucky had become Frederick Schreck—Nosferatu—and Schreck had become Markov.

And his grip on the Markov persona was crumbling. The Poe quote on the wall of his studio flashed in Quinn's mind:

My terror is not of Germany. It is of the soul.

Markov recovered his stoic demeanor and continued. "The only thing I can say with certainty is what happened. Kong leapt onto Johnny's shoulder and bit her ear. I immediately threw off the gloves and goggles and Kong disintegrated. I have given you my theory about the soul being captured on film, which I am convinced is not theory but fact. Beyond that, no one can say with certainty how these things can be. Maybe it was his way of showing affection. Perhaps some of an ape's primal urges had been instilled into Kong by his creators, and those primal urges overtook him. Or—and this I do not like to think—some digital bits of mine intermingled with his during the extraction process and something in my twisted psyche overtook him. Perhaps the heightened magnetism of this infernal miasma has brought the phantasms of my netherworld to life. Perhaps, perhaps, *perhaps*.

"Whatever the case, my monsters are developing wills of their own. Even the digital versions I have destroyed sometimes retain a physical substance and appear out of nowhere. A fitting irony, don't you think? That a man whose lifelong obsession with the undead may have somehow created digital undead? Who can say what evil might lurk in the darkness between the pixels?

"And this is why I warn you for the last time: We can never be sure what is a special effect totally under my control, or a creature that has escaped its bonds and taken on a life of its own. In the worst-case scenario it could be a version of myself, unable to control my monsters from the id."

Each revelation deepened Quinn's understanding of the truly warped family he had discovered. Whatever lingering resentment Johnny felt toward her father for maiming her must have turned to hatred after the Kong incident. As Markov he had promised to protect her, but couldn't keep one of his digital creations from chewing off part of his daughter's ear.

Daughter. When had Johnny ceased to be his daughter and become his caretaker? His servant? Markov had said she was twenty-something when they moved into the castle in 1960.

"How old is Johnny?"

"We stopped counting birthdays long ago. Somewhere in her seventies, I suppose."

"She looks fifty. You are over a hundred, and you could pass for sixty. How is that possible?"

Markov hesitated, tried to give him the stare.

Quinn was having none of it. "Cards on the table, remember?"

The stare softened. "Old habits die hard. Very well. The next card awaits in the Chamber of Horrors. The one that will answer your question. The one that started it all."

CHAPTER 26

Johnny sat in front of the control panel that took up much of one wall in her apartment, watching the monitor that showed the two men exiting the screening room and rounding the corner to the next corridor. Behind them, the skull of the Grim Reaper swiveled. Digital eyeballs deep within the empty sockets watched the two men proceeding down the hall—security cameras checking for any unauthorized presence. Johnny had added the Reaper's earlier video of Quinn to the database of approved visitors, so the harvester of souls took no further action.

She watched them walking side by side. Ever since this stranger had come out of nowhere, with his knowledge of film and filmmaking and love of horror, Markov's belief in destiny had become stronger than ever. In his mind, fate had sent him Adam Quinn to bring about her father's long overdue ending.

After years of recording the bizarre events of their unwholesome existence, his glorified home movie was almost finished. Before Quinn's arrival, she'd asked Markov how their guest could be worked into the climax, especially on such short notice. Markov had said the ending could not be revealed, that it would ruin a surprise better than the shower scene in *Psycho*.

However it ended, it wouldn't be the ending Johnny wanted.

Because she believed in destiny too, and for fifty years had clung to her vision of a happy ending—not for Markov's sick movie that had destroyed their lives—but for this sham of a life.

How much control *did* a person have over their own destiny? After a lifetime of being controlled, it was time to find out.

CHAPTER 27

In the storm cloud of ominous thoughts gathering in Quinn's brain, Markov's revelation that Johnny was his daughter had been a thunderbolt. Now, as the two men walked down the long corridor toward the Chamber of Horrors, Quinn forced those thoughts aside to prepare himself for Markov's dramatic reveal of what started it all.

They came to an alcove on the right that led to a large wooden door. To the left, a stone staircase spiraled down and out of sight. Straight ahead, the corridor continued past this intersection into darkness. At the top of the staircase, a suit of armor stood at attention, its gauntlet-covered fist gripping a halberd as if poised to repel invaders from below. The unmistakable shadow of Nosferatu, creeping up the stairs, had been painted onto the wall of the staircase.

Quinn gestured at the black outline and tried to lighten the grim mood. "Since beheading is one of the ways to stop a vampire, if I were Nosferatu I'd find another way in, rather than try to get past this knight and that wicked axe."

"One never knows what might happen in a world where dark shadows come to life." Markov nodded toward the staircase. "I know I have said you are free to move about the castle and its grounds, but the one place you may not go is down those stairs. As a fellow lover of the Gothic, I am sure you know that every castle must have its secret chamber. The one below is mine. The suit of armor and the shadow of Nosferatu are my sentinels."

Markov's insistence that Quinn never go to the very place where he'd felt a disturbing presence only strengthened his resolve to explore it fully at the first opportunity.

Markov led them into the recessed entryway of the Chamber of Horrors. On either side of the oak door, two flickering gaslights in 19th-century glass sconces cast disturbing shadows on the face painted above. A lurid demonic gargoyle, replete with pointed ears, lolling tongue, and glowing pupils, eternally leered down at all who dared to enter. Above its face were the words *Le Chambre du Horreurs*.

Quinn said, "I remember seeing something like that in the beginning of *Mad Love* with Peter Lorre."

"You are an astute cineaste. That was my inspiration. Karl Freund directed it and invited me to the premiere."

Quinn felt a twinge of regret at his mention of Freund. Markov's recollections of the legendary cinematographer who'd shot *Dracula* was one of many discussions he'd been looking forward to, but after the sinister turn his visit had taken, he saw those discussions slipping away.

Markov went on. "I think the French lends a nice atmospheric touch, since my collection—my entire approach to horror—is very Grand Guignol."

"From the moment your carriage picked me up, I've felt like I'm being pulled into those movies I've watched so many times."

"Prepare to be pulled even deeper." Markov held up the skeleton key. "Other than Johnny, you are the first person I have ever let into my Chamber of Horrors. I am sure you will find my collection of oddities fascinating, but the main attraction—the darkest of my dark secrets—will challenge all credibility. Keep an open mind."

"You don't do what I do for a living and not be prepared for things that defy rational explanation."

Markov unlocked the door and beckoned Quinn into an utterly black void, save for a faint patch of light beyond the threshold where the gaslight barely reached. The flick of a switch revealed a room that was an assault on the eyes.

Embedded along each side wall of a carpeted space about thirty yards square were several glass-enclosed showcases, each with its own spotlight shining on the exhibit within. Scattered throughout the center of the room were shockingly lifelike re-creations of classic movie monsters, all posed with hands outthrust, eager to clutch their next victim. After the initial jolt, Quinn thought of all the happy Halloween birthdays he'd spent with his father watching these creatures on the screen. It was as though he'd walked into a macabre reunion of old friends. That feeling quickly dissipated as he was struck by the more disturbing aspects of the scene.

Dracula, Frankenstein's Monster, the Wolf Man, the Creature from the Black Lagoon, and several other classic monsters each stood in their own tightly focused spotlight, surrounded by impenetrable darkness. The overall effect was of an army of inhuman beings, emerging from some impossible nightworld, to wreak havoc on the human beings they despised.

"I have much planned for our time together," Markov

said, "so this may be my only chance to show you my collection. We will save the best—or worst, depending on your viewpoint—for last."

He led Quinn to the showcases along the left wall. "I have arranged the exhibits in chronological order, according to the release date of the movie they were in, so you can trace the development of horror cinema."

The first display was a wax sculpture of an oversized severed hand with long fingernails, frozen in the classic horror pose of reaching to close on a throat. "This one has particular sentimental value," Markov explained. "It is from *Eyes of Mystery*, the first Tod Browning movie I saw and the reason I sought him out. It was a spooky 'old dark house' chiller that had everything I love: hidden chambers, shadowy figures skulking around, and, of course, hands reaching out from behind curtains to strangle hapless victims. You might say this is the hand that reached out and led me here."

Next came an iconic mask. "Is that…?" Quinn asked.

"Yes. Lon Chaney's mask from *The Phantom of the Opera*."

"That would have to be one of the most sought-after pieces of movie memorabilia ever. How were you able to obtain it?"

"I got many of my pieces through connections I had at the time, but not this one. This and several others I got through a rather ghoulish system I developed. I would trace the provenance of artifacts I coveted until I found the person who had ended up with it—usually someone associated with the production, or a collector. I would call and make an offer. Sometimes they needed money and a deal was made quickly. If they refused, I would keep tabs on them until I saw their obituary. I knew that family members often sold off collections when the owner died, so I would wait a respectful amount of time—not too long, I didn't want to be beaten out—and make a generous offer they were usually eager to accept."

He led Quinn to the next case, where a prosthetic arm ended in a black-gloved fist.

"Don't tell me," Quinn said. "The arm the Monster ripped off Lionel Atwill in *Son of Frankenstein*?"

"The very same."

"That was a great touch. *Son of Frankenstein* is my favorite of all the Frankenstein movies."

In the next case, a large butcher knife was perched on a stand at a 45-degree angle. "From the shower scene in *Psycho*," Markov said.

If this was genuine, Quinn was looking at a prop that had attained its own screen immortality by terrifying a generation. He had to ask the inevitable question. "How can you be sure this is the one?"

"*Psycho* was a Universal picture, and I knew a man from the old days who had worked his way up to being the head of the property department. The moment I walked out of the theater after watching it, I knew I was going to do everything possible to get that knife. The prop man told me it was a common kitchen knife available at stores. He had come to Universal in the '30s, a humble young man just starting out. But in 1960 he had two children reaching college age and mentioned that tuition was going to be a problem. For fifty thousand dollars, I persuaded him to buy a duplicate knife to put in storage and sell me the original. Of course, one can be absolutely certain about very little in this life—particularly the honesty of human beings—but one thing about this knife convinced me that the prop man had indeed sold me the original. Some dark substance had gotten into the crevice where the blade joined the hilt. I had it tested."

A dramatic pause. "Chocolate syrup."

Quinn had seen it coming. "Hitchcock's substitute for blood."

"It would have been an easy thing to fake, but this man was very salt of the earth. I am convinced the knife is genuine."

Bernard Hermann's classic screeching violin sound track came into Quinn's head as he continued to stare at the knife. Markov got his attention and they moved to the life-sized figures in the middle of the room. Front and center, hands outstretched, was the Creature from the Black Lagoon. It had been played by a man in a suit, so there had to be some kind of internal framework for it to stand like this without any visible support.

"The Creature is one of the all-time great man-in-a-suit monsters," Quinn said. "Your collection wouldn't be complete without it. Is this the original?"

"In a sense, yes, although it was not used in the movie. Prior to shooting, they were testing it underwater and it got snagged and torn." He pointed to the calf of the left leg. A lighter-colored, veinlike line zigzagged across a few of the otherwise smooth and uniform large scales that covered the Creature's body. "The suit in the movie was actually the second one. They kept this one in wardrobe for backup, but it was never used. Their loss turned out to be my gain."

After an admiring stroll through the others, they moved to the showcases along the opposite wall. The first several held props from films that were lesser known but fondly remembered by buffs. The next-to-last case contained another horror movie icon.

It was an exact replica of Regan's head from *The Exorcist*, in the throes of satanic possession.

"This was a mock-up they used to see how the makeup would look before they began shooting," Markov said.

Eyes frozen open in that soul-chilling demonic stare, the head slowly began a three hundred and sixty degree turn. When it faced front again, the eyes shifted focus to lock onto Quinn. A black forked tongue lolled out, then flicked at him.

Markov held out his hand. In the palm was a small remote. "A parlor trick," he said.

"Very effective."

It occurred to Quinn that the knife from *Psycho* and Regan's spinning head had left two of the deepest scars on audiences in cinema history.

They moved to the last showcase. "The pièce de résistance," Markov said.

On a rotating pedestal sat a small leather carrying case, open to display its contents: nose putty, face paint, eyebrow pencils, brushes. Gold lettering on the lid had the name of the owner:

LON F. CHANEY
HOLLYWOOD, CAL.

"This can't possibly be the original," Quinn said. "Lon Chaney's makeup kit would have been guarded like Fort Knox—especially after he died. It had already become legendary."

"I can say with absolute certainty that it is. I know, because … once again, my obsessions overtook me and … I took it."

Quinn remembered Irving Thalberg's memo to Tod Browning, cautioning him about his assistant, who had been seen rummaging around in Lon Chaney's makeup kit during the shooting of *London After Midnight*. "How?" he said.

"I had planned it for months. I waited until everybody was occupied with shooting one of his scenes, then slipped into his dressing room with a camera to get shots of his makeup kit from every angle. I bought an exact duplicate of the carrying case, had it engraved, and used the photos to match every scuff, every scratch. Then, when I was ready to make the switch, I took more pictures of the contents to make sure that the replacement makeup would be the exact same. I filled the case with pencils that were worn to the same length, tubes squeezed the right amount, and arranged everything in its exact same position. No forger was ever more meticulous. I checked the photos one last time before I made the switch. It was impossible to tell the difference.

"So here it is: the prize possession of a good man whom I betrayed."

Thoughts of this level of betrayal, and what it said about Markov's obsessiveness, tempered Quinn's awe at being the first outsider to see movie treasures that included this, the Holy Grail.

"Is this your 'darkest secret'?"

"Not quite."

Markov gestured for them to continue to the far corner of the room. He flicked a switch and a recessed overhead light revealed an armchair and small table facing a large wooden panel, held in place by grooved rails along both sides. This time Markov showed him the remote so there would be no surprise.

"The figure who, in a sense, started the whole Dracula/vampire mythos. Tod would have been proud."

He pressed a button and the panel slid up to reveal a shadowy outline in the glass-enclosed showcase. He pushed another button and a spotlight shone on the very lifelike sculpture of a head resting on a pedestal. It was a famous historical figure Quinn recognized at once. Anyone researching the origins of the Dracula story had seen the painting of this man, with his large mustache, aquiline nose, and intense eyes. Markov had even gone to the trouble of duplicating the ceremonial headdress and royal garb the man wore in the famous portrait. Unlike the portrait, however, the eyes on the sculpture were closed, as in death. Another, more drastic difference was that Markov had chosen to display the head as having been severed. Ragged flesh ran along the neck. On the velvet cloth that lined the bottom of the display case was an area a shade lighter than the rest, in the shape of a sword.

Markov stated the obvious. "Vlad the Impaler."

Quinn nodded. "The original Dracula. Son of Dracul. Very realistic sculpture. Is it wax? If it is, Madame Toussaud would have loved to have it for her museum."

Markov gave him the Lugosi stare.

"It is not a sculpture. It is real."

CHAPTER 28

Quinn understood but couldn't accept it. "*What?* What are you saying?"

"I'm saying this is the actual head of Vlad Dracula III. Vlad the Impaler. I'm sure a folklorist with your love of the macabre knows the story."

Quinn nodded and looked back at the severed head, recalling the exhaustive research he'd done into the Dracula legend. Years of dealing with murders prompted by the most outrageous superstitions had conditioned him never to rush to judgment, but the notion that a five-hundred-year-old severed head could still exist, in this pristine condition, was preposterous. Nevertheless, he quelled that thought and recited what he knew of the legend with scholarly objectivity.

"Documentation confirms that Vlad Dracula was indeed beheaded after a battle against Ottoman Turks in 1476. Most likely near the monastery at Snagov. Some accounts say that monks found the body, but not the head. One legend has it that the sultan had ordered for the head to be brought to him in Constantinople. It was dipped in honey to preserve it, then put on display to prove that the Ottomans' evil archenemy had been vanquished. That may or may not be true, but the fact is that no one knows what happened to the head."

"Until I tracked it down in 1945."

"Markov. Come on."

"I completely understand your skepticism. I'm asking you to believe something—many things—that are far beyond the laws of nature. But there are two things you need to factor into your thinking: My obsession with the Dracula legend, and the fact that I had access to a trailblazer no one else had: Lugosi. He was born and raised in a land steeped in the Dracula legend, going back centuries, to Vlad's days as Prince of Wallachia—the region that included Transylvania.

"Lugosi was born in 1884, and Bram Stoker's book came out in 1897. Until then Vlad Dracula III was merely a ruler Lugosi had learned about in history class. To some, Dracula was seen as a hero for repelling the Turkish invasion. But then Stoker's novel came out, giving Vlad's name to the infamous vampire, and the legend began.

"Lugosi told me what a sensation it caused in Transylvania. He and his teen-aged friends devoured the book. It affected him deeply, to the point where he wondered if the original Dracula might have ever engaged in vampirism. Lugosi researched it off and on for years, even more intensely when he got cast in the part in the stage production that preceded the film. He was a serious actor who always did his homework, and he poured himself into that role, feeling it was the one he had been born to play. He combed the records, looking for descendants. He went to the town where Dracula had spent five years in prison and sought out the local historian. This historian had collected every shred of information he could find about their most infamous prisoner, which included the prison log with the names of Dracula's visitors.

"The name of one particular woman kept appearing that didn't appear in any of the other documents. The historian had traced her to a remote village some distance from the prison. Romanian oral tradition is very strong. Often it is all we have to go on in the centuries before records were well kept."

"Welcome to the world of a folklorist," Quinn said.

"Indeed. So we can imagine this historian talking to the villagers, armed with only the name of this woman and her apparent connection to Vlad Dracula. Eventually he found someone who recognized her name. The scandalous story had been passed down for generations. She'd had a son but never gotten married. The father was said to be Vlad Dracula. According to the villager, legend had it that, years later, the son was at the battle where his father was beheaded with his own sword. He had somehow retrieved the head and sword and escaped to England.

"Lugosi had to abandon his search at that point, because after *Dracula* came out, his career took off. And that could have been the end of it. But Lugosi's fateful path had brought him to someone far more obsessive about the Dracula legend—me. The chance, however remote, to actually possess the head of Vlad Dracula himself took my obsession to a whole new level."

At first Quinn had considered Markov's talk of Dracula and dark secrets to be simply manifestations of his movie-influenced tendency toward melodrama. But now Quinn was beginning to see the aptness of his references. Whether or not he was staring at the actual head of Vlad the Impaler, he felt himself being pulled into Markov's "infernal miasma."

"I told Bela I would follow the trail he had blazed. He let me copy the records he had kept, and gave me his blessing. His research had uncovered the illegitimate son's name: Viktor Flaviu."

In the quick glance Markov cast at the severed head before going on, Quinn thought he saw a trace of affection.

"And so began a quest that took nearly fifteen years. Since the villager had told the historian that the son had escaped to England, I went to London and scoured the records: births, deaths, marriages, passenger lists, military records, land records—everything. Viktor had gotten married in 1502 and had two sons. He died in 1521. I won't bore you with the countless dead ends, but this is where—some would say luck, I would say destiny—plays a part. Finally, after following a bloodline that had trickled down to a few drops, in 1945 I found a Romanian man who had the head. He was living in a rundown flat in Manhattan. Irony of ironies, only a few miles from where Lugosi had starred in the stage version of *Dracula*. I was awestruck at having succeeded on such a far-fetched quest, but the scene was not one for rejoicing.

"To see this eighty-nine-year-old shell of a man, sitting in his ratty armchair with the stuffing coming out … faithfully executing a duty he probably had never really wanted or understood, doing whatever needed doing to preserve the five-hundred-year-old remains of Vlad the Impaler. I pictured his whole world just sitting in that room, tending to what was left of Dracula: a severed head in a glass case, showing no sign of life, yet still powerful enough to command his one remaining loyal subject to do his bidding."

The same thing could be said about you, Quinn thought.

"Looking at the man's cadaverous frame," Markov continued, "I couldn't help but think that, if not literally, certainly figuratively, Dracula had sucked the life out of him."

As he has done to you.

"I asked for proof, and he gave me a letter establishing provenance and giving instructions to each custodian on what must be done to preserve Vlad's head. The letter had been written by the first caretaker. His son Viktor."

"You have the letter?"

"Yes. And one thing more had been passed down along with the head and the letter. The sword that had supposedly been used to behead Vlad Dracula. His prized sword that had belonged to his father. It had the Dracula crest on the hilt, but even so, I knew this could all be a hoax. The sword could be an imitation. The letter could be a forgery, the head a fake. But the scene of the withered custodian watching over these relics had me in no mood to argue, and on some visceral level I was convinced. Technically I owed this man nothing, but I already had more money than I could spend in several lifetimes, and wanted to do something to ease whatever days the poor wretch had left. He almost went into shock when I wrote him a check for fifty thousand dollars—a fortune in those days. I promised to follow the prescribed treatment and perpetuate the legacy." Markov nodded toward the head that, if genuine, had deteriorated very little since posing for that famous portrait five hundred years ago. "And here he is."

"An astounding tale, to say the least," Quinn said. "I see a bare spot on the lining at the bottom of the case in the shape of the sword. Did you remove it for some reason?"

"No. Max absconded with it." Markov's face sagged under a weary regret. "My son. He knew it was my most precious possession. It had traveled with the head all those centuries. An expert confirmed that it was a Toledo sword from the 1400s. It is a matter of record that after Vlad Dracul was slain, his sword was retrieved from the battlefield and given to his son. Dracula—which means 'son of Dracul'—treasured it and used it for the rest of his life. When DNA testing became reliable, I scraped a small sample of dried-up blood from the sword and collected a vial of blood from the head. I had them tested and they were identical. The blood on the sword was the blood of Vlad the Impaler."

Quinn remained skeptical, but let it pass.

Markov went on. "The final irony was that the sword Dracula used to behead so many was used to behead him in the end."

"Why would your son take the sword?"

"Because he despises me." He made an impatient wave. "Another twisted branch in my family tree. I'm not in the mood for that particular story right now. Perhaps later."

Quinn added it to the growing pile of questions pummeling to get out and gestured at the head. "How can tissue that's been dead for over five hundred years not have decomposed? The only deterioration I see is those bumps, or ridges, where the skin has apparently sagged or drooped."

"We cannot possibly know everything that has happened in the passing along of this head for five hundred years. We can only hypothesize."

"So what is your hypothesis?"

"When I first gained possession, I carefully removed one of those bumps and had it examined. It was not flesh. It was dried-up honey. With a trace of formaldehyde." Markov took a beat to let that sink in. "Honey was a common preservative in Dracula's time. Even today it is still used in some of the more primitive cultures. I believe the early custodians continually replenished the honey until formaldehyde became the scientifically accepted alternative.

"Whatever the case, to fully answer your question I must first show you the letter from Viktor. It is his eyewitness account of how this came to be, and his instructions on the proper care. Only after reading that can you fully understand the things I will tell you. Even then credibility will be stretched to the breaking point. I would not believe these things myself if I had not experienced them firsthand."

Quinn recalled something he'd said to a detective after assisting on the case involving satanic child porn and sacrifice: nothing shocked him anymore. But….

Vlad the Impaler's head preserved for five hundred years?

Markov went to a small safe in the corner and removed several sheets of paper. He carefully arranged them into two piles on the small table, then gestured for Quinn to sit in the armchair.

Leaning over him, Markov explained. "This is the original." He indicated the pile on the left, three pages handwritten on yellowing parchment paper sealed in plastic sleeves. "Written in Latin, which the Romanians inherited from their Roman conquerors." He gestured at the typewritten pages alongside the letter. "This is my translation. For the sake of readability, I took a few liberties in rendering his sometimes archaic language into a more modern form, but in no way has any of the meaning been altered."

"You know Latin?"

"And Romanian. And five other languages. Living like Morbius for fifty years has given me ample time to learn many things. Not as many as his Robby the Robot, who knew 'one hundred-eighty-seven languages, along with their various dialects and sub-tongues.' But then again, Morbius was a philologist. I am a filmmaker."

Quinn made a small appreciative nod at Markov's word-for-word delivery of Robby's line from *Forbidden Planet*, at the same time wondering how deep into madness a hundred years of obsessive filmmaking delusions—the last fifty on his own Forbidden Planet—had taken him.

"I have another matter to tend to," Markov continued, "so I shall leave you alone to read the letter. I will return in good time."

He stood and held Quinn's gaze for a long beat—a stock actor's trick for punching up an exit line. "Viktor describes the origin of a species. One that Darwin never dreamed of."

CHAPTER 29

January 12, 1477

Vlad Dracula is dead but not dead.

I am his illegitimate son, Viktor Flaviu, born in 1456. Those who search for a record of my existence search in vain. Our relationship has been hidden from the world. In the remote village of my mother he arranged an upbringing equal to one of his rightful heirs. In the privacy of his secret home I received the finest education, and in the hidden forests I was trained in the skills of the warrior.

This document is the sole testament and decree regarding the fate of my father and myself. It shall be passed on to future custodians of Vlad Dracula's ~~mortal~~ immortal remains, to instruct them in the proper procedure for preserving them. These instructions must be followed in the strictest manner to keep what is left alive until science can find a way to make him whole again.

First there must be an explanation of what God and science tell us cannot be.

Vlad Dracula had long understood that the blood is the life. He had watched it flow out of the many he had impaled, and knew well the tales the villagers told, of vampires who

166

had roamed the wilds of Transylvania for centuries. Creatures of the night, in whose veins the blood of the living intermingled with the blood of the undead to become the source of eternal life.

During his reign as Prince of Wallachia, Vlad Dracula knew his enemies would attempt to assassinate him as they had his father, Vlad Dracul. And so he made Transylvanian alchemist Baron Dimitru a part of his court, commissioning him to unlock the secret that gave unhallowed immortality to the undead.

The Baron gained the trust of the vampires and was allowed to live among them, they as eager as he to understand how they were able to cheat death by sucking the life from the living, to understand this evil practice that gave them life but cost them their souls.

Through bloodletting the Baron began to combine the blood of the vampires with the blood of aged villagers, willing participants in an experiment that might make them young again. After years of adjusting the admixture, adding elements whose properties are known only to the practitioners of this Hermetic science, he observed their revitalization. Long after the barrenness of old age, they began to have children. Samples of their altered blood proved that the alchemical processes of the human body had fully transmuted the admixture into the blood of immortality.

The Baron had created a new bloodline. A race of half-human, half-vampire, in whose veins flowed the elixir of life.

One fatal flaw remained.

The vampire blood was becoming dominant. For this new race to overcome death without having to prey upon the living, more human blood was needed to purify the strain.

In 1462, Vlad Dracula was captured and imprisoned. The Baron visited him often, each time smuggling in some of the new blood to drink, and drawing a sample of Dracula's blood to test at his laboratory. The tests confirmed that his blood was becoming the elixir.

Upon his release from prison he resumed his reign. Only the Baron and myself knew that my father was no longer simply Vlad Dracula, Prince of Wallachia.

He was Dracula, patriarch and perpetual ruler of a new race that could cheat death.

Immediately upon his accession to the throne he summoned me to the castle. He confided that I was his favorite son and the only one he could trust. As his most highly skilled warrior, he wanted me by his side in the upcoming campaign to repel the invading Turks. I was introduced as one of his Moldavian bodyguards and known only by my *nom de guerre* as Andrei. He charged me to preserve his immortality in the event of his earthly demise. We drank a small amount of each other's blood each day to keep our bloodline strong. The Baron instructed us that human blood must also be ingested once a month to maintain the proper balance of the elixir flowing in our veins. This could be done through simple bloodletting rather than the gruesome violation of the vampire. It became my duty to collect this blood—either from a peasant for a token payment, or from the impaled.

A month ago bitter enemy Mehmed II, Sultan of Constantinople, sent his army to usurp the Wallachian throne. As always, I was by my father's side during the battle. To my eternal shame, an assassin, disguised as one of us, bulled his horse through our phalanx and beheaded my father with his most prized possession: his own sword, which had belonged to his father, Vlad Dracul.

In one fell swoop the villain escaped with head and sword, shouting, "Trophies for my Sultan!"

I collected as much of my father's blood as I could and rode like the wind for Constantinople. When I reached Mehmed's palace, my father's head was staked upon his sword for display. Under cover of darkness, I hid my horse and slit the throats of the two guards.

The elixir had kept the head alive, and it had been dipped in honey so that it would keep. I secured head and sword and fled for home, stopping often to let my father drink the life-giving elixir.

And so began the eternal vigil to keep Dracula alive. No longer Prince, he is now something much greater: Patriarch of the new race of immortals.

I shall seek out the Baron to see if his magic can find a way to attach the head to some other body. Whether yes or no, I must take whatever remains and disappear. If that is with only the head, I will do all I can to keep it alive.

I will have children, and they will have children, and though they will not bear the name of Dracula, they will be of his blood, and they will be charged with the sacred duty of maintaining his bloodline. The head shall be passed on to these descendants in a chain that must not be broken, along with the sword and the log containing the Baron's formula and record of his experiments.

These are the instructions for keeping Dracula alive until one day science can find a way to make him whole again:

Preserve the head in honey, which must be replenished when it begins to lose its strength. Each day let him drink of the elixir. Test the elixir once a month to ensure that the elements are properly balanced according to the Baron's formula. Should the vampire blood again begin to dominate, human blood must be added.

This blood must be gotten from willing subjects, never through the foul bloodsucking of the vampire. If the quest for immortality is to be worth pursuing, the inhuman practice of stealing the life of an innocent to perpetuate the life of a fiend must be expunged from this new race. The evil ways of the vampire cannot be ours.

I close this decree with a forlorn hope.

I have succeeded, but is it too late? Have I condemned my beloved father to an eternity of torment? Is this life? To keep the brain alive but not the body? Not the soul?

May my watch not become a wake.

CHAPTER 30

Sitting at the control panel in her apartment, Johnny had been watching and listening on the monitor that continually recorded the area around Vlad the Impaler's showcase. When Markov had left Quinn alone with the letter, she'd seen her chance to talk to him privately.

She'd barely gotten out her door before Markov intercepted her.

"Come with me," he said.

When they passed the entrance to the Chamber of Horrors, her heart fluttered in despair at the thought that Quinn was in there but she couldn't get to him.

Now father and daughter sat facing one another in the seating area of his quarters. Markov dispensed with his customary formalities and abruptly began.

"The moment of truth is upon us, Johnny. The arrival of this particular person, at this exact moment, is the hand of fate sending us the lead for the climax of our film. I have given him the option to leave, but I know his curiosity will not let him. He is a seeker of monsters, and he knows that what he might find here will exceed anything he can find in the real world. He is in our movie now. The sun is coming up, and I need some time to write him into the ending. I want a climax that will make *Frankenstein Meets the Wolf Man* look like child's play."

He leaned forward and gave her his most intimidating stare. "I need you now more than ever to make sure all is in readiness. Minutes are going to count. Everything must be gotten on the first take. Nothing must be left to chance. If the ending of our movie goes as planned, we will both be free."

Our movie. It was never their movie.

"Free," Johnny said, a hint of mockery in the word. "To sleep? Perchance to dream?"

She saw him wince and knew that the words from Hamlet's famous soliloquy had pierced the armor around his heart. All the nights they'd read Shakespeare or Poe together, all the movies they'd watched, laughing as they'd acted out the parts…. It had not all been horror. There had been some happiness, even moments of hope….

Ancient history. The only thing left was to prepare for the end.

"We'll get plenty of sleep when we're dead," Markov said.

"'Tis a consummation devoutly to be wished," Johnny said.

Markov impatiently waved the repartee aside. "We have both learned our lines well. But rehearsals are over. It is time to shoot the ending."

"How can I play my part when I haven't even seen the script?"

"I haven't finished it. I'm trying to concoct a scenario that will put our guest in grave peril without harming him, but when one creates monsters, there are risks. The Blood

Moon is fast upon us, and the creatures are beginning to stir. I cannot be certain that whatever comes after him will be under my control."

"What exactly are you asking me to do?"

"Your role may be more as my head of security. No matter how carefully I plan, other forces are at work. Have your complete arsenal at the ready for whatever mayhem might develop: magnetic wristbands, bear spray, wolfbane, garlic, stakes, silver bullets, even the spear gun."

Whatever mayhem might develop. For him to describe his monster rally that way—and to specifically mention those weapons—powerfully reinforced what Johnny already knew: there was no way she could stop him and his monsters alone. Her only hope was to find Quinn as soon as possible and see if he would help. "I'll take care of it," she said.

"I assume you've been keeping a close watch on the Garden."

"Since our guest's arrival, the … *flowers* … have been more lively." She made no effort to remove the contempt from her voice.

"Check on them every few hours from here on out. This man's energy waves have upset the delicate electromagnetic balance. I have not come this far not to have the ending that will give me true immortality. It is the culmination of my life's work, and nothing or no one shall keep me from it. Is that clear?"

He waited, unblinking, for a response.

A small reluctant nod.

"Are all the doors locked?"

She nodded again while staring at the floor.

"You must check all the props, the robotics, the special effects to make sure everything is working properly."

"I understand."

He leaned closer, their faces barely a foot apart. "Do you? Since our guest arrived you have seemed distracted."

Johnny's gaze shot up to meet his. "Perhaps if I say it as Renfield it will reassure you: I am loyal to you, Master!"

Markov recoiled from the defiant response but recovered quickly. "Very amusing. But of course Renfield was lying. He had already betrayed his Master."

"He was a fictional character. This is real life. Events will unfold as *destiny* has decided they must."

"Indeed," Markov said. "And I am the master of my destiny." He stood. "I shall leave you to tend to your duties, while I tend to mine."

CHAPTER 31

Quinn re-read the five-hundred-year-old letter and considered the bizarre light it cast on one of the many missing links in the elusive history of Vlad Dracula III—*if* the letter was genuine.

Markov conducted himself with such authority that everything he said had the ring of truth. But there was also madness in the air, and its dark clouds were thickening. His Dracula-obsessed mind could easily have driven him to create that bust—worship it—and to have written this letter, all as backstory for his movie. Concocting such a scenario might also have been a salve for his conscience, allowing him to claim that his "bad deeds" were done at the behest of Vlad the Impaler.

Or ... the unthinkable—Markov's entire story, including this—could somehow be true.

Quinn was mildly startled when Markov eased into the seat at the opposite end of the table.

"So?" Markov said.

"Now I understand your comment about the origin of a species Darwin never dreamed of. Not the *dhampyre* of folklore, which result from the union between a vampire and a human. Viktor claims Dracula's race of semi-vampires, if they even existed, achieved their immortality asexually—by ingesting a blood mixture created by the one alchemist who had succeeded, where countless practitioners of that pseudoscience had failed for centuries. The one alchemist who had achieved the goal that humans had been seeking before alchemy even existed. He had created a magic potion that would keep us from getting old and dying. The elixir of life, no less. When you sum it all up, it sounds rather far-fetched, don't you think?"

"I fully understand your skepticism," Markov said. "I can only tell you the path I have taken since becoming custodian. As we venture ever deeper into the nethermost regions, we get further from things the world would consider possible. All horror stories require a willing suspension of disbelief. Mine will put yours to the supreme test."

"As one who spends his life investigating and debunking the most bizarre legends and superstitions," Quinn said evenly, "I always require undeniable proof before I can declare them to be fact. Which is almost never. But be assured I am willing to suspend my disbelief if you can furnish that proof."

"Fair enough. I shall present the evidence that made a believer out of me. And that I am confident will make a believer out of you.

"The first thing I did when I got the head home was to remove a tissue sample from the ragged flesh along the neck and examine it under a microscope. I'm no biologist, but I know enough to recognize live cells from dead ones. Not only were the cells continuing to reproduce, but when I removed the sample, there was bleeding.

"This went a long way in convincing me that the story in

Viktor's letter was true. That the alchemist's elixir had kept Dracula alive, at least on a cellular level. Since blood is the key ingredient, I quickly made myself an expert in the handling of blood. I purchased equipment for drawing it, testing it, preserving it, and so on. I then began mixing my blood with Dracula's, according to the instructions in the letter."

He stifled a sigh. "I could not resist the lure of immortality and began to increase the percentage of vampire blood in the elixir. I can offer no greater proof that it works than what you can see with your own eyes." Markov leaned so the light fell more fully on his face. "I am over a hundred years old, yet I have scarcely aged for the last fifty years."

"I *can* see that. If everything you are telling me is true— that you've been ingesting Vlad Dracula's blood—then, in a sense, that would make you his descendant."

"Yes. Almost like a son, since some of his genetic material now flows through me. And while I take full responsibility for my actions, I have always felt that— despite Viktor's noble instruction against the 'foul bloodsucking' of the vampire—it was the Dracula blood in the elixir that drove me to the same wanton disregard for life he proudly displayed against his enemies. I have always been enthralled by the Dracula mystique, yes, but I was never overcome by my 'mindless primitive' until …" he nodded toward the head "… that came into my life."

He made a dismissive wave. "And yet … some other force compels me to do the things I do. Something that comes from *me*. As the elixir in my veins has gotten stronger, I have come to believe that some of Vlad the Impaler's bloodthirsty soul has mingled with the digital bits of Lugosi's Dracula inside me, to create the vampiric monster *I* have become. A digitally remastered and enhanced Dracula."

"You seem to be avoiding the word vampire, choosing to call yourself vampiric instead."

"I am *not* a vampire, but the vampire's craving for blood sometimes overtakes me. When I can no longer resist, I roam the woods at night. Sometimes as Dracula, sometimes as the Wolf Man, and …" shame flickered across his face "… I *feed*. On sleeping campers, hunters. Never with the intention of killing them or turning them into vampire slaves. Whatever spark of human decency still burns within me prevents that. When I finish, I simply leave them there and hope my violation will not have dire consequences."

Quinn pictured drained souls staggering out of those deep woods after having their blood sucked—if they made it that far. For all he or anybody could know, Markov's vast private forest could be littered with bodies. As that grim thought coiled itself around Quinn's brain, he felt himself being drawn into exactly the type of atrocity he had come here to escape.

What other atrocities might Markov have committed? His talk of feeding on campers as the Wolf Man or Dracula had taken his story far beyond the eccentricities of a strange recluse and his enslaved daughter. Quinn had worked on cases where murderers, claiming someone else inside them did the killing, were later diagnosed with multiple personality disorder. That had to be what was afflicting Markov. Despite his very well-reasoned and persuasive explanations of what he believed were monsters inside him, he couldn't possibly be the actual Wolf Man or Dracula.

Another thought occurred to Quinn. Perhaps Markov's explanation of his vampiric tendencies was merely dialogue for a scene. The things he was saying might be true, or he might just be taking dramatic license to get a reaction from Quinn for the hidden cameras. Quinn decided to play along and see where this went.

With a disturbingly clinical detachment, Markov continued.

"You said that the head has been kept alive. Yes and no. The fact that blood still flowed meant there was some semblance of life. But the eyes remained closed; there was never any movement, no indication of any brain or muscle activity. So I tried an experiment.

"For the last several years, I have been using the latest technology in an effort to fully re-animate the head. Much in the manner of Mesmer and Galvani."

"Have you gotten any results?"

"With electric current I achieved what Galvani did, to make the dead twitch. Two hundred years ago that was thought to be life, but we now know that it is merely the danse macabre of dead nerve tissue simulating life. But more recently I have introduced another element that has given me pause."

Quinn waited.

"Magnetism," Markov said. "I have added magnetic flux to the current and gotten dramatic results. The eyelids flutter. The lips move, as if trying to speak. At first this could all be considered the same simple reflexive movement we might get from a frog in biology class, but lately…. I could swear I have heard sound issuing from the mouth. Nothing intelligible, perhaps it is only air being released, but…."

Quinn followed his gaze until they were both staring at the head. It remained utterly still. Markov seemed disappointed.

"It would take some time to set up the apparatus," he

said, "but I can show you my experiment. An opinion from a neutral party could be valuable."

Quinn felt any sympathy he had for Markov—George Tilton—melting away at the thought that he might be feeding on hapless souls who happened to wander onto his property. Whether Markov was delusional or not, he believed he was drinking the blood of Vlad the Impaler and that it was keeping him young. There was no denying the fact that he and his daughter looked decades younger than their ages.

"Does Johnny also drink the elixir?"

"She and Max both did when they were younger, but at my behest more than by choice. Max refused to drink it long ago, and Johnny did too, some years later—when what was left of her will asserted itself."

A hot burst of anger burned away Quinn's last shred of sympathy. "You forced your madness on your kids?"

In an instant Markov's benign expression changed to one bordering on ferocity.

"I *loved* my family, sir. I wanted to bring them with me on my journey to immortality, but first I had to see if the elixir worked. I had to make sure there were no harmful effects and that I had gotten the balance of human and vampire blood right. So for years I kept them completely in the dark about my experiment, administering the elixir only to myself."

"How could you keep the head a secret?"

"I know this is the hoariest of movie clichés, but movie clichés are the story of my life. Wherever we lived, I always had a laboratory that was never to be entered by anyone but me."

His gaze softened. "The experiment began in 1945 when

I procured the head. It had to be long-term, to measure aging and to be sure there were no negative side effects. In ten years the calendar said I had gone from forty-four to fifty-four, but my body had not aged a day."

"How could you know that?"

"It was clear in every way such a thing could be measured. If anything I was younger, stronger. My skin became less wrinkled. It had the glow of youth. I needed far less sleep—a side benefit I loved, because it gave me much more time to study and pursue my work. My teeth began to regenerate themselves. New ones came in and pushed out the old ones. Broken veins in my legs disappeared. I had a sexual prowess far beyond anything I had ever had, even at the peak of my virility."

"Ten years is a long time to keep a secret like that," Quinn said. "I did a lot of homework to prepare for our meeting. There's a record of your son, Max, being charged with attempted murder in 1954. Does that have something to do with why he despises you?"

Markov's sudden flare of anger at the mention of Max's name quickly melted under a flush of remorse—remorse that struck Quinn as the inevitable result of a family neglected to pursue an unwholesome, unfulfilled dream. George Tilton, the father, overtook Markov long enough to say, "In a sense, yes." His gaze drifted toward the floor. "Not entirely without cause."

"What happened?"

His normally resonant voice took on a hollow quality, as if coming from a crypt somewhere deep in his soul. "The continuation of my dark destiny. A path that had led me to become inextricably linked to Tod Browning and *Dracula*, and to become an eager participant in the power you spoke of: the power of movies to affect real life."

CHAPTER 32

Sitting in his inner sanctum, overseen from above by the closed but undead eyes of Dracula, Markov turned over the next card from the Tarot deck of his life.

"1954," he began. "Unlike Poe's narrator in *Ulalume*, it was not my most immemorial year. I remember it vividly. We were living in Boston, and a local movie theater found out that I had worked on *Dracula* and *Freaks* with Tod. They wanted to show them as a double feature on Halloween, make it a gala event with me as their guest of honor. Dolores—my first wife—Johnny and Max were with me, reveling in all the attention.

"Until a man who had been in the audience came up to me at the reception, raving about the way the so-called pinheads had been presented in *Freaks*. You remember them?"

"Yes. They had misshapen heads that almost came to a point."

"A condition known as microcephaly. This man's young daughter had just died from it. He grabbed a knife from a food table and tried to stab me, but I moved out of the way and the blade went into my wife instead. Max yanked the knife out and stabbed the man. He lived but my wife died. Since Max had acted out of self-defense, the charges were later dropped."

The Markov persona continued to crumble as the fatherly part of George Tilton broke through. "I was left to live with my children alone. Without my wife's sensible feminine influence, I could see that imposing my twisted worldview was damaging them. Again, the intertwining of my life with Tod Browning's had played a hand. His films had brought me to the screening on what turned out to be a very fateful night in my life. It resulted in the death of my wife, but it also introduced me to the woman who would become the helpmate I desperately needed, lest I slip irredeemably into madness and take my children with me.

"Elinore was her name. She was the organizer of the gala, a lover of film whose background meshed perfectly with mine. She had fallen in love with horror movies as a child, as I had. *Dracula* was one of her favorites, so she was thrilled to meet someone who had worked on it. We started dating. She loved my idea of building a castle and studio for making horror films. We married and I moved my new family here, rationalizing that seclusion and fresh air would help cleanse our souls—all the while building a home where no soul could ever be clean.

"In this movie world I had created, my fetters of reason were cast off, Mr. Quinn. My obsession with immortality and Dracula was given full rein. At first it was just cinematic immortality. But as the Dracula blood got stronger, and I saw myself not aging, I convinced Elinore to begin drinking the elixir with me. I had hoped that we might live together forever."

He hesitated, and Quinn watched his authoritative air

melt away. When he spoke again, his tone was that of someone resigned to an ill-chosen fate.

"And so began the inevitable fall of the House of Markov. We were never a normal family, but our first years here were the closest we ever came. We had moved here in 1960. Johnny and Max were both in their twenties then, and could have gone out on their own, but they seemed content to learn everything there was to know about filmmaking. We stayed busy setting this place up as a studio and movie set, shooting some of the establishing scenes for our movie. But, eventually, the piper had to be paid."

"As he always must," Quinn said.

"Indeed. The vampire blood in the elixir constantly absorbed the human blood, making it virtually impossible to maintain the proper balance. There would be brief periods when my wife and I would succumb to the vampiric urges coursing through our veins. We would prowl the woods at night to feed…. Small animals at first, then the occasional camper or hunter. We would satisfy our cravings, then leave them to fend for themselves. We should have stopped drinking the elixir, but the lure of immortality had become too strong.

"As I got deeper into my Markov persona, my twisted psyche began envisioning myself as the patriarch of a race of immortals, directly descended from Dracula himself. I had used the basic idea in *Blood of Dracula*, but now—*now*— I had everything I needed to make the plot of my movie a reality. To create an *actual* race of immortals, as Viktor had described in his letter."

Markov's eyes narrowed as they stared inward, apparently at a memory he was hesitant to reveal. After a long pause he said, "I decided it was time to begin giving the elixir to Johnny and Max. Ours would be the family that blazed the trail into that brave new world."

Quinn took a measured breath to quell his rising anger. "A world where—despite Viktor's decree never to engage in the foul bloodsucking of a vampire—that's exactly what you were doing. Surely you could see that."

"I turned a blind eye."

"Ah," Quinn said, his patience all but gone for Markov's lame rationalizations of his soul-stealing behavior. "So you brought Johnny and Max into your *vampiric* fold."

"Yes. But as I said, not by their choice. They submitted to my domineering will—with the full support of Elinore, who found it exciting to be pursuing immortality by perpetuating the bloodline of the actual Dracula.

"Johnny was more malleable. I took advantage of her gentle nature and the pact I had forced upon her—that we would be together forever. She drank the elixir for years. Enough to greatly retard the aging process. But she could not turn a blind eye to the inevitable urges. Whenever they became too strong, Johnny would stop taking it. She never engaged in bloodsucking. Even so, I still managed to turn a lovely young lady into a cringing servant. My Renfield."

"You were assuaging your guilt over having ended the life your daughter might have had—with another Faustian bargain. The promise of immortality in exchange for her soul."

Markov used his perfect Lugosi voice to paraphrase Dracula's line when Van Helsing exposes him with the mirror: "For one who has not lived even a single lifetime, you are a wise man, Mr. Quinn."

Quinn was not in the mood for snappy repartee. "What about Max? What was his reaction to the elixir?"

"Max fought me on it every inch of the way and finally flatly refused to drink it. From the very beginning he abhorred my cheating death by sucking the life out of the living. He became my nemesis. My Van Helsing. To the point where he could no longer ignore the late-night wanderings of Elinore and myself.

"Eventually he confronted us after one of our rambles. We told him we simply enjoyed walks in the moonlight, but he knew we were lying. He had followed us and saw what we did. His hatred for me had been growing ever since the night his mother was killed. And he never forgave me for getting remarried. Unlike Johnny, who eventually accepted Elinore as her new mother, Max hated her.

"After that confrontation, I found a mallet and stake under his bed. I left them there, wanting to see how far his hatred might take him."

"I suppose that makes a kind of twisted sense," Quinn said. "But why would he take the sword?"

"He had loved his mother dearly and made it clear that he held me responsible for her death. One night he came into my room, sword in hand. Max's attempt at poetic justice. To use the same sword to behead Vlad Dracula's spiritual descendant—me—and bring the 'accursed bloodline'—his pet phrase—to an end." His lips compressed into a small sardonic smile. "But we Draculas know there are many who wish to destroy us, so we are light sleepers. I sprang up before he reached my bed. He held me at bay, calling me a 'psychic vampire', raving about how being constantly immersed in the world of horror had sucked everything good out of him. He vowed to make me pay for what I did to him. And to his mother."

Markov's soul-weary sigh spoke of a battle he no longer

wanted to fight, no longer believed in. "His 'psychic vampire' comment hit home. I hadn't sucked my family's blood, but ... some of their souls? I had built an impenetrable wall around that part of my psyche. In the carefully edited movie of my life, I would only allow myself to see the things that made me the hero. I was the devoted father, and Max the ungrateful son. I was teaching him everything there was to know about movies, grooming him to take over my work and my collection when I was gone. If nothing else, he could have been a director.

"But the damage had been done." Markov's eyes narrowed as the anger returned. "My son left home and I haven't seen him since."

Quinn waited while Markov gathered himself, wondering uneasily where his unburdening of his soul would take them.

"I have received two letters from him in the last forty years. The first came in 1973, updating me on his situation. He had gone to Boston and gotten into acting. He railed against directors who couldn't spot the obvious talent he deluded himself into believing he showed in auditions. He called them psychic vampires as well. The notion of psychic vampires had become his way of scapegoating others for his shortcomings. He could never accept that, in the world of acting, there are king actors and there are butlers. Alas, Max was doomed to be a butler."

Markov's expression took on a gloating air. "He closed his portentous epistle by saying that only a final reckoning between he and I could fully exorcise the demons I had bred into his soul. His flair for melodrama."

A chip off the old block, Quinn thought. "Maybe after all these years he's forgiven you."

"Hardly. The second letter came a few weeks ago.

Ravings about my days being numbered. He said my head would soon be resting on a stake beside Vlad the Impaler's. I doubt that he has the backbone to follow through."

Until now Quinn had considered Markov's description of his castle as a shrine to madness part of *his* flair for melodrama, but now he realized it was true. Dysfunctional didn't begin to describe this bizarre family. They had created an alternate reality that existed in a land that time forgot.

"What about your second wife. Is she … did she…?"

"Sadly, the vampiric urges kept getting stronger in my beloved Lady Elinore, and … I had to put her away." In the slight movement of his head, little more than a twitch, Quinn saw George Tilton trying to shake off what had to be one of the most painful memories in a life filled with pain. The moment lasted only a few seconds before Markov was back.

"This concludes the tour, Mr. Quinn. Now we come to the moment of truth: stay and live forever in the movies, or leave and rejoin the parade of mortals shuffling to an earthly and unremembered demise."

Quinn thought of Markov's description of his life as a descent into the maelstrom, a whirlpool of madness and death. He pictured Johnny being pulled into the vortex, hands reaching up in desperation, looking for someone to save her from being sucked down into her father's personal Hell. With that image swirling in his brain, he only half-listened to Markov's patently absurd plan: that he was ready to write, storyboard, direct, and shoot the ultimate monster rally sequence—in one day.

"I have written a draft of the ending with you as the lead," Markov said. "Should you decide to stay, I need to work out the shooting script. If you decide to leave, it will have to be on foot. To borrow once again from Morbius, I must ask you to forgive the ill manners of an old recluse, but I cannot spare Johnny just now. The Blood Moon is upon us and there is still much to do. I can give you a little time to make your decision, but not much."

Quinn didn't need any more time. He'd seen enough to suspect that this *was* a house where evil dwelled.

"I'm staying."

"Excellent," Markov said. "I will need a couple hours, more or less. You should use that time to explore the castle and grounds—within the limitations we have discussed. Greater familiarity with the set could save us time when we shoot the final sequence."

Quinn had been thinking the same thing—but for a different reason. He wouldn't be scouting out a location. He'd be looking for an escape route.

"I'll do that," he said.

"I will contact Johnny when I am ready to begin the final shoot. From that point on we will be on a very tight schedule to wrap before midnight. She will let you know when and where to report."

"Fine," Quinn said. "I'll start with a walk around the grounds."

"Think of it as my back lot. Go freely, but do not venture too far into the woods. I have seen many of its four-legged denizens on the prowl during my midnight rambles. Even though it is daylight, we cannot be certain that they are entirely nocturnal."

Just the natural predators on a heavily wooded property this large would be dangerous enough, Quinn thought. Coyotes, bobcats, bears…. If Markov was also one of those four-legged denizens….

CHAPTER 33

Standing in the porte-cochère at the entrance to the castle, Quinn zipped his fleece jacket against the morning chill and took a moment to decide which way to go. The unpaved access road the carriage had used to bring him here continued past the porte-cochère to the left, toward the back of the estate. Running parallel to the side wall of the castle, at barely ten yards wide, it was more of a lane than a road.

He headed down it, counting his paces as he went. Every bit of information he could gather about the layout of this massive estate, and the distances between its various parts, could turn out to be vital if … he resisted the phrase *if he needed to escape* … if Markov's game became truly dangerous.

He reached the rear corner of the hulking pile and stopped to get his bearings. He pulled a notepad and pen from his pocket and jotted *49 from entrance to rear corner.*

A large clearing had been established around the castle, but no landscaping had been done. The weedy growth had simply been mowed. Clumps of wild brush too hardy to mow were scattered here and there. With such a vast estate, Johnny undoubtedly had far too many things to do to be overly fussy about lawn maintenance.

The lane continued straight ahead through a stand of trees about thirty yards away. To the right, a footpath perpendicular to the lane ran through the woods in the direction of the lagoon.

The humanoid shape Quinn thought he'd seen rising up from the lagoon still nagged. Even allowing for an imagination conditioned by a lifetime of watching horror movies, this was a world where the laws of nature didn't apply.

The body of water warranted a closer look.

He decided to stay on the lane to see what was beyond the stand of trees ahead, then explore the lagoon on his way back.

Twenty-seven paces later, the lane continued through an opening in the trees. Quinn made a quick note and continued into the opening. He was struck by how well it had been cut to form a precisely defined walkway. Overhead, branches extending from the trees lining each side of the path met to form a natural roof. Quinn imagined that in the summer, when the growth was full, the branches would convey a soothing feeling of walking through a leafy tunnel. Now, however, the bare, gnarled branches appeared more like long bony fingers poised to clamp down on unwary trespassers.

He emerged from the trees into another clearing. In the middle stood a large, weather-beaten barn. He went to take a closer look.

Although the sliding door was pulled shut, the padlock hanging on the hasp was unlocked. Had Johnny purposely left this open for him? Simple forgetfulness was possible, but when Quinn remembered her stopping him with a gun in the forbidden chamber, and later urging him to explore any unlocked doors, that seemed highly unlikely.

Quinn removed the padlock and slid the door open. Late morning sunlight coming through windows on all sides brightened the gloomy interior enough to see. He entered and went to the left to begin his inspection. As he approached the rear wall, he smelled the horses before he saw them. One whinnied as he rounded the corner. The horses in each stall watched him intently. The carriage was parked beside the stalls. Bridles, harnesses, and other tack items were neatly hung and arranged beside the carriage. In the corner were two ATVs, two snowmobiles, and a sidecar, all spotlessly clean and precisely lined up side by side.

Quinn began walking along the other side wall to complete the circuit that would take him back to the front door. Partitions had been attached to the wall to create several large bays.

In the first was a black Hummer H1. Quinn had researched GM's civilian version of the military's Humvee when they first came out, thinking the rugged vehicle might be just what he needed to handle the primitive terrain he often encountered in tracking down legends. But with a price tag of over a hundred thousand dollars, and fuel economy around ten miles a gallon, he had quickly dismissed the idea. This one was several years old and still looked in excellent condition.

The final bay held tools and an odd assortment of items. The diving equipment got his attention first. Air tanks, flippers, facemasks, a wet suit, dry suit, and other miscellaneous diving supplies were neatly laid out. Given their reclusive lifestyle, it seemed unlikely Johnny would be a recreational diver. This had to be for the lagoon. The item propped in the corner brought a frown.

A spear gun. What possible use could they have for a spear gun? Despite Markov's ominous talk of monsters, it was impossible to think there was a creature in his black lagoon.

No. Maybe Johnny went spear fishing somewhere. Or maybe they used it to hunt game instead of a bow and arrow.

Next to the spear gun was a scythe. A scythe made sense, but considering how carefully everything else had been grouped together, why wasn't it with the lawn implements? A few rust-colored patches marred the otherwise immaculate razor-sharp cutting edge. Wondering if they were rust or blood, Quinn rubbed his fingers across one of the spots, looked at the tiny bits that had flaked off, then sniffed.

It proved nothing. Bits of rust and dried-up blood could look and smell the same. "What am I? CSI all of a sudden?" he muttered. Nevertheless, he made a mental note to see if the Grim Reaper was still holding his scythe.

Several paces farther along, he came to a shelf that held life-sized replicas of instantly recognizable heads.

Lon Chaney's Hunchback and Phantom, Max Schreck's hideous Nosferatu, Lugosi's Dracula, Karloff's Frankenstein Monster, Lon Chaney Jr.'s Wolf Man, the Creature from the Black Lagoon, Robby the Robot, King Kong. Beside the head of the Creature was one of its clawed hands that had reached up from the lagoon to strike fear into Julie Adams and generations of movie fans.

Quinn walked back and forth, admiring how perfectly the replicas resembled the originals while wondering where Markov could have gotten them.

He picked up the head of Kong and looked inside, imagining that someone might have worn it during the actual filming. But instead of the hollow interior of a mask, he saw a network of wires running from the various facial features into a hub that must somehow have been the source of power. He checked the others and found the same apparatus in each. These masks had not been meant to be worn. They had been meant to be animated.

Markov had boasted of his advanced special effects and how he had incorporated them into his filmmaking. These might have been some of his early attempts. More questions to add to the rapidly growing pile he had for his mysterious host.

There were wristbands in the spaces between each of the heads. Quinn picked up the one between Dracula and the Frankenstein Monster. Both heads moved slightly toward him as he pulled the wristband away. He moved it slowly back toward them, and they slid closer. When he got to within a few inches, the heads shot forward and stuck to the wristband.

Magnetic. He'd heard of golfers using them to combat arthritis. Maybe Markov had experimented with using them as a better way to move the heads around than stop-motion animation.

On another shelf were several open cardboard boxes. He went to the first and looked inside. It was filled with more magnetic bracelets. At least two dozen. The next three boxes held several dozen more. The final two boxes were filled with large canisters of bear spray. Their purpose was easier to guess. Johnny's security duties included nightly patrols of the woods, and this was bear country. Next to the boxes was an unusual-looking gun and several darts whose shafts were clear glass cylinders for holding medication.

A tranquilizer gun. Quinn wondered what Johnny might use it on. The horses?

He continued past the shelf to the front door. Stepping from the gloomy barn into bright morning sunshine and a clear blue sky, he slid the door closed as though sealing off troubling thoughts and looked at his watch.

He probably had an hour left before Markov would need him. Spending it looking for signs of a shape emerging from the lagoon—a shape that almost certainly had a simple explanation—would be a waste of time. He needed to use that time to explore inside the castle. Markov would undoubtedly be staging his climactic sequence there. And having seen how Markov's mind worked, Quinn felt sure the sequence would include a shocking reveal. Whatever unfolded between now and midnight, Quinn couldn't let himself get cornered in the place that must hold Markov's darkest secret.

It was time to find out what was hidden away in the forbidden chamber.

CHAPTER 34

Quinn headed for the staircase by the Chamber of Horrors that led to the forbidden chamber below. As he rounded the corner guarded by the Grim Reaper, he pulled up suddenly.

It was still holding the scythe, but—was its head facing in a different direction? He thought it had been looking in the direction of his door. Now it was looking the other way, down the long corridor that ended at the Chamber of Horrors. Growing frustration at his inability to know what was real and what was a special effect propelled him around the corner. A short distance down the next corridor, he came to a door he wanted to check. Johnny's quarters.

Quinn tried the handle. The door opened. Had Johnny intentionally left it unlocked? When he'd summoned her this morning after the pterodactyl incident, she'd said, "I wish I could help you more," and made a point of encouraging him to take full advantage of his chance to enter any unlocked doors. As eager as he was to know what was hidden away in the secret chamber, he also needed to learn as much as he could about the human being behind the crumbling mask of Markov's oddly-named *daughter*.

Quinn went in and clicked on the lights.

He stood for a moment, scanning the overall layout. Johnny's quarters were, in effect, a huge apartment. Unlike the square layout of Markov's laboratory, this was a long rectangular space, about twenty-five yards wide and twice that in length. The high ceiling and open floor plan added to the feeling of vastness. After taking it all in, Quinn was drawn to the array of equipment and readouts running along the left wall, eager to see Johnny's level of control over the workings of the castle and the digital creatures that haunted it.

It quickly became apparent that her workstation was a virtual duplicate of Markov's. Aside from providing Johnny the ability to remotely operate and monitor all of the castle's systems 24/7, the duplication of Markov's editing/special effects studio made perfect sense. There was no way he could do everything himself; in their many years together, he must have taught his daughter everything he knew. Aside from her countless duties as steward of such a large estate, just the ways in which she could assist him in his filmmaking were endless. Clear evidence of her involvement in that aspect of their lives sat near the large monitor of the editing console: exact copies of the gloves, goggles, and mouse Markov used to manipulate his digital creations.

Whatever he could do, she could do.

Just beyond the left end of the workstation was a door. Quinn had noticed a door in about that location in Markov's laboratory/studio, which was the next space after Johnny's. This must be the other side of the same door, put there for easy passage back and forth between the two adjoining rooms, facilitating communication when they were working on projects together.

He tried the door and wasn't surprised to find it locked.

To the left of the door, the panel was divided into sections for controlling the different automated components of the castle. A section labeled Kitchen included buttons for starting the coffee and pre-heating the oven.

The next section, Lighting, included buttons for Torches and Candles. He pushed the button for Candles, and a monitor showing his bedchamber blinked to life. A subset of buttons under the monitor controlled all the candles and torches in the castle. Although he'd seen real candles and torches at various locations, these had to be artificial, probably lit by gas.

Quinn shifted his attention to a section with a much more intriguing label: Robotics. Among the buttons in that section were ones labeled Robby, Kong, and Reaper.

Reaper? Maybe he wasn't imagining things when he thought the Reaper's skull had been looking in the opposite direction.

His attention was drawn to two larger labels, the only two he'd been able to read on Markov's panel: GARDEN and LAGOON. As on his, the labels were under two larger monitors positioned side by side, and both screens were dark.

Quinn pushed the on/off button for the LAGOON monitor. The screen remained dark. He followed its cord to make sure it was plugged in. It was.

Dismissing it as a technical glitch, he shifted his attention to the GARDEN monitor. He pushed its power button.

Nothing. It too was plugged in.

It seemed beyond coincidence that among Markov's advanced technology these two monitors would be the only things to malfunction. Further evidence that the garden— and possibly the lagoon—must hold the darkest secrets of the castle. Secrets that apparently were being guarded very closely.

When Quinn had gone down that hidden staircase in his bedchamber, Johnny had intercepted him at gunpoint and warned him never to come down there. But that aborted encounter had left him with the nagging memory of a strange moaning and smell, coming from a chamber sealed off by a locked gate, over which was the inscription *Les Fleurs de Mal.*

The Flowers of Evil. Flowers grew in gardens. Was the GARDEN monitor blacked out to keep any prying eyes from discovering what horrors were being kept in that secret chamber?

He moved to the final section of the control panel: Security. The first labels that caught his eye were Front Door and Cameras. Under the label for the front door were buttons marked Open, Close, and Lock. That solved the mystery of how the door was able to open when no one was around.

Quinn pushed the button under the label for Cameras. Fifty thumbnail images came up on the large widescreen monitor, one for each camera, showing the area it covered. He found the one for his bedchamber and clicked on it. A full screen image of his bed came onto the screen.

Each camera's movements could apparently be controlled by a single cluster of buttons beside the one he had pushed. They were labeled Tilt, Pan, Zoom, Dolly.

Dolly? Markov couldn't possibly have an apparatus for dolly shots on all these cameras. He must have them on some kind of extendable mounts that made simulated dollies possible. Quinn pulled up the monitor that showed the Grim Reaper standing in his corner. He pushed *Dolly* and got an error message: NOT AVAILABLE ON THIS CAMERA. There were two buttons for panning—one with an arrow pointing right, the other an arrow pointing left. He pushed the one pointing right.

The Reaper's head swiveled to the right. Johnny must have panned it toward his door for some reason. *Or had she?* Since Markov's instrument panel was a duplicate of this, that meant at any given moment either of them might be in control. Either way, it was disturbing to know that the Reaper was robotic. What else was it capable of?

He quickly scanned the other thumbnail images and saw that there were two for his guest quarters—one showing his bedchamber and the other showing the oriel. He pulled each one up and moved their cameras in all directions, looking for blind spots. There weren't any.

Quinn stepped back to look at the control panel in its entirety, and realized that Markov had not exaggerated his genius for technology. The software program alone that he must have developed to control all this would put him in the genius category.

A small shelf extended out from the base of this section of the control panel. Resting upright in the center of it, as though to make sure it wouldn't be overlooked, was a cell phone. Next to the phone was a large skeleton key—the master key for the entire castle.

As the person in charge of security, it was conceivable that Johnny would place two of the most important security-related items by the word Security to always know where she had put them—but it was a stretch. Had she left the phone and key laid out for him to find?

He picked up the phone, turned it on, and dialed his home number as a test. After the usual three rings he heard his answering machine message loud and clear.

He stuck the phone and key in his pocket. With a heightened sense of urgency, he went on with his exploration of Johnny's apartment.

The overall décor was in keeping with the Gothic theme, but she had added many feminine touches to brighten the gloom.

Wall hangings depicted colorful birds in beautiful seasonal landscapes. Here and there were tastefully arranged bouquets of wildflowers in handcrafted vases. A living room, kitchenette, and modern bathroom made this a self-contained unit with everything Johnny needed to live independently. Apparently none of her quarters would appear in Markov's movie. In most other areas of the castle, anything not in keeping with the Gothic set design was kept hidden. In here, concessions to modern living were plainly visible.

The rear third of the cavernous apartment was her bedroom. Angled into the corner was a king-sized canopy bed, impeccably made and set off by a stunning royal burgundy satin coverlet. Near the large fireplace to the side of the bed, she had set up a cozy seating area consisting of two high-backed chairs and a small desk. Atop the desk were a few books, some stationery and a quill pen. Recessed into the rear wall was a large wardrobe, the castle version of a closet. Its contents were nothing fancy: simple functional clothing for the various tasks she might need to perform, neatly grouped together and arranged by color. At the far end of the wardrobe, a separate section a few feet wide had been partitioned off. A simple folding door concealed what was inside. Quinn knew he needed to keep moving, but couldn't resist seeing what was behind that door. He opened it and flinched in surprise at what hung there.

It was a stunning, floor-length white dress fit for a ball. Or a wedding. A royal burgundy sash circled the waist, and a matching velvet choker with a cameo brooch hung on a peg. At the bottom of the dress, a pair of embroidered and bejeweled slippers poked out.

Did she dress up in this outfit—Cinderella waiting for her Prince to save her?

A Prince that would never come.

Quinn closed the door with a gentle, regretful respect, as though closing the lid of a coffin and not wanting to disturb the final rest of what lay within. He turned away in disgust at a stolen life and moved to leave the room.

He stopped at a large screen television positioned at the foot of the bed. In the compartments built into its base were several state-of-the-art, audiovisual components for downloading movies and listening to them in surround sound. In this windowless room, the television was her window to the world, a world she had hardly experienced.

Quinn felt a dull ache settling in his chest, a mixture of sadness and anger at a life spent in this gilded prison, a life un-lived in Markov's world of the un-dead. Feeling like a looter of treasures of the heart, Quinn turned to leave.

A soft grating noise stopped him. He snapped his head to find the source.

It was coming from the fireplace. As he stared into the dark shadow, a familiar figure emerged and began walking toward him.

CHAPTER 35

Rather than approaching in her usual hunched subservient posture, Johnny walked toward Quinn as fully erect as her damaged leg would allow, carrying two large canvas bags. As she reached him, Quinn looked around her toward the fireplace. "Another secret passage?"

"My direct access to the Garden below. I keep a close eye on it." She set the bags down. "We need to talk."

"I've been thinking the same thing."

They moved the two high-backed chairs around and sat facing one another. She began with uncharacteristic directness.

"I have been wanting to speak with you alone since you got here, but the opportunity never presented itself. I was hoping you'd pick up on my veiled invitation to come in here."

"Can Markov see us in here?"

"No. If there is anything sacred in this unholy place, it's our agreement never to violate the privacy of each other's apartment. This is the one place where the all-seeing eye of *Milord* is blind."

"Then we may speak freely."

"Yes."

Quinn took a few seconds to decide where to begin. "Markov has been telling me the story of your lives, which included showing me his film. *The Blood of Dracula*."

"I know. I was watching from the projection booth. It was the first time I had ever seen it."

"That must have been painful."

"Very. But it was exactly what I needed to compel me do whatever must be done to end this obscene travesty of life. This shameful denial of my very own soul so I could be his ... Renfield, his Igor—whatever embarrassing horror movie cliché I have let myself become."

As uncomfortable as it was to watch her lifetime of anguish spilling out, Quinn was glad to see that she was finally casting off the yoke of Markov's oppression. "You are his—George Tilton's—daughter. He told me the whole story. About you and your brother Max, the accident that maimed your leg, what happened to your mother, his re-marriage to Lady Elinore."

"Has he told you of his belief in destiny?"

"At great length."

"He and I disagree on a great many things, but his belief in destiny is one I happen to share. I believe you have been sent to us for a reason, though not the same reason he believes—as someone to help him with the climax of his accursed film." *Accursed.* That word again. "I believe you are a lifeline we have been thrown. The voice of sanity from the real world. Our last chance before we sink to the bottom of the abyss."

"I'm not a savior, Johnny. Far from it. I came here to escape my own abyss. I've been looking forward to losing myself in a weekend that lovers of Universal horror can only fantasize about: the chance to hear the stories of someone who worked on one of the all-time classics. But it has taken a drastic turn. Now that we're speaking honestly, let me give you my impressions of your very bizarre lives."

Johnny nodded, never taking her eyes from his.

"Until now the dialogue from both of you has sounded like lines from movies. Which is not surprising, since for fifty years, neither of you has had much practice in conversing with real live human beings. It's like you're both playing parts in an old black-and-white haunted castle movie, where you think you have to keep the audience— me—in suspense until the final twist is revealed. Don't get me wrong. I love haunted castle movies—where the threats are make-believe. But you and your father have both been telling me that some of the threats in here might be real."

"Has he explained to you about how some of his creations seem to be developing lives of their own?"

"Yes. But both of you have also said there's madness here. His arguments are very persuasive, but they could also be the ravings of a madman. I'm not sure what is fact and what is fiction."

"I wish it were only fiction," Johnny said. "But there are evils in this castle that must be stopped."

"Listen. I work with law enforcement on some of the sickest murder cases. The atrocities I've seen have made me vow never to turn a blind eye to evil. So if there is genuine evil here, I'll do what I can to stop it. But I didn't come here for some madman to make me part of his snuff film. If it comes down to kill or be killed, I'll do whatever it takes to survive."

"Perfectly understandable," she said.

He tried to read the face of someone who had been

scarred not only physically, but deep down in her soul—by her father. Quinn saw defiance rising up from pride too long swallowed. "Can I trust you, Johnny? Are you on my side now?"

She answered without hesitation. "Yes."

He wanted to believe her, but couldn't help wondering if a lifetime of brainwashing could be undone so quickly—if at all. For now he had no choice but to take her at her word.

"Then let's dispense with all the play-acting and bring me up to speed on what's really going on here. It's bad enough that your father keeps talking of monsters—real and virtual—stalking the castle, but much worse is him saying the Universal monsters have gotten inside him, that his blood is mixed with Vlad the Impaler's, that it makes him feed on humans in the woods."

Quinn's gaze was a probing searchlight from which there was no escape. "Have innocent people died? Have we got a serial killer on our hands?"

Johnny winced. "His feedings left them not quite dead, but…. Yes. Some eventually died."

"What about you? He said you drank the elixir for years but stopped. I can see that it slowed the aging process, as it did in him. He said you're in your seventies. You look fifty, at most. Have there been any lingering effects? Any 'vampiric' urges?"

"No. There were when I was drinking it, and for a while after I stopped, but something in my nature never let me succumb. Finally I found the courage to stand up to him and said no more. Over time my system has purged the poison from my bloodstream."

Her cell phone beeped. She held up a finger for Quinn to wait and pressed a button. "Yes?" She hesitated before saying, "Out by the barn. Finishing my patrol of the perimeter. Then I was going to check on the Garden." Johnny listened a moment and then said, "I understand. Yes. I will tell him."

She clicked off and turned back to Quinn. "Markov's growing paranoid."

"Why did you lie?"

"I was buying time for us to finish our talk. His rewrite is giving him problems and taking longer than expected. He wants you to use the time to familiarize yourself with 'the set,' to save time later when he's setting up the scenes."

"This gives me time to explore the areas I haven't gotten to. Particularly the Garden. He's forbidden me to go down there, but, frankly, at this point, I don't give a shit. Whatever his Flowers of Evil are, they need to be weed-whacked. His reign of terror is over."

"My thoughts exactly," Johnny said. "With his deadline fast approaching, I know he's going to be calling me constantly for one thing or another. We have to seize our opportunity now to come up with a plan to stop him."

"And for you to show me the Garden."

"Absolutely." She spread her arms to indicate the entire castle. "He has turned this infernal pile—and himself—into an incubator for vampires and monsters. This place and everything in it must be destroyed."

CHAPTER 36

As Johnny's darkest secrets gushed forth from their imprisonment in the nethermost dungeon of her soul, they washed away the last of Quinn's reluctance to accept a world that defied all reason. She couldn't be just making all this up to further her own agenda. The horrors Markov had created here were not just the special effects of a deranged imagination. They were *real*.

"He has long been determined to end his movie on the night of the Blood Moon," Johnny said. "He'll almost certainly use the horror movie cliché of having midnight as his deadline. By the time he finishes his rewrite and blocks out all the action, we might only have a few hours to stop him before all hell breaks loose."

"I don't see any possible way he can do everything he needs to do by midnight. Do you?"

"No. But he can certainly wreak havoc trying. He probably thinks he can just put you in peril and record whatever happens, then figure out a way to edit it all into the final cut. It's insane. It always has been." She waved the thought aside. "Regardless, whatever ending he comes up with will undoubtedly make him the hero. I cannot let that happen. I will *not* let him emerge triumphant after all the lives he has destroyed. Like Renfield, I cannot live with all those innocent souls on my conscience."

Johnny looked around as though scanning for signs of surveillance, despite Markov's promise that the privacy of her quarters was sacrosanct. She pulled her chair closer, until their knees were almost touching, and lowered her voice to barely above a whisper.

"My father is the carrier of what I've come to think of as the Dracula Virus, and he—it—cannot be allowed to escape into the world. Ebola would pale by comparison. As bad as it is, at least Ebola has no human awareness. No evil design. The Dracula Virus does. It has all but obliterated its host—George Tilton—my *father*—and is taking him to the end stage, beyond Markov. To becoming a monster who would knowingly create a race of vampires, with him as its lord and master, to ensure that Dracula lives forever. He must be stopped, but I cannot do it alone. I know this is too much to ask, but … will you help me?"

Quinn had been anticipating this moment. "Yes. I'm not leaving until this is over."

Hints of the gentle soul long buried inside her rose up to shimmer in her eyes. Her small nod was one of deep gratitude for someone willing to put his life on the line to save hers. He returned it, and she blinked away the emotion before going on.

"Then we must come up with *our* version of the ending now. He thinks fate sent you to be the lead in his big monster rally sequence. That's how he justifies maybe getting you killed. After all he's put me through, he couldn't let me be the one getting chased by his monsters. He needed someone else. Someone who wouldn't bother whatever is left of his conscience." She hesitated but never broke eye contact. "Someone expendable."

"Finally," Quinn said. "The truth comes out."

"In this infernal pile, truth is buried under a mansion of lies. Now it must be exhumed." She slid the canvas bags around by her feet. "I have weapons in here that will help protect us, but I can give no guarantees. He has many at his disposal as well. The digital special effects and robots are dangerous enough, because he is losing control of them."

"I know. He told me."

"Then he may also have told you about the monsters that live within him."

"He has."

"They are much worse. Predators without a conscience. And they are getting stronger. I believe he is actually encouraging the evil part of their natures, so they will be more convincing in the climax."

"But if they come from inside him, he can't use them all simultaneously. Can he?"

"No, but he could combine whatever monster escapes from him with digital or robotic versions of the others to confuse us."

Quinn shook his head. "Whatever ending he has in mind, you've both been telling me it will be dangerous. We can't let it get that far."

"Agreed," Johnny said. "So let's come up with a plan to stop him."

CHAPTER 37

"Where is Markov doing his rewrite?" Quinn asked.

"In the Chamber of Horrors. He always goes there to write his darkest scenes. It inspires him."

"When we finish in the Garden we could go in together and overpower him."

"Do not underestimate him. He is still quite strong—and resourceful. We would need the element of surprise."

Quinn thought of the bruisers he'd knocked down playing rugby, and couldn't imagine not being able to handle a hundred-year-old man, no matter how strong. "We could discreetly get into position on both sides of him, give each other a nod, and take him down. Then restrain him with whatever we can bring that will do the job: rope, chains, handcuffs."

In the curt shake of her head, Johnny's fierce determination made her almost unrecognizable as the formerly cringing servant. "When he becomes enraged, the creatures that live inside him try to break out. So far they haven't, but if any of them do they could overpower us."

"So what can we do to keep that from happening?"

She gestured toward her control panel. "Before we get

into all that: I left a cell phone and a master skeleton key over there for you. You need to take them with you in case we get separated."

Quinn smiled. "Thought so. They're in my pocket."

"Good. If you need me for any reason, just press 1 and the call button. That will get only me. I'll leave it on vibrate, so he won't hear your call if he's with me. If he is, just leave a message and I'll call you as soon as I can get away."

"It sounds like you inherited your father's knowledge of technology."

"He has taught me since I was at his knee. From the day we moved here he has shown me how to do everything he does, so I can serve as his backup for all the systems of the castle. Everything he can do, I can do." A hint of melancholy flickered across her features. "I am very much Daddy's little girl."

In a blink, her grim determination to bring this all to an end was back. Staring into the defiant face that might once have been beautiful, Quinn saw the indomitability of the human spirit. "Consider us the antibodies that will stop the Dracula Virus," he said.

"Yes!"

She yanked the canvas bags around and with a few fierce swipes unzipped their compartments so Quinn could see their contents. "I knew this day would come so I have gathered up some weapons. There are essentially two types of threats he has at his command: digital and real. Against the digital, we have magnets. These are the most powerful on the market."

She slid up her sleeves. There were magnetic bands around each of her wrists, fastened by Velcro. "I always wear two on each wrist and ankle. In effect, they create a force field around you that will keep any of his digital creations at bay. Wearing these is your first line of defense."

"Meaning you need a second line of defense?"

"Usually they disintegrate right away, but they are clearly getting stronger. Coming closer. They always stop several feet away, but lately a few have started to advance again." She nodded at the open canvas bag. "There are four dozen more in there. Wherever you go, carry extras. If the ones you're wearing haven't stopped them, start throwing them. I'm not sure exactly what happens, but since the digital monsters are computer-generated, and magnetism can fry computers, so far that has shut them down."

"So far," Quinn said. "It doesn't sound like they'll definitely do the job."

"They might not. Especially if these things keep getting stronger." She unzipped the large side compartment. It was full of canisters about an inch thick and five inches long. "Bear spray."

"I saw some of that in the barn."

"I order it in bulk and always keep plenty on hand. Hunters use it to stop bears. Take the bag with you. And carry extras—of the bands and the spray. As many as you can fit into your pockets without arousing Markov's suspicion."

Quinn looked at the sweatpants he was wearing. They only had two small pockets. "I'll have to swing by my room. I'll change into cargo pants and grab a couple things that could come in handy."

Johnny made a curt nod.

"What about the real threats?" Quinn said. "Physical realities?"

"This is where the line between the real and the unreal

gets blurred," Johnny said. "Part of Markov's humanity is seeping into his special effects. I've started preparing myself to fight the digital and the real. And the real—as impossible as it sounds—could include the monsters he might become."

She opened the main compartment of the other bag and pulled out something that looked like it might be for killing weeds in a garden: essentially a short pipe with a nozzle at the end and a pistol grip with a squeeze trigger. A handle was attached to the top; underneath was a small fuel tank.

"What's that?" Quinn said.

"Another of Markov's paranoid inventions. A propane-powered flamethrower. Nothing on the market pleased him, so he made his own."

"To use against what? I can only remember fire being used against the Frankenstein Monster."

"Exactly."

Quinn shook his head at the insanity of it all. "So, if it came time to use it, that would mean you torching your own father."

"Sick, isn't it?"

"That would be one word for it."

"A discussion for a later time. For now, the stupid thing might come in handy." She showed him how the flamethrower worked. "It only has a maximum range of about five feet, so keep that in mind. There's a spare tank of fuel in this bag. Also a pistol loaded with silver bullets in case he becomes the Wolf Man."

"*If* the myth about silver bullets stopping werewolves is true."

"He's Lon Chaney's Wolf Man. Lawrence Talbot. And in that movie, silver bullets killed him. There's also a box with two dozen extra bullets. If he changes into his vampire persona, there's wolfbane, garlic, and a hammer and stakes."

"This is all well and good, Johnny, but it seems like our primary objective should be to disable Markov before he gets to use any of his monsters—digital or real. Then it's over."

"You're right. He's the source of all their power. Of everything. But overpowering him might be easier said than done. He's more unbalanced than I've ever seen him. He's possessed by the need to finish his film tonight. He'll stop anyone or anything who tries to get in his way. But—yes. If we can disable him, it should make his creations powerless."

If. Should. Quinn still didn't like it, but he had to trust Johnny. After all these years, she had to know his every weakness, be able to anticipate his every move. Even so, he could see that something was still troubling her. "What?" he said.

"Disabling him and his digital minions is only the first step. I cannot stop until this place has been destroyed. If the horrors he has locked away in the Garden somehow got loose, all our efforts would be for naught."

"How do you plan on destroying the castle?"

"I am going to burn it to the ground."

"That could start a serious forest fire."

"The clearing around the castle should keep the fire contained."

Quinn started to say she couldn't be sure about that, but the ferocity of her expression told him the matter was not open to debate. He let it pass. "Whatever we do to overpower his monsters, there may be no way around it: We might have to kill your father."

Johnny seemed unfazed. "If it comes to that, so be it."

They took a few minutes to walk through precisely how they were going to get on either side of Markov and take him down in the Chamber of Horrors. "Then that's the plan," Quinn said. "We need to get moving so you can show me what's in the Garden."

He started to stand but stopped when he thought of another complication. "Markov told me your brother Max recently sent him a letter, threatening to come here and kill him. Talking about his 'days being numbered.' Are you aware of that?"

"Yes. He showed me the letter."

"Is there any chance Max will follow through on his threat?"

"A chance, I suppose. His hatred has been simmering for years. The fact that he was driven to write that letter after all this time tells me it might have reached the boiling point. I've been keeping an eye out for him ever since."

"It's probably a long shot that he would show up," Quinn said, "but stranger things have happened."

"Even if Max is planning something, all we need is for him to drag his feet for a few more hours. Then whatever he has planned will be too late."

Quinn held out his hand. "For you it is not too late, Johnny. Together we can make it a happy ending."

"A happy ending." Tenderness softened her expression as she gave his hand a gentle squeeze. "Something I have fantasized about my whole life." She released his hand, and her steely determination was back. "Time to bring about *my* version of destiny."

Destiny.

Markov had repeatedly mentioned his belief in it, but to Quinn it had sounded like a way of justifying the Dracula

216

obsession that had led to his murderous cravings: if he was only a helpless pawn in the clutches of an inescapable fate, he couldn't be held accountable. Now, hearing Johnny saying she believed in it too, he thought about it for a moment. If there was such a thing, maybe this was his: the first real test of his vow never to look away from evil again.

"Whatever you want to call it," he said, "let's get this done."

Johnny was leading him to the secret passage in the fireplace when her cell phone rang. Her determined expression started to melt as she listened to what the caller was saying. "I still have to check the Garden. Then I was going to run a test on all the cameras, make sure we don't have any technical problems once shooting starts."

Quinn couldn't hear Markov's response, but as Johnny listened, her expression hardened. "Yes. I will."

She ended the call with an angry stab of the button. "Full moons have been affecting him more and more, and there have been many Blood Moons over the years, but this one … on this night…. He's obsessed with making sure there are no interruptions. He's particularly paranoid about someone wandering in from the woods, so he's ordered me to check the perimeter again. He'll undoubtedly be monitoring my movements." She shook her head. "You'll have to go to the Garden alone."

Quinn gave a curt nod. "We have to be prepared for the worst-case scenario, Johnny. Which could be us running for our lives. After I finish in the Garden, I still want to look around some more outside. The more I know about the possible escape routes, the better."

"Agreed," Johnny said. "The easiest thing would be to take you on my patrol now and show you, but if he sees us together, he'll know we're up to something—if he doesn't already." She shook her head in frustration. "He's going to be keeping me on a short leash from here on out. Finding the time to do everything we need to do is going be tricky. We need to stay in close contact so we can set up a time and place to meet and launch our attack."

"Where can we make our calls so he can't see us?"

"There are a few blind spots. One is in the Garden." She thought for a moment. "Maybe we won't have to make any calls. My patrol of the perimeter shouldn't take more than fifteen minutes. Unless he calls me for something else, I can meet you in the Garden before you go outside."

"I'll be looking for you."

"Leave your cell phone on in case I need to reach you."

"I will."

Johnny's iron resolve had fully returned. "We need to leave the bags in here for now. It's the one place where we can be sure he won't see them."

Quinn hesitated.

"What?" Johnny said.

"If I go to my room for cargo pants, then have to come back here for the wristbands and spray…. It would make more sense to take the bag with me and use the stairs in my chamber to get to the Garden."

Johnny shook her head. "We can't let him see us carrying those bags around. I was taking a chance just getting them in here."

"Okay. But once I'm back here, the quickest way to the Garden will be the staircase by the Chamber of Horrors. That's a lot of time out of your room where he can see us."

"I can disable the cameras, but I can't leave them off for long."

"How long?"

"Ten minutes, at most. Even then, if he's watching and gets suspicious, he could override my command and turn them back on. There's just no way to be absolutely certain you won't be seen."

"Disable the cameras. I'll be quick. And hopefully lucky."

Johnny's already intense gaze narrowed. "Forget Markov's cute little description of his life as a descent into the maelstrom. You will be descending into the bowels of Hell, Adam. Remember what I said about staying fully alert."

"I will." Quinn didn't want to say what he was thinking, but he had to. "You do the same. Markov is no dummy. If he smells a conspiracy—"

Johnny held up a hand. "Don't worry. If he tries anything, he'll have another monster to deal with: the Monster from *my* Id. It's been growing since that sword hit my leg. If it gets loose, God help the bastard."

CHAPTER 38

Having been born and raised in a world of movie horror, it did not escape Max Tilton that the neglected church graveyard outside Boston was the perfect setting for the scene he was in. Against the backdrop of gathering storm clouds in the darkening sky, the jagged brown limbs of the leafless trees looked like the decomposing skeletal fingers of giants, reaching out from beyond their graves to drag unwary souls from the land of the living into the land of the dead.

Max stood directly under one of those trees in the most isolated corner of the graveyard. In the years since he had escaped his father's reign of terror, he'd made this pilgrimage every year. This would be his last.

The feeble sunlight filtering through the leafless branches on this chill October afternoon was still strong enough to cast stark spidery shadows on his mother's tombstone:

DOLORES TILTON

1912-1954

Beloved wife and mother
Peaceful slumber in life denied,
She sleeps with angels by her side.

He and his father had argued over the inscription. Max had not wanted "beloved wife" on there, because he'd never believed his father had loved her enough. As a compromise, Max had been allowed to write the verse.

Crouching, he placed a vase of flowers next to her tombstone. He gently patted the ground beneath which she was buried, then pressed his palm on the patch where he imagined her heart would be, keeping it there to convey his loving reassurance as he spoke softly.

"I shall be coming to join you soon, Mother. This painful sequel to *Dracula* that has been our lives will finally have a happy ending. I have one last familial duty to perform, one I have postponed far too long. The polluted blood that flows through the Tilton veins must be cut off at its source. Only then can we be free."

When he reached his car to leave, he glanced at the back seat. What lay there brought a grim smile.

Vlad Dracula's sword. After all those years of hearing his father's tiresome lectures about how making a movie of their lives at the castle was a fulfillment of his destiny, Max was going to make a last-minute change to the script—a fantastic twist that would give *George Tilton* a destiny far different from whatever one he envisioned for himself. As Markov, he had often said that ending his movie on the night of the Blood Moon would be the perfect culmination of his life's work.

Which made this the perfect night for Max to change the ending. Tonight it would be *his* destiny that would be fulfilled, not Markov's.

Before getting in the car he looked up at the thunderclouds getting blacker in the ominous sky, and felt a moment of anxiety over all he had left to do. He had a couple scores to settle before he headed for the castle, and they would take time. By the time he reached that trail through the woods that led to the castle—which was treacherous in the best of circumstances—it would be dark, and he'd almost certainly be driving his beat-up old sub-compact, with its worn-out tires, through a thunderstorm. As dangerous as that might be, picturing that final scene brought another grim smile.

The gothic horror story that had been their lives would end on a dark and stormy night.

CHAPTER 39

Markov sat in his studio staring blankly at the scriptwriting program on his computer screen, feeling as though his head was about to explode. He had been rearranging shots and scenes for hours and gotten nowhere. He got up and began to pace, grappling with the numerous problems they needed to overcome before he could write a shooting script for the final sequence.

His plan had been simply to record Quinn as though he were being chased by the various monsters, then edit them into the sequence later. But he was losing control—not just of his monsters, but of Johnny and Quinn. They weren't fooling anyone. He saw the furtive glances. They had both been out of view for some time now, so he suspected they were together somewhere. They were forming a bond, and that could only lead to trouble. That realization brought his pacing to an abrupt halt.

Whatever script he came up with, they couldn't be relied upon to stick to it. As if he didn't have enough to worry about, he needed to keep a close eye on them. Even so, one way or another, he had to get the final sequence shot before everything got completely away from him. He had until midnight to wrap his movie. His life.

He looked at the clock. Almost four. He'd been up for twelve hours and accomplished nothing. He had often storyboarded entire scripts in a day. Now, on a single sequence—the most important one of his life—he was blocked.

After a few more minutes of trying to work out a sequence that would include everything he wanted in it, he finally stopped pacing and faced the inescapable truth:

It was too complicated. There wasn't enough time to bring all the different elements together. It was almost with relief that he heard himself saying, "The ending cannot be scripted. It will have to be *cinéma vérité* in its purest form."

Standing in front of the large monitor he used to manipulate his special effects, he noticed that its built-in camera projected him onto the screen. Even though he was standing perfectly still, there was movement.

The only thing moving was his face.

It bubbled and stretched as the moon-driven monsters inside him fought to get out. The split-second glimpses of his inner demons faded until one face stared at him.

Vlad Dracula.

Staring at the face on the screen, Markov finally accepted another truth, one he'd been denying for decades: Despite his efforts to maintain the proper balance of vampire and human blood in the elixir, over the years the vampire blood had taken over, becoming the dominant element in his very life force. Gradually—inevitably, Markov now realized—it had made Dracula the ruler of the monster brood growing inside him. Now he felt the vampire stirring.

Dracula's mouth suddenly opened wide in what looked like a silent scream. A head erupted from the mouth and began pushing frantically against the screen, as though trying to escape the realm of cyberspace. The screen stretched and warped but did not yield to the maniacal pushing. Finally the head managed to poke through.

It was the head of George Tilton, darting eyes ablaze with terror. The head kept jerking around to look behind itself, as though being chased by some demon from Markov's virtual world. Finally the eyes looked directly at Markov.

"Save me!"

Gazing into the pleading eyes of his former self, Markov felt a twinge of pity, but that quickly passed as he stared at the overall image: Vlad Dracula's face frozen on the screen, with George Tilton's head jutting out. A mutant hatchling trying to break free from its egg.

Suddenly Dracula's eyes glowed a hotter red, and the mouth swallowed George Tilton in one gulp. The vampire's cheeks rippled and his lips twitched as Tilton fought to get out, but in seconds the battle was over and the face became still.

A small sadistic smile came onto the lips, and the glowing red eyes bore into Markov.

Last night the power of Dracula growing inside him had willed him to bring the impalement stake from his bedchamber to the studio. Now the mesmeric power streaming from the eyes in the mirror was willing him to use it.

Staggering away from the monitor, Markov went to retrieve the stake. When he came back, he saw no traces of himself in the monitor, only glimpses of the monsters steadily overtaking him. Instead of alarm, the montage brought a feeling of peace.

He didn't need a script. He didn't need Johnny.

I am an auteur.

He could simply leave all the cameras on, and they would record the ultimate truth of his life.

He was the monster rally.

CHAPTER 40

Max had seen the Grim Reaper do many digital beheadings at the castle when his father and sister were working on their special effects, but this was no special effect. *He* was the Grim Reaper now.

He knocked on the door of the downstairs unit in a small duplex apartment just outside Boston.

A man's voice came from behind the door. "Who's there?"

"I have a package for Mr. Owens."

"Can you just leave it at the door?"

"No, sorry. I need a signature."

Max readied himself as he heard the chain being removed and a lock being unlatched. The door opened a few inches and Max bulled his way in, knocking the frail man backwards and quickly shutting and locking the door.

"Who—? What—?" the man stammered.

Max swung Dracula's sword with all his might, slicing cleanly through the man's neck. His severed head tumbled across the floor of the small apartment and wedged in the corner. Max walked toward it, smiling at how fitting it was for the head to come to rest there. On the walls behind the head were posters from plays the idiot had directed last year at a small theater outside of Boston.

With their last spark of life, the director's eyes followed Max as he put the sword aside and sat on the floor beside the head. He grabbed it by the hair and turned it to face the poster of *Macbeth*.

"Remember me?" he said. "I auditioned for Macduff. The one who must behead Macbeth to stop his insane quest for power. I *lived* that part, fool. I *am* Macduff. Yet still you did not cast me. I was compelled to show thee the error of thy ways."

He turned the head to face him and leaned close, delivering his lines with his best Shakespearean diction to the final flicker in the fast-dimming eyes:

"Double, double toil and trouble. Fire burn, and cauldron bubble. Cool it with a baboon's blood…."

He filled his fountain pen with the blood still flowing from the neck, pulled a piece of paper from his pocket, and scribbled hastily.

There are many vampires among us. Those who suck blood are easier to detect, but it is the psychic vampires, who suck the life force from us, who do the most harm. Bloodsuckers like this one. Who have no talent but presume they can recognize it in others.

They must be stopped. I have begun the grim task. You can follow my trail of head crumbs instead of bread crumbs—ha HA!—but it will do you no good. By the time you find me, the worst of the vampires shall be headless, and I will happily join him in death.

The un-dead shall live no more.

CHAPTER 41

In the Chamber of Horrors, Markov stood looking up at Vlad the Impaler like a worshipful follower. He spoke to his Prince in Latin.

"I can no longer serve you. The time has come for me to fulfill my—"

"Destiny," Dracula breathed in the raspy voice of the grave.

"You know about my belief in destiny?"

"Yes. We all have our destiny. From the first moment of this unnatural existence, I knew mine was to wear the Crown of Dracula until a worthy successor could be found. Someone to perpetuate the line of Dracul."

Dracula III's eyes bore into those of his disciple. "My destiny and yours have become one. All these years, I have only been able to listen as you came to me—torn, seeking guidance, because you used your vampire blood to vanquish invaders into your territory. Now that I can speak, here is my decree:

"All who try to usurp our Crown must die. By whatever means necessary. I chose impalement. You chose the way of the vampire. Even better, because it gave us the blood for the elixir that kept us alive. The blood that will make us a race of beings to reign supreme for eternity. Not just over Wallachia, but *over all.*"

A hint of affection softened the fierce gaze. "You were the most loyal of my followers, and have become like a son unto me. Therefore, I hereby pass the Crown on to you."

Markov stood transfixed, awestruck by the realization that his love of Dracula had led him to this. Returning Vlad's affectionate gaze, Markov held up a finger. "Please, give me a moment, Milord. I have something for us."

He opened a cabinet beneath the showcase and pulled out two small vials of the elixir, then walked around to the access panel on the back. He opened it and stepped through to stand facing the head. He removed the caps from the vials and held one near Vlad's lips. "A toast to the new world kingdom of Dracula."

"I hereby proclaim you Dracula IV," said Dracula III. "My reign is at an end. Drink them both to give you the strength you will need to go forth and fulfill *our* destiny."

Markov did as he was commanded and emptied the vials in two swallows, then reverently removed the crown and placed it on his own head. He felt the elixir surging through him as the vampire blood began to overtake the human. More of George Tilton's soul was absorbed into the pit of darkness that was Dracula's soul.

The eyes in the severed head bore into him. "The man you call Quinn mocks you. He cannot be trusted. Neither can your Johnny. They both must die."

Markov—Vlad Dracula IV—grinned. "I will see to it forthwith, Milord."

"Wear the crown well," Dracula III said, a hint of a smile flitting across his lips. "You must see that our line never dies."

Markov felt the weight of the crown settling onto him. Before leaving the Chamber he retrieved the impalement stake and looked at himself on the overhead monitor.

All traces of Lugosi were gone.

He was Dracula now.

CHAPTER 42

Standing in the wardrobe of his bedchamber, Quinn finished changing into cargo pants. From one of the suitcases he fished out the multitool he always brought with him when he was working in the field. A Boston detective had given it to him as a Thank You for helping crack one of their more difficult cases.

"Our SWAT teams use these," Jack Thompson had said. "They're like a Swiss Army Knife on steroids." It had come in handy so many times on Quinn's explorations he'd come to consider it a good luck charm. Thinking they'd need all the luck they could get, he inserted the tool into the pocket for concealing valuables—a cushioned zipper pocket inside the back of the waistband. He adjusted its bulk until it rested comfortably just below the small of his back, then stuffed Johnny's cell phone and the skeleton key into the pocket with his flashlight.

Back in Johnny's apartment, he fastened two magnetic wristbands around each wrist and ankle, then filled his baggiest pockets with as many wristbands and canisters of bear spray as he could without looking conspicuous. He left the bags of weapons in Johnny's apartment for now—the one place that was off limits to Markov's cameras.

Quinn exited Johnny's safe haven and hesitated in the recessed entryway outside her door. Johnny had said she'd disable the cameras, but after ten minutes, Markov might get suspicious. The ten minutes had to be almost up. The cameras might be back on. Quinn wanted to sprint, but he'd have to walk at a normal pace in case Markov was watching.

He took a deep breath and entered the corridor.

CHAPTER 43

Quinn had barely entered the corridor when something clamped onto his ankle.

He looked down in disbelief at a severed hand.

It was one of the webbed hands of the Creature from the Black Lagoon. He'd seen one in the barn with the models of heads.

One.

It couldn't be digital. The hand had clamped itself over the two magnetic bands on his ankle and they were having no effect.

But it couldn't be real. The original Creature had only been a man in a suit.

The clawed fingers were squeezing hard enough to cause pain. Alarmed, Quinn stooped to pry them loose. As he reached for them, he took a quick glance into the opening at the wrist to see if there was a mechanism he could disable.

Thin wires ran down into the fingers.

Robotic.

No time to figure it out.

The hand squeezed harder. Its long sharp claws dug into his flesh. He doused it with a forceful stream of bear spray.

The jolt sent the hand flying. It landed palm up, clutching and flexing until it flopped itself over and began scrabbling erratically across the floor. Burrowing itself into a corner of the entryway, it kept flexing while rubbing itself against the wall, as if trying to scrape away the pain. Finally it came to rest on its back.

It couldn't be entirely robotic if the pepper spray affects it….

The hand began to stir. Struggling for a few seconds, it managed to flip itself over. It advanced a few inches toward Quinn, then stopped and retreated to the safety of the corner, apparently wary of getting sprayed again.

Quinn moved to douse it with more spray. The hand must have sensed him coming, because it scrambled past him and skittered down the corridor. Quinn gave chase for a few steps before stopping. He had no time for chasing a mechanical hand all over the place.

Was Markov controlling it? Was this his way of trying to keep Quinn from discovering what was in the Garden?

He retreated into the entryway, hoping he wouldn't be seen while he considered his situation. Markov had said these things were taking on a life of their own. Whatever, whoever was controlling it, the hand was not just another harmless example of his genius with special effects. Those claws had been intent on inflicting serious physical harm.

The questions still nagged. Had it merely been defending its territory? Or had Markov been sending a message—the director letting his actor know there must be no deviations from the script?

It didn't matter. The only thing that mattered was meeting Johnny in the Garden and carrying out their attack.

Markov had repeatedly warned him not to go down the stairs by the Chamber of Horrors, but that was the quickest way to the Garden. He'd have to risk being seen.

Quelling the urge to sprint, he walked down the long corridor at a normal pace. It occurred to him that the attack by the hand could have been the beginning of Markov's monster rally sequence, so he continually scanned the floor and his surroundings in case the hand or anything else might suddenly appear. A moment later he reached the top of the staircase. Standing in front of the suit of armor, Quinn took a last look around for any lurking monsters, then turned his attention to the staircase that led to the Garden.

He'd only taken a step toward it when from behind he heard a *whoosh*.

Something was sailing through the air toward him. He ducked. A rush of air ruffled the hair on his head. He sprinted a few steps down the stairs and turned back to look for the source of the sound.

The suit of armor had just swung its halberd. If he hadn't ducked, it would have decapitated him.

The weapon returned to its upright position, and the suit of armor became still.

Quinn's heart pounded an angry warning in his chest.

Did Markov just try to kill him? Or was this another case of him losing control?

Quinn pulled a magnetic wristband from his pocket and made his way back up to the landing. As he cautiously moved toward the suit of armor, he saw two spots of red glowing through the eye slits. He extended an arm to direct the full force of the two magnetic bands on his wrist at them.

The spots began to dim. He looked for any hint of movement from the halberd. There was none, nor any other signs of life. He snatched the halberd from its gauntlet-covered fist and opened the visor. The dimming red spots quickly went out. The suit was empty.

Had the red spots been eyes? Or was the suit of armor just a cleverly disguised part of Markov's obsession with security, the red spots merely sensors programmed to maim trespassers who dared to use the stairs?

Quinn shoved the thought into the messy pile of questions that he now knew would never get answered. All that mattered now was for he and Johnny to execute their plan to bring about *The End*.

He dropped a wristband into the suit of armor for whatever good it might do, and moved the halberd several yards down the corridor to get it out of the armor's reach.

Unless the armor could walk....

Quinn dismissed the thought with an impatient shake of his head. He couldn't anticipate every conceivable possibility in a world where the laws of nature no longer applied.

He crossed the landing to head below.

He had just placed his foot on the first step when the shadow of Nosferatu separated from the wall to block his path. The black silhouette did not morph into a full physical being, but even as a razor-thin shadow, the unmistakable features were still chilling: the hunched creeping posture, the pointed ears, the aquiline nose, the long, pointed fingernails. Standing ten feet below Quinn on the next landing, the vampire shadow kept cocking its head as though confused by what it was seeing.

Or is it waiting for its next command? Has Markov sent another of his digital minions to keep me from discovering his secrets?

Quinn used the shadow's hesitation to decide on what action to take.

The shadow couldn't be real. It had to be digital. But how much of Markov's spirit was in control? Max Schreck's portrayal of Nosferatu had obviously affected him profoundly. If Markov's theory that some of his essence had seeped into his digital creations were true, that animating force might be especially strong in even a shadow version of Nosferatu.

The black silhouette began creeping up the stairs, arms extended in the familiar gesture of the vampire about to envelop its victim. When it came within a few feet, Quinn held out both wrists.

The shadow vampire stopped, wavering as if uncertain of the danger. The magnetism must be having an effect, but apparently it wasn't strong enough to completely overpower one of Markov's darkest shadows.

Quinn decided to try something. He yanked three wristbands from his pocket and used their Velcro fastenings to join them into one long one. Securing this around his neck, he enticingly exposed his jugular while pulling a canister of bear spray from his pocket.

The apparition kept leaning forward then pulling back. Finally, unable to resist the river of blood pulsing beneath the flesh, it closed in. Against every instinct, Quinn held his position, finger poised to shoot a stream of spray. The phantom mouth opened as it came ever closer to his neck.

Six inches. Five. Four. Three....

The head sprang back. Quinn moved toward the shadow of the vampire. As the specter reluctantly backed down to the next landing, something happened that didn't make sense. Even though the head was closest to the magnets, it began to disintegrate from the feet up.

Maybe the head is the most powerful part....

The disintegration continued until only the disembodied head hovered in the air. One bulging eye materialized, the vertical slit of its jaundiced yellow pupil fixing Quinn with its baleful stare. Finally it, too, fell apart, until it joined the countless black bits of decomposed remains scattered about the floor—the digital ashes of a digital vampire.

Just as the tension began to drain from Quinn's body, another horror assaulted his eyes.

Some of the bits began to twitch and wriggle about. Only a few at first, but their numbers rapidly grew until the movement spread like a nest of conqueror worms tunneling under the skin of their corpse. What had looked like a jigsaw version of a Rorschach inkblot began to take a more definite shape.

The shadow Nosferatu was coming back to life.

Quinn dropped another wristband into the middle of the coalescing pile.

The movement subsided as a small ripple of concentric waves flowed outward from the wristband. In a minute, all was still again. Quinn glanced up the stairs to make sure nothing was coming at him from that direction, then watched the decomposed metallic remains to be sure they would not come back to life. He left the wristband in the pile—a magnetic stake through the heart of the digital Nosferatu.

As he moved to head the rest of the way down the stairs, he wondered how much of what had just happened was controlled by Markov—or if none of it was. Or if reality lay somewhere in between. Whatever the case, in the fleeting glimpse which that malignant eye had given him into the soul of Nosferatu, Quinn had fathomed the depths of an evil that originated in the nethermost regions of the Pit.

CHAPTER 44

Markov had gone to his apartment to choose the costume for his final scenes with Quinn and Johnny. But on the way to his wardrobe, he'd seen Quinn on the monitor that showed the stairs leading to the Garden—clearly getting ready to head down, even though he had been expressly forbidden to do so. Burning rage at such treachery had consumed any thought of including him in the final sequence.

I *am the star of this picture, not that double-crossing son of a bitch!*

Thinking like a director, Markov had instantly come up with a new scene to fit the situation:

Decapitate Quinn with the halberd, then put his head beside Vlad Dracula's as a brilliant display of irony: the obsessed pursuer of the origin of Dracula legend who had succeeded in his quest. *Be careful what you wish for....*

But Quinn had ducked, then defeated the shadow Nosferatu. Markov looked at the special effect gloves and goggles that lay on the floor where he'd tossed them in disgust after his digital creation had fallen apart.

Quinn was proving to be a formidable foe. And Johnny could be. The two of them were not fools. If they *were* plotting against him, with her intimate knowledge of the inner workings of the castle—*and my mind*—they were clever enough to devise a plan that might work.

Johnny might be meeting Quinn in one of the blind spots to work out their scheme. I have to find a way to observe what's going on without being seen.

Whatever they were up to, his best defense would be to keep them apart. Divide and conquer. He'd have to catch them each alone and eliminate them—by whatever means necessary. But they might even be anticipating that....

I'm going to need reinforcements. Strength in numbers.

It was time for Dracula to round up his strongest minions.

He went to his wardrobe to get into costume. Carefully taking off his crown and placing it on a shelf, he knew which costume would give the final sequence its maximum dramatic effect, but he forced himself to take a moment to consider all his options.

There was no getting around it. He put on tux and tails and went to his full-length mirror to see how he looked.

What he saw made him flinch. His instinct had been correct. His Dracula was disturbing on many levels, not the least of which was that such a hideous creature would actually think that stylish dress would make him acceptable in polite society.

The costuming choice was good, but the fact that he could see himself bothered him. A vampire should cast no reflection. His was faint, but he could still see it. He knew what was keeping the transformation from completion: the dying whispers of conscience from George Tilton.

Markov defiantly placed the Dracula crown back on his head. The whispers died out and he focused on what had to be his first priority as the new ruler: eliminating those who would usurp the crown.

He looked at the clock on his nightstand. Past five. After making a quick calculation on how long it would take to do everything he needed to do, he called Johnny's cell phone. He spoke in his own voice, but it was Dracula who told her to tell Quinn to meet him in the Chamber of Horrors at six to go over the final sequence. "Tell him from here on out he'll have to tend to his own needs. I need you to finish your rounds so you can help with the shoot."

He hung up before she could respond. There was no time for snappy repartee. He needed to gather his prize Flowers, then eliminate Quinn and Johnny so he could consummate his life's work without having to look over his shoulder. As dangerous as the confrontation scenes were sure to be, envisioning them brought a grim smile. They would add yet another layer of perfection to his version of Dracula. Quinn and Johnny would be his Van Helsing and Renfield, coming to vanquish the vampire. But in a final stunning twist, Dracula would vanquish them.

He needed to find out where they were and plan his strategy accordingly. The monitors would be no help; Johnny knew how to stay one step ahead of him on those.

Most likely they were in the Garden. He'd start there.

He opened a window and effortlessly climbed through it. The sun had already sunk behind the trees. Clinging to the castle wall, his gaze was irresistibly drawn to the moon. The werewolf inside him was not yet strong enough to get out, but it was strong enough to make the vampire open his mouth and let out a long, ululating howl.

Dressed as though going to a premiere, bathed in the red glow of the rising Blood Moon, the ancient drinker of blood fell into a predatory crouch and crept on all fours along the castle wall.

CHAPTER 45

Ten minutes after crossing the Vermont state line, Max pulled off the Interstate and into the parking lot of the Olympian. He parked out of sight behind the theater.

His timing was perfect. There was only one car in the parking lot, and he recognized it as the director's from the fading bumper sticker advertising some obscure Shakespeare Festival. After getting out of the car he stood looking at the sky for a moment.

The distant storm he'd noticed when he was at his mother's grave was getting stronger and closer. It was still many miles away, but it was darkening the sky and bringing nightfall early. Hopefully he could outrun it. Most of the trip from here to the castle was Interstate; driving on the highway in the rain was no problem. It was those last ten miles through the woods that worried him. They were never fun, but in a storm … and the dark.…

He shook his head to cast out the negative thoughts and opened the trunk. He pulled out the sword and strode confidently toward the rear stage door, as though he were someone connected to the latest production. People in Vermont were trusting souls, so the door would probably be unlocked.

It was. He went in and took a moment to make sure no one was around, then headed through the scene shop to the hallway that led to the director's office. Halfway down the hallway was a bulletin board with reviews of the previous season's productions. The review of the one he'd auditioned for got his attention.

Last year he had swallowed what was left of his pride to come up here and audition for this community theater production of *Dracula*, drawn by the chance to play another of the roles he'd been born to play: Van Helsing, the vampire killer. But the director was a gutless stooge who cast the arrogant star of the company, a rank ham, in the role. The spineless amateur had sent his stage manager to offer Max— a professional—the minor role of the buffoonish guard at Seward's sanitarium. Seething at the indignity of not getting yet another part he was perfect for, he'd turned it down and vowed revenge.

He eased down the wide hallway and stopped just short of the open door to the director's office. He heard rustling inside, the sound of someone at their desk. Max called out the director's name, to be sure he had the right person. "Walter?"

"Yes?"

"Hello," Max said, remaining out of sight while placing both hands on the hilt of the sword and raising it into the ready position.

"Hello?" came the director's voice.

Max said nothing and remained still, waiting.

"Hello? Who's there?"

"The Grim Reaper."

A chair scraped as the director got up to come see who it was. The instant he came through the door, Max took a vicious swing.

The sword sliced cleanly through the director's neck. His body toppled back into the doorway and his head fell straight to the floor. Max knelt down to stare into eyes open wide in shock.

"Arrogant fool. You had a chance to cast someone with the blood of Dracula himself running through his veins."

The eyes showed confusion just before their light went out. Max watched as a film came over them like a curtain coming down. He felt no remorse, only satisfaction that another psychic vampire would no longer be sucking the creative juices of others to enrich his own. Max knew he needed to get going in case the police were on his trail, but couldn't resist taking a moment to savor the expression of ultimate defeat on a face that had been so smug and condescending.

He filled his fountain pen with the blood spilling out from the neck and left his final note:

By the time you read this it will be too late to stop me.

Since a severed head has perpetuated the bloody reign of Dracula, it seems fitting to use beheading rather than the stake on this stealer of souls. Especially fitting when the beheading is done with the blood-soaked sword used by Vlad Dracula himself.

The final swing of this accursed sword shall remove the head of the last loyal subject of Vlad Dracula, the twisted follower who carries out his bidding.

My father.

And then we all must die. The foul vampiric bloodline of Vlad Markov must end.

He stuck the note on the bulletin board on top of the Dracula review.

CHAPTER 46

Now aware that any manner of horror could appear at any time, Quinn clicked on his flashlight and followed the spear of light down into the black gloom of the staircase. Other than unlit gas torches along the walls, nothing revealed itself among the eerily dancing shadows created by his light. As he continued his winding descent, he thought of the labor and expense required to carve this staircase out of the solid rock upon which the castle had been built—more stark evidence of Markov's crazed pursuit of his demented vision.

Quinn rounded another coil of the spiral and his beam revealed the last section of the staircase. At the edge of his light, he could see the earthen floor of the castle. He descended the final stairs and entered the forbidden chamber.

A few steps onto the barren hard-packed dirt, he stopped to get his bearings. Somewhere to his left, far beyond the range of his light, was the staircase he had come down before, the one that led to his bedchamber. He estimated the distance between here and there at fifty to seventy-five yards. This staircase had deposited him close to the castle wall that faced the access road and the lagoon.

The same faint moaning he'd heard on his previous descent began to penetrate the tomblike silence.

As he strained to determine the direction the sound was coming from, he detected the same smell he'd noticed before. Earthy. Some kind of weed or plant matter.

He pulled out a canister of bear spray and followed his flashlight toward the sound, staying close to the wall to keep from becoming disoriented in the black void. He knew from his walk outside that this wall was about fifty yards long. Forty-six steps later he reached the back wall.

The moaning grew louder, coming from somewhere to the left, farther along the rear wall. As he walked toward it, the smell became more pungent, and made Markov's description of whatever was in his Garden as Flowers of Evil seem more apt. This was not the pleasant bouquet of a flower. More like the offensive odor of a weed.

He came to a wrought iron gate. It was so large he needed to move several steps back to get a better perspective.

Through the bars, at the edge of a shallow antechamber, he saw a large opening. Another set of stairs, much wider than the others, continued the descent.

Quinn pulled the skeleton key from his pocket. Expecting a lock that might be frozen from years of neglect, he was surprised when the key turned easily and he heard a click. The hinges groaned a mournful protest as he pulled the gate open.

He crossed to the opening beyond and looked down. A short section of stone steps led to a landing. Quickly scanning for anything unusual, he saw nothing and went down. The landing opened onto another, larger chamber carved into the rock. As he cast his light about, a disturbing sight met his eyes.

A dungeon. The barred doors of three large cells ran along the wall to his right. At first he thought the moaning might have been coming from a prisoner, but the cells all appeared to be empty. The moaning was coming from somewhere to the left.

He went to the nearest cell and unlocked it. The woeful groan of these hinges was worse than the sound of the gate, almost as though the soul of the last inmate were crying for release.

As he got deeper into a cell about thirty yards square, he saw something on the floor near the rear wall. Several steps later he was looking down at a horror that triggered a memory: Markov's response when Quinn had asked him what haunted his castle.

"Bad deeds. Remnants of things I have done."

Moldering remains lay on the floor, a collapsed pile of bones and dust clad in the moth-eaten clothes someone had died in. The fetter that had held the prisoner chained to the wall hung loosely around one skeletal ankle. The decaying clothes—tie-dyed T-shirt, jeans, hiking boots—sparked another memory.

In researching this area before coming, Quinn had found mention of a hippie commune that had disappeared in the early '70s.

How far back and how deep did Markov's sickness go?

Quinn shone the flashlight on his watch. 5:19. He closed the door to the cell and made a quick inspection of the others to make sure no one alive was in them, then hurried along the rear wall of the castle toward the sound of the moaning. Forty paces later, he came to a much larger wrought iron gate and aimed his light between two of the bars. It penetrated ten yards or so into the gloom and revealed only barren earth. Faint light glowing from a considerable distance beyond gave Quinn the sense that this antechamber opened into a chamber that was huge.

The moaning was louder. The smell had become almost smothering.

He stepped back to aim his light at the ornate lettering he had noticed atop the gate when Johnny had intercepted him before:

Les Fleurs du Mal

Quinn stuck his key in the lock.

CHAPTER 47

The raspy moan of the hinges as the gate slowly opened was like the death rattle of the damned. The sound left icy trails on Quinn's scalp and back as he tucked the pepper spray into his waistband. Flashlight in hand, he quickly crossed the craggy stone floor of the antechamber, stopping at the short set of stairs that led down to the sunken Garden. Light from stands placed throughout the vast space, combined with the flickering gaslight from torches along the walls, enabled him to put away the flashlight.

What lay beyond that threshold was the ultimate realization of Markov's mastery of set design: a meticulously created burial chamber for the dead.

The moaning seized his attention and made him revise the thought:

Or the undead....

Several stone steps led down to the Garden. Peering out over the vast chamber from this higher vantage point, Quinn looked for Johnny. She had not yet arrived.

As he continued to scan the macabre scene in the pit below, he thought of Dante's concept of the Inferno as having ever deeper and more agonizing levels.

Markov's Garden of Evil was the nethermost level of his own private Hell.

Dozens of precisely arranged wooden coffins filled the space. Each rested on its own wooden bier to keep it off the dirt floor. All the lids had been left off and were propped against the coffins.

In the center of this underground necropolis, a single stone coffin rose higher than the rest. Its lid was in place, and what appeared to be a sculpture of some sort rested atop the lid. On all four sides, precise aisles running through the coffins ended at a neatly cleared perimeter around the stone coffin, as though the sarcophagus were the Capitol in this city of the dead.

The entire burial ground was situated under an elaborate dome-shaped vault, supported by four columns that created pointed arches on all sides. Obviously the work of skilled stonemasons, the structure conveyed the jarring air of a blasphemous cathedral, consecrating its unhallowed dead. Quinn wondered if the cobwebs scattered throughout were real or more set decoration.

The moans continued to ripple through the sea of coffins. Remembering Johnny's warning that he would be entering the bowels of Hell, Quinn continually scanned his surroundings as he warily descended the last section of stairs and made his way to the nearest aisle. Through a mullioned window high up on the castle wall, red-tinged moonlight shone down.

The pungent odor finally overpowered his jumble of sensory impressions. It had to be coming from the small plants in stands interspersed here and there in the gaps between the coffins. Quinn instantly recognized the flowering shrubs from a Dracula tour he had once taken through the remote villages of Transylvania.

Wolfbane.

It could only be here for one reason: to keep the undead at bay. The lights on stands placed throughout the chamber were not for illumination. They were the growing lights for Markov's botanical Garden of Evil. Their soft artificial glow combined with the flickering gaslight from the torches along the walls to create an eerie, writhing pulsation. Quinn became momentarily spellbound by the throbbing illumination, struck by the notion that it was the fluttering heartbeat of the light, locked in an eternally losing battle against the darkness.

Finally he began to move slowly between the rows of coffins on either side of the aisle, hoping the wolfbane would keep the restless dead from rising as he struggled to believe what he was seeing.

None of the bodies had completely succumbed to decomposition. Some were badly gone, with parts of the skeleton showing. On others the skin had remained intact, but had the desiccated, shriveled appearance of mummies. Some had ruddy cheeks and looked fresh....

The range of decay was probably the result of the bodies having been harvested over a long period of time, but another factor might be that the elixir worked better in some than it did in others.

Although all the eyes were closed, moaning escaped from some of the mouths. Standing in the middle of four coffins on either side of the aisle, he noticed that the moaning wasn't coming from all of the mouths. Sometimes one would fall silent, then another that had been still would emit the mournful sound. Throughout the massive chamber, moans erupted then died out, as though some invisible torturer of souls were floating through space, insinuating itself into one semi-corpse, then another, making sure they never rested in peace. It was like walking through a waiting room for the souls of the damned, trapped at the moment of their death throes, moaning to be released—either to complete their journey into the abode of the dead that waited below, or back into the world above to seek vengeance on the living.

As Quinn made his way through the coffins, the way the bodies were dressed added to his confusion. Their clothing was not the typical somber raiment of the dear departed. Some wore the attire of hunters or hikers; others wore nice casual clothing. He came to a dozen bodies grouped together that were dressed like hippies. T-shirts and jeans predominated. Some shirts were tie-dyed. On the front of one was the badly faded slogan: Make Love Not War. On another, a peace symbol.

The hippie commune that had disappeared…. Forty years ago….

As he continually scanned the vault for Johnny, he kept a wary eye on the corpses, half-expecting one of the undead to latch onto his arm and pull this new source of blood into its coffin. Just as he had convinced himself he was being paranoid, one opened its eyes and licked its lips. A jolt of fear shot through Quinn as he realized the full horror of Markov's secret chamber.

No special effects could be this good. These things were *real*.

Pale hands began reaching out to grab him as he hurried past the coffins. A few managed to snatch at his shirtsleeve, but they were too weak to hold on. Thankful for the wolfbane, he finally he reached the end of the aisle.

The elevated stone coffin lay several steps ahead, further

offset from the others by a perimeter of smoothly-packed earth that had been left completely clear—even of wolfbane—for easy passage. Curtailing his speculation about what it all meant, he urged himself forward to get an answer to his most pressing question:

In the twisted movie that had become George Tilton's life, who was the star attraction entombed in that stone coffin?

Quinn thought he knew the answer but hoped he was wrong.

Much wider than a normal coffin, the tomb rested on a trapezoidal stone bier several feet high. The nameplate on the bier confirmed his worst imaginings:

LADY ELINORE

1919-

Markov's beloved second wife. The one whose "vampiric urges" had become so strong he'd had to "put her away."

No death date....

Quinn went up a ramp at the end of the bier and stood on a wide ledge that ran on all four sides of the tomb. He became momentarily transfixed by the sculpture atop the lid of the coffin.

A Weeping Angel.

He'd seen many versions in his graveyard investigations, usually draped across or sitting beside an above-ground sarcophagus, a poignant expression of sorrow on its face.

This angel, however, did not convey the comforting feeling of a guardian from Heaven eternally protecting or grieving for a loved one.

This angel conveyed a sense of dread. The way she had thrown herself face down across the wide coffin lid, arms outstretched to their fullest extent so she could clamp her hands over the edge, looked like it had been an act of desperate urgency—as though she had needed to hurry before an evil spirit could get in.

Or was she trying to keep an evil spirit from getting out?

The expression on the angel's face conveyed another, much more disturbing feeling. It was an image like none Quinn had ever seen in a graveyard. Despite the beautifully sculpted wings on the prostrate figure's back, it was not the face of an angel. At least not the face of any good angel.

The eyes were open wide and showed only the stone equivalent of the whites, as though the eyes had rolled back in her head and a demon were taking over. The lips were parted far enough to reveal the teeth.

The incisors were elongated into fangs. Black stains trickled down from each corner of the mouth.

More evidence of Markov's mad set design? Or—like the polluted blood that flowed through his veins—had the castle's poisonous atmosphere seeped into the sculpture, replacing its original benevolent purpose with the soul-stealing thirst for blood?

The heavy stone lid of the coffin had shifted a few inches until the stone fingers the angel had clamped over the edge had broken off.

The tomb had been opened.

From the inside or outside?

Behind him the familiar voice slashed through the preternatural silence.

"There you are."

CHAPTER 48

"Jesus Christ you scared me," Quinn said as Johnny came up the ramp to stand beside him.

"Sorry," she said, "but pretty much everything is scary down here."

"Tell me about it. Are the cameras disabled?"

"Yes. Unless he overrides my command."

Quinn gave a sharp impatient shake of his head. "We can't keep playing that game, Johnny. Obviously it's better if we can take him by surprise, but if not, so be it. We still need to be as careful as we can, but whatever happens, happens."

"You're right. And you know what? Fuck him. If he sees us, he sees us. If the two of us can't kick his ass, then we deserve to die."

Despite the grimness of the situation, Quinn couldn't suppress a tight smile at the sudden outburst of profanity he wouldn't have thought she had in her. "I'm with you, Johnny. Except for the dying part."

"I know. I haven't lost my mind. Yes, we still need to be careful, but—whatever it takes—his reign of terror ends tonight." She quickly scanned the space around the bier, and

Quinn wondered if she thought one of the undead might have risen from its coffin. There were still the occasional moans, but nothing moved. "Wait here a second," she said.

She went down the ramp and disappeared under the bier. When she returned a moment later, her accelerated breathing seemed to stem from the excitement of getting ready for battle, rather than exertion. "Now the whole Garden is a blind spot."

"What did you do?"

"I bought us some time. I cut the cables to the cameras. I knew this day would come, so I hid some wire cutters down here."

"Good thinking," Quinn said.

"Now if Markov notices the cameras down here are off, he'll have to come down and fix it."

Quinn nodded, but didn't relax. She'd bought them minutes, at most. "Have you finished everything you need to do?"

"No. I still need to get to the barn to gather up the rest of the things we need for our attack."

"I thought you already did that with those two bags full of stuff you showed me."

She shook her head. "The things in the bags were only what I could carry. I left a lot of the bracelets and bear spray behind. Also the spear gun. Even with all that, some of the things that will come after us are not going to just keel over and lie there. Especially the monsters that live inside him. There might be situations where we only temporarily weaken whatever we're up against. Which is why I also want to get some things from the barn we can use to restrain them with."

"That all sounds good, Johnny, but we're running out of

time, and it still sounds like too much to carry. And even if you could, Markov might see you between the barn and here."

She shook her head again. "This is where Markov's paranoia helps us. He wanted to be able to shuttle things around without being seen, so there's an underground passage connecting the barn to the passage that leads from the lagoon to the Garden. And there aren't any cameras in either one. I can load up one of the ATVs and use those passages to get everything to the castle, then disable the cameras in the Garden just before I get there. I only need to leave them off for a couple minutes so I can go up the passage from the Garden to my fireplace. From there I can get everything ready in the privacy of my chamber, so we're ready to go when it's time to unleash the hounds of hell."

She looked at her watch. "It's almost five-thirty. Markov wants you to meet him in the Chamber of Horrors at six to go over the final sequence."

Quinn nodded. "I want to take a quick look around outside. He told me to familiarize myself with 'the set,' so if he sees me, I'll just be doing what he told me I should do. That still leaves us time to meet in your chambers and get everything ready. Can you be there by quarter to six?"

"I'll be there."

"We need to get moving," Quinn said, "but I can't leave here without answers to a few more questions. You can give me the short versions."

Johnny gave a curt nod.

Quinn pointed at the coffins he'd just walked through. "There's a section over there where people are dressed like hippies. I read about a commune that disappeared up here in the '70s. I'm guessing your father had begun to hunt. Am I right?"

"Yes. He justified it by saying they were on his land. First he would fetter them in the dungeon, giving them transfusions of the altered blood. When their blood had fully mutated into the elixir, he moved them into the Garden and kept them in this state of half-life so they would keep producing it. Over the years he kept adding people who had the misfortune of coming onto our land to create this netherworld of half-vampires."

"A heavy price to pay for trespassing," Quinn said.

"To him they aren't even human. They are just producers of the elixir that keeps him from aging. Markov sugarcoats the method by which he injects it into his victims by calling it 'vampiric'."

She impatiently waved the euphemism aside and leaned forward. "He bites them on the fucking neck, okay? Which turns them into hosts for replicating the Dracula Virus. They've become inhuman … *things*, that live only to drink blood. If any of them somehow escaped, they could spread a vampire plague that would destroy the human race."

"The Dracula Virus."

"Yes. What is now just a Garden of Evil would become a Forbidden Planet of Evil."

That image sent an icy chill skittering across Quinn's back. Confirmation that her father had been preying on humans for decades, in a demented quest for vampiric immortality, made it all the more imperative that he must be stopped. "That takes things far beyond anything I could have imagined, Johnny." He glanced out over the mass of coffins to make a quick estimate of the number. "There's at least a hundred of them, and only two of us. Plus whatever crawls out of Markov's id. Maybe it's time to call the police. And anybody else we can think of."

"*No.*" She said it with a vehemence that left no room for debate. "I cannot watch any more innocent people die. You've seen the monsters he has at his disposal. Outsiders couldn't begin to cope with the things he would throw at them. It would only bring confusion and death." She shook her head. "No. This is a fight that only I can finish." Her ferocity lessened a hair. "With you by my side."

Quinn was reluctant to abandon the idea of calling in help, but there was logic in her reasoning, and when she put it like that….

He reined in his runaway imagination to stay focused on their immediate priority. Even though Markov couldn't see them, he'd made it clear that the Garden was always his biggest area of concern. Whatever extra time Johnny had gotten them, it still couldn't be much longer before he'd come down to see what was wrong.

"We're in this together, Johnny." Instead of the tender look he expected, Quinn saw concern. "What's wrong?"

"He made a point of telling me to tell you that you're on your own. He wants me to keep making rounds, to make sure nothing interrupts the shoot. If we walk into the Chamber together, he'll be suspicious."

"Even if he is," Quinn said, "he wouldn't instantly launch an attack. He'd observe us first, to see if his suspicions were correct. We only need a minute or so to get on either side of him, give each other the nod, and take him down."

She shook her head. "I know him too well. I think he already suspects us of joining forces against him, and is trying to keep us apart. With everything that's at stake, he's going to be fully alert to the possibility of sabotage."

"Then two things have to happen," Quinn said. "We

have to give the acting performance of our lives when we walk in there—give him no clue that we've turned against him. And we need to pounce immediately, before he senses that something's up."

"I've spent my whole life acting. Piece of cake. And I am so ready to pounce."

"Good. There's just one more thing we need to deal with before we leave here." He pointed to where the lid on Lady Elinore's tomb had shifted. "When you walked up, I had just noticed that her coffin has been tampered with."

"Not tampered. Even though the love we had has turned to hate, I move the lid to tend to her needs."

"She's *alive*?"

"Yes."

"How does she breathe?"

Johnny pointed to ornamental rosettes sculpted along the sides of the tomb. "Those aren't just for decoration. In the middle of each one is an air hole." She paused long enough for Quinn to process that bit of information, then went on. "You said you needed to know what was down here to fully understand what you are up against. Nothing will show you better than letting you see what the Lord of the Manor has turned his beloved wife into." She nodded at the tomb. "My adopted mother. Above she was the Lady of the Manor. Down here she's the Queen of the Undead."

Johnny stepped toward Lady Elinore's tomb. "Help me with the lid."

Quinn marveled at her strength as they each grabbed an end and maneuvered the heavy concrete slab. They tilted it carefully over the edge and propped it against the tomb. Quinn's attention instantly became riveted on what lay within.

Although the body was wrapped in a bandage that appeared fresh, the head was completely exposed.

Lady Elinore lay on her back, eyes open and fixed straight ahead, apparently doomed to spend eternity staring up at the lid of her coffin, imprisoned alive in her final resting place that gave her no rest.

Her cheeks were ruddy and there were no signs of decomposition. Her bandaged hands, crossed over her heart, held a large ornate crucifix. A rosary hung around her neck. Despite these talismans to ward off evil, there was a demonic glow in her eyes.

The fiery glow burned hotter, until the eyes fixed their burning gaze on Johnny. In the few seconds that mother and daughter stared into each other's soul, Quinn saw the vaguest hint of a loving pity on Johnny's face. Only hatred glowed on Lady Elinore's. He wondered why it was there, and guessed that at least part of the reason was bitter envy: Johnny was still among the living, while she had been sentenced this obscene mockery of life.

"Why the rosary and crucifix?" he said.

"Because she's evil. The elixir has kept her alive, but the vampire blood keeps getting stronger—which has made her stronger. Before I put the rosary and crucifix in there, she had tried to escape. The Weeping Angel was not always as you see her now."

"What are you saying?"

"When we first put Elinore in her tomb, the Weeping Angel was the classic one I'm sure you've seen: sitting by the tomb, keeping a sad vigil over the soul of the dear departed. But several months ago, when I came down to give Elinore her nightly dose of the elixir, the angel had thrown herself across the tomb, and the lid had been moved." She closed her eyes and rubbed them, as though trying to erase the nightmare vision. "On Walpurgis Night."

The rational part of Quinn's brain wanted to protest the absurd notion that a stone sculpture could come to life, but the things he had seen and heard since coming here had begun to make him believe anything was possible. And Johnny was not delusional or making things up.

"April 30th," he said. "The night legend says that a portal opens between the natural and supernatural worlds, and witches and demons gather for a night of unbridled debauchery. The night when evil rules, according to some interpretations. It's the highest holy night in the modern Satanic calendar." He pointed to the angel. "One thing is undeniable: That's not the face of a loving protector."

"It was, originally. But for at least a year the vampiric emanations from Elinore have become so powerful, they've apparently begun seeping into the angel. Powerful enough so that on Walpurgis Night the angel tried to set her free."

"Free? In her condition? Free to do what?"

"To join Markov for his Grand Finale. They were deeply in love once. Kindred spirits, joined by their love of Dracula. He has been strengthening the dosage of the elixir, hoping to make her strong enough to be by his side at the end. The Mummy for his monster rally."

Quinn felt a chill as Lady Elinore's gaze slowly shifted to him and hardened. Her parched lips twitched, struggling to open. Johnny pulled a small water bottle from her pocket. She held it to the mouth, pulling the lips far enough apart for some of the liquid to dribble in. A low scraping moan began, as though air had begun to flow though frozen pipes. Johnny forced a little more water into the mouth, then moistened the lips.

She put the bottle away and pulled out a small vial. Moving her head so Elinore couldn't see, she made a face for Quinn, meant to convey that she had to do this in case Markov was watching. Turning back to Elinore she said, "Time for your medicine."

The liquid inside was red. She removed the cap and emptied the contents into the greedy mouth. An obscenely healthy pink tongue emerged from the wizened face to sensuously lick the lips.

The mummified remains stared at Quinn with distrust. Finally she emitted a hoarse whisper from the hollow depths of the grave.

"Who … is he?"

"His name is Adam. He is a guest."

"Then we must make him feel at home." Lady Elinore licked her lips again.

Johnny winced. "Ah. Yes. There's no place like home."

Their eyes locked onto each other in an unwavering stare. In that brief moment, Quinn saw Johnny's metamorphosis from cringing servant to independent woman reach completion. The loving pity he'd noticed when she'd first looked at Lady Elinore was gone. In its place was a blazing fierceness that left no doubt about the thought that fueled it: The grinning obscenity in the coffin was no longer the woman she had once called mother. It was a loathsome subhuman thing that needed to be destroyed. Quinn stood transfixed as he watched the hate streaming from Johnny's eyes burn away the last vestiges of the Johnny persona.

Johnny was dead.

She looked at Quinn and made a covert beckoning movement of her head. "Excuse us for a moment," she said to Elinore.

Quinn followed her to the end of the bier. "We need finish here and take care of Markov," she said, "before he gets suspicious and comes down. Once we eliminate him, we can come back here and turn this into a funeral pyre. Purge it of its evil."

"What about Elinore?"

"She is part of that evil. It is time for both of their unnatural lives to end."

"Are you going to tell her?"

"No. If Markov comes down here before we get to him, she could warn him. We have to maintain the element of surprise. Let's just say our good-bye and finish this."

They returned to the coffin and stood looking down at Lady Elinore. She must have sensed that whatever they'd needed to discuss privately could not bode well for her, because her defiant gaze of a moment ago was now one of fearful apprehension. Her eyes scanned their faces, apparently searching for clues to whatever conclusion they had reached. Finally her gaze regained some of its defiance and settled on Johnny. Lady Elinore spoke in that sepulchral voice.

"I know Markov's *destiny* is at hand. He has said as much during his midnight visitations, that it must happen tonight on the Blood Moon. Our mortal lives will end and our immortality shall begin."

In the brief moment that they stared deeply into each other's eyes, Quinn sensed that mother and daughter were searching for some last remaining spark of the love they'd once shared. If so they searched in vain. Only a cold indifference showed in their eyes now.

"Good-bye, Elinore," Johnny finally said. "I shall leave you to whatever fate Markov has decided for you."

"I think he was hoping I could make a cameo appearance in his monster rally climax."

"He's the director," Johnny said. "I'll leave that to him. Whatever happens, may we all rest in peace. Good-bye."

Without waiting for a response she motioned for Quinn to help her replace the lid. Just before they had it all the way closed, they heard a hollow whisper from within.

"This isn't over...."

Johnny walked away without showing any reaction. Quinn caught up with her in the aisle that would take them to the passage from the Garden to her apartment. Never slowing, they continued to walk briskly past the coffins lining the aisle. Johnny spoke loud enough to be heard over the sporadic moaning.

"I know we said to hell with Markov, but I still think you should give me a couple minutes head start when we get outside, in case he's watching. If he sees us together it won't help our cause."

"I'll wait. Then we'll have to take our chances."

"The second we finish with Markov, I'm coming back down here to light that fire, and the undead can finally sink into the earth." A flicker of emotion surfaced in her eyes, but her fierce determination quickly burned it away. "My father and I often read to each other over the years. Poe's *The Fall of the House of Usher* was his favorite. I just realized that the last line will make a fitting epitaph:

'The deep dank tarn ... closed sullenly and silently over the fragments of the House of Markov.'"

"Poe gets the last word," Quinn said. "Perfect."

CHAPTER 49

Markov stood on a ledge and watched them through a window high on the castle wall. Even from that considerable distance, as Dracula his supernatural night vision enabled him to see them having a private conversation at Lady Elinore's tomb. He saw them clearly enough to know that he was being betrayed by his own daughter. He couldn't let her throw some last-minute twist into his ending.

She can no longer be trusted. She is his now. And she can go to hell with him.

Whatever monsters got loose could go after them both. It would make the monster rally that much more exciting. The aura of red moonlight around Markov burned brighter, as he began envisioning possibilities for the best way to stage their comeuppance scene.

It wouldn't be easy. Johnny knew him well enough to anticipate his every move, and Quinn was obviously on her side. Two against one. He needed to monitor their movements and come up with a reason to keep them separated so he could deal with them one at a time.

First he needed to finish in the Garden.

Exerting all his will, he turned to fog and seeped through

the cracks along the window's edges. Once inside, he resumed his human form and scampered lizardlike down the castle wall. He quickly made his way through the dozens of coffins, gathering up all the wolfbane. By piling it into a mound at the bottom of the staircase that led to Johnny's apartment, he accomplished the dual purpose of allowing the undead to regain their strength, while keeping them from coming up the stairs and causing unforeseen problems. When he was done he walked through the coffins, looking for signs of returning vigor.

He was not surprised when he saw very few signs of it. The half-dead, purposely weakened for so long, would need some time to regain enough strength to move about. Some, he saw, might be too far gone to ever rejoin the living. Whether they did or not was of no concern to Markov. His only concern was the six newer, younger, stronger specimens he had brought into the fold—three men and three women he had hand-picked to start his new race. He had grouped them together to make them easy to check on, and he headed for that section now to observe their progress. He stopped short when he noticed something extremely disturbing.

Four of the nearby coffins were empty.

Had the missing bodies somehow gotten strong enough to escape? Or was this Johnny's doing? Had she revived them enough to wreak havoc on his movie?

He cast an uneasy glance around the Garden to see if they might suddenly emerge from the shadows and come after him. Nothing moved. Wherever they were, there was nothing he could do. They could have disappeared into the woods, or be wandering the castle. Instead of increasing his concern, that thought calmed him.

More monsters for the rally.

Feeling very much like he was in a horror film, he went to check on his chosen six.

All their eyes were open and alert. All gave him a knowing eager look when he approached.

They weren't strong enough to rise yet. But they would be. Soon.

He would come back to round them up after he checked on the movements of his betrayers.

CHAPTER 50

Quinn stood in the porte-cochère, giving Johnny her head start so they wouldn't be seen together.

He watched her quickly receding into the distance along the lane that led to the barn. As soon as she was out of sight, he headed down the lane in the same direction. A minute later he reached the rear of the castle and veered onto the perpendicular footpath that led to the lagoon. He looked up at the darkening sky.

A half hour of daylight at most.

"Do not venture too far into the woods," Markov had said, warning him about four-legged predators that may or may not be nocturnal. Quinn had no intention of venturing into the woods. He would be scanning them as he went for possible escape routes, but he didn't have much time, and his priority was getting a closer look at the lagoon. He wanted to see if there was any evidence of the shape he thought he'd seen rising up from the water last night. The more he knew about his battleground before he and Johnny went to war against Markov, the better.

About thirty yards along the footpath, it cut through a dense stand of trees before opening onto a swath, roughly ten yards wide, that had been cleared around Markov's version of Usher's tarn. Quinn kept going until he reached the thicket of reeds and aquatic plant life that shielded the lagoon. He stood perfectly still for a moment, acclimating his senses to this new environment.

Last night's storm had moved through, and though he could see another one blackening the sky in the distance, at the moment the grounds were utterly still and silent as the evening turned gray in the dying light. No birds sang. No breeze stirred the trees. The spreading cloak of darkness was turning the flat surface of the water black.

The calm before the storm, he thought.

Whatever he'd seen had been at the far end of the lagoon, about fifty yards from where he stood. He walked along the water's edge, scanning the dark surface and the tangle of brush for signs of anything unusual.

A few insects left tiny ripples as they skimmed the surface. The mouth of a large fish broke through the water to snag a bug, but the fish wasn't big enough to have been the thing Quinn thought he'd seen. The ripple caused by the disturbance quickly disappeared. By the time he reached the end of the lagoon, the water was glassy calm again. No underwater rocks created any swells, no plants protruded through, no debris of any sort floated on the smooth surface. Whatever he'd seen from his window last night could easily have been a trick of the light, the wind, or an overheated imagination. He walked along the edge of the woods that surrounded the lagoon, looking for anything unusual or possible escape routes. He saw only dense, untouched forest.

"I'm beating a dead humanoid," he muttered to himself. Wanting to cover as much ground as he could, he picked up his pace as he circled the end of the lagoon.

He didn't get far before something else caught his eye. Several yards from the water's edge, a small cluster of bubbles appeared on the surface, lingered briefly, then disappeared. Another cluster bubbled up a few seconds later, then another. He stared at the spot for another minute, but no more came up. His first thought had been that something was down there breathing, but if that was the case, why would the bubbles stop?

Maybe whatever it was had swam away. Or maybe it was gas escaping from an underground deposit. Or maybe—

He cut the thought short. Standing there speculating was a waste of time. Diving was the only way to know for sure if anything lurked in the lagoon. As far as he could tell, nothing did.

"Give it up," he muttered to himself, and got back onto the footpath to return to the castle. Halfway there he saw something he hadn't noticed on the way to the lagoon. A few yards to the right of the path, partially covered by weeds, a large rectangular panel was embedded in the ground. The padlocked handle made it obvious that it was the entrance to some underground space.

Johnny had mentioned an underground passage from the lagoon to the Garden. This might be a hatch for moving equipment in and out. She'd also said there were no cameras in the underground passages. Having access to it if they ended up outside might come in handy.

He looked at his watch. 5:37. He could spare a few minutes and still make his 5:45 meeting with Johnny. He pulled out his multitool and began sawing the u-shaped shackle of the padlock with the six-inch hacksaw blade. He made quick progress and was almost through when a large shadow gliding over the panel made him look up.

The pterodactyl.

With its enormous wings spread, it circled lazily overhead, like a buzzard homing in on prey. Quinn eyed the creature warily, wondering if Markov was just toying with him or if the pterodactyl had taken on a life of its own.

He quickly considered his options.

He could try to finish cutting the padlock and getting into the underground passage, but that could take another couple minutes, and it would leave him completely vulnerable with his back turned to the monster. It made no difference whether the pterodactyl or Markov was in control. Either way it could be on him in seconds.

The pterodactyl was getting closer. Too close to finish the padlock. He quelled the urge to run. It might look like he was trying to escape and trigger the pterodactyl's predatory instincts. Walking quickly he could reach the castle in a few minutes.

He'd have to take his chances.

He got onto the footpath, frequently looking up to make sure the prehistoric beast wasn't swooping down.

In the thick forest that bordered the footpath, a light wind whispered through the trees. Ahead, high on the castle wall, a single light glowed through the rectangular window of Markov's apartment. Quinn thought he saw a shadow glide past it. From this distance it was impossible to tell if it was inside or outside the window. Wondering if he was somehow being watched, and if Markov had sent the pterodactyl to let him know there was no escape, Quinn moved as quickly as he could without breaking into a run.

The whisper of the wind had become a steady moan, emanating from deeper in the woods. Hidden by the darkness, there was something of suffering and despair in the sound, as though the trees themselves were crying out to be rescued from a realm where evil ruled. Somewhere in that impenetrable gloom, another sound began fluttering through the moan of the wind.

Quinn froze, listening.

Invisible in its world of shadow, something skittered across fallen leaves.

An animal.

Four-legged.

Running. Fast. Parallel to the footpath.

The racing footsteps started from far behind him, in the darkness beyond the tree line. In a matter of seconds they streaked ahead—as though whatever it was meant to cut him off, maybe confront him. Moving fast, the sound quickly died out. Quinn remained still, listening to hear if the animal might be closing in, or if there were any others. Where there was one there might be a pack.

The darkness seemed to be holding its breath. Quinn thought he saw a hulking shadow streak across the clearing around the castle. At length, a sound coming from the general direction of the porte-cochère pierced the night.

A howl.

Markov's *troublesome* wolf? Or was it just him showing off again?

Quinn pulled the pepper spray from his waistband. He had to get back into the castle, and the only way he knew to do that was through the front door. There had to be other ways in, but there was no time to look for them.

Just before he stepped from the footpath onto the main access road, he heard what sounded like a motorized vehicle zipping along underground. It had to be Johnny, driving the

ATV with the supplies into the castle. He pressed the button on his watch that illuminated the dial.

5:43. He was supposed to meet Johnny in her chambers in two minutes. If Markov or one of his creatures was waiting for him at the front door, the plan to overtake him in the Chamber of Horrors at six would obviously be off. Quinn would have to have to improvise, and hope Johnny would figure things out and do the same.

Finger poised over the trigger button of the bear spray, flashlight in his other hand, Quinn hurried up the access road toward the porte-cochère.

CHAPTER 51

This morning when Max had been at his mother's grave and seen the thunderstorm coming, he had thought it would be fitting for the Gothic movie of his life to end on a dark and stormy night.

But this was no movie, and now his piece-of-crap car with its worn-out tires was slipping and sliding all over the place in the rain and mud. He was a bundle of raw nerves as he bounced through another section of potholes in the old logging road that led through the woods to the castle. Living there all those years, he'd made this trip many times, but that had always been in a sturdy four-wheel drive vehicle built to handle rough terrain. In his crapmobile, every time he hit a severe bump, or his wheels got caught in old tracks left by logging skids, he expected an axle to break or something bad to happen.

The thunderstorm that had been brewing in the distance had finally caught up to him, and was rapidly turning the pitted dirt road into a quagmire. The combination of heavy downpour and nightfall had reduced visibility to less than ten feet. Every severe bump or encounter with the logging tracks made him have to fight his way out of a fishtail, forcing him to slow to a crawl.

He tightened his grip on the wheel as he approached the narrow ridge through the quarry. Even in ideal conditions and a sturdy vehicle, the deep man-made gorge was intimidating. The ridge the excavators had left standing in the center for Markov to use as his Borgo Pass was only several feet wider than a car on either side—which made staying in the middle essential.

As Max eased his way onto the ridge, the poor visibility made it almost impossible to tell how close he was to the edge. He couldn't go much slower or he might get stuck in the mud, but the car was still fishtailing, even on the fairly smooth stretches. If he went over, the fall to the bottom would almost certainly kill him. Max was fighting back panic as it became harder and harder to keep from skidding out of control.

He was about two-thirds of the way across the muddy ridge when his tires fell into ruts left by an old logging vehicle. Sliding into ruts left by other vehicles on slippery unpaved roads was common in Vermont, and drivers quickly learned to ride them out. If you fought it, you could either damage your vehicle or come out of the rut suddenly, forcing you to make a quick correction that could lead to oversteering yourself into a tree or ditch.

Max knew all this. But unable to tell if he was in the middle of the ridge, and worried that, in these slippery conditions, the ruts might take him over the edge, panic finally overtook him. The wheel was pulling to the right, so he turned hard to the left.

The car lurched out of the ruts and went into a skid to the right. Max tried to correct by whipping the wheel all the way to the right, to no avail. The car kept sliding to the right, and even in this poor visibility, he saw the edge of the steep precipice fast approaching.

His heart almost exploded when he felt the rear wheels thump over the edge.

CHAPTER 52

Following the powerful beam of his flashlight as it pierced the darkness, Quinn neared the oasis of light in the porte-cochère.

Several feet short of the sheltered entryway, at the farthest dim reach of the light, he stopped to remain hidden from whatever might be waiting there. He clicked off his flashlight and shoved it into a rear pocket. He already had two magnetic bracelets on each wrist and ankle, but from another pocket he pulled out two more to use as projectiles if necessary. He also pulled out a canister of bear spray, then began walking silently along the path until he reached the edge of the porte-cochère. He eased his head just far enough in to see if anything lurked.

A man-shaped beast crouched in the shadows. It must have heard or smelled him, because it froze and whipped its head in Quinn's direction.

Its burning gaze locked onto him.

The lips receded, exposing rows of ferocious teeth. Deep in the beast's throat, a low savage growl began to rumble.

The things Quinn had seen and been warned about had conditioned him to be ready for anything, but still he wasn't prepared for this.

The portable control panel clipped to the waist told Quinn this was Markov. He was strangely dressed in the torn remnants of formal wear, but there was no doubt that he was now the Wolf Man. As in the movie, the forelegs were partially covered by the sleeves of a shirt, torn at the shoulders and open in front. The hind legs were covered by shredded trousers that barely reached below the knees.

Something was happening to the face.

It blurred exactly as Lon Chaney's had in the movie, when a series of dissolves showed the transition from wolf to human. But as Quinn continued to stare, different faces appeared in rapid succession, as though forces within were fighting for dominance.

Chaney.

Markov.

Chaney.

Markov.

As the fur and other werewolf features slowly disappeared, Lon Chaney as Lawrence Talbot gradually regained control. That face lasted only a few seconds before dissolving into Markov again.

Every instinct told Quinn to run, but this was the confrontation he and Johnny had wanted. They had planned on handling it together, but that hadn't worked out. If he ran, it would be a betrayal of Johnny, and Markov would have won.

Fight or flight.

He had grave doubts about the power of his weapons to stop the Wolf Man, but he had to trust them. They were all he had. Heart pounding, he released the breath he had been holding and stepped into the porte-cochère.

Another series of dissolves began and Markov quickly

became the Wolf Man again. He rose up on his hind legs and took a step toward Quinn, then another, until the beast towered over his prey, blocking the steps that led to the front door.

Quinn threw the bracelet. It bounced off. A growl rumbled in the werewolf's throat, much louder and angrier than before. The beast picked up the bracelet and studied it for a few seconds before flinging it aside.

The werewolf leaned down until its face was only inches from his. Quinn was about to shoot pepper spray into the inhuman yellow eyes when the sound of the front door opening seized both men's attention. The groan of the hinges sounded like Dracula's death moan when Van Helsing drives the stake into his heart.

Johnny stepped into the doorway, holding the spear gun. She shouted a taunt down to Markov. "Who's the impaler now?"

Rage contorted the Wolf Man's face as he drew himself up to his full height. He looked from Johnny to Quinn, clearly trying to decide how to deal with them both.

The Wolf Man began turning into Dracula.

In the seconds it took for the change to take place, Quinn's mind raced to make the adjustment from fighting a werewolf to fighting a vampire, going through a lightning quick inventory of the supernatural powers ascribed to vampires: they could transform themselves into werewolves, and back into vampires; they could become bats; turn into fog, even control the weather. But Quinn couldn't be sure about any of it. The Dracula legend was mythology created by writers and filmmakers. And the vampire's powers varied from book to book and movie to movie.

The Vlad Dracula that had inspired Stoker was a 15th-century ruler. Prince of a region that included Transylvania. Vlad Dracula—Vlad the Impaler—had been bloodthirsty in the extreme, but he was not a vampire. *Or was he?*

Markov believed that he was. He claimed to have preserved Dracula's severed head and his vampiric bloodline. Even claimed that he might be on the verge of bringing him back to life.

Was that what was happening now?

As Quinn watched the last traces of the Wolf Man disappear, he was certain about only one thing:

The magnetic bracelet had bounced off the wolf. Which meant the creature was a physical reality, not a digital illusion. And now Markov's version of Dracula stood before him—the hideous version from *The Blood of Dracula.*

"Come!" Johnny shouted down at him, brandishing the spear gun. "Take your chances against me!"

Dracula looked up at her. A sinister grin formed on the vampire's lips as he pushed a button on the control panel at his waist. He turned his gaze to Quinn. "I'll leave *you* to take *your* chances against the creature that once fought King Kong."

The pterodactyl landed just beyond the end of the porte-cochère. One deliberate, lurching step at a time, the creature began circling the porte-cochère, wings tight against its sides. "Good luck," Markov said before turning back to Johnny.

"Father against daughter," he shouted up at her. "So it has come to this."

As she swung the spear gun around to aim it at him, he turned into a giant bat and flew out of the porte-cochère. Quinn sprinted to see where he was going. Markov flew up to his apartment window, changed into fog, and seeped inside.

Quinn started to run toward Johnny so he could warn her, but the pterodactyl now stood between him and the front door. Unblinking predatory eyes bore into him—pools of primeval savagery born eons ago. Staring back, resisting every urge to run, Quinn extended both arms to get their magnetic wristbands as close as possible to the creature.

Unfazed, the monster took a lurching step toward him. Maybe it was too far away for the magnetism to reach.

Or maybe it's real.

"Run!" Johnny yelled.

"Markov is inside!" Quinn yelled back. "In his apartment!"

"I'll deal with him. Run!"

Quinn back-pedaled out of the porte-cochère as fast as he could. The pterodactyl continued its lurching march toward him.

As it got within striking distance, Quinn pulled out the pepper spray and aimed at eyes narrowed for the kill.

The creature emitted a soul-ripping shriek that drove Quinn back. One flap of its enormous wings propelled it above his head before he could release the spray. In the next instant he felt talons digging into his shoulders. The pain was so intense he dropped the spray to free his hands and try to pull the talons off.

The pterodactyl was flying away with him.

They were headed in the direction of the lagoon and the forest beyond. He had to do something fast, before they got too high or too far.

He reached up and pulled on one of the talons. It dug deeper. Shards of moonlight glittered on the surface of the lagoon. They'd be there in seconds.

My knife.

Forcing himself to remain calm, he reached behind,

unzipped the security pocket in his waistband, and pulled out the multitool. The lagoon was seconds away. Quinn extracted the knife from its slot and slashed one of the talons. The pterodactyl shrieked and released its grip on that shoulder, squeezing harder on the other.

Quinn dangled from the beast's claws at least fifty yards above the water and getting higher every second. Hitting the water from this distance could cause serious injury, might even kill him, but hitting the trees or the ground would be worse. The water was his best chance, and they were halfway across the lagoon, approaching the end where he thought he'd seen a shape. They'd be over the trees in seconds.

He slashed the talons gripping his shoulder. With another soul-chilling shriek the pterodactyl released its grip. As Quinn saw the water zooming toward him, he curled himself into a ball and covered his face to prepare for the impact. It sounded like a gunshot when he slammed into the water, but the need to breathe obliterated any thoughts of pain. Quinn uncurled himself as he sank to the bottom. He landed on his feet in soft mud. The impact bent his legs at the knees, and from that crouch he launched himself toward the surface. As he shot upward, he glimpsed something partially concealed by a tall thicket of seaweed, as though hiding. It looked like a much more sinister version of the Creature from the Black Lagoon. Its eyes were closed, its body limp. There were other alien shapes floating at the bottom among the kelp. Quinn guessed this must be a dumping ground for Markov's failed attempts at creating movie monsters. But why were chains fettered around their ankles?

Just before the Creature disappeared from view, its eyes opened. Even in the dim glow of the moonlight, there was no mistaking it: Their demonic red glow was trained on him.

CHAPTER 53

Max's car teetered like a seesaw, half on and half off the ridge. Heart thumping, he opened the door and threw himself onto the flat surface of the ridge.

The car wobbled for a moment before coming to rest. Most of the trunk hung over the edge. The next gust of wind could slam against the open door and send the car falling.

The sword. He couldn't finish this without the sword. It was in the trunk.

Max scrambled to his feet and pushed the button on the door that opened the trunk. His heartbeat raced as he waited to see if the force of the lid popping open would upset the precarious balance. Several seconds went by without any movement. He released the breath he'd been holding. He went to the trunk and opened the lid as gently as he could.

The sword had come to rest at the rear of the trunk, which hung several feet over the edge. He couldn't reach it from where he stood.

He had to have that sword.

He looked down to see if there was anywhere he could step to get closer. An outcropping of rock extended a few feet beyond the ridge. Two, three steps would get him there.

Rain splashed against his face. Max took one tentative step onto the outcrop, then another. He moved his feet slightly to test his footing, ready to jump back onto the ridge if they started to slip. They didn't. He was only another step or two from the side of the trunk. Just as he lifted his foot to take the first one, he heard a loud grinding noise.

The car inched farther over the edge.

Max hurried to the trunk as fast as he dared and leaned in. The loud grinding became a roar as the car began to topple over the edge. Max's fist closed on the hilt of the sword. He jumped back, a split-second before the car disappeared into the abyss. The jostling made him lose his footing. He twisted his body and threw his weight backward as he fell. He landed on the outcropping, inches from the sheer drop. Clutching the sword, he scrambled on hands and knees back onto the flat surface of the ridge. He crawled several feet to get away from the edge and collapsed.

He lay in the mud and rain for several moments, catching his breath and gathering the strength to move on. Finally he stood and looked at how far he had left to go. About fifty yards to the end of the ridge. The castle was a mile beyond that, and now he'd have to get there on foot, soaking wet. The rain was tapering off, but jagged bolts of lightning still exploded above the castle.

In the flashes of intermittent light, Max saw a dim red glow over the castle, obscured by the massive black storm cloud. Slowly, a hole began opening in the section of cloud that concealed the glow. Having been trained from childhood to see the world through the eyes of a filmmaker, Max envisioned the hole as an iris fade-in for the climax of Markov's movie. When the source of the red glow was fully revealed, the hole stopped expanding, as though framing the focal point of the shot.

The Blood Moon stared down like the eye of Satan, beaming its demonic energy into Markov's accursed pile. The image became so powerful that, standing there clutching the sword, Max began to envision himself as a lone Crusader, the one man who could reclaim this land from someone who worshipped—wanted to *be*—a character whose name meant Son of the Devil. A surge of self-righteousness propelled Max forward. Stepping carefully along the muddy ridge, when he finally made it across and began the mile-long march to the castle, his stride became a cocky strut.

The lightning continued to shred the sky above the castle, but the rain had stopped, and for the first time since leaving home this morning, Max felt sure he was going to succeed in his quest. He threw off his wet jacket and increased his pace. He was soaked to the bone and cold. The exercise would warm him. When he reached the castle he could get dry clothes from Johnny's wardrobe before dealing with Markov.

Halfway to the castle a flash of lightning illuminated something about thirty yards ahead. What Max saw brought him to a sudden halt.

From each side of the thick woods that hugged the lane, a shadowy figure emerged and began shambling toward him. Despite their unsteady gaits, the pair rapidly came together to block his path. At first Max thought they might be drunken campers or hunters, but as they came closer, their cadaverous frames and tattered clothing made it clear they were much worse.

They were *flowers* that had escaped the Garden. Or—

Maybe they hadn't escaped. Max thought of the letter he

had sent, telling Markov he was coming to kill him. Maybe Markov had revived the undead enough to act as sentinels. They certainly weren't behaving like half-dead corpses that had languished in their coffins for years. They moved into the best position for cutting him off—too close together for him to bull through, and too close to the woods for him to go around—with a surprising quickness that showed a sharpness of mind and intense focus on their task.

Max had to do something fast. They were barely twenty yards away now.

Striking off into the woods wasn't an option. More of them might be waiting in there—or if not them, some of Markov's other "creatures of the night." And as dark as it was, Max would essentially be blind.

He couldn't retreat. That would take him away from the castle, costing him time he didn't have. And it wouldn't solve his problem. He would still have to get around these things to get to Markov.

A rustling noise behind him made him snap his head around.

Two more were shuffling toward him. Retreating was no longer an option.

He would have to stand and fight.

As the undead closed in around him, uncertainty came into their eyes when they saw the sword. Seeing their hesitation, Max let out a maniacal yell and began thrusting and slicing with controlled fury. The attack took them by surprise. Years of inactivity had dulled their reflexes. One lunged at him, but could make only a feeble sidestep to avoid his parrying thrust.

The sword ran straight through the attacker's chest. It was dead when it hit the ground.

Max kept the rest of them at bay with maniacal swings of the sword. Finally another of the undead gathered enough courage to make a lunge. Max countered with a vicious swipe.

The sword almost took its head off. Still attached by a few inches of flesh, the head flopped onto the chest. Blood spurted like a fountain as the eyes closed and the thing collapsed into a lifeless pile on the ground.

The eyes of the remaining two lit up when they saw the blood draining from the defenseless corpse. They fell to their knees and pressed their mouths to the huge gash.

Max quelled his revulsion at the loud slurping noises. He wanted to kill the foul bloodsuckers, but it might not go quickly, and others might show up to block his path. This wasn't the battle he had come here to fight.

The sky over the castle had cleared. The red moon shone down on it with full force, and even though the rain had stopped, bolts of lightning still bombarded it as though hurled by a wrathful God. Again feeling like a lone Crusader, the one chosen to administer the killing blow to evil, Max hurried toward the castle.

CHAPTER 54

Markov stopped at the landing in front of the Chamber of Horrors to begin his search for Johnny. He had to be careful. She had the advantage. The spear gun could kill from a distance. The impalement stake couldn't. There were other weapons he could use, but....

A spark of tenderness flared up from the embers of his love for his daughter, but was quickly extinguished by the ever-stronger vampire blood replicating itself in his veins.

Wear the crown well, Vlad Dracula had said.

Markov was the vampire prince now. If he could not defeat a mere mortal with her toy, he did not deserve to wear the crown.

His grip on the impalement stake tightened.

It has to be this way.

He plucked the control panel from his hip and quickly scrolled through the castle's monitors. Johnny was nowhere to be seen, which didn't surprise him. She knew all the blind spots, and was much too smart to let him find her that way. And she had her own control panel. She could search the monitors just as he could and stay one step ahead of him.

He took his eyes off the corridor to clip the master

control back onto his waistband. When he looked up, Johnny was just rounding the corner guarded by the Grim Reaper. She halted when she saw him. She had the spear gun.

Fifty yards of corridor stretched between them as each calculated their next move.

He had been with her when they'd picked out the spear gun several years ago. Since it was only going to be used in the lagoon, they had decided on one that was lightweight and easy to handle. It had turned out be awkward and difficult to aim, and the line attached to the shaft gave it a maximum range of only ten yards, but still—he had to get it away from her before she got that close.

Markov's head swiveled skyward, in the direction of the Blood Moon that he knew was growing ever larger above the castle.

He pushed a button on his master control.

The Grim Reaper stepped down from its pedestal. The cameras in the eyeless sockets locked onto Johnny. Both skeletal hands gripped the scythe to administer the killing stroke. One swipe of its razor-sharp blade could easily remove her head.

The grinning, black-robed skeleton began following her up the corridor. Johnny's cautious advance allowed the lumbering Reaper to gain on her. It was about five yards behind. Markov waited until she was about twenty yards away.

"The moment of truth," he said.

Seeing his hand moving toward his master control, Johnny quickly looked around to see what he was activating.

The Grim Reaper was almost on top of her. She swung the spear gun up to fire. Markov pushed a button. The

Reaper swung the scythe. It hit the spear gun just as Johnny fired and the spear skittered down the hall. The Reaper brought the scythe back into an upright position and stood at attention, awaiting its next command.

Johnny dropped the spear gun and turned back to face Markov. He stood several steps away with the impalement stake pointed at her.

"Did you really think you could defeat your master?" he said.

"I do, yes."

"Prepare to face your destiny." Markov took a step toward her.

"Two can play the destiny game." Johnny pressed a button on her master control.

The Grim Reaper began moving again. Johnny stepped aside, and the black-robed skeleton continued advancing toward Markov. The skeletal hands brought the scythe into position for the kill. Keeping a wary eye on the blade, Markov backed along the corridor. He pushed the button that would stop the Reaper.

It kept coming. The relentless approach of Death, as it made its ungainly, hitching way toward him, was made even more chilling because it came without making a sound.

When he had put enough distance between them, Markov stopped backing and pointed the stake at the Reaper's chest. He would hate to lose one of his favorite set pieces, but this thing was hell-bent on killing him.

And he was Vlad Dracula, he reminded himself. Draculas didn't run. They made others run.

Death kept coming. Markov thrust the stake at the spot where the heart would be, knowing it didn't have one but allowing for any possibility in the virtual world he had created—a nightmare blend of the digital and the real, swirling around him like a gathering maelstrom.

The Reaper's jerky movements made him miss, and the stake shot through the space between two ribs. Unexpectedly finding no resistance, Markov stumbled forward and slammed head-on into Death. Its backward stagger, combined with Markov's instinctive recoil, withdrew the stake. Markov scurried backwards to get beyond the range of the scythe, but Death could let no one escape. It quickly regained its balance and lunged forward, bringing the scythe around with a vicious swipe.

It sliced through the stake, missing Markov's hands by inches. Markov threw the stub at the Reaper and backed hastily up the corridor.

Johnny stepped out from behind the Reaper. She pushed the button to deactivate it and quickly closed on Markov. Before he could react she shot a blast of bear spray. Frantically rubbing his eyes, he let out a roar so loud it seemed like it might crumble the stone walls. His hands grew larger and hairier. He was turning into the Wolf Man.

Johnny aimed the spray again but he slapped it from her hand. She turned to run, but his huge paw clamped onto her neck and spun her around. Hatred blazed in the werewolf's eyes as he blinked away the final effects of the spray. His voice was hoarse and guttural through the altered vocal cords. "Your pathetic little rebellion has failed. Quinn is carrion for the pterodactyl, and now I must treat you like anyone else who tries to overthrow the crown."

He dragged Johnny to the Reaper, who stood motionless, awaiting its next command. The Wolf Man slammed Death to the floor, then savagely pulverized its grinning skull with repeated blows from his huge paw.

Still holding Johnny by the neck, he bounded to the end of the corridor and dragged her down the stairs to the subterranean chamber.

CHAPTER 55

Quinn broke through the surface of the lagoon gasping for breath. The image of the demonic eyes of the Creature burned in his brain. There had been *life* in those eyes. Predatory life. Whether the thing down there was real or virtual, if it was capable of movement, he was directly above it.

He began swimming toward the nearest shore as fast as he could. His heart pounded as much from fear as the need for air. If he looked back to see if the amphibian thing was following him, it would slow him down—but he had to know. If it *was* coming after him, he could at least try to defend himself or take evasive action. Still swimming furiously, he looked back.

Just below the surface, a hulking shadow was streaking toward him like a torpedo. From its shape there was no mistaking what it was. He was only a few yards from shore, but the Creature was closing fast.

Quinn scrambled up onto land. Chest heaving, he stood and faced the lagoon to see if the Creature would leave the water to continue the chase.

Its head broke the surface. The demonic eyes locked

onto him. Backpedaling, Quinn pulled a canister of bear spray from his pocket. The eyes burned a hotter red just before the Creature sank out of sight beneath the water.

Keeping a wary eye on the lagoon, he pulled the phone from his pocket that Johnny had said would get her and only her. He speed-dialed 1.

Nothing.

He tried again.

Dead.

The water must have ruined it. Or—

Markov might have caught her and destroyed hers.

He took off running as fast as he could. He stopped when he came to the hatch that opened into the tunnel connecting the lagoon to the Garden. It wouldn't take long to finish sawing through the lock, and the tunnel was the quickest way to the staircase that led to Johnny's apartment.

He knelt and began sawing where he had left off. A minute later the lock popped loose. He opened the panel enough to ease himself onto a set of makeshift wooden steps, then silently closed it behind him. He descended the few steps until he stood in the middle of the passage.

No light or sound penetrated the gloom. Quinn pulled out his flashlight and clicked it on. As powerful as the small light was, it only reached about fifteen yards into the darkness. Aiming it first in the direction of the lagoon, then in the direction of the Garden, Quinn saw nothing but the earth walls and ceiling of the passage. A few scattered puddles glistened on the dirt floor. Here and there were pieces of seaweed that must have washed up from the lagoon.

Soaking wet, eager to get into dry clothes, he had barely started heading toward the Garden when he heard faint sounds. He stopped to listen.

A dragging sound, followed by a clanking sound. Coming from the direction of the lagoon.

Shhhht.

Clank.

It kept repeating at regular intervals.

Shhhht.

Clank.

Each repetition brought it closer.

Quinn aimed his flashlight beam in the direction of the sound. Two red pinpoints of light emerged from the gloom and grew steadily larger.

The demonic eyes of the Creature. It shuffled toward him, dragging the chain it had broken loose from whatever had anchored it.

Quinn turned and sprinted toward the Garden. Behind him he heard the Creature continuing its relentless advance, but the sounds gradually faded as the distance between them increased.

Ahead, the light coming from the Garden allowed him to click off his flashlight. As he crossed the threshold, unexpected movement brought him to a sudden halt.

Three of Markov's "Flowers of Evil" had risen from their coffins. They had appeared to be aimlessly shuffling about, but at the sound of Quinn's approach their heads snapped around.

They began weaving their way through the coffins, apparently with the intention of heading him off. Quinn ran down the nearest of the four aisles that that terminated at Lady Elinore's tomb. As he approached her coffin, something was very wrong. He needed to keep going to the aisle on the other side that would take him to Johnny's staircase, but he couldn't ignore what he was seeing. He slowed to a walk and and proceeded with extreme caution. If the undead managed to get ahead of him he'd have to deal with it.

He and Johnny had placed the lid back on Elinore's tomb. Now it was propped against it. The lid was extremely heavy. Who could have taken it off? Those three? Markov as one of his superhuman monsters?

Lady Elinore?

No. She could not possibly have gone from her near-dead state to being that strong.

Quinn thought of the impossible things he'd seen since coming here. *This isn't over*, she had said.

Maybe….

The three undead were slowly catching up. The one leading the pack ran a tongue across its lips, exposing its fangs.

Quinn had to keep moving. Find Johnny. But he had to know if Elinore had gotten loose.

He ran up the steps of the bier to look inside her tomb.

It was empty.

He staggered back and quickly looked around. The only thing moving was those three. The leader broke away and headed up the ramp to the bier. The others kept going toward the far side of the Garden, probably to block the entrance to Johnny's passage—the only other way out.

The leader stepped onto the bier and shambled relentlessly toward Quinn. It was blocking his path to the ramp. Quinn backed away and looked to see how far it was to the ground.

Far enough to make a jump risky.

The undead thing reached out to grab him.

He jumped.

Ignoring the pain as he crumpled to the ground in a heap, he scrambled to his feet and sprinted up the next aisle.

When he reached Johnny's staircase, the two undead were looking at each other in confusion as they backed away from a large mound that blocked the entrance.

That wasn't there before, Quinn thought. *What was it that had them afraid?*

Whatever it was, it seemed to be holding them at bay. They were to the right of the mound, so Quinn went to his left. As he got closer to the mound he recognized the look and smell.

Wolfbane.

Markov must have removed it from the Garden to set his minions free. Which meant more could be loose.

The undead eyed him from the other side but came no closer. Quinn stuffed as much of the wolfbane into his pockets as he could and squeezed past the mound onto the stairs. He bolted up the staircase, ready to barrel past anything that got in his way.

A moment later he was in Johnny's fireplace. Just as he was about to emerge from that shadowy void into her bedchamber, something clamped onto his ankle. Instantly thinking it was the severed hand, he pulled out a canister of bear spray. But when he looked down, the hand was covered in bandages. And it wasn't severed.

"I told you this wasn't over."

Lady Elinore's voice was much stronger now. And her grip was like a vise. Quinn took several awkward steps into Johnny's apartment, dragging Lady Elinore with him. She finally released her grip and struggled to her feet, stumbling slightly before she stood facing him. The hatred he'd seen in her eyes when she was in the tomb burned hotter now.

"How did you get out?" Quinn said.

"My husband set me free."

"After all these years? Why?"

She motioned to her body wrapped in bandages. "He thought having a mummy for his monster rally would be a nice touch. He has other reasons, which I can't divulge. He's the director, and he insists on being the one to reveal how the ending unfolds. I can tell you this: When this picture is wrapped, he plans to do a sequel. Do things better this time."

"With the movie or your lives?"

"They are one and the same."

Markov had said the same thing. His brainwashing had been thorough. "Where is he?"

"Going after Johnny. We both are. She's been a bad girl. She must be punished." Her lips parted in the mockery of a smile. Among her rotting teeth Quinn saw two glistening white fangs. The elixir was taking over.

He had to find Johnny. He looked across the room to her control panel, thinking he might be able to see her on one of the monitors. All were dark.

Elinore responded to his puzzled look. "Markov turned them off. He doesn't want you to see what we're doing. The ones in his apartment are still on. We can see without being seen."

"I'll find her."

"You're probably too late." She smiled the obscene smile again.

Quinn needed to find something to restrain her with before he left. Even in her weakened state, she could pose a threat. He grabbed her by the arm and squeezed. "Come with me."

She swung her free arm at him. He blocked the feeble attempt and squeezed harder. "You can make this hard or easy. But I don't care if you're in league with Satan himself, you're coming with me." He squeezed harder. She howled in pain as he dragged her to the kitchenette. Still holding onto her arm, he rummaged through drawers and cabinets. When he opened the knife drawer, she shot her free hand into it and tried to grab a knife. He slammed the drawer on her hand.

She let out a sound that was half moan, half scream, and looked at her hand as though she thought it might fall off. Rage blazed in her eyes. "You'll pay for this."

He ignored the threat and kept searching. Under the sink he found a clothesline still neatly coiled in its original cardboard holder. He jammed it into his waistband and dragged her to the four-poster bed. He swept her up onto it, then pinned her by sitting on her with his knees on her arms. Her feeble struggle lasted only a moment before she became still. Quinn pulled out his knife and cut the line into four pieces, easily overcoming her resistance as he tied her by the wrists and ankles to the four posts.

At the foot of the bed he took a last look to make sure she was secure. "Rest in peace," he said, and headed for the door without waiting for a response.

On the way to the door he noticed the two canvas bags full of weapons he and Johnny had left there. One was filled with magnetic bracelets and bear spray; the other had a hammer and stakes, wolfbane, garlic, the flamethrower, an extra can of fuel, and the pistol with the silver bullets.

Wanting to be ready for anything, he grabbed the bags and exited the chamber.

CHAPTER 56

As eager as he was to find Johnny and finish Markov, Quinn needed to get out of his wet clothes first. They were sticking to him and impeding his mobility, which could get him killed.

He sprinted down the corridor in the direction of his chamber. As he neared the corner where this hallway intersected the next, a warning jolt of adrenaline brought him to a sudden stop.

The Grim Reaper was gone.

Markov had removed the wolfbane so his undead could escape ... freed Elinore to become his mummy ... the Creature from the Black Lagoon was alive ... the pterodactyl ... now this....

Clearly Markov's monster rally had begun. And he was in the middle of it.

Moving warily past the Reaper's empty pedestal, he eased around the corner just far enough to see if Death was waiting for him.

The corridor was empty. Quinn moved cautiously to his door several steps away. He hesitated before entering, thinking of all the things that could be waiting on the other side of the door: the Grim Reaper with its scythe; the suit of armor with its halberd; the severed hand. The undead could have come up the secret stairway and be hiding behind the bookcase.

Anything was possible. Nowhere was safe.

He had to press on and find Johnny.

He set the bags down and pulled out his flashlight. He opened the door to his chamber slowly, probing the darkness before entering. When he saw nothing moving and heard no sound, he followed the beam of light a few cautious steps into the room. To his right, on the far side of the chamber, faint moonglow in the oriel was the only other illumination. Everything else was cloaked in darkness. He pulled the bags inside and closed the door. Continually casting his light about, he went to his wardrobe and reluctantly set the flashlight on a shelf to free his hands.

He grabbed a towel and dried himself off, then quickly changed into a dry version of what he'd been wearing: long-sleeved T-shirt under a pullover, cargo pants, fresh socks and hiking shoes. He transferred the multitool from the wet pants to the security zipper pocket inside the waistband of the dry ones. When he reached the door, he opened the bag with the magnetic bands and bear spray. He fastened three fresh bands around each wrist and ankle, filled his pockets with the bands and spray, and closed the bag. Before exiting, he made one more attempt to reach Johnny on her cell phone, knowing it would probably be futile.

It was. The line was still completely dead. He put the phone in an empty pocket and took a moment to decide where to begin looking for her.

They had originally intended to overpower Markov in the Chamber of Horrors. Even though that plan had been shot all to hell, it was the only thing he had to go on. He would start there. He picked up the canvas bags, exited his chamber, and began moving quickly down the long corrridor. A short distance past the entrance to Johnny's apartment, a disturbing sight made him stop.

The Grim Reaper lay in a lifeless pile on the floor, its skull smashed to dust. Johnny's spear gun lay nearby. It had been fired. A little farther down the corridor was the scythe Death used for harvesting souls.

Johnny must have confronted Markov here.

A horrible vision of her writhing on his impalement stake inflamed Quinn's seething anger. He kept it in check by telling himself she might be somewhere safe, that she might have defeated him.

He pulled a canister of spray from his pocket and shoved it into his waistband, then continued down the hallway, hesitating when he reached the entryway of the Chamber of Horrors. As much as he needed to have the weapons with him, if Markov was in there, and saw him walk in with the bags, the element of surprise—Quinn's only real advantage—would be gone. Markov might even be lying in wait on the other side of the door, which made it imperative that Quinn have both hands free from the moment he walked in.

He pulled out the flamethrower and left it within easy reach. He shoved the pistol with the silver bullets into his waistband beside the bear spray and concealed them under his pullover, then placed the bags in the far corner and went to the entrance.

Flickering shadows cast by the gaslights animated the painted gargoyle leering down into an eerie semblance of life. Dante's inscription at the entrance to the Inferno flashed in Quinn's mind: Abandon hope all ye who enter here.

He tore his attention away from the lurid mural to prepare himself for whatever might await beyond the door. Steeling himself against the possibility that Markov might already have defeated Johnny—and was waiting inside to do the same to him—Quinn entered cautiously, pausing inside the door while his vision adjusted to the movie monsters forever poised on the brink of attack. In Markov's impossible otherworld, any one of them might start moving … might even come after him.

He scanned the shadow-filled room for any sign of movement. Nothing seemed to be amiss. For a moment he was struck by Markov's skill at lighting. In the discreetly hidden and carefully focused illumination, his collection of monsters appeared to be—like Nosferatu—emerging from a sinister world of shadow on an eternal hunt for humans to satisfy their unnatural cravings.

As he weaved his way through the Chamber, Quinn's senses remained on full alert, even as he thought of the thousands of hours Markov must have spent in here. His movie world, his forbidden planet, inhabited only by monsters and demons. At the far side of the room, Quinn approached the exhibit that represented the origin of the Dracula mythos, and its continuation in the warped vampiric realm of his spiritual descendant. Set apart from the others in the far corner, the internally lit display case cast a surreal glow. The stark contrast between the lighted showcase and the surrounding darkness made Quinn think of the infamous tenant as a disembodied soul, doomed forever to be poised at the threshold between the dead and the living.

He reached the exhibit and peered into the gloom to see if Markov was lurking there. He wasn't. Quinn's attention was drawn into the showcase of Markov's most prized relic.

Even with its eyes closed, the face behind the glass exerted a mesmeric pull. Quinn wondered how much of the irresistible attraction was due to simple fascination with the Dracula story, and how much had to do with Markov's claim that this was the severed head of Vlad Dracula himself.

The subdued spotlight brought the faintest trace of color to the deathly pallor, but there was no sign of life. Still, Markov had insisted this was not a sculpture, but the real thing. And that it had been kept some semblance of alive for over five hundred years.

If Markov's story were true, Quinn was staring into the face of a ruler whose altered blood continued to flow in the veins of a demented carrier of his vampiric bloodline. A ruler who, besides lopping off countless heads himself, had spilled a sea of blood during a reign of unspeakable cruelty. A reign that had included thousands of impalements, the stakes usually driven through the anus or vagina and coming out the mouth.

He tried to pull himself away to continue his search for Johnny, but as he probed the face for any sign of life, his gaze kept being drawn to the eyes. With his focus narrowed onto the closed eyelids, he wasn't sure if he'd seen a slight movement lower on the face.

Had the lips just twitched?

Perhaps it had been a shadow caused by a flicker from the spotlight bulb. He kept his attention centered on the mouth while widening his field of vision to include the bulb.

It continued to burn steadily.

This time there was no mistaking it.

The lips were moving.

Another movement behind the eyelids.

They sprang open.

Accusatory eyes locked onto Quinn.

The mouth opened and a long, shuddering groan oozed out. The fierce gaze sharpened into a piercing beam of hate.

The mouth spoke with a Romanian accent.

"You … must die."

CHAPTER 57

A rustling noise made Quinn jerk his head around. Markov emerged from the shadowy void beyond the showcase, dressed in his familiar black.

Oh Christ. Where's Johnny?

Markov wasn't wearing the glove and goggles he used to animate his creations, but his portable master control was attached to his hip.

Vlad could still be one of his special effects. And whatever else he might have running around loose.

Quinn pulled out the bear spray. His finger was poised over the trigger button. "Stop right there. Where's Johnny?"

"Wait!" Markov held out his hands to show he wasn't holding a weapon. "I am not here to harm you."

"Bullshit. I've just barely escaped being killed by a bunch of your monsters, while you were going after Johnny as Vlad the fucking Impaler. *Where is she?*"

"Below. I came to my senses at the last second. I locked her away to keep her safe while I came here to pull myself together."

"Locked her away?"

"In the dungeon."

Quinn wanted to empty every canister of spray he had on this madman, but that would enrage him, and rage was one of the triggers that could turn him into the Wolf Man or Dracula. If they were part digital, even the silver bullets might not stop them.

It took every ounce of self-control for Quinn to quell his anger. He shoved the bear spray back into his waistband. "Vlad just opened his eyes and looked right at me. He told me I must die. Is he one of your robotic creations?"

"No. This is what I wanted you to see for yourself. It cannot be just magnetism or some outside influence." Markov nodded at the severed head that still watched them. "Who knows what forces I ... he ... *we* have unleashed in this cauldron that draws the lightning—as though my home were a relay between a digital Heaven and a digital Hell?

"All things generate energy. Perhaps the electromagnetic waves I have released into the ether have combined with— not only the electromagnetic and neurochemical impulses of my body, and the vampire blood of the elixir—but with my psychic emanations as well."

Fire came into Markov's eyes. "The energy coming from my very soul, Mr. Quinn. The essential It." He thrust his face forward. *"The animating force of life itself."*

Before Quinn could respond, Markov went on, pointing at the severed head.

"*He* is inside me now. Joining the others in taking on a life of his own. And it has been getting worse with each full moon. I particularly dread this one."

"Why? You said ending your film on the night of the Blood Moon would add the final note of perfection."

"And so it will—but only if all goes as planned."

"Are you saying it might not?"

"I can no longer say anything with certainty—except that the monsters within me have been stirring."

"The Wolf Man came after me an hour ago. Looking a lot like you."

"It *was* me."

"And then you became Dracula."

"Yes. But that wasn't the first time. I had made his lizard crawl from my chamber to the window of the Garden. I saw you and Johnny plotting against me."

So he knew. "The Garden. A very cute name for the place where you've hidden dozens of people you've stolen to prolong your unnatural existence."

"I did what I had to do."

"And so must Johnny and I. I've seen glimmers of the battle you seem to be fighting against the forces that drive you to kill. A battle you are clearly losing, which is forcing Johnny and I to do what must be done."

"Can a soul be reclaimed from the Devil?" Markov asked.

"Yes. But the owner of that soul has got to want it. Which means that this alter ego you've created must cease to exist."

Quinn's gaze plumbed the depths of whatever the "essential It" was that had turned this man into Markov. "George Tilton," he said, "if you are still in there, you must regain control of yourself before anyone else is harmed."

Steeling himself against any reaction, Quinn waited to see if whatever was left of George Tilton was strong enough to overpower the Dracula blood coursing through his veins. Markov's attempt at the defiant Lugosi stare quickly melted into acceptance of the truth. "Once again you have cut to the core of the matter. From the moment you arrived, Mr.

Quinn, your voice of sanity and reason—your *humanity*—has made the Monsters from my Id feel threatened."

He paused, not for dramatic effect this time, but simply to gather himself. His iron composure was crumbling, but he quickly regained it. "The toxic atmosphere I have created permeates the castle. It has seeped into Johnny and myself." He gestured toward Vlad Dracula. "In that brain that I have so diligently kept alive, his brainwaves have become inextricably connected to mine. And try as I might,

> Neither the angels in Heaven above,
> nor the demons down under the sea,
> can ever dissever my soul from the soul
> of the hideous Dracula Three."

He was paraphrasing Poe again. *Annabel Lee*. The clever rhyme on the last line sounded memorized, not ad-libbed. Which meant that he'd been aware of losing control long enough to come up with and memorize the line.

Before Quinn could react, Markov went on, shaking his head as if saying no to a voice inside it.

"You are right, Mr. Quinn. I have let myself come under his spell. Somehow I must break it, or the consequences will be dire."

He pushed a button on his master control and the ambient lighting came on. Combined with the backlighting coming from Dracula's showcase, it cast Markov's face half in shadow, half in light, creating the disturbing impression of the war between good and evil seething inside him. He gave no indication that the effect was intentional, merely nodding toward an area a few feet from where they stood. "Look."

A high-backed chair and small table sat in the corner from which he had emerged. The knife from *Psycho* rested on the table. A pile of wood shavings had accumulated at the foot of the chair. Propped upright in the corner, a wooden stake, nearly ten feet long, had been whittled into a fearsome point.

"He had me preparing that for your impalement."

Quinn discreetly moved his hand into position in case he needed to snatch the bear spray or the pistol.

"Somewhere in me a last spark of decency still burns," Markov said. "I have told you of my belief in destiny. I refuse to accept that mine is to be a depraved murderer. I must cast off this Markov/Dracula persona and return to my rightful self—if it is not too late. Even in this windowless room, I can feel the pull of the moon."

A sudden tremor coursed through him. The time-lapse transformation of Lon Chaney/Lawrence Talbot into the Wolf Man began. Fur sprouted across his hands. He brought them up to his face as if trying to keep the werewolf from getting out.

Watching the beast return, Quinn took a few anxious steps backwards and looked toward the door, wondering if he could escape before the werewolf attacked. He moved his hand close to the pistol, but when he turned back to face Markov, the fur had begun to retreat. Several seconds later it was gone, leaving Markov clearly shaken, but himself again.

"I have tried to warn you," he said. "I am *not* evil. I have no wish to kill. Like Larry Talbot, I have a conscience. But … the soulless monsters that live within me do not."

"This all sounds very noble," Quinn said, doing his best to stay calm, "but reality is a very elusive commodity in your world. And we have come to the moment when reality must trump fantasy." Markov opened his mouth to protest but

Quinn waved it aside. "We are far past the time for noble speeches. You have much more pressing problems than the full moon. Not the least of which is that you have removed the wolfbane in the Garden, which means your Flowers of Evil are starting to rise up, while Johnny—*your daughter*—is locked in the dungeon."

Markov stepped in front of the display case to face Quinn. From its perch several feet behind, the head of Vlad the Impaler now hovered in space beside Markov's.

As Vlad Dracula's unwavering gaze bore into the back of his most loyal subject's head, Quinn saw Markov's commanding presence begin to return. In that moment, Quinn knew he was watching the death of any hope for the redemption of George Tilton.

He needed to free Johnny so they could end Markov's nightmare movie. Fast.

Quinn was trying to think of the best way to get to her when the door to the Chamber burst open.

CHAPTER 58

Max stood there, the sword hanging down by his side.

Markov calmly retrieved the impalement stake from the corner. While his back was turned, and Max's attention riveted on his father, Quinn eased closer to the door.

Holding the stake in front of him like a spear, Markov began a slow advance toward Max. "The prodigal son returns. I cannot offer you a fatted calf, but"—he brandished the stake—"perhaps something else can be roasted on this spit."

"*You.*" Max stepped into the Chamber. "On your funeral pyre. The vampire beheaded and burned. The perfect ending for your loathsome *Dracula* sequel." He assumed a fencing stance.

"Ah. So you are a swordsman now?"

"I have taught it in theater departments all over Boston."

"Impressive," Markov said. "But you forget that *I* taught *you.*"

"As usual, you flatter yourself, *George.*" Max made a slash through the air. "You and your piece of wood do not stand a chance." He took another step forward.

"*No.*" Markov pointed the stake at him. "Not in here. In

the corridor. There is more room, and my collection will not be damaged."

"You would rather damage your family."

"Ah. Still wallowing in self-pity, I see."

Quinn was looking for an opening to get away and free Johnny. They'd have to improvise a new plan for disabling Markov.

Or maybe not. If Max was any good with that sword, maybe he'd do it for them.

Max seemed to notice him for the first time. "Who the hell are you?"

"Someone to help put an end to all this."

"Then you are on my side."

"We have a common enemy. Your psychic vampire father must be stopped."

"Enough!" Markov's bellow stunned them into silence. "This is *my* picture. *I* will decide how it will end." He slid a caressing hand along the stake. "We have a new opening for our climactic sequence, Mr. Quinn. It shall now begin with the most gruesome scene in cinema history—while staying true to the story and the dark prince who inspired it."

He held the stake up to Vlad the Impaler in salute. "Until now people have only been able to imagine the horror of impalement." He looked back toward his son. "When I finish with this misguided avenger, they will no longer have to imagine. They will see." He let out a small sigh of pity. "After a lifetime as a coward, at least you will be able to die like a man."

He pointed the stake at Max. "So. You have been teaching swordplay. Let us step into the corridor and see if the pupil can defeat his master."

Markov herded them through the door at the point of

the stake. "Stay out of the way," he said to Quinn as he backed Max up the hallway. "Lest you become collateral damage."

Max assumed a fencing stance and the duel began. Locked in mortal combat, swinging wildly, they didn't see Quinn ease back into the entryway of the Chamber of Horrors. He stuffed the flamethrower into the canvas bag with the wolfbane, garlic, hammer and stakes, and a spare tank of fuel. He started to grab the other bag with the wristbands and spray but reconsidered. He and Johnny were already wearing wristbands, and he had extra canisters of spray in his pockets. With everything he might be up against, two bags would be too much to carry. They'd have to come back for the second bag if it came to that.

He hefted the other bag and stuck his head into the corridor to see if he could cross the landing to the stairs without being seen.

Their fierce battle had taken Max and Markov farther up the corridor. As Quinn crossed the landing, he saw that the suit of armor was once again holding the halberd he had removed after it tried to decapitate him. Markov must have put it back. Quinn snatched it from the gauntlet-covered fist. It wouldn't hurt to have a weapon in hand if something came out of nowhere.

The sounds of a fight to the death echoed through the hall as he descended the stairs.

CHAPTER 59

Markov quickly backed his son to the top of the stairs. Max stood perilously close to the edge of the staircase, parrying every thrust of the stake. He sidestepped one and countered with a vicious swipe that missed Markov's neck by inches. Before Max could regain his balance, Markov thrust the stake again.

Max felt a sting of pain. A spot of red blossomed on his shirt. Growling, he lunged for the kill with the sword outthrust like a bayonet. Markov blocked it with the stake, but the deflection bounced off and slashed his forearm. He threw his head back and let out an inhuman growl. A lightning bolt of fear shot through Max as he backed away.

Markov's clothing began to come apart at the seams. Coarse hair quickly covered his face and body. His ears grew pointed and his teeth sharpened into daggers.

Max made another desperate thrust, but the werewolf easily sidestepped it and closed a hairy fist around the blade. His roar as it sliced into his palm shook the corridor. He yanked the sword from Max's hand, flipped it and caught it by the handle.

Max tried to escape down the stairs, but with one leap

the werewolf was on him. A half-human paw clamped onto his neck while the other still held the sword. As the Wolf Man dragged his son below, the sword clanked against the stone steps like a death knell.

CHAPTER 60

Quinn sprinted to the dungeon. Markov had locked Johnny in the last of the three large cells, as though he had wanted to keep her as far away as possible. Quinn opened the door with his skeleton key and quickly brought her up to speed.

"Our original plan is off. Max is here—locked in a duel with Markov. We need to get ready in case your father wins. Even if your brother kills him, Markov's monsters may still run amok." He pulled the flamethrower from the bag. "You take this. I'll hold onto the halberd for now."

"What else have we got?"

He showed her the pistol and bear spray in his waistband. "Plus wolfbane and garlic in the bag. A hammer and stakes. An extra box of silver bullets and a spare tank of fuel. Here." He pulled a canister of spray from his pocket and gave it to her. "We need to get up there and make sure Markov is dead. If he's still alive, I'll start pumping bullets and you torch his ass."

"Before we can do that, there's something else we need to deal with."

"What?"

"Since I've been in here, three of the undead have come

out of the Garden. They came straight for me—licking their lips." She paused, clearly still shaken by the encounter. "They tried to pull the door open, but they weren't strong enough. Finally they gave up and headed up the stairs."

"Markov's removed all the wolfbane. The three you saw might be the same three I dealt with in the Garden—or it might be three different ones. Either way the shit is hitting the fan. Eventually all the ones with enough life left in them will rise up. If they make it into the countryside—"

Johnny finished his thought. "They could spread the Dracula Virus."

Quinn made a single grim nod.

"All the more reason to burn this place down," Johnny said.

"As soon as we finish with Markov." She started to leave. Quinn held up a hand. "Wait. There's something else."

"What?"

"Lady Elinore somehow got out of her tomb."

"What?"

"Her tomb was empty when I came through the Garden. I went up the passage to your chamber and she had made it up to the fireplace. She was strong enough to try and stop me. I tied her to the bed, but if Markov wins, he'll find her and untie her."

A fierceness came onto Johnny's face that was almost frightening. "Mommie dearest. If ever any creature needs killing, it's my stepmother."

"I'm with you Johnny, but let's keep our heads together."

"Don't worry. My head has never been more together. Now let's fucking go."

On the way to the door she picked up her portable master control that had fallen onto the floor and stuffed it into the bag.

They exited the dungeon and were almost to the staircase that would take them to the Chamber of Horrors when they heard metal clanking down the stone steps.

"Something's coming," Johnny said.

Quinn tugged her arm and led them into a shadowy recess behind the staircase.

Seconds later the Wolf Man loped past. Dragging Max by the neck, sword in his other hand, he quickly disappeared into the gloom.

"He's either taking him to the dungeon or the Garden," Johnny said.

"Let's follow him."

He started to move but she grabbed his arm. "We have to be extra careful. When he sees that empty cell, he'll know we're after him. And his senses are much better than ours. In this feeble light he'll have the advantage."

"I have a flashlight, but if we use it, he can see us coming."

"Not a good idea," Johnny said. "Leave it off. The lighting will be better in the dungeon and Garden with the wall torches. Wherever he ends up, he's very good at lying in wait for his prey. And when he strikes, he's lightning quick."

"You've got the flamethrower. I'll have the pistol and the halberd. As soon as he makes any kind of move, we send him to Hell." He looked for any sign that, despite her tough talk, she still might have a problem with killing her father.

"Don't miss," she said.

"With six shots, I won't. And don't you."

"I won't. The minute he hits the ground, we start the fire that will give this movie a happy ending." Johnny held up a hand as though gesturing at a movie screen. "The House of Markov. Going up in flames. And him with it."

CHAPTER 61

Still gripping the dazed Max by the neck, the Wolf Man scampered to the last dungeon chamber. His ungrateful son could keep his ungrateful daughter company while he tracked down his ungrateful guest.

Johnny was gone.

Quinn.

They were together now.

The werewolf's preternatural senses became fully alert. He stood up on his hind legs and scanned the surrounding area: an ambush predator searching for those who would ambush him. His nostrils twitched as he tried to pick up their scent. He pricked his ears and listened for the slightest sound. He detected nothing, but primal survival instinct told him he must finish here quickly and go after the others.

He laid the sword on the ground to get the skeleton key from his pocket, but his forepaw was too big. He ripped the pocket and the key fell out. He snatched it up, opened the door, and angrily flung his son across the large cell. Max bounced once before crashing into the far wall and crumpling to the floor. He struggled to get up, but with a few quick bounds the Wolf Man was on him. The beast

322

clamped both forepaws onto Max's neck and forced him onto the floor, squeezing until he went limp. Satisfied that this vermin posed no threat, the werewolf released him and went to the fetters attached to the wall.

Max shook himself out of his daze enough to lift his head and assess his situation.

He was inside one of the dungeon's cells. The Wolf Man's back was to him. He was unlocking the fetters.

He's going to leave me here to die.

Max looked around frantically. The sword was just outside the open cell door. He got up and moved as quietly as he could toward it.

The werewolf snapped its head around. Two bounding strides later the beast slammed Max to the stone floor and held him pinned by the throat.

Max saw no trace of his father in the yellow eyes, only savage bloodlust. Knowing he was about to die, he unleashed a stream of venom from the poisoned tarn at the bottom of his soul.

"You vile excuse for a father. You doomed us all from the start. I hope you burn forever in Hell!"

"If I do," came the guttural rumble, "you'll be there with me." The Wolf Man pulled his son up by the hair and picked up the sword. A moment later he loped into the darkness, blood dripping from the blade.

CHAPTER 62

When Quinn and Johnny reached the cavernous dungeon chamber, they saw the open door of the cell Johnny had been in and stopped.

"Markov's been here," Quinn said. "I closed that door when we left."

"He may still be close. Watching us."

"There's something inside the cell. On the floor." In their quickly exchanged glance, Quinn knew they were both thinking the same thing.

They advanced warily, Quinn gripping the pistol and halberd, Johnny the flamethrower and bag of weapons. With each step into the cell the horror deepened, until they stood at the rear wall looking at what was left of Max Tilton.

Fetters attached to the wall by three-foot lengths of chain had been clipped to the corners of his mouth to keep his severed head suspended. The stretched rictus made it look like Max was laughing at his own death. In a brain permeated with movie images, Quinn envisioned Conrad Veidt's frozen grin in *The Man Who Laughs* and wondered if Markov had been going for that effect.

Max's dead eyes staring at them cut the thought short.

A moan came from some long-abandoned region in Johnny's soul. She dropped the canvas bag and covered her mouth to keep a sob from escaping at the sight of her dead brother. Ruthlessly murdered by their own father.

Keeping an eye on the darkness beyond the open cell door, Quinn laid the halberd down and placed a hand on her shoulder. He thought of all the pain that was in the droplets trickling down her cheeks.

"Somewhere in my father was a conscience," she said as she wiped the tears from her eyes. "Even as Markov, there was always a spark of decency." As she continued to stare at the severed head, the sob she had been trying to hold back finally came out. "That is the son he once read bedtime stories. My brother."

There was a lifetime of sorrow and regret in the small shake of her head. Her gaze went to the headless corpse on the floor, then back to the grinning atrocity on the back wall. Quinn watched her expression harden until all sentiment was gone. When she turned back to him, he saw only a burning desire for revenge.

"Our father is dead. He is not 'the son of the Devil.' He is the Devil himself."

The sound of the door clanging shut made them snap their heads around.

Markov stood inside the door, holding an impalement stake upright by his side, as though striking a warrior pose. The blood-stained sword rested against his hip, secured by a cord tied around the waist.

His voice was Markov's, but his dialogue was Dracula's.

"If I am the Devil, then I bid you welcome."

CHAPTER 63

"The pit of this hellish pile is very fitting for the Devil's final resting place," Johnny said.

Markov seemed amused. "My, aren't you the liberated female. It seems your new friend has been putting ideas in your head."

"The ideas are all mine."

"My poor deluded Johnny. Knowing how thoroughly I have prepared my monsters for this night, you still think you can defeat me."

She motioned toward Quinn. "Together we can."

"Together we will," Quinn said.

"No, you won't. There are two of you. I have an army of monsters. I am them and they are me. And our survival instincts are very strong. When one of us is threatened, any one of the others might take over to eliminate the threat." He sighed for comic effect. "I try to be a good host, but … being a Monster Maker is risky business."

"Listen to yourself," Quinn said. "You call your daughter deluded, while you turn a blind eye to the evil monster you have turned yourself into. Look." He pointed to the butchered corpse on the floor. "Look what you've done to your own son."

"The die was cast for Max and I long ago. For all of us. This moment had to come. Now, it's time for his sister to join him." Markov took a step toward her.

"Stop right there." Quinn picked up the halberd. "Or your head is going to be in the Chamber of Horrors beside your idol's. Dracula and Son of Dracula."

"Your bravado is very unwise, Mr. Quinn. You cannot defeat us all. Aside from all my weapons, reinforcements are coming. Look."

He gestured at the area beyond the open cell door. Several of the undead from the Garden were shuffling toward them. Markov saw Quinn's look of surprise when he realized that Lady Elinore was leading them.

Johnny gasped. A chill skittered down Quinn's back.

Markov grinned. "Surely you didn't think I would release my beloved from her tomb and then not check on her progress. She was too weak to resist when you tied her up, but she is getting stronger every minute. Strong enough that I have appointed her my new assistant director." He shot a look of scorn at Johnny. "Now that my blood can no longer be trusted."

Elinore and her vampiric followers had gotten within ten yards of the cell when Markov shouted to her: "Take the extras to the studio and get everything ready."

She veered off in the direction of the staircase. The undead followed close behind. Quinn counted them. "I don't think six 'extras' will be enough."

"There will be others," Markov said.

Quinn let the halberd drop to the floor and pulled the pistol from his waistband. "I think I can save us all a lot of aggravation." He gave Johnny a nod and she ignited the flamethrower, spitting an orange-blue flame in her father's direction.

Still holding the impalement stake, Markov growled and moved backwards to get out of her range. A barely perceptible ripple fluttered across his forehead. A vein swelled near his temple.

Something erupted from the top of his head and landed on the ground near his feet. Quinn and Johnny looked in disbelief as it streaked toward them. Quinn aimed the pistol at it, but the severed hand of the Creature from the Black Lagoon was too fast. It launched itself and clamped onto his wrist, squeezing until the pistol fell to the floor. While he struggled to pull the hand off, Markov dropped the impalement stake and reached for the gun. Quinn kicked it across the floor. Johnny backed Markov into a corner with the flamethrower.

The assault was bringing out the Wolf Man.

Quinn managed to get a canister of spray from his pocket. He shot a burst onto the hand. It fell to the floor, scrabbling about wildly until it reached the stone wall and began rubbing its back side against it, trying to scrape off the stinging spray.

Quinn rushed to grab the impalement stake. As he picked it up he heard soft popping noises.

The flamethrower started to sputter. It was running out of fuel.

Markov's transformation into the Wolf Man was complete.

Quinn held the stake in front of him like a lance and charged. The werewolf swatted it aside. Quinn's momentum kept him going forward. A vicious backhand from the huge paw sent him sprawling across the stone floor. The stake clattered to a stop several yards away. Dazed, Quinn struggled to get up.

The werewolf shifted his attention back to Johnny. She had abandoned the spent flamethrower and retrieved the pistol. She aimed directly at Markov's heart. He snarled and fixed her in his bestial stare, watching her struggle to find the strength to kill her father. That part of his brain raced to think of something that might stop his daughter from shooting him. He latched onto one of the strongest bonds they shared: a love of Poe. All the Halloweens, when they'd recited "The Raven" in the oriel....

He delivered the line from the poem with all the intensity his altered vocal cords would allow. It came out as a guttural plea, whispered from the deepest recess of an abandoned lair.

"Is there ... *is there* ... balm in Gilead?"

Her expression softened. Somewhere there *was* balm in Gilead. There had to be.

Johnny looked into the jaundiced eyes of the Wolf Man, searching for the man who had held her on his knee and read Poe to her. Her eyes filled with tears just before she pulled the trigger.

A red hole opened in his chest. As she watched the Wolf Man stagger and fall, a single word echoed in her head, each reverberation a wave washing more of the stain from her soul:

FREE! Free! Free ... free....

Quinn came up beside her, impalement stake in hand. As Johnny stared down at her slain father, the Wolf Man melted away until the body of Markov lay there. The bullet hole in his chest slowly closed.

"Did you see that?" Quinn said.

Johnny nodded and went down on one knee, probing for the hole. It was gone. She lifted one of Markov's eyelids. The glazed yellow eye stared lifelessly at nothing.

Suddenly the eye became human and riveted onto her.

Markov's hand shot up and snatched the gun.

Quinn made a rush but Markov swung the gun around. Quinn halted, staring down the barrel.

"Drop your weapon and back away," Markov said, getting to his feet.

Quinn dropped the stake and took one grudging step, then another.

Markov looked down at Johnny with a mixture of sadness and anger. "You killed the Wolf Man, but I am Dracula. I cannot die."

His long sigh sounded like the final exhalation of whatever love he'd still had for his daughter. The sound burrowed into the gaping wound in her heart where her love for her father had once been. His next words were salt in that wound. "Now that you have revealed your true feelings," he said, "you must be confined."

"You have your destiny," she said defiantly. "I have mine."

"You are the *supporting* actor in our movie, dearest daughter, not the lead. There can be only one outcome now. The one I have been preparing for since we got here. This is not the way I had it scripted, but a good director is always ready to improvise. First I must go to the studio and do a hasty edit of the monster rally footage. Everything else is done. Then I will invite you to the premiere."

He took a step back and addressed them both. "Sadly, until then, I can no longer trust either of you. You shall both remain here in your new guest quarters until I am ready."

A noise made them turn their heads.

It was coming from behind the open gate of the Garden

of Evil. From this distance the noise was faint, but growing louder. Quinn recognized the dragging sound at once.

Shhhht.

Clank.

Shhhhht.

Clank.

The familiar figure came through the gate. It paused, as though getting its bearings, then began shambling toward the dungeon chamber.

"Your Creature from the Black Lagoon," Johnny said. "The magnetism seeping into the water has brought it to life."

Markov's attention was on the relentless approach. The chain it had broken trailed from its ankle.

Shhhhht.

Clank.

Johnny scrambled to her feet and stood next to Quinn.

The amphibious Creature had gotten close enough for them to hear its labored breathing as it struggled for air in its new environment. It paused at the entrance to the cell. In a face of some impossible humanoid demon from beyond any ocean depths, blazing red eyes searched the faces staring back at it and quickly locked onto one:

Markov.

The Creature let out a breathy howl and moved toward him, much faster than it had been moving before. Markov pointed the gun at it. Never slowing, his misbegotten creation reached out to choke the one who had left it in a watery dungeon to die.

Markov fired.

The shot knocked the Creature back but it quickly recovered. A hollow groan escaped as it gasped for air. It fully extended its arms and charged.

Markov fired again but missed. The Creature clamped its long webbed hands onto his throat. Johnny seized the moment to get the spare tank of fuel from the bag and onto the flamethrower.

The claws digging into Markov's flesh triggered a defense reaction. Metal bolts shot out from the sides of his neck, startling the Creature into removing its hands. The red eyes of the amphibious beast watched in stunned amazement as the rest of the transformation took place.

Markov's brow thickened as his eyes receded in their sockets. A large scar formed over the right eye. His slicked-back Dracula hair rearranged itself into a style with bangs that resembled a skullcap. A slight movement of his head revealed another long scar along his left jaw line. His hands grew larger and his arms lengthened, extending several inches beyond his shirtsleeves until they exposed stitching around the wrists. Hints of Boris Karloff were mixed in with Markov's facial features when the transformation was complete.

Johnny and Quinn backed away.

The Frankenstein Monster and the Creature from the Black Lagoon, both well over seven feet tall, stared each other down, waiting to see who would make the first move.

CHAPTER 64

The Monster spoke to the Creature in the perfect English of Mary Shelley's novel, rather than the broken English of the movie. "Aside from the fact that you have turned against your maker, you would be a jarring anachronism in my monster rally. I must leave you on the cutting-room floor."

Whatever life force might have seeped into his Creature, Markov had seen that bullets wouldn't kill it. Which meant it was still more robotic than real. He would have to try magnets, if he could get to them. He shoved the pistol into a pocket.

The Creature used the split-second hesitation to charge. The Monster's ferocious backhand swipe sent it flying backward. The beast staggered and fell to the ground in a heap. A sound of alien savagery rumbled through its hollow gasps for air as it struggled to its feet.

The Monster countered with his familiar growl. "RRRRRRRRRRRR!"

The Creature came at him again. They clamped onto each other in a fierce wrestling match that was a blur of throws, choke holds, body slams, and wild windmilling arms. In the confusion Quinn grabbed the stake, Johnny the flamethrower. She went straight for the Monster, but the approaching flame only enraged him more.

With a defiant roar he hurled the Creature aside and walked into the flame. Two steps later he ripped the flamethrower from Johnny's hands and threw her across the cell. She slammed against the bars and collapsed onto the stone floor, where she lay utterly still. The Monster tossed the flamethrower aside and frantically brushed sparks from his shirt. The Creature struggled to its feet.

Quinn hesitated. He needed to check on Johnny, but with the monsters distracted, he might have an opening to end this.

He sprinted to the flamethrower.

The Monster reached into his pocket for the pistol. The Creature charged. The Monster rushed his shot, and the bullet hit the Creature in the shoulder. It staggered backward.

Quinn adjusted the flame to its maximum five-foot range. The sound of the gas-powered rush made the Monster whip his ahead around. He pointed the pistol at Quinn, unaware that the Creature had recovered and was coming up behind him, arms outstretched, reaching for his neck.

"Drop it," the Monster said.

"Fuck you," Quinn said.

The clawed hands clamped onto the Monster's neck.

Quinn seized his opening and directed the flame at the hand holding the pistol. The Monster dropped it and flew into a rage, twisting and contorting his body to avoid the flamethrower while pulling at the hands that were strangling him.

The tip of the flame reached the Monster's chest. Instead

of subduing him, it inflamed his instinct for self-preservation into white-hot fury. The strength and rage of all the monsters inside him combined to rip the webbed hands off his neck. Fiercely gripping the Creature by the arm, Markov swung it around like a whip, smashing it into Quinn. The flamethrower went flying as he and the Creature tumbled across the floor.

While they were both dazed, the Monster retrieved the pistol and flamethrower. Seeing that neither Quinn nor Johnny posed an immediate threat, he went to the Creature. On the way he saw a canister of spray on the floor. He stuffed it and the pistol in his waistband, then looked down at the Creature with contempt.

It lay on its back, large fish-lipped mouth wide open and chest heaving as it gasped for breath. The Monster knelt and shot a stream of spray into the mouth. The hollow gasps became desperate choking coughs. The scaly chest heaved as though it might explode.

The red eyes dimmed; the choking gasps became weaker; the scaly eyelids began to come down. Just before they closed completely, fiery sparks appeared in the eyes—futile parting bursts of hate. They penetrated the soulless shell of the Monster and flared briefly in the fog-shrouded moor that was Markov's brain. In that sickly flash of reason, Markov couldn't tell if the hatred came from the Creature, bitter at being aborted just as its soul had begun to form, or from the bits of his own soul that had seeped into it—self-loathing at the awareness that he was killing a part of himself. When the Creature's eyes finally closed, the Monster became Markov again. His clothes hung on him in tatters.

He cast a quick glance at Johnny. She showed no signs of life.

Quinn had gotten to his feet. He couldn't tend to Johnny until he dealt with Markov. He made a move for the stake. Markov stopped him with the pistol in one hand and the flamethrower in the other. "Move."

He backed Quinn to the rear wall until they stood on either side of Max's suspended head. Markov set the flamethrower down and ripped one of the fetters from a corner of Max's mouth. The head fell a few feet until the chain of the other fetter became taut. The head jiggled and bobbed, finally coming to rest with its sightless eyes looking at the floor. While Markov stared remorselessly at the remains of his son, Quinn slapped the pistol from his hand and bolted.

Markov touched a button on the remote attached to his hip and the cell door slammed shut. He calmly retrieved the pistol.

"You cannot escape," he said as he walked toward Quinn, "and I have no more time for your misguided heroics. *Move.*"

Again he herded Quinn to the back wall. He kept the pistol trained on him while he pulled a key from his pocket. He unlocked the fetter hanging from the wall, snapped it shut around Quinn's wrist, and went to check on Johnny.

He lifted an eyelid, felt her pulse. "She's alive."

He carried her to the back wall and laid her down. He ripped Max's head from the other shackle and unceremoniously dropped it to the floor. It landed with a squishy sound on the soft ragged tissue of the neck. Max's milky dead eyes gave baleful witness to the further desecration of his rude grave.

Johnny began to stir. Markov scooped her up and chained her to the wall. She sagged when he let her go, but the pressure on her wrist quickly brought her to attention.

Markov picked up the impalement stake and faced his prisoners. "I and my army cannot be defeated. Now, If you'll excuse me, I have a movie to finish. For you two, this is a wrap."

He took a deliberate step to Quinn and raised an eyebrow to give him the Lugosi stare. "When we first met, you said you didn't believe in monsters. So I shall leave you with Van Helsing's famous line from his closing curtain speech:

'Remember: *There are such things.*'"

CHAPTER 65

Markov slammed the cell door shut and quickly disappeared into the darkness.

Johnny held up her shackled wrist and whispered to Quinn, "I have spare keys for this and the cell door in the bag, but we can't get to them."

"Not necessarily." Quinn reached into his hidden zipper pocket and brought out the multitool. He flipped the six-inch blade up from its slot and showed it to her. "Hacksaw. Very sharp."

He inserted the blade into the shackle's loop and began sawing with machinelike speed. A few minutes later he was free.

"The keys are in the small compartment on the side of the bag," Johnny said.

He got the keys and removed the shackle from his wrist, then freed Johnny. "We've got to figure out a new plan," he said. "We can't go hand-to-hand with him. He's got the pistol. And the stake."

"And 'reinforcements,'" Johnny added. Her brow furrowed as she tried to think of a solution. She held up a finger. "Wait a minute."

She pulled her master control unit from the bag, scrolling until she found what she wanted. Filling the screen was the corridor that ran in front of her apartment. She held it out for Quinn to see.

"What?" he said.

"The spear gun. It's still there where I left it. We can get that and charge into the studio through the door inside my apartment. I can harpoon him before he knows what hit him."

"If you don't miss, that should do it."

"I've had plenty of practice with all these things. I won't miss. Once I take care of Markov, I'll get the pistol off him."

"We'll still have the others to deal with," Quinn said.

"Without their ruler they'll be confused, but it won't stop them from going after what they need to live—fresh blood. Which means us."

"There's a box of extra bullets in the bag," Quinn said. "I'll take the flamethrower and the halberd."

"Even if the bullets don't kill them, it's got to slow them down."

"While you're pumping them with lead I'll be slashing and burning."

"Then we start the hellfire," Johnny said. "The End. The. Fucking. End. Roll credits."

Quinn went to get the halberd and flamethrower. Johnny met him just inside the gate with the canvas bag. She set it down and started pulling out wolfbane and garlic. "Put this on you wherever you can. Hopefully it will keep his reinforcements off us."

They stuffed the banes into pockets, waistbands, socks. "We're going to need some light," Johnny said, "and you're going to need both hands free." She reached into a separate compartment and pulled out a light with an elastic headband attached. "I always keep these handy. I use them for my dives in the lagoon, but also whenever I'm outside at night."

Quinn snugged the headlamp into position, then unlocked and opened the gate. They took a moment to assess the conditions before entering the battlefield.

About fifty yards from where they stood, a dim glow from the light inside the Garden spilled into the main chamber. Between where they stood and that glow, all was darkness.

"This is the moment of truth, Johnny."

She made one small grim nod. "Be ready for absolutely anything. We've got to get through the Garden and up the stairs to my apartment."

Quinn rested the halberd on a shoulder and picked up the bag. "I've got this," he said. "You take the flamethrower."

He aimed the beam of the headlamp into the eerily silent gloom. They followed the ten-foot shaft of light into darkness where every step might bring them face to face with death—or something worse. About halfway to the Garden, Quinn stopped suddenly and held out an arm to restrain Johnny. He pointed to something straight ahead. At the farthest reach of his light, two red dots were slowly coming toward them. Their eerie reflective glow left no doubt what they were.

Nocturnal eyes reflecting the light.

Quinn moved the light around to see if there were others.

Two more eyes glowed a short distance behind the first two. Escapees from the Garden were coming toward them.

"Start the flamethrower," Quinn said. "You take the second one."

He held out the halberd to use the pike that rose above the battle-ax like a spear. Johnny adjusted the flame to its maximum five-foot range.

The undead sensed danger and stopped just beyond the range of the weapons. The light showed demonic blood hunger melting into confusion.

"Now," Quinn said.

He charged and thrust the pike into something no longer human. Blood spurted from its chest as it fell to the ground. The other one turned to run but had only taken a step before Johnny set it on fire. Agonized moans filled the chamber as it collapsed to the floor in a flaming heap.

"We have to keep moving," Quinn said. "Let's close the gate so nothing else can get out. Then we can see what we're up against in the Garden."

They looked to make sure these two were dead.

All that remained of the one Johnny had torched was a smoldering charred carcass. Quinn shone the light on the other.

Its eyes were open. They shifted toward the light.

"*God damn you!*" Quinn plunged the pike into the same hole in the chest, furiously agitating it around as though trying to scrape away any last vestiges of life. He yanked it out and raised it again, ready to do the same thing to the eyes.

Johnny grabbed his wrist. "*Wait.* Look." The eyes slowly closed. "It's done. We need to get going."

Almost hyperventilating, Quinn aimed the light straight ahead and they went on.

A moment later they shut the gate to the Garden from the inside. "It's time to round up the herd," Johnny said.

Quinn held her gaze for a few seconds, continuing to

marvel at her transformation from cringing servant to fierce warrior.

They crossed to the final short set of stairs that would take them down to the Garden. Light from the gas torches that dotted the walls of the vast subterranean chamber was enough for Quinn to turn off his headlamp. He handed it to Johnny and she put it back in the bag.

The horror unfolding in Markov's crypt for the undead kept them momentarily riveted to their spot. Strobelike flashes from the lightning storm outside added sinister animation to the nightmare scene in the pit below.

Some of the undead had risen and were moving about the Garden. One was bent over a coffin. From this distance it was impossible to tell if it was giving mouth-to-mouth resuscitation to one of its undead brethren, or draining the last drops of blood from a weaker inmate. A few that had not gotten strong enough to walk wriggled along the floor, like Poe's conqueror worms, searching for whatever sustenance they could find in the scraps of dead flesh that might have fallen between or under the coffins.

Three had gathered at Lady Elinore's empty tomb in the center of the necropolis and were looking around in apparent confusion. The image struck Quinn as worker bees just emerged from their hive, wondering where their queen had gone. Isolated thoughts floating in his brain suddenly coalesced in a flash of understanding.

Whatever cameras Markov had down here would be recording this macabre scene. He had said he wanted to make the ultimate horror film, to "out-Tod Tod." Browning's climactic scene in *Freaks*—the freaks stalking and slithering through the storm for revenge—had sent many moviegoers fleeing from the theater. The real-life scene unfolding below made Browning's look like quaint horror movie hokum.

"We need to start the hellfire *now*," Quinn said. "Before any of these things have a chance to get out of here and join forces with Markov."

Johnny started the the flamethrower. "We can go down the center aisle. The coffins are wood. I won't have to torch them all. They're close enough together that all I have to do is get some of the ones along the aisle started. They'll spread it to the rest."

"We've got to get to the aisle on the other side of Elinore's tomb that will take us to your apartment. I don't think those loyal subjects hovering around it are going to just stand there and let that happen."

"Then you slash and I burn," Johnny said.

Quinn looked along the aisle and made a quick calculation. "There are about a dozen coffins on each side of the aisle. Even if you only light a few, they could take too long to catch fire. We could use some kindling."

"The clothing on the corpses will be my kindling," Johnny said.

Quinn dismissed the thought of people being burned alive with a curt nod. The sympathy he'd originally felt toward them as innocent victims had been smothered by seeing what they'd become. They were no longer human. They were mutant abominations that needed to be exterminated.

His brain was so permeated with lines from movies that even the worst situations could bring one to mind. As he watched the hideous mockery of life shambling and wriggling about, the Monster's famous line from *Bride of Frankenstein* popped into his head:

"We belong dead."

Quinn gripped the halberd. "While you're starting the fire I'll be watching for anything coming after us. Hopefully the wolfbane and garlic we have on us will keep them away, but—if not I'll be doing some Grim Reaping."

Johnny reached for the bag but Quinn shook his head. "I'll carry this. You need both hands for the flamethrower."

"If these things come at us, you're going to need both hands too."

Quinn picked up the bag. "I'll put this down when I have to."

Movement in the Garden got their attention. Two more of the undead were struggling to get out of their coffins.

"You ready?" Quinn said.

Johnny made one quick nod.

They descended the stairs and plunged into the Garden of Evil.

CHAPTER 66

They entered the nearest of the four aisles that converged on Lady Elinore's tomb. "Torch the ones with their eyes open first," Quinn said.

Johnny ignited the flamethrower. She went to the first body with its eyes open—a thick-chested man wearing the camouflage of a hunter.

Before she could squeeze the trigger, his hand shot up and grabbed the barrel of the flamethrower. The fierce tug of war lasted only a few seconds before he wrested it from her hands. Apparently able to use only one arm, he struggled to turn it around so he could use it on Johnny. She snatched it back just as Quinn came up with the halberd.

Johnny thrust the flame a few inches from the thing's face. A bottomless howl of pain erupted as the fire caught and quickly spread. She spoke loudly to be heard over the final groans of a long-postponed death.

"Kindling," she said. "I'll have to be more careful."

Quinn retrieved the canvas bag and they went to the next pair of open eyes. No hands came up as Johnny shot fire into the coffin. Shuddering moans mingled with the crackling of the flame as the undead corpse writhed in agony. Johnny showed no emotion and moved on to the next. Quinn walked beside her, continually scanning the Garden. They were about twenty-five yards from Lady Elinore's tomb when he saw movement ahead.

Her minions had left the bier and were shambling toward them. The first had just entered the aisle. The other two were close behind.

Quinn turned to get Johnny's attention. She had just started the fourth fire. The three she'd set earlier were spreading. The howls from the burning undead grew louder. One sprang up in its coffin. Encased in fire, it groped about wildly before falling back out of sight. As the hungry flames continued to devour coffins, more of the undead caught fire. Their agonized wails were merging into a rising crescendo of death.

All three of Elinore's undead minions had entered the aisle. Twenty yards ahead and coming toward them. "Get ready," Quinn said. Ten yards away, they began slowing down. "The wolfbane and garlic we have on us must be having an effect."

"Maybe," Johnny said. "Whatever it is, let's hit them while they're confused."

They charged.

Johnny set the first one on fire. Screaming, it staggered through the coffins, knocking several over as it frantically tried to brush off the flames. Quinn stormed toward the next one. It held out its hand to protect itself, but Quinn knocked the hand aside with the halberd's blade and plunged the pike into the thing's heart. Surprise flitted across a face that was more bone than flesh. A hollow gasp escaped the lipless mouth when Quinn yanked the pike back out, but the thing made no further outcry as it fell to the floor.

The last one started backing away. Johnny passed Quinn to go after it. Before she got there a hand shot out from a coffin and grabbed her shirt.

Quinn came up beside her and brought the battle-ax down, severing the hand at the wrist. Still it held on. He stabbed it with the pike. It released its grip and fell to the floor, still clutching. "Look at that," he said, pointing to the blood and dust spilling out from the wrist.

"I've seen it before," Johnny said. "It's the natural forces of life and death fighting it out. Parts of them decompose, parts of them don't." She blasted the hand with fire until it lay still.

The last of the undead continued its retreat, weaving its way back among the coffins.

"Looks like he doesn't want to play anymore." Quinn picked up the bag and they entered the clearing, stopping to see if anything else was moving to intercept them before they could get to the continuation of the aisle on the other side.

Johnny reduced the flame to conserve fuel, then pointed to an area about twenty yards to the right. "Look." Two of the undead were clambering out of their coffins.

Quinn nodded. "There's another one over here." To the left, several rows from where they stood, one had just gotten out of its coffin and was looking around in a daze, as though it hadn't gained full control of its faculties. "We've got to get to those stairs before any of these things can pull themselves together."

They crossed the clearing and entered the aisle that would take them to Johnny's staircase, slowing only long enough for her to torch two more whose eyes were open. Ten yards from the end of the aisle, something darted out from under one of the coffins to block their path.

A half-corpse, gone from the waist down, began wriggling toward them.

Quinn was upending the halberd to stab the squirming thing with the pike when it suddenly reared up and launched itself, clamping both hands onto his neck. He dropped the halberd to pull them off but their grip was too strong. Johnny started to use the flamethrower but she couldn't without burning Quinn. She set it aside and grabbed the atrocity by the waist, pulling with all her might.

Still it held on.

Quinn saw what she was doing and tried to help by pushing on the thing's shoulders while she pulled.

The hands held fast.

Johnny's fierce tugging ripped the torso from the arms at the shoulders. She stumbled backwards and fell. The torso landed on top of her, stumps wriggling as though trying to wrap arms that were no longer there around her. She shoved the undead freak aside and scrambled to her feet.

The arms that had been ripped off hung down in front of Quinn as the hands still held on. Blood and dust trickled from the ragged ends of the severed limbs. No longer connected to their life-giving source, the hands finally released their grip and the arms fell to the floor.

Johnny had retrieved the flamethrower and was aiming it at the torso.

"Wait." Quinn pointed to the legless, armless remnant of a human being. The last spark in the eyes went out and a milky curtain came down. "Save the fuel."

The two that had been rising from their coffins had just entered the aisle behind them. The one that had seemed dazed was focused now, weaving his way through the coffins to join the others. Quinn picked up the bag and halberd. "Let's go."

They moved quickly across the final clearing. Between them and the stairs was the mound of wolfbane. "Markov must have put this here to keep these things from getting up the stairs and disrupting his work," Johnny said. She swung the flamethrower around. "If we set it on fire, the pungent smoke will make it even more effective."

They looked behind them.

More undead had entered the clearing and were continuing their relentless advance.

"Do it," Quinn said. "Quick."

Johnny squeezed the trigger. A small fire fluttered to life, searching for oxygen in the dense tangle of wolfbane. While Johnny waited to see if it would catch, Quinn kept an eye on the undead.

They were twenty yards away. The flames spreading behind them made them look like demons emerging from Hell.

"We've got to go," Quinn said.

Johnny's attention was on the flame still struggling to stay alive. "The fire might not catch."

He pointed to the approaching horde of undead. At least ten of them now. They had begun to slow as they got closer to the mound, finally stopping several yards away. "The natural fumes are having an effect and the coffin fires are spreading. That'll have to do. We need to get out of here."

Johnny extinguished the flamethrower to conserve fuel. She and Quinn squeezed through the space between the mound and stairs. Before heading up they took a last look at the Garden.

The fire kept spreading. In the orange haze of smoke,

several more of the undead had risen from their coffins. Some were encased in flame and howling in agony. Others that had escaped the fire were weaving their way through the coffins. One was missing an arm; another half its face. A few of the remnants, gone from the waist down, had emerged from nooks and crannies and were wriggling along the floor.

Loyal subjects to the end, Quinn thought. *Conqueror worms.*

"If Markov's cameras are still recording," Johnny said, "he couldn't have written a better scene to show his deepest level of Hell."

"Time to change the ending."

Quinn had the halberd and bag of weapons, Johnny the flamethrower, and they headed up the stairs like angry villagers storming the castle.

CHAPTER 67

Senses fully alert for anything lurking in the shadows, they moved through the fireplace that led to Johnny's apartment. They stopped at the threshold before entering the bedchamber, scanning to make sure none of the undead or Markov's creations were on the loose.

All was still and appeared undisturbed.

Even though no threats were visible, Johnny spoke in a whisper. "If the spear gun is still in the corridor, I'll go in first and harpoon Markov. Then I can get the pistol off him."

"Once we open that door, we've got to be fast. And ruthless."

"I've got a lifetime of pent-up anger. Ruthless will not be a problem."

"You'll have your hands full with the spear gun. I'll open the door, you charge. I'll be right behind you with the halberd and flamethrower. You finish Markov, I'll torch Elinore. Once we eliminate the Lord and Lady, their followers won't know what to do. We can't give them a second to breathe."

She nodded. "This is the moment Markov has been

aiming for his whole life. He'll be super alert, and he won't go down without a fight."

"Got it," Quinn said.

They took a last look around to be sure nothing was stirring, then quickly made their way through the apartment and into the corridor.

The spear gun was still lying where Johnny had dropped it when fighting the Grim Reaper. She re-armed the gun with the spear, and they continued down the hall until they stood at the door to Markov's studio. They set the things they were carrying down and Quinn pulled the skeleton key from his pocket. Johnny slid her finger onto the trigger of the spear gun.

Quinn eased the key into the lock and gave her a nod. She nodded back. In one swift movement he turned the key and opened the door. Johnny charged in. Quinn shoved the bag of weapons inside with his foot and followed fast behind with the flamethrower and halberd.

Twenty-five yards away in the long rectangular room, Markov sat at his editing console with his back to them. His hands played over the keyboard and oversized mouse like a pianist lost in the crescendo. Standing beside him, looking very much like a mummy in her grave wrappings, Lady Elinore was absorbed by whatever was happening on his computer screen.

The six undead she had brought from the Garden moved to block the charge. Much sturdier and more nimble than the ones below, they formed a protective phalanx with such quickness and precision it looked as though they had been handpicked and trained for exactly that purpose. Within seconds they stood shoulder to shoulder, showing no fear.

Johnny stopped several yards short of the inhuman wall.

Seconds later Quinn was by her side. He put the halberd and bag of weapons down and ignited the flamethrower. Just beyond the line of bodyguards, Markov sat unfazed with his back to them. At the far end of the room, the full-sized movie screen showed him editing the last of the new footage onto his film: Quinn and Johnny escaping the dungeon and fighting their way through the Garden.

They watched Markov casually move his hand from the mouse to pick up the pistol that lay beside it. Next to the pistol sat the gloves and goggles he used to manipulate his special effects. Next to them sat Vlad Dracula's crown. He slowly swiveled his chair around to face them.

He was wearing Lon Chaney's mask from *The Phantom of the Opera*. Perfectly re-creating Chaney's iconic moment in horror cinema, he stood and ripped it off.

Quinn and Johnny stared in shock at the repulsive thing that Markov had become.

He was the hideous Dracula from his own movie—*The Blood of Dracula*—which was actually Lon Chaney's from *The Un-Dead*.

The madness had won.

Quinn shook himself out of his daze. He backed the undead out of the way with a five-foot jet of flame, waving it from side to side.

Markov and Lady Elinore stood unprotected. Johnny raised the spear gun. Markov aimed the pistol at her.

"Drop it," he said.

"You first."

The spear hissed through the air. It went through Markov's heart with such force it pinned him to the wall. Johnny followed the spear and went to watch her father die. Twitching death throes began. The pistol fell from his hand.

Elinore moved to pick it up, but Quinn backed her away with the flamethrower and grabbed it. As he held Elinore at bay, he was stunned to hear Johnny taunting her father with words from Poe's *Conqueror Worm*:

"It writhes! It writhes!"

Elinore lurched toward her. "Using the Poe he taught you against him. You ungrateful witch."

Quinn jammed the pistol in his waistband and swung the flamethrower around. He looked at Johnny before squeezing the trigger that would incinerate her adopted mother.

"*Do it,*" Johnny said.

The burst of fire turned Elinore's bandages into a flaming death shroud. The waxy exposed flesh above the neck began to melt, until only a charred skull was left. The two fangs were still white and glistening in the rows of rotting teeth.

The skull made a creaking sound as it swiveled to face Johnny. Elinore used the last gasps from her soul to repay Johnny's taunts of her husband. Staying in the spirit of the moment, she retaliated with Poe's words from his poem to his adopted mother:

"In the Heavens above … the angels can find no term of love … so devotional as that of Mother.…"

Johnny got as close to Elinore's charred skull as the flames would allow. *"You turned on me when I needed you most! You were no more a mother than he was a father!"*

Elinore collapsed to the floor. Only her skull remained intact in the center of the smoldering pile of cinders. A final burst of flame sprang up from the ashes to do a fiery dance of death on the last of her mortal remains. Rather than screams of pain, the fire brought a hint of a smile to

Elinore's frozen rictus. With another creaking sound, the mouth opened.

"I'll be waiting for you in Hell."

Johnny raised the spear gun to smash the grinning skull. Before she could bring it down, one of the undead slapped it away and shoved her into Quinn. The impact knocked the flamethrower from his hand. As Quinn pulled the pistol from his waistband, Markov's loyal minion yanked the spear from his master's chest. The others hovered several yards away, waiting to see if removing the spear would bring their master back to life.

Markov's remains fell to the floor as a red mist. The mist quickly separated into thousands of digital bits, blinking and fluttering like the tiny eyes of a swarming horde of demons.

"Dear God," Johnny said. "The red is blood. He's part human, part digital."

As Markov turned to digital dust, another horror appeared. The severed hand of the Creature from his Lagoon materialized in the pile.

Johnny spoke in a barely audible whisper. "*He was right. His soul and the Creature's are mingled together.*"

The hand shot up and clamped onto her throat. She tried to pry it off but couldn't.

The minion that had removed the spear started toward her. Quinn fired.

The silver bullet did its work. A look of disbelief came onto the undead thing's face as it saw the blood and dust spilling from its chest. Seconds later it fell over dead.

Johnny's face was reddening as she frantically tried to pull the hand off her neck.

"Move your hands," Quinn said. As soon as they were out of the way he pressed the pistol against the Creature's hand and fired. It fell to the floor on its back side, struggling to get turned over. He handed Johnny the pistol. "Keep an eye on them."

Quinn pulled the hammer and a stake from the bag. With three vicious blows he nailed the wriggling hand to the floor. Finally it stopped moving. "That's enough of that bullshit," he said.

One of the undead charged. Johnny fired. It staggered toward Quinn. He stepped aside and it fell beside Markov's mutated remains. Either the silver bullet had not hit a vital spot, or this one was stronger than the first, because it was still alive and struggling to get up. *Or maybe silver bullets don't kill them.*

The four others hovered a few yards away. Johnny went to help Quinn.

"Use the rest of the wolfbane and garlic," he said. "Get it all around them while I take care of this one." He pulled another stake from the bag. "Then we can finish the rest together."

Johnny created a circle of wolfbane and garlic around the four remaining vampiric creatures. They backed away from the toxic fumes and huddled together in the middle.

The wounded one had gotten to its knees. A ferocious kick sent it tumbling backwards. Quinn was on him in an instant with the stake poised over his heart.

The thing's red eyes blazed at Quinn. "Our master will not let us die," came the defiant whisper.

Quinn leaned to within inches and returned the stare. "Your master no longer has anything to say about it." A vicious blow from the hammer drove the stake home.

A hollow shuddering moan erupted as blood bubbled up around the base of the stake. Quinn pounded like a man possessed until the eyes closed and the abomination lay still.

He picked up the sputtering flamethrower and started toward Johnny. Odd movement along the floor stopped him. "What the—?"

Johnny followed his gaze.

Markov's disintegrated remains were starting to re-integrate themselves. One leg started to form, then the other. The flesh knitting to cover the legs slowly crept upward. Before it got above the waist, Quinn and Johnny saw the skeleton and internal organs taking shape, as though looking at an animated x-ray.

The rib cage slowly formed. The puncture from the spear was clearly visible in the lifeless heart.

The hole began to close. The heart twitched.

A beat. Then another. And another. The heartbeat became steady. The pace of regeneration quickened. Flesh covered the torso in seconds. The mouth began to reconstruct itself. First came the gums. Slowly, two fangs pushed through.

White. Glistening.

Johnny stammered out, "Dear Christ … the magnetism…. It's mixed with the elixir. God only knows what he is now. Part human, part digital … *part vampire*."

The regeneration was almost complete. Markov was recognizable as himself. As he got stronger so did the undead that were still inside the circle of wolfbane and garlic. Their signs of decomposition were disappearing. They appeared younger, stronger. They inched closer to the wall of toxic vapor.

Quinn raised the flamethrower. The flame sputtered and went out. Several attempts to re-ignite it failed. Johnny had the pistol, but three rounds had been expended. The pistol held six, but Quinn wasn't sure if it had been fully loaded. There might be three rounds left—or there might be none. However many were left, they weren't enough to stop Markov and his four protectors if they got loose.

The extra bullets were in the bag.

"Look," Johnny said.

Markov had fully recovered. The eyes of his four remaining minions were locked onto him—loyal subjects awaiting their command. As Markov had regained strength, their rejuvenation had continued. Now they were the young strapping physical specimens they had been in life. Markov extended an arm toward them, as though he were a hypnotist establishing control.

"My power is now in you. Come!" With his palm facing up, he drew them to him by simultaneously closing his hand and pulling it closer to himself. They left the wolfbane-and-garlic prison—not as shambling half-dead, but as sure-footed warriors going into battle. They quickly formed a protective semicircle around Markov. He drew himself up to his full height and spoke with a triumphant air.

"Do not waste your time trying to stop me. I am no longer something that silver bullets or fire can destroy. Do you remember my hypothesis, Mr. Quinn? That the magnetism seeping into me during all those years of remastering had further altered my body chemistry—which had already been drastically altered by the elixir?

"My hypothesis has been proven correct. The magnetism pulled all the animating forces inside me together to create a new life form. I'm talking about altering the molecular structure of my very *soul*. The essential It that drives us all."

A look of satisfaction welled up from the depths of his remastered soul. "I have succeeded in both of my goals: to bring Dracula back to life, and to eliminate the boundary between movies and reality."

He turned his attention to Johnny. "You are right, dearest daughter. I am part human, part digital—part vampire." He gestured at the goggles and gloves. "I no longer need those. Now *I* have the power. The digital part has given me control over my body down to the atomic level. I can modulate the energy waves of my body however I wish. Even amplify their power to a superhuman level. I can synchronize them with the energy waves of the material world.

"Do you comprehend what I am saying? Through sheer will, I can adjust my wavelengths until they are in phase with wavelengths of surrounding matter. I have achieved the goal attained by Morbius's mighty Krell on Altair 4: *creation by mere thought*. Gloves, goggles, a mouse—they are no longer needed. *I* am the input device. The ultimate interface between man and matter. I can manipulate reality with the energy emanating from my bare hands. Watch."

On one of his editing monitors, he had frozen the confrontation in the dungeon between his Creature from the Lagoon and the Frankenstein Monster. They stood glaring at each other in a face-off.

Markov inserted his hands into the monitor and pulled them out. He plucked off their heads and put the Creature's on the Monster and the Monster's on the Creature, then re-inserted them into the dungeon. His expression became almost childlike.

"All the horrors ever shown in the movies will be available to me. I can cut and paste them to create any alien lifeform I wish. Think of the possibilities!

"I have created a new Dracula for the digital age! A

Dracula infused with the genius of Markov—Maker of Monsters!"

His moment of triumph was cut short by the smell of smoke. It was coming from the corridor. Markov shot a glance in that direction. "What have you done?"

"Started the hellfire," Johnny said.

They all looked at the monitor of the Garden.

The vast chamber was a raging inferno. Dozens of the undead staggered around encased in flame.

The smell of smoke was getting stronger. "This hellhole will burn to the ground," Johnny said. "Your reign has ended."

"My reign *here*," Markov placed the crown on his head. "I shall begin a new reign as Vlad Dracula IV." He gestured at the four remaining undead. "I have what I need. Two strong men and two strong women, specifically cultivated in the Garden to continue the Dracula bloodline. My breeding stock.

"Don't you see? Bits of my soul and Dracula's have become part of the elixir that flows through them. Their veins are conductors of our psychic energy. We have total control, because our commands don't just come from some detached other. They flow from our mind to the mixture of myself and Dracula that flows through them. It has made the elixir much more powerful. It compels them to do whatever it takes to keep the bloodline alive. Mesmer would be proud. I have turned his animal magnetism into the ultimate mind control."

Johnny raised the pistol.

Markov shook his head and looked at her with pity. "You still do not understand. Your silver bullets will do you no good. I am indestructible."

"We'll see about that."

She fired the three remaining rounds into him. He winced as each one hit him, then pulled up his shirt to look at the holes in his chest. Very little blood came out. He calmly inserted his fingers into each hole, pulled out the bullet, and flung it at her feet.

"You are nothing if not stubborn, Johnny." A hint of something like affection flickered across his face. "You get that from me."

A crackling noise made them all turn their heads.

Tongues of flame were licking the bottom of the door to the corridor.

"That's our cue," Markov said. "We must leave you now to fulfill our"—he looked at Johnny—"you know."

His minions maintained a protective barrier around him as he went to his editing console and made a few clicks on his specially designed mouse. "A camera on the roof has recorded the Blood Moon," he explained, "and the cameras in here have recorded our final confrontation." He unplugged a pocket-sized external hard drive from a USB port. "I just downloaded it all onto onto this. Along with all the other edited footage." He held the hard drive up as though submitting it for Best Picture consideration.

"I have arranged for my masterpiece to premiere on Halloween—at the Orpheum in Los Angeles. The same theater where *Dracula* was shown in 1931. The teaser ad campaign I started weeks ago has created such a buzz they are expecting a sellout. Seating will be general admission, but of course as director I was able to reserve two seats for my guests of honor. In medieval times they would have been the King's seats: front and center in the balcony. Just go to Will Call. To avoid confusion they are under the name Quinn."

His need for an audience brought a trace of humanity to his expression. "I know the three of us have had our … differences, but as my co-stars, you simply must be there to see the *Citizen Kane* of horror pictures."

The crackling noise was getting louder.

The flames had gotten inside. They would reach the door connecting the studio to Johnny's apartment soon.

"We've got to go," she whispered. "That door is our only way out of here."

Markov saw them looking at the growing flames. "The fire is spreading and—" he pointed to the monitor showing red-tinged moonlight streaming through the windows of the great hall—"the Blood Moon is high. I feel the Wolf Man trying to get out. If he does, he will rip you to shreds. Come. We have just enough time for me to show you my last bit of movie magic."

He shoved the hard drive into a pocket and they all hurried to the the full-sized screen at the far end of the room. Markov took center stage in front of the screen.

"My work here is done," he said. "I can finish my final edit where no one can get at me."

He stuck both hands into the movie screen and spread them as though opening curtains. A portal opened in the frozen image of the great hall. Markov stepped into the screen and beckoned for his minions to follow.

The four specimens he had so carefully tended and nurtured entered the portal single file. With a dramatic wave of his hand, Markov closed the portal. Quinn and Johnny pressed their hands where the portal had been, but the screen did not yield.

Markov addressed his audience of two from the safety of his movie castle.

"This is why movies are better than real life. In here I can finish my work in a perfectly controlled environment, rather than in the annoyingly unscripted real world. Go. Save yourselves, mortals. Live to see the premiere.

"By the way, I have changed the title. It is no longer *The Blood of Dracula*. It is now *Dracula Lives*. Much more fitting. Because … you must attend the premiere to find out."

A sweeping motion of his arm caused the screen to go black.

CHAPTER 68

Quinn and Johnny were in a race against fire. They sprinted to the connecting door. Quinn brushed sparks off her as she fumbled to get it open. They coughed in the smoke. Finally they got through and closed the door behind them.

The fire hadn't gotten into her apartment, but they could feel the heat through the wall of the studio. They raced to the door that opened into the corridor.

"I can feel the heat from the other side," Johnny said.

Quinn nodded. "We don't know how far the fire has gotten down the corridor. It could be right outside the door."

"We've got to chance it. There's no other way out."

Quinn nodded again. "If it's out there, as soon as we open the door, it'll come rushing in, looking for oxygen."

"Backdraft."

"Right. And there's not enough room in the entryway for us to avoid it."

"Wait a second," Johnny said. She ran to the bathroom. A moment later she came rushing back with two large wet towels. "We can wrap these around ourselves."

He gave her a skeptical look. "It's the best we can do."

He motioned for her to stand back. "If there's fire when I open this, we've got to cover our faces and bull our way through it."

"Let's do it."

They wrapped the towels around themselves. Johnny pressed herself against the wall. Quinn got behind the door and opened it. The flames rushed in with a loud *whoosh*. "Let's go!"

They covered their faces and plunged through the fire. It was coming from the right. To the left the corridor was clear.

"Let's get the hell out of here!" Quinn said.

They jammed the towels into their waistbands in case they needed them again, then ran as fast as they could. Fires were springing up in the nooks and crannies of the great hall, but nothing blocked their path to the front door. They opened it and scanned the porte-cochère for any lurking threats. Nothing moved as far as they could see in the moonlit darkness. They cautiously made their way down the stairs and through the porte-cochère. When they were safely on the other side of the access road, they silently watched as the Blood Moon shone down on the fall of the House of Markov.

Finally Johnny spoke. "Good riddance."

As the hellfire swallowed the castle into its greedy throat, reflections flickered across Johnny's face. They struck Quinn as the victory dance of the fire she'd started, rejoicing at her escape from Markov's Hell. But when he focused on her face instead of the reflections, he saw sadness. "What's wrong?"

Johnny kept watching the blaze. "For the first time in my life, I'm finally free." A feeble smile made its way through the sadness. "But I'm also homeless."

"No, you're not," Quinn said, throwing his arm around her. "You'll stay with me until we figure something out."

She looked at him and her eyes moistened. They hugged, then probed each other's gaze as though searching for answers.

"Did what we just saw actually happen?" Quinn said. "Can Markov and his vampire breeding stock be walking around in a virtual House of Markov?"

"We can't have imagined what we just saw," she said. "He's good at creating the illusion of reality, but he's not that good. He has come up with a way to enter a movie. The question is: can he and his vampire whatevers come back out?"

"He can't have done everything he's done, just to rule as Vlad Dracula in a make-believe movie world. This isn't over. Somehow he's coming back to start his new race. And knowing his flair for showmanship, I've got to believe he's going to make his grand entrance at that premiere."

"You're right. One way or another, he'll be there. That gives us one more chance to stop him." She paused, apparently considering possibilities.

"What?" Quinn said.

"I'm thinking about what you said. His flair for showmanship. There's nothing a showman loves more than a big audience reaction. After spending his whole life obsessed with making the ultimate horror movie, you're right. There's no way he'll miss that. Which means that— unless he's figured out a way to hear it from inside the movie—he might already have re-entered the real world and be in the audience at the premiere."

"If there's anything I've learned in the last twenty-four hours," Quinn said, "it's that anything's possible. Which means we'll have to not just be keeping an eye on the screen, but watching out for any strange movements in the theater."

"After living in a haunted house all these years, I'm good at having eyes in the back of my head." Johnny glanced up at the Blood Moon. "We need to get to Los Angeles. Fast."

"Right. But we've some details to work out first."

"Such as?"

"Such as the fact that all my cash, credit cards, ID—" he pointed to the House of Markov going up in flames— "everything we have is in there."

"I've always kept a spare credit card in the Hummer, just in case. That will take care of everything."

"Then what are we waiting for?"

Five minutes later they were standing inside the barn.

"Before start winging our way to Los Angeles," Quinn said, "we've got to have something to stop him with when we get there." He nodded at the boxes of wristbands and bear spray on the table inside the door. "Something better than this." He pointed to the tranquilizer gun. "What about that? What were you using that for?"

"I haven't used it yet. I ordered it on-line and it got here just before you did."

"What were you going to use it for?"

"When I saw Markov's monsters trying to break out, I didn't think magnets and bear spray would be enough." She reached into an open box and pulled out a packet of something. "So I figured I'd try getting this into his system. It's a clotting sponge to stop bleeding in an emergency. I thought I could wet the sponge, then squeeze the water with the clotting agent into the darts. There are two dozen sponges and two dozen darts. I don't care how invincible he thinks he is, if we can get this into his bloodstream, it's got to do *something*. Something that couldn't be good."

"Good thinking. We've seen that silver bullets didn't do it. He can just pull them out. But something in his bloodstream—he can't pull that out. This needs to be part of our arsenal."

"We'd never get it on the plane. Or the other stuff for that matter."

"We don't have to," Quinn said. "We can just box everything up and take it with us. FedEx it overnight and have it held for us at FedEx in Los Angeles. It'll be waiting for us when we get there." He paused as another idea occurred to him.

"What?" Johnny said.

"The tranquilizer gun is going to be our best shot. It would be better if we both had one. You said you got this on-line?"

Johnny nodded.

"When we get to the airport, we'll find a computer and see if we can order another one. It's a long shot, but we might get lucky. Get them to ship it overnight to the same FedEx office. If that doesn't work out, we can try to get one in Los Angeles."

"Whatever happens," Johnny said, "he's not leaving that theater."

CHAPTER 69

Quinn and Johnny had gotten into Los Angeles late last night, rented a car, and checked into a hotel within a few minutes walking distance of the Orpheum.

Now they stood under the neon-lit marquee.

SPECIAL HALLOWEEN SHOWING
ONE NIGHT ONLY
DRACULA LIVES
DOORS OPEN 7 PM TONIGHT

They had gotten to the theater at 6:30 so they could be first in line and have ample time to get everything ready for the eight o'clock screening.

Five people had gotten there before them. In the nearly half an hour since, the line had rapidly grown.

They stood close together and spoke softly so the others in line couldn't hear them. "I have to give the devil his due," Johnny said. "His publicity campaign must have been brilliant. He predicted a sold-out premiere, and it looks like he was right."

"I looked up the Orpheum before we came out. It seats

over 2000. At the rate these people are coming, if it's not sold out, it'll be close."

"Markov couldn't have found a more perfect place for his premiere," Johnny said. "His family lived a couple blocks away. He grew up going to movies at the original Orpheum, which was only a little farther down on Broadway."

"I know," Quinn said. "He told me movies were his escape from a rotten home life. He said he'd sit in the Orpheum for hours, wishing he could go through the screen and into the movie, because their lives were always much better than his. And even though this isn't the original Orpheum, it *is* the one where *Dracula* debuted in Los Angeles. Which definitely makes it the perfect place for him to release what amounts to his long-delayed sequel."

The line of people with tickets, mostly in costume, had disappeared around the block. Another line was growing at the box office. Both lines were abuzz with excitement. Johnny and Quinn had dressed for the occasion. Both were disfigured hunchbacks. Quinn pointed to the poster in the glass case.

"Somewhere, William Castle is smiling," Quinn said.

"Markov is nothing if not a showman."

They heard the sound of the lobby doors being unlocked. Quinn looked at his watch. "Right on time."

As they walked through the ornate lobby, Quinn again tried to suppress bittersweet memories of his father. Seeing a horror movie on Halloween—his birthday—had been their annual father-son ritual, full of love and laughter ... until the last one. When he'd been killed by a crazed fan. Of the movie *Halloween*.

Tonight could be as bad. Maybe much worse.

The sight of the attendant in Will Call triggered another memory of his father, this time a happy one. In his cheesy Dracula getup, the attendant reminded Quinn of the host on the creature features he and his father would watch on Saturday nights when he was little: Dr. Paul Bearer.

"Ah," Dr. Bearer said. "Igor and Bride of Igor." He took a beat before adding, in a very bad Bela Lugosi, "I bid you welcome." His smile showed yellowing teeth. No fangs.

"Thank you," Quinn said. "You have two tickets for us. The name is Quinn."

"Ah. Yes." He had the envelope with their tickets ready on his desk. "Guests of Mr. Markov."

"Yes. But I was wondering if you could do us a favor."

"Certainly, if I can."

"I think Mr. Markov reserved us seats on the balcony. I know they're good seats, but with our eyesight, we'd rather sit downstairs. In the front row, if possible."

"Oh, that's no problem. Those seats are too close for most people. This early you can have your pick. Just a second." He pulled two passes from his desk and stamped them. "Just give these to the usher."

"Thanks. You're a credit to the name Dracula."

"Thank *you*. Go freely, but"—he raised an eyebrow and slipped into his bad Lugosi—"watch out for creatures of the night."

"I guess we need to get out of here then," Quinn said, "since that would include you."

The attendant smiled and turned to wait on the next in line.

Quinn handed Johnny her pass and they made their way through the beautifully restored lobby of the movie palace. The glittering chandeliers, white marble walls, and plush carpet made Quinn think how much he would enjoy seeing a movie here under normal circumstances. That thought quickly faded as he kept picturing the horror that might unfold in the next few hours. When they entered the theater and he saw the screen, he wondered if *Dracula Lives* would be the last movie ever shown here. He used the walk down the aisle to clear his head, and by the time they reached the front row, he was completely focused on what they had come here to do.

There were a few people in the second and third rows, but the first was completely empty. They sat in two seats closest to the middle aisle. "You go first," Quinn said. "I'll wait here."

Johnny gave him a small, tight nod and went through the side door nearest the stage. After making sure no one was around, she took off her costume shirt and quickly shrugged out of the knapsack she had been using as a hump, then put her shirt back on and rejoined Quinn.

"Be right back," he said.

He went through the same door and quickly removed his knapsack/hump. A minute later he was sitting beside Johnny. The knapsacks contained the things they had FedExed to themselves—including the second tranquilizer gun.

The theater was filling up rapidly, but only a couple more people had come into the front row. They sat several seats in, on the other side of the aisle.

As discreetly as possible, Quinn and Johnny peeled the scars from their faces and began pulling their weapons from the knapsacks. They put six magnetic bracelets on each forearm, over the shirtsleeves rather than under them. More than just for protection, they could quickly be pulled off and either thrown at or attached to whatever was coming after them. They stuffed wolfbane, garlic and canisters of spray into pockets for whatever good it might do. The tranquilizer guns they slid under the seat. Finally they pulled out ammo belts they had bought this morning at a local gun shop. Each belt held twelve darts filled with the clotting agent. They clipped them on and concealed them under their shirttails.

The theater was almost full, even the front row. The excited buzz of the Halloween menagerie was like the roar coming from a zoo of monsters. A large percentage of Goths and vampires made black the predominant color.

Speaking softly so they wouldn't be overheard, Quinn and Johnny went over their plan one last time.

The house lights dimmed. Quinn made pointed eye contact. "You ready?"

"I am so ready," Johnny said. "Whatever he is, he's not Superman. One way or another, he's going down."

Dr. Paul Bearer went up on stage to introduce the movie.

"Creatures of the night, I bid you welcome. The movie we are about to watch, no one has seen—not even us here at the theater. Markov, the director, said it would ruin the surprise. So whatever horror awaits us, we are all in this together. All we know is that he has promised a new experience in horror, with special effects beyond anything ever shown. He also asked me to end my introduction with these lines from the original stage production of *Dracula*. They are from Van Helsing's closing curtain speech."

Dr. Bearer delivered his lines as though he were Van Helsing:

"When you get home tonight, and the lights have been turned out, and you are afraid to look behind the curtains, and you dread to see a face appear at the window—why, just pull yourself together and remember that, after all: *There are such things.*"

He held for the giggly reaction, then strutted off the stage to raucous laughter and howls of approval. The house lights went out, and the audience became silent.

The movie's opening was a reworking of the opening from Markov's Poverty Row masterpiece, *The Blood of Dracula.*

A screeching violin straight out of the shower scene in *Psycho* slashed through the darkness. The title burst onto the stark white screen:

DRACULA LIVES

Throughout the movie, moans and gasps of genuine terror mingled with nervous laughter. Markov couldn't have hoped for a better reaction.

Some of the sicker moments got the loudest response. Markov's beheading of Max and fettering the head to the dungeon wall got applause.

Quiet moans came from Johnny as she watched fifty years of her life boiled down to a two-hour highlight reel of terror. Each time her father became the hideous vampire from *Blood of Dracula*, a soft moan would escape, and Quinn would look to see if she was alright. Watching her face harden after each manifestation, he realized that the movie was making her stronger. He didn't need to worry about her; she would be ready for battle.

When the moment came for the head of Vlad Dracula to be revealed as still alive, Quinn remembered Markov saying how he had agonized over making that moment plausible in *Blood of Dracula*. The way this crowd had been reacting, Quinn expected howls of laughter. Instead, when Markov turned on the spotlight in Vlad the Impaler's showcase, there was spellbound silence. It lasted all through their scene, where Vlad passed the crown on to Markov. From that point on the only audible reactions were frightened gasps.

The final scene began, where Johnny and Quinn tried to defeat Markov and his undead followers in the studio. Markov had edited it brilliantly, cutting the nonessential exchanges and asides, leaving only the battle between the two opposing forces. There had been a shocked outcry when the spear had turned Dracula into digital dust. Now there were gasps and apprehensive murmurs as the digital remains began re-integrating themselves. Markov had not cut Johnny's line as she watched it happening:

"Dear Christ … the magnetism…. It's mixed with the elixir. God only knows what he is now. Part human, part digital … *part vampire.*"

The final blackout after Markov and the undead entered the movie screen lasted only a few seconds before fading back in. Standing in the great hall of the movie castle, Markov centered himself in the frame and looked straight into the camera to give the audience the full effect.

Lon Chaney's monstrous Dracula had become Markov's Dracula, updated for the digital age. Swollen veins zigzagged along each temple and both sides of the neck. Orbits of bone encircled the eyes. The thin black lips parted to reveal a set of jarringly perfect teeth. Two fangs suddenly popped down—curved white needles like the fangs of a snake. The eyes widened into a mesmeric stare far more intense than Lugosi's, until it seemed they would burn through the screen. Markov pressed his palm against his heart and delivered the line he had waited his whole life to deliver:

"*I* am Dracula."

The audience erupted into a standing ovation. Security and theater personnel had stationed themselves in all the aisles to maintain control of a potentially volatile situation.

The movie did a slow iris fade, holding on Dracula's face before going to black. The blackout lasted only a few seconds before fading back in. Markov's hideous Dracula still stared at the camera, but now he was an actor at his curtain call, basking in the rousing applause. When it finally died out, Dracula held his arm out to the side, as though to draw something offscreen to him. In his most commanding voice he said, "Come … here."

His vampire breeding stock came to stand beside him. The two males and two females Markov had so carefully nurtured in the Garden showed no signs of having been raised from the dead. They were now gorgeous physical specimens.

Dracula stuck his hand through the screen and opened a portal. "Go," he said. "*Feed.* Feed on them all."

They stepped from the screen with Dracula close behind. A loud cry erupted from the audience—a mixture of fear and excitement. Some ran, but most stayed. Many of the Goths and Halloween vampires hurried to the steps on either side of the stage, like groupies waiting for their rock idol.

Quinn and Johnny rushed up onstage with their tranquilizer guns. Security and ushers were fast coming down the aisle. The four undead formed a protective line in front of their master. Quinn and Johnny fired. The darts lodged in one of the males and one of the females. They staggered back a step and looked in confusion at the darts.

"*Go!*" Dracula said to the other two, gesturing for them to use the stairs on the other side of the stage. "*Feed!*"

They did as they were told. By the time Quinn and Johnny finished reloading they were out of range. One of the female Goths had come up the stairs and bared her neck. The male vampire fastened onto her throat, while the female continued on to the blood feast that eagerly waited at the bottom of the stairs.

The sound of approaching sirens began to fill the theater.

The two that had been hit had removed the darts and seemed to be regaining their strength. Moving cautiously past them, Quinn and Johnny raised their guns to kill whatever Markov had become.

He had seen them coming and hurried toward the screen. They fired just as he reached it. Both darts hit him in the back. He staggered and fell, groping for the darts but unable to reach them. He crawled on hands and knees toward the screen while Quinn and Johnny reloaded. They reached him just as he reached the screen. The male they'd hit staggered in to protect his master while the female pulled the darts from Markov's back.

Markov extended his hand. A portal opened in the screen and he crawled toward it.

Sirens blared and footsteps scurried everywhere.

Standing side by side, Quinn and Johnny raised their guns.

Dracula's two loyal subjects closed ranks to shield their master.

"You take her!" Quinn said. Johnny's dart staggered the female. Quinn's dart did the same to the male. They started to reload, but stopped.

It was too late.

Whoever—whatever—Markov was had crawled into the screen. He stayed on his hands and knees without moving for an agonizingly long moment. Johnny held her breath as she waited to see if the darts had been in long enough to finish him, or if they might have killed Dracula but left Markov alive.

Slowly, keeping his back to the camera, he drew himself up to his full height. Ever the showman, he began a slow dramatic turn. When the turn was complete, he held the pose for the audience to get the full impact.

Johnny felt the leaden beat of her heart as she stared at the monster that had once been her father.

All traces of Markov were gone. His hideous Dracula stood there. An evil grin bared his fangs.

Suddenly his head poked through the screen. His hypnotic gaze scanned the screaming audience as though searching for prey. Finally it came to rest on Johnny and Quinn. Staring straight at them, he delivered his final line with gloating menace:

"I live."

THANK YOU for reading *Dracula Lives*.
I know everyone's minutes are golden, so if you have time
to leave a review, that would be greatly appreciated.

ABOUT THE AUTHOR

I was born and raised in the D.C. where tourists don't go—a land of soul food and Scrapple.

We lived directly behind the neighborhood movie theater, and as a kid I couldn't wait for the Saturday creature features. Atomic mutants running amok, the monsters of Ray Harryhausen, Roger Corman's Poe films, and the unabashed frightfests of William Castle were among the early influences that warped my writer's muse into a breeding ground for—to borrow a line from Morbius in *Forbidden Planet*—my "Monsters from the Id." In Castle's *The Tingler*, when Vincent Price told us all to scream because the Tingler was loose in the theater, you better believe I screamed. On the literary front I followed the trail Edgar Allan Poe blazed into the "ghoul-haunted woodland of Weir." Instead of his Tales of the Grotesque and Arabesque, I call mine Tales from the Shadowland. I hope to see you there again.

Best Regards, Robert Ryan

www.ingramcontent.com/pod-product-compliance
Lightning Source LLC
Chambersburg PA
CBHW021430240626
47153CB00001B/92